# To Joy

## March - August 1872

*Book # 18 in The Bregdan Chronicles*

*Sequel to Renewed By Dawn*

**Ginny Dye**

*Journey To Joy*

*Journey To Joy*

## March – August 1872

Copyright © 2021 by Ginny Dye

Published by Bregdan Publishing
Bellingham, WA 98229

www.BregdanChronicles.net

www.GinnyDye.com

www.BregdanPublishing.com

ISBN# 9798461569341

All rights reserved. No portion of this book may be reproduced in any form without the written permission of the publisher.

Printed in the United States of America

Book # 18 of The Bregdan Chronicles 3

## For Iqra Ahsan

I can't imagine doing my books without my amazing Pakistani graphic design artist. She has done all 50+ books I have published.

She somehow manages to take my random mumblings about what I see in my head and bring the book covers to beautiful life - making them even better than what I saw.

Through the years she has become my "little sister" and my beloved friend. Iqra, her husband, and her three children (all added to her life during our years working together) are a vital part of my life.

I love you, Iqra!

## A Note from the Author

My great hope is that *Journey To Joy* will both entertain, challenge you, and give you hope to walk your own Journey To Joy. I hope you will learn as much as I did during the months of research it took to write this book. Once again, I couldn't make it through an entire year, because there was just too much happening. As I move forward in the series, it seems there is so much going on in so many arenas, and I simply don't want to gloss over them. As a reader, you deserve to know all the things that created the world you live in now.

When I ended the Civil War in *The Last, Long Night*, I knew virtually nothing about Reconstruction. I have been shocked and mesmerized by all I have learned – not just about the North and the South – but also about the West.

The things I learned while writing *Journey To Joy* blew my mind!

I grew up in the South and lived for eleven years in Richmond, VA. I spent countless hours exploring the plantations that still line the banks of the James River and became fascinated by the history.

But you know, it's not the events that fascinate me so much – it's the people. That's all history is you know. History is the story of people's lives. History reflects the consequences of their choices and actions – both good and bad.

## Book # 18 of The Bregdan Chronicles

History is what has given you the world you live in today – both good and bad.

This truth is why I named this series The Bregdan Chronicles. Bregdan is a Gaelic term for weaving: Braiding. Every life that has been lived until today is a part of the woven braid of life. It takes every person's story to create history. Your life will help determine the course of history. You may think you don't have much of an impact. You do. Every action you take will reflect in someone else's life. Someone else's decisions. Someone else's future. Both good and bad. That is the **Bregdan Principle**...

> **Every life that has been lived until today is a part of the woven braid of life.**
> **It takes every person's story to create history.**
> **Your life will help determine the course of history.**
> **You may think you don't have much of an impact.**
> **You do.**
> **Every action you take will reflect in someone else's life.**
> **Someone else's decisions.**
> **Someone else's future.**
> **Both good and bad.**

My great hope as you read this book, and all that will follow, is that you will acknowledge the power you have, every day, to change the world around you by your decisions and actions. Then

I will know the research and writing were all worthwhile.

Oh, and I hope you enjoy every moment of it and learn to love the characters as much as I do!

I'm constantly asked how many books will be in this series. I guess that depends on how long I live! My intention is to release two books a year – continuing to weave the lives of my characters into the times they lived. I hate to end a good book as much as anyone – always feeling so sad that I must leave the characters. You shouldn't have to be sad for a long time!

You are now reading the 18th book - # 19 will be released in early 2022. If you like what you read, you'll want to make sure you're on my mailing list at www.BregdanChronicles.net. I'll let you know each time a new one comes out so that you can take advantage of all my fun launch events, and you can enjoy my BLOG in between books!

**Many** more are coming!

Sincerely,
Ginny Dye

## Chapter One

**March 7, 1872**

Carrie shivered as she dashed into the barn through a deluge of frosty raindrops. She turned to glare at the offending clouds hovering over a landscape that was beginning to take on the brilliant green she so loved. "Did someone forget to tell Mother Nature that it's spring?"

Miles looked up with a patient smile, his ebony hand never stopping its gentle stroke as he groomed one of the Cromwell horses. "It's spring sure 'nuff. Which means there's got to be one more good blast of winter 'fore it loosens its hold. Besides, we done be two weeks away from real spring. I reckon winter has a right to have one last say."

Carrie loved her old friend's constant patience but simply wasn't in the mood for it today. She pushed back the black curls that had escaped her braid. "I don't have time for this," she retorted. "I wanted to take No Regrets and Granite out for a walk this morning before I head to the clinic."

Miles chuckled and waved his hand. "I don't reckon a little bit of icy rain gonna bother those two. And I don't figure you be sweet enough to melt, Carrie Girl." His brown eyes sparkled with amusement.

Despite her irritation with the weather, Carrie couldn't suppress her laugh. "I suppose you're right," she admitted. Still, she didn't relish walking in sleet.

Miles nodded toward the tack room. "You put on a slicker and take those two outside. My Annie will have a hot breakfast ready for you when you get back."

Two impatient whinnies sounded from the stall in front of Carrie. No Regrets, a tall bay mare, stuck her head over the door and whinnied again. A higher, shriller whinny followed.

"That little boy don't like that he don't be able to see over the stall door," Miles observed. "He figures he oughta be full grown by now."

Carrie laughed as she moved forward to release the latch on the stall door. "At the rate he's growing, it probably won't be long."

"Ain't never seen a colt grow this fast," Miles agreed. "It's like he wants to be big enough so you can ride him again. *Right now.* Ain't a lick of patience in that one."

Carrie swung the stall door open and gazed at the colt prancing in anticipation of her arrival. She knew she would never cease to be awed by the reality of Granite's return. His mother, No Regrets, nuzzled Carrie's shoulder and stepped aside to let Granite push his head into Carrie's chest.

Carrie wrapped her arms around his neck and stroked his muzzle. "Good morning, boy." She stood silently as she savored the love they shared. Granite calmed immediately, his whole body relaxing as Carrie caressed him. Finally, Carrie stepped back. "Ready to go for a walk?"

Granite bobbed his head and began to prance again.

Carrie slipped a leather halter onto No Regrets' head and then snapped a smaller one onto Granite. She clipped a lead line onto the mare's halter, struggled into the leather slicker Miles handed her, and moved through the barn door.

Even with the icy rain pelting her, she felt a surge of familiar joy. She hadn't missed a morning at the barn since Granite had been born on Christmas Eve. In the two and a half months since he'd returned, her wonder had done nothing but increase. He was used to his halter, and he would lead easily, but during their morning jaunts she let him run free, knowing he wouldn't go far.

As they headed down the road toward the tobacco fields that would be planted in one week, Granite cavorted and played, his hind legs kicking high in the air as he bucked and danced. No Regrets watched him with a tolerant look before gazing at Carrie as if to ask where her son got his energy.

"Get used to it," Carrie said quietly. She smiled as she watched Granite. He had not quite shed his winter coat, but she could see patches of gray coloring showing through the brown. His regal head and his flashing eyes were complete replicas of the gelding she had loved for many years. As if called by her thoughts, Granite hopped to a standstill and turned to meet her eyes. He snorted, danced over to her, and shoved his head into her chest.

Carrie lowered her head until their foreheads met. She breathed in his smell as she gazed into his eyes. "I love you," she murmured.

Granite nickered his reply, waited a moment longer, and danced away again.

Carrie turned her attention to the men working in the fields. They worked steadily, not bothered by the icy rain dotting the fragrant brown fields which stretched as far as she could see. She breathed in the rich perfume of freshly turned earth, knowing she would never tire of the comforting aroma.

"Good mornin', Dr. Carrie!"

"Good morning, Miss Carrie!"

The men greeted her as she walked along the raised road above the fields. They were used to her early appearance every morning. The seedlings currently nestled in their beds behind the drying barns would soon be planted in the rows prepared for them. A winter crop of rye, as well as a coating of oyster marl, had been tilled back into the soil, ready to provide needed nourishment for the fledgling plants.

Two weeks of warm weather had caused the trees to burst into life, but Moses had known better than to plant the tender tobacco seedlings so early in the season. As usual, he had been right. He and Miles both agreed this was the last spurt of winter before spring would truly return to Virginia. The seedlings would be planted in celebration of a new season.

Carrie lifted her face as the icy rain ceased. Spots of sunlight burst through the gray clouds, creating a patchwork quilt that floated overhead. She smiled as the wind pushed the dark clouds further west.

"Gonna be a right pretty day, Miss Carrie!"

"You're right, Booker." She slowed and smiled at the young man hoeing one of the rows. "The planting will begin soon."

"Yes, ma'am," he replied. "I reckon this gonna be the best crop yet."

Carrie hoped he was correct. The flood two years before had destroyed most of the crop, swallowing the fields a week before it was due to be harvested. Last year's crop had been wonderful, but she knew Moses and her father had not fully replaced the financial reserves it had taken to carry them through the loss. They were counting on this year's crop to build the reserves again. "I believe you're right," she called back confidently.

She walked for an hour, talking quietly to No Regrets as Granite ran up and down the road. When she returned to the barn, her stomach was growling noisily. She fed the horses, laughing as Granite eagerly shoved his nose into his grain.

"That boy needs a lot of food to keep him growing this fast."

Carrie turned as Susan, her friend and business partner, appeared at her side. A quick perusal of her glowing eyes told her Susan was regaining her full strength after an almost deadly bout with the flu that winter. "That he does," she agreed.

Susan's blue eyes observed the colt. "He's growing faster than any colt I've ever seen."

Carrie nodded. "I know, but I'm not going to ride him until he's three. He may end up being taller than my first Granite, but his bones and muscles are going to need that time to grow strong."

"There are lots of people who ride horses, even race them, when they're two," Susan teased.

"And we both know it's not good for the horses," Carrie retorted "Their ability to carry riders at that age doesn't mean it's good for them." She knew Susan agreed with her. "Why are you mentioning this?"

Susan shrugged. "I know you're eager to ride him again."

"I'm counting the days, but for right now it's enough to simply be with him. He was grown when Miles gave him to me the first time when I was fourteen. It's a joy to be able to experience him at this age. I'm quite content to ride No Regrets until he's old enough. I'm in no hurry."

Susan eyed her. "I actually believe you mean that."

Miles walked up, carrying a bucket of grain. "You might believe my Carrie Girl ain't got no patience, but you be wrong. She likes to pretend she ain't got none, but she be chockful of patience about the things that matter most."

Carrie threw her arms around him. "Thank you, Miles." The old man who had started out as a slave on Cromwell, escaped to Canada for many years, and then returned to work on the plantation he loved, was one of her favorite people. "Coming from you, that means more than you know. However, my stomach is telling me it's beyond time to eat. I have no patience to wait for food."

"I just came from the house," Susan replied. "I smelled bacon and pancakes. If I hadn't eaten with

Harold at home, I would be up there eating a pile of them myself."

Carrie's stomach growled again. "They're calling my name," she announced. "I have barely enough time to eat and change before I have to leave for the clinic." They were expecting a lot of patients that day. Now that she'd had her time with Granite, she was ready for them.

"Mama, is Daddy coming home today?"

"He's coming home tomorrow night," Carrie told her daughter Minnie.

Minnie twisted her mouth into a pout, her blue eyes darkening below thick red hair. "But I miss him right now."

"Me too," Frances chimed in.

"As do I," Carrie agreed, smiling at her oldest daughter. "He's only been gone five days, though."

"It seems longer," Frances answered, her brown eyes flickering with sadness.

Carrie hesitated before taking another bite. She was alone with the girls eating breakfast in the large dining room. Everyone else had already eaten, and Annie was in the kitchen baking pies.

"Is something wrong?" she asked softly. Her daughters loved their father, but they were used to him leaving for short stays in Richmond to oversee the stables he owned.

Frances opened her mouth, but only shook her head.

Carrie held her gaze. She had learned her oldest needed time to express her feelings. Pushing Frances for emotions seemed to make it harder for her to communicate.

Frances looked away before swinging her eyes back. "I'm worried."

"Me too," Minnie announced.

"Worried?" Carrie asked with surprise. "Why?"

Frances and Minnie exchanged a long look.

It was Minnie who provided the answer. "We heard you talking."

Carrie frowned, wondering what they had overheard. "Talking about what?"

"About being robbed," Minnie answered. "We heard you and Daddy talking about the letter that came from Mr. Willard."

"Telling Daddy that the stable was being robbed," Frances added. "We're worried something is going to happen to him while he's there."

Carrie understood. Both of her adopted daughters had experienced immeasurable loss in their young lives. "I'm sorry you overheard our conversation."

"Are *you* worried?" Frances demanded.

Carrie was relieved she could answer honestly. "I'm not."

"Why?" Minnie pressed. "What if Daddy catches someone stealing and they try to hurt him?"

Carrie didn't miss the accusing tone in her daughter's voice. She kept her tone gentle. "I'm not worried, because nothing big has been stolen. If someone were out to cause harm, they would have taken much more." She knew her daughters were remembering the attempts to burn Riverside Carriages down when there was great resistance to the Bregdan Clinic in Richmond. "This isn't like before," she said soothingly. "Your daddy, or Willard and Marcus, will figure out what's going on. I don't believe there is anything to fear."

Minnie stared into her eyes. "Do you *really* believe that?"

"I do," Carrie said firmly.

Finally, the girls relaxed.

Carrie filled her mouth with pancakes, hoping her eyes didn't reveal the anxiety she had successfully hidden behind her confident words. She knew she would never fully get over her first husband, Robert, being murdered. It was hard not to worry, at least a little, every time Anthony was gone. Truth be told, she was counting the hours until her husband returned.

Anthony Wallington stood at the door of River City Carriages and looked down the hill toward the sparkling waters of the James River. The last five days had been quite productive, but the mystery hanging over their heads had cast a pall over the stables.

"You sure you want to stay here tonight?"

Anthony nodded as he turned toward Willard, one of the stable managers. "I am."

Willard's eyes turned serious. "I can stay with you."

Anthony appreciated the offer, but his gut told him they weren't looking at anything serious. "I don't believe I'm in any danger. I simply want to get to the bottom of this before I go home."

"Someone is out to hurt us," Willard said more firmly. "You know what happened before."

Anthony had vivid memories of the intense efforts made to burn the stables by the men determined to get Carrie, Janie, and Elizabeth to close the Bregdan Clinic. "I haven't forgotten," he acknowledged. "This feels different."

"How?" Willard demanded. "Something seems to be missing every week. Last week, it was three different times."

"But nothing taken is ever valuable. Which tells me someone is desperate," Anthony said thoughtfully. "If they were trying to hurt us, they would take something major. Whoever it is hasn't destroyed anything, and they haven't hurt any of the horses."

"No, but food is disappearing," Willard argued. "Bridles are gone. Halters have disappeared. They may be small things, but the cost to replace them is adding up."

"I'm not debating that point," Anthony agreed, grateful his stable manager was concerned about costs. "Which is why I'm going to stay here tonight to try and clear up the mystery." He recognized the stubborn look in Willard's eyes. "Go home," he commanded. "You've been here since before dawn."

"You're armed?"

Anthony nodded. "I'll be careful." Since he could not truly say why he was certain there was no danger, he didn't try to explain.

"I'll see you in the morning."

Willard looked uncomfortable, but he eventually nodded. "I'll see you in the morning."

Anthony watched as his friend's broad shoulders descended the hill toward the river, gradually disappearing around a corner that would take him to his house. Willard and his wife, Grace, had lived in a small home on the outskirts of the city, driven there by people who couldn't accept his marriage to a black woman. When Grace died tragically in the Christmas Eve fire at the Spotswood Hotel more than two years earlier, Willard had stayed in their home. When the success of River City Carriages had provided him the income, he had fled the memories that haunted him daily, buying a new home closer to the stables. Willard's smile came more easily these days, but sadness lingered in his eyes.

With Willard gone, Anthony turned back into the stables. There were a few drivers out with carriages and horses, but the majority had brought their rigs in for the night. He strolled down the stable corridor, feeling the familiar sense of contentment as he listened to the munching of horses eating their allotment of hay and grain. As always, he took great pride in the gleaming coats that revealed the excellent care his horses received.

The icy cold morning had been swallowed by sunshine that produced an almost balmy afternoon. A soft breeze blew down the corridor, bringing with it a sense of peace. Whatever was going on at River City Carriages, he would figure it out. The business venture, shared with his father-in-law, Thomas Cromwell, had succeeded far beyond their expectations. In the beginning, it had been necessary for him to be at the stables far more often. As the business grew and prospered, he had been able to designate the daily responsibilities to Willard and Marcus. He spent most of his time at the plantation with Carrie and the girls, but a thriving business could not be ignored. He came into Richmond when he believed it was necessary.

Two hours later, when nightfall had blanketed the city, swallowing all but the regular noise of the trains rolling in and out of Broad Street Station, Anthony pulled out the bedroll he had carried in that morning. Since most of the missing items seemed to be from the tack room, he moved a few saddle racks to make space in the far corner away from the door, laid out his bedroll, and settled in to wait.

Anthony realized his efforts might be for naught. Things didn't go missing every night, and there seemed to be no discernible pattern. The sole result from the long, cold night he was facing might be nothing more than a sore back.

As the night hours wore on, the only sounds he heard were horses nickering and the movement of restless hooves. Most of the horses were bedded down in thick straw, sleeping peacefully. It was too dark to look at his pocket watch, but he thought it must be about three in the morning. He was exhausted and suspected his uncomfortable night was a complete waste of effort, but he forced himself to stay alert. The sun would lighten the horizon in a few hours. He had kept his eyes open this long, surely he could stay awake until dawn.

He kept himself vigilant by thinking about the plantation. He envisioned Carrie's sparkling green eyes and the black hair that fell in waves past her shoulders. Try as she did to tame it, dark curls found a way to escape whatever confines she created. He smiled as he thought about her steady determination to achieve whatever she wanted. He wondered what patients she had treated today at the Cromwell Clinic. It had been hard for her, Janie, and Elizabeth to close the Bregdan Clinic here in the city, but the people around the plantation were thriving because of their decision.

Janie was working with his wife at the plantation clinic. Elizabeth had returned to Boston to work with her father in his medical practice.

His thoughts turned to Frances next. His fifteen-year-old daughter was a complete joy. Determined to be a doctor like her mother, she showed the same hunger for knowledge that Carrie did. No one who saw them working together would ever guess Frances had been adopted three years earlier, after her family died in a flu epidemic. The two of them worked as a seamless team. If it were up to Frances, she would work full-time at the clinic, but she had many years of schooling to accomplish before that could happen.

Minnie had been a surprise for them. Her mother, Deirdre, had been their cook while Carrie was completing her surgical internship in Philadelphia two years earlier. A disastrous fire had killed Minnie's entire family, sparing the little girl because she had chosen to stay late at their home with Frances.

Neither he nor Carrie had found it necessary to discuss what they would do. Minnie became their daughter. Her constant good humor and bright enthusiasm was a ray of sunshine for everyone on the plantation.

Despite his determination to stay awake, Anthony could feel his eyes drooping in defeat. Even a couple hours of sleep would make the day easier. Drivers would start arriving as soon as the sun rose, starting their routes throughout Richmond. He stretched out onto the bedroll, pulled another blanket over his shoulders, and allowed his eyes to close.

Moments later, an odd sound caused them to pop back open. He eased off the blanket and sat up quietly.

He listened closely, trying to determine if it was caused by one of the horses. The sound of the tack room door easing open told him the noise was caused by a human. The door hadn't been locked, since he had no way of locking it from the inside, but past thefts told him their thief wasn't thwarted by something as simple as a lock. Hopefully, he would believe the unlocked door was caused by forgetfulness.

He tensed, waiting to see what would happen. If it were one of the drivers arriving early, they would light a lantern and reveal themselves.

Soundlessly, Anthony reached for his gun. He had the element of surprise, but he wasn't going to be careless. The inky darkness of the tack room provided him the perfect cover. He would wait until the right moment to make his move.

He heard the scratch of a match. Bunching his muscles in preparation to spring toward the thief, he held his breath so it wouldn't give him away.

A light flared brightly in the room. Moments later, a candle produced a soft glow.

Anthony's mouth dropped open as he caught his first glimpse of their thief. He waited quietly while he watched the thief reach toward a bridle hanging on a peg, the metal bit glittering in the candlelight.

## Chapter Two

"Looking for something?" Anthony asked sternly.

The thief gasped and turned to run, dropping the candle in his attempt to flee.

Anthony leapt forward, grabbed the thief by the arm, and snatched up the burning candle with his other hand. "What are you doing?" he demanded.

"I... I..."

Anthony glared down at the small boy he held in his tight grip, easily holding him in place despite the youth's frantic attempts to escape. "Stand still," he said sternly.

The boy stiffened and stood as still as a statue.

Anthony could feel the tremors in the slight body he had subdued. Without saying anything else, he turned and marched the boy across the tack room, down the corridor, and into his office. He closed the door, locked the latch, and led the boy to a chair. "Sit down."

The boy sat down without a word.

Anthony quickly lit the lanterns, casting a bright light into the room. Now that there was more illumination, he strode over to the boy and stared down at him.

Defiant brown eyes stared back. Now that the boy had gotten over his shock at being grabbed, he seemed to have recovered some of his courage.

"Who are you?" Anthony asked.

"Who's asking?" the boy asked belligerently, a slight tremor sounding in his voice.

"My name is Anthony Wallington. I happen to own the business you have been stealing from."

The boy continued to stare at him. "Ain't been stealing from you," he muttered. "Just tonight."

"You're not merely a thief," Anthony said grimly. "You're also a liar."

The boy opened his mouth to protest, but closed it without uttering a sound. He shrugged and looked away.

"How old are you?" Anthony had seen many street urchins since the end of the war. Children, left parentless by the devastation, roamed the streets, looking for a way to survive. The boy sitting in front of him appeared to be quite young, but malnutrition might be the reason for that.

"Go ahead and do it," the boy shot back as he stiffened in the chair.

"Do what?" Anthony asked.

"Beat me. Go ahead and get it over with."

Anthony didn't miss the fear mixed with the defiance. Slowly, he sat down in the chair across from the boy. "I'm not going to beat you."

"Why not?"

"I don't beat children."

The boy stared at him, brown eyes glimmering under dark, wavy hair, and shrugged again. "What you gonna do to me?"

Anthony thought about the question but didn't have an answer. "How old are you?" he asked again.

The boy looked as if he wouldn't answer, but eventually did. "Ten," he said grudgingly.

Anthony absorbed the knowledge that such a young child was evidently an accomplished thief. "What's your name?"

"What does it matter? What you gonna do to me?"

"I haven't decided," Anthony answered honestly. There was something about the boy that pulled at him. "What is your name?"

The boy gazed around the room as if looking for an escape. Realizing there was none, he answered. "Russell."

"Russell who?" Anthony pressed.

The boy stiffened again. "Don't matter none. Ain't got no mama or daddy, so I don't reckon I got to have a last name."

Anthony felt a surge of sympathy. "What happened to them?"

"Don't matter," Russell grumbled.

"It matters to me," Anthony said calmly. "And since you're my prisoner in the business you were stealing from, you might as well tell me."

Russell glared at him for a long moment. "My daddy died during that dumb war. Reckon it was the third year, but my mama hadn't seen him since he left in the first weeks. He never knew about me. My mama did the best she could. She was with some new man a couple years back, but when she ended up pregnant, he lit out of here lickety-split. Mama and my little sister died when she was born."

Anthony's heart softened with sympathy. "You've been on your own ever since?"

Russell stared around the office. "I didn't have nobody else," he said simply.

"That's why you're a thief?"

The defiant look melted away as Russell's eyes fell to the floor. "Didn't know what else to do," he admitted.

"What are you doing with the things you steal?"

"Sellin' em," Russell answered. "I make enough to eat."

Anthony gazed at the stick-thin figure of the boy in front of him. "You must not eat much," he observed. "Why aren't you stealing more things?"

That got the boy's attention. He gazed up with a look of disbelief. "My mama wouldn't like it that I steal things. I don't take more than I got to."

Anthony felt another surge of sympathy. He couldn't quite imagine what he would have done if he found himself in the same situation. "Where do you live?"

Russell seemed to shrink down into the chair. "Don't live nowhere. I find me a place to sleep at night."

Anthony knew things were bad for many children in Richmond, but he had yet to any personally. There were agencies trying to help, but the sheer number of war orphans was daunting. He sat silently as he considered his course of action.

Silence stretched through the room for long minutes.

Russell was the one to break it. "What you gonna do with me?" He took a deep breath. "If you let me go, I promise I won't come back to steal nothing from you."

"Just from other places of business," Anthony observed wryly.

"I do what I gotta do. But I won't do it here again."

Anthony's mind worked furiously.

"You gonna keep me here forever?" Russell finally demanded. "If you gonna take me to the police, go ahead and do it."

Anthony knew that was exactly what he should do, but he found himself shaking his head slowly. "I'm not taking you to the police."

Russell looked confused. "Then what are you gonna do with me?"

Anthony smiled slightly as he recognized the answer. "I'm going to give you a job."

Russell's mouth dropped open. "What?"

In truth, Anthony was as surprised as the boy. "I'm going to give you a job," he repeated.

"Why?" Russell asked. "I've been stealing from you."

"That's true," Anthony agreed. "But in all honesty, I might have done the same thing at your age, if I was on my own." He smiled again, before infusing sternness into his voice. "Can I trust you to quit stealing if I give you a job?"

Russell considered the question carefully. "How much you gonna pay me?"

Anthony bit back his laugh. He had to give the boy credit for cleverness. "Twenty-five dollars a month and a place to live. That's the going rate for laborers. You'll work Monday through Friday."

Russell's mouth dropped open.

Before the boy could respond, Anthony continued. "You can keep your wages each month, but you have to work on Saturday and Sunday for free, to make up for all the things you stole." He could see the boy's eyes narrow in thought. Whomever his mother had been, she had raised him to be a thinker. "For one year," Anthony added. "I figure that should repay the debt. After one year, you can continue to live here, but you'll work five days a week."

Russell eyed him. "What am I gonna do?"

"Clean stalls and oil the tack every day," Anthony replied. "And whatever else needs to be done. I don't really need to hire an extra worker now. Since I'm going to, you need to make life easier for the drivers."

"They drive, *and* clean stalls, *and* take care of their tack?"

"They do," Anthony assured him. "If you're going to be on your own, you need to learn how to work like a man."

Russell mulled over Anthony's words before nodding. "I reckon that sounds like a good thing," he said slowly. His eyes revealed the deep relief he felt.

"No more stealing?"

"No more stealing," Russell promised. Suddenly his seriousness evaporated beneath a huge grin. "I got me a real job," he said proudly, before he sobered. "I reckon my mama, wherever she is, would be real glad." He stood up and held out his hand. "I'll work real hard for you, Mr. Wallington." He hesitated. "I like horses a whole lot."

Anthony swallowed the sudden lump in his throat. "You do?" he managed.

"Yep. My daddy left before I was born, but my mama's brother helped us make do. They said he was too sick to fight. He had a horse named Rocky. He taught me how to ride when I was five, but he died a year later. When things got real bad, my mama had to sell Rocky and move here to Richmond."

Anthony recognized the pain shining in Russell's eyes. "Broke your heart, didn't it?"

Russell didn't look away. "I reckon it did."

Anthony felt a surge of affection for the boy. "Let me show you where you're going to sleep." He reached over to unlock the office door.

The first drivers were arriving for the day. They didn't seem surprised to see Anthony emerging from his office with a young boy. They nodded, smiled, and called out greetings.

Anthony lifted his hand in response. "Good morning," he called.

Russell followed him down the aisle.

Anthony stopped in front of a door and pulled it open. He knew what he would find: a storage room crammed with old tack that needed repair. It was one of the many things he was trying to get around to.

Russell stared into the gloom. "Don't look like there's a place for me to sleep," he said doubtfully.

"Not yet," Anthony agreed. "Your job for today is to clean out this room. We have an extra stall down at the far end of the stables. I want you to carry everything down there, and clean this room. You can sleep in it tonight." He waved his hand toward the tack room. "You'll find some buckets and rags in there. Make good use of them. I'll make sure you have a bed for tonight."

Russell looked up at him, for the first time looking like the little boy he was. "Why are you doing this?" No longer defiant, he simply looked confused.

Anthony leaned down, put his hand on Russell's shoulder, and smiled. "Because I can," he replied. "The whole country is hurting right now, and we all have to do our part to make things better. This is something I can do." He straightened. "Besides, I'm not giving this to you. You're *earning* it." He instinctively knew the boy needed to feel a sense of pride. "You're going to work hard, and you're going to make life easier for other men who work hard. I need you."

Russell straightened as his eyes took on a shine. "I'll work real hard," he said firmly.

"I know you will."

"You gonna be around here all the time?" Russell asked hopefully.

Anthony felt an unexpected pang as he shook his head. "No," he answered. "I have to go home to my family tonight. I live several hours from here."

Russell looked alarmed. "Who's gonna tell me what to do?"

At that moment, Willard and Marcus walked into the stables.

Anthony beckoned them over. "Good morning," he said cheerfully. "This is Russell. I've hired him to clean stalls and take care of the tack. He starts today. He's also going to be living here."

Russell gazed up at the two men as he shifted uncomfortably.

"Russell, this is Willard and Marcus. They co-manage River City Carriages. You'll do whatever they tell you to do."

Russell didn't look happy, but he nodded willingly. "Yes, sir."

Anthony waved his hand toward the open door. "He's going to clean this room out today. Marcus, will you have Hannah pull together some blankets for him? Willard, will you take care of getting him a bed and a lantern?"

Willard and Marcus stared at him wordlessly, and slowly nodded their heads. "Yes, Anthony."

Anthony hid his smile. He would explain everything to them later. He turned back to Russell. "Get started cleaning your room. I'll check on you before I leave this morning."

Russell nodded and turned away, but turned back. "Mr. Wallington?"

"Yes?"

"Will it be alright if I brush the horses sometimes?" Russell's voice was serious. "I promise I'll be real careful. My uncle taught me how to do it."

Anthony nodded, swallowing another lump in his throat. "I know the horses would like that," he said quietly. He laid a hand on the boy's shoulder again before turning away to the office, confident Marcus and Willard would follow him.

"The boy is going to live here?" Willard was the first to break the silence when Anthony closed the door to his office.

"He's the one who been doing all the stealing?" Marcus asked.

"Yes, and yes," Anthony answered, remaining silent while he waited for their response. He could imagine what was racing through their heads.

"Why?" Willard asked. "What's his story?"

Anthony explained Russell's plight, waiting as softened sympathy replaced their skepticism.

Marcus frowned when Anthony finished speaking. "What's the boy going to eat?" He answered his own question before Anthony could respond. "I reckon my Hannah can send extra food for him."

"That would be good," Anthony said gratefully. "He can help pay for the food."

"You paying him?" Willard asked keenly.

"Twenty-five dollars a month and a place to stay. That's our agreement."

Willard and Marcus nodded thoughtfully.

"And you believe he can be trusted?" Marcus asked.

Anthony shrugged. "I think so, but only time will tell. I'm counting on the two of you to keep an eye on him and make sure he stays busy. He's been on his own for a while. He's resourceful, but he needs some men in his life."

"A woman, too," Marcus retorted. "Me and Hannah will have him over to our place sometimes for dinner."

"I will too," Willard offered.

Anthony smiled. "I know he'll be in good hands."

Willard turned to leave but swung back around. "You did a good thing here, Anthony. A real good thing."

The warm glow in Anthony's heart told him Willard was right. "I'm leaving in a few minutes. I'm eager to get home."

"Anthony will be home tonight?"

Carrie nodded as Rose settled down in the rocker across from her. "He's supposed to be." She turned her eyes back to the horizon, listening closely for the sound of hoofbeats.

"You're worried."

"I'm trying not to be," Carrie answered honestly. She told Rose about Frances' and Minnie's concern.

Rose listened closely. "Why didn't you tell me about this before?"

"Neither Anthony nor I thought there was any real reason for concern," Carrie answered.

"But you do now?"

Carrie lifted her hands and allowed them to fall. "I don't have any reason to." She realized she wasn't making any sense, but she didn't know what else to say.

Rose nodded, her eyes never leaving Carrie's face. "Why are you thinking about Robert?"

Carrie's eyes filled with tears. Leave it to Rose to get straight to the heart of the matter. "I don't know. Maybe because it's spring?"

"It's been almost five years," Rose said softly.

"April 27, 1867," Carrie whispered. "Robert and Bridget both died." She shook her head. "I have much to be grateful for now. Anthony. The girls."

"Which doesn't replace what you lost," Rose replied gently. "They are new blessings, but the pain of your loss will always be there."

Carrie absorbed her friend's words as a soft breeze blew across the porch. "I'm still afraid," she admitted.

"Of course you are," Rose answered. "But you don't let your fear stop you. You don't keep Anthony from doing what he needs to do. You're letting your girls grow into independent, strong women. That's what counts."

Carrie smiled. "You sound like your mama."

"I hope I do," Rose replied. "The older I get, the wiser I know my mama was."

Carrie couldn't have agreed more. "Do you think the fear will ever completely go away?" she mused.

"Probably not," Rose answered promptly.

Carrie frowned. "That doesn't sound very hopeful."

"But truthful," Rose retorted. "I'm afraid every time Felicia goes back to college. I'm afraid for her to travel with Sojourner Truth this summer. I know what can happen." Her voice trembled slightly. "So does Felicia."

Carrie reached over to take her best friend's hand. "Sojourner will take care of her."

"I know she'll do the best she can," Rose responded. "That doesn't always keep things from happening."

Carrie knew how true that was. "Are you changing your mind about Felicia going?"

Rose shook her head decisively. "As much as I would love to, Moses and I won't do that. That's my point. I don't believe I'll ever quit being fearful of what can happen to each of my children. To Moses." She drew a deep breath and looked out over the pastures. "I have to keep taking actions based on faith, not fear." A slight smile lifted her lips. "And keep praying."

Carrie knew she was right. She relaxed against the back of the white wooden rocking chair and gazed out over the plantation. Warm sunshine had chased away the pewter clouds that had dumped sleet on them the morning before. Brilliant blue sky embraced everything she saw. As if the countryside knew winter had delivered its last blow, the land had erupted with even more vibrant life.

The tight buds of the massive oak trees that bracketed the house were unfurling, promising rich shade. Lilacs were beginning to release their sweet fragrance, purple and white blooms swaying in the breeze. Massive banks of daffodils surrounding the boxwoods that lined the driveway danced with delight.

Carrie sighed with pleasure, and turned her eyes to the pasture when she heard a shrill whinny.

"Granite sees you," Rose said with amusement.

Carrie's heart swelled as she watched her colt run up and down the pasture fence. His tail, lifted high, floated behind him like a banner. "He's showing off."

"With good reason," Rose replied. "He's absolutely beautiful."

Carrie nodded, watching as Granite kicked his hind legs out and ran over to join his mother. "I'll be glad when the other foals are born. He needs someone to play with."

"Soon?" Rose asked.

"The first ones should start dropping next week," Carrie said happily. She was confident this year's crop of foals would be magnificent. The new mares they had purchased the summer before would all be giving birth soon. Nevertheless, Carrie and Susan wouldn't be able to meet the growing demand for Cromwell Stables stock. Letters of intent to purchase had been coming in since last fall. The knowledge filled Carrie with deep satisfaction. Abby had taught her the truth of supply and demand. Increased demand would keep the value of their foals high.

The goals she and Susan had set for their business had been aggressive, but she suspected they would make even more money than projected. She had learned to appreciate the financial aspects of their partnership, but her true joy came from the horses.

A sound in the distance brought her to her feet. She moved to the edge of the porch and looked down the winding driveway. The sight of a horse rounding a curve made her smile. "Daddy is home!" she called toward the open door of the house.

Moments later, Frances and Minnie appeared at her side, both of their faces bright with anticipation.

Anthony caught sight of Carrie, Rose, and the girls as he drew closer to the house. He hoped he would never stop being thrilled by the sight of his family. He knew how fortunate he was to have such a glorious home to return to.

The three-story house gleamed white in the afternoon sun. The trees, not yet decked out in their full foliage, revealed the guest house they had built the year before. The barn shone red against lush, green pastures full of dazzling horses. Rich brown fields, waiting for the tobacco seedlings, stretched out in the distance.

Anthony inhaled, relishing all the smells swirling around him. As soon as he had turned in through the brick pillars of the plantation, he had slowed his horse to an easy trot so it would be cool after the long ride, but his impatience caused him to break his gelding into a canter.

Carrie was waiting on the ground, her face lit by a brilliant smile, when he reached the house. He leapt off, threw his reins over the hitching post, and wrapped her in his strong arms.

"Welcome home!" Carrie cried.

"It's good to be home," Anthony answered. He kissed her warmly before he turned to sweep his daughters into his arms. "I am the luckiest man in the world."

"That you are," Carrie replied. "And we are the luckiest women."

Minnie giggled. "I'm not a woman, Mama."

"Not yet, but you're well on your way," Carrie teased.

"Daddy, is everything alright in Richmond?" Frances asked seriously.

"Of course," Anthony replied, exchanging a quizzical glance with Carrie.

"The robber didn't hurt you?" Minnie demanded, stepping back as if to examine him for wounds.

"The robber?" Anthony wondered how the girls could have known about the problem at River City Carriages.

"They overheard us talking about someone stealing from the stables," Carrie explained.

Anthony understood immediately. He pulled his daughters into his arms again. "Everything is perfect. I actually caught the thief."

"You did?" Minnie's eyes were huge. "Did he try to hurt you?"

Before he could answer, Clint, the stable manager, appeared behind him. "I'll take care of your horse, Anthony."

Anthony nodded his head with gratitude. "Thank you, Clint. He has definitely earned some extra feed."

"I'll take good care of him," Clint promised as he turned and led the gelding away.

Anthony glanced up toward the house when he heard the front door swing shut. He smiled as Annie approached with a tray of lemonade and cookies. He grabbed Frances' and Minnie's hands. "How about if I tell the story while we have something to eat?" He rubbed his stomach dramatically. "Your daddy is starving!"

"You better eat those cookies before Moses and John get home," Rose said with a smile.

Anthony strode over, leaned down to give Rose a hug, and reached for a cookie. "Not to worry, Rose. I know to eat my fill before your husband and son arrive on the scene. I'm not sure which one of them eats the most. Thank goodness Jed doesn't seem to be trying to keep up with them."

Moses' and Rose's newest adopted son, Jed, was small for his age, but wiry and strong.

Annie placed the tray on a chairside table. "Moses used to eat exactly like John when he was a boy. Course, food weren't so easy to come by then. Moses woulda probably been even bigger if he ain't gone hungry so much."

Anthony nodded soberly. Moses and his entire family had spent most of their lives as slaves. The fact that Moses was now half-owner of Cromwell Plantation was a remarkable thing.

"Which means John will probably be bigger than Moses," Carrie said with amusement. "It's a good thing you love to cook, Annie. He's going to eat a lot of food."

Annie nodded, a look of warm satisfaction in her eyes. "Ain't nothing gives me more joy than fillin' a body with food."

"Which is something all of us are eternally grateful for," Anthony said fervently.

"Daddy, tell the story," Minnie demanded impatiently. "What happened with the robber? Was he a real mean man?"

"Not exactly," Anthony said as he reached for the platter. Despite Minnie's impatience, he took the time to eat two warm sugar cookies. He wiped his mouth with a napkin and took a long swallow of lemonade before he answered. "More like a scared little boy."

Carrie's eyes widened with surprise. "A little boy?"

"His name is Russell. He's ten years old."

"The same as *me*?" Minnie asked breathlessly. "He was stealing from you? Why? Where are his mama and daddy?"

Anthony told the story. "He was desperate," he finished.

"What did you do to him?" Carrie asked, her eyes soft with sympathy.

"I gave him a job," Anthony responded, explaining the entire situation.

Minnie grinned. "He has a place to eat and he's going to have money. I'm so glad you did that, Daddy!" She sobered. "That could have been me, if you and Mama hadn't adopted me."

"And me," Frances added.

Anthony knew how right they were.

"What about his education?" Rose asked.

Anthony turned to Rose, his heart sinking as he realized he had missed one very important part of the whole equation. "His education..." His voice trailed off as he shook his head. "Of course, he should be in school."

"In time," Rose agreed with a smile. "I think the most important thing is to give him shelter and food. Can he read?"

"I have no idea," Anthony admitted. "I'll find out when I return next month. Hopefully he won't still be as skinny as a rail when I get there."

"He won't be if Hannah has anything to say about it," Rose replied. "She likes to feed people almost as much as Annie."

"*Almost* would be the right part of that," Annie snipped. "We should get that boy out here to the plantation. I'd fatten him up in no time."

Anthony sucked in his breath as Annie spoke the words he had thought about all the way home.

"Could we, Daddy?" Minnie asked. She leapt up from her rocking chair and stood in front of him, her blue eyes latched on him like a beacon. "There's room out here for one more little boy, isn't there?"

Carrie reached over to take her daughter's hand. "Would you like to have a brother, Minnie?"

## *Chapter Three*

Anthony watched the exchange carefully. He and Carrie had talked about adopting more children. He knew there was endless need, but both of their children seemed to have been meant purely for them. Surely, catching Russell as a thief gave them a special connection, but they all had to agree as a family before they adopted another child. John and Hope had both been eager for Moses and Rose to adopt Jed last fall after his father died from a terrible beating by the Ku Klux Klan in South Carolina.

Minnie thought about the question for a moment. "It might be a little strange to have a brother my same age, but he sure sounds like he needs a family. Just like I did," she added seriously. "I wonder sometimes what would have happened to me if you and Daddy hadn't wanted me after my other family died in the fire. I was real lucky."

"We were the lucky ones," Carrie said fervently.

"I was too," Frances said, her eyes as beseeching as Minnie's. "If you hadn't come to the orphanage to find me, I don't know what my life would be like now. I do know I wouldn't have my own horse, I wouldn't live in a beautiful place like the plantation, and I wouldn't have the chance to be a doctor." She took a deep breath. "It sounds to me like Russell needs the same chance. I'm glad he has a place to live and a job, but that's not the same as having a real home and family."

"Besides," Minnie added. "It's how we do things around here."

Anthony leaned forward. "What do you mean, sweetie?"

Minnie turned her small face up to him. "Well, you adopted me and Frances. Rose and Moses adopted Felicia and Jed. They didn't have anyone either. Me and Jed were talking last week, and we decided Cromwell Plantation is meant to be a place where things like that happen." She smiled brightly. "I think we have room for a brother."

"I do too," Frances added, but glanced back at the house. "*Do* we have room for him?"

"We'll always make room for children in need," Carrie said reassuringly. She turned her eyes back to Anthony.

Anthony suspected he should wait until he and Carrie could have a real conversation, but he also recognized the look of certainty in her eyes. She met his gaze with a smile and a nod. They would work out the details later. "So I'm going back to Richmond?" he asked.

"It looks like you are, my dear."

Anthony felt a surge of joy that practically took his breath away. He was thrilled with his family of daughters, but he could also acknowledge his longing for a son. Since it was dangerous for Carrie to have any children, he had known adoption was the lone option, but he had never dreamed he would find his son stealing from his business. The irony of it brought a smile to his lips.

"You like him, don't you, Daddy?" Minnie asked, breaking through his thoughts.

"I do," Anthony said gladly. "He's smart and resourceful. He's also full of spirit." He smiled warmly. "He's special, just like you two are."

"Do you think he'll want to come to the plantation?" Frances asked anxiously. "What if he wants to stay in Richmond?"

"We have to let him make that choice," Anthony replied. He hoped that wouldn't be the case, but Russell had been forced to grow up quickly. He had lived in Richmond with his mama until she died. Though he'd never known his father, the combination of the war years and losing his mother was a lot for one little boy to handle. He might not want to leave that connection. "Regardless, we'll make sure he's taken care of."

"But you'll try to convince him, won't you?" Minnie pressed.

Anthony smiled again. "I promise I will do my best."

Rose listened to the conversation quietly. The look in Anthony's eyes when he had first talked about Russell already revealed to her what his true desire was. There was no surprise in the decision they had made. She exchanged a long look with Carrie. "Cromwell Plantation is becoming much more than we dreamed."

Carrie nodded. "I've quit trying to guess what's coming in the future. I'm learning to live one day at a time and see what happens." She smiled, but immediately sobered. "I know the need is vast. The war and disease have left many orphans all over the country. I wish we could take all of them, but I know that isn't possible."

"No," Rose agreed, "but there are many people stepping up to help."

At that moment, Abby and Thomas walked onto the porch and settled down in the chairs next to Carrie.

"Stepping up to help with what?" Abby asked as she reached for a glass of lemonade and a cookie.

"War orphans," Carrie answered, and then told her what they'd been talking about.

Abby and Thomas smiled happily.

"You're going back to Richmond tomorrow to bring us a grandson?" Thomas asked.

"I'm going to do my best," Anthony assured him.

"That's good news," Abby said, clapping her hands joyfully. She turned to Rose. "Have you heard about the Friends Asylum for Colored Orphans in Richmond?"

"I know very little," Rose answered. "Other than they opened their doors last year. How do you know about that?"

"Last week, while Thomas and I were in Richmond, I met with the founder, Lucy Goode Brooks. She asked me if I would consider having the Bregdan Women's group here on the plantation donate some of their quilt earnings to help the orphanage."

Rose was surprised. "How did she know about the Bregdan Women's group?"

"Mrs. Brooks has worked with the local Quaker Society of Friends to buy the land at the corner of Charity and Saint Paul streets and establish the asylum. The head of the Society of Friends is familiar with what we're doing out here. Nancy Stratford and I met with her when Nancy was here. They're long-time friends from New York City.

"Mrs. Stratford who was here for Christmas, Grandma?" Frances asked eagerly. "The one who has invited me for a visit in New York City?"

"That's the one," Abby assured her. "I'm going to talk to the women tonight at our meeting."

"I'm sure they'll help," Carrie said.

Abby nodded. "I believe so too, but it will be up to them. They're working hard to provide money for their families. There may be some who don't feel they can contribute. I'll understand."

Rose was intrigued. "Tell us more about the asylum."

"The story really begins with Lucy Brooks," Abby replied. "She is quite a remarkable woman. She's mulatto, born to a slave mother and a white man. She grew up in slavery. At some point, she met another slave named Albert Brooks. She taught him to read and write so they could write passes to see each other."

Rose smiled, thinking of the secret school she had operated in the plantation woods. She'd taught Moses how to read and write.

"Lucy's master died when she was twenty. She was bought by another man who allowed her to marry Albert the next year. He even allowed them to live together, though she worked at his house during the day. Albert's owner allowed him to operate a livery stable. He collected rent, but he allowed Albert to keep the additional money until he had enough to buy his freedom."

"What about Lucy?" Rose asked.

Abby frowned. "She remained a slave. Although her master at the time, a man named Sublett, allowed her to be with Albert and their nine children."

"Nine?" Carrie asked with surprise. "They all stayed together?"

"Until 1858," Abby answered. "I realize how unusual that was. When Sublett died, his heirs threatened to sell Lucy and her children to different masters."

"The father obviously didn't pass his compassion down to his children," Carrie observed sardonically.

"Unfortunately, he didn't," Abby agreed. "Lucy and Albert were determined to keep their family together, though. Lucy went down to the tobacco warehouses and negotiated with merchants there. They purchased her children but allowed them to live with her as long as they showed up for work every day." Abby's eyes turned sad. "Except for Margaret Ann."

Everyone sat quietly, intent on hearing the rest of the story.

"Margaret Ann was seventeen when she disappeared one day. She left for work, but never came home."

"She was sold," Rose said flatly. She had seen it often enough to know how the story ended.

"She was sold," Abby agreed. "She was sent to Tennessee, where she died two years later."

"That's terrible!" Minnie cried.

"Yes, it was," Abby agreed in a soft voice. "That's why Mrs. Brooks is passionate about children now."

"What about her other children?" Rose asked.

"When Margaret Ann disappeared, Lucy and Albert worked extra hard to buy Lucy's freedom, as well as all the children's. Lucy's new master owned her and the three youngest boys, but allowed Albert to pay for their freedom in installments. It took four years, but in 1862, their freedom was granted."

"One year before the Emancipation Proclamation," Rose said softly.

"Yes, but we know it couldn't be enforced down here until the war ended. That's when the three older boys were freed. Their two daughters were already free."

Abby paused to let the story sink in. The sun was disappearing below the horizon, casting an amber glow over the barn and fields. A flock of Canada geese, heading north for the summer, flew overhead in a V formation, their loud honking filling the air.

Abby continued. "Lucy cares deeply about helping children who have been separated from, or lost, their parents. She's worked hard since the end of the war. In the beginning, the Freedmen's Bureau helped with food and care for abandoned children, but that was short-lived."

"They wanted local relief efforts and benevolence societies to carry the burden," Rose observed. "At the very time almost everyone was suffering from the consequences of the war. Unfortunately, it hasn't changed much in the last seven years."

"That's true," Abby agreed. "Lucy has worked long and hard to pull the funding and support together for the asylum. The city council approved the plan, and the building's location was authorized five years ago. It took them time to gather the money, but they opened their doors last year."

"What a remarkable woman!" Carrie's eyes sparkled with admiration.

"That she is," Abby said.

"The need is huge," Rose said ruefully. "And it will be for a very long time."

"For both races," Thomas observed. "There are as many white orphan children as there are black – perhaps more. Most of the Confederate soldiers who fought during the war didn't have much to begin with. Four years of war took practically everything away...not to mention all the men who died."

"Many women died as well," Abby added sadly. "Disease and hardship killed them. There are very few families in the South who aren't suffering right now, but as usual, the children pay the highest price. People are working hard to provide for them, but far too many are like Russell, being forced to survive on their own in whatever way they can."

"You know," Annie said thoughtfully. "Ain't nobody got a lot right now, but most folks could take on just one more mouth to feed."

Rose swung her gaze to her mother-in-law, caught by the intensity in her voice.

Abby looked up, obviously hearing the same thing Rose had. "Go on, Annie. What are you thinking?"

Annie shrugged. "Everybody workin' here on the plantation done got plenty to eat. The tobacco crops be providin' jobs for right many folks. The greenhouse makes sure people don't go hungry during the winter. Most folks 'round here know just how good we got it. I wonder how many of them poor chilluns in Richmond could find a home around the plantation?"

Everyone stared at her.

"You talk to all the Bregdan Women about givin' up some money, Miss Abby," Annie continued. "I figure I'm gonna talk to each of them about addin' one more child to their family. If everyone who could, did a little, we could make things a heap better. At least for the chilluns we could bring out here."

Abby jumped up and rushed over to give the woman a warm hug. "Annie, that's a wonderful idea!"

Annie shrugged and looked away, but not before Rose saw the pleasure shining in her eyes.

"I completely agree," Carrie added, her voice thrumming with excitement. "Everything is here. Food, schooling, medical care. Annie, you've come up with a splendid plan."

"Well," Annie replied. "I guess we'll see how many of these families think it's a good idea. Sometimes people forget that they oughta be givin' back when things be good. Too many of these families been beat down for so long, they ain't learned how to give yet."

Abby smiled. "I have no doubt you can talk some sense into them. You say it precisely like that, and I believe they'll agree with your idea."

Moses had a broad smile on his face as he listened to Anthony recount the story of his trip to Richmond. The children, thrilled by the first truly warm night of spring, were playing chase in the yard, their calls and laughter ringing through the air.

"Then Minnie asked if there was room enough for another little boy on the plantation," Anthony said.

Moses slapped his massive hand on his knee, his laugh booming over the noise from the children. They all stopped their playing and stared up at the porch. "Let me guess, you're going back to Richmond to bring Russell home?"

"If he wants to come," Anthony replied, a grin concealing his anxiety. The decision had been made two hours ago, but he already felt like Russell was the son he had always wanted.

Jed ran up the steps to the porch. "Who you going back to Richmond for, Mr. Anthony?"

"Who *are* you going back to Richmond for," Moses corrected.

Jed rolled his eyes. "Mama isn't here, Daddy."

"That doesn't mean you don't have to speak correctly, son," Moses said good-naturedly. "She's not the only one who happens to believe it's important."

Jed grinned and shook his head slightly before he turned back to Anthony. "Who *are* you going back to Richmond for, Mr. Anthony?" he asked clearly and succinctly.

"A boy your age, Jed," Anthony answered. "His name is Russell."

"He's ten?"

Anthony remembered the grief that had swallowed Jed the previous summer when his father died as a result of a savage beating, shortly after his mother had been murdered in the same attack. Carrie and

Janie had done all they could to save his father, but in the end, infection had ravaged his body. It had been a lot for a little boy to handle. Anthony relished in the easy grin and confident shine in the boy's eyes now. "That he is."

"Is he needing a home?"

Anthony swallowed the lump in his throat. "He is, Jed. He lost his daddy during the war. His mama died about a year ago."

Jed absorbed that knowledge with a knowing nod. "Do you want me to come with you? So I can tell him he'll be happy here?"

The lump in Anthony's throat grew tighter. "I appreciate that Jed, but I think I need to have a man-to-man talk with him. He'll need to make his own decision."

Jed frowned thoughtfully. "Like Daddy and Mama did with me when they let me make my own decision."

"That's right," Moses agreed, reaching over to put a hand on his son's shoulder.

Jed cocked his head. "Does he like horses?" His voice grew more serious. "That's important out here, you know. I want Russell to go riding with me and John."

Anthony smiled. "He likes horses."

Jed grinned. "You tell him about all the horses, Mr. Anthony. He'll want to come live here."

Anthony hoped he was right.

Carrie smiled when she saw Moses, Anthony, and her father waiting on the porch. She, Rose, and Abby had let Annie off at the door to the barn and waited until she climbed the stairs to join Miles in their apartment. "Good evening!" she called.

The three women climbed out of the carriage and waved their thanks to Jeb, their driver and guard. There had been no trouble on the plantation for a few years now, but everyone knew it would be unwise to lower their guard. During the day, Jeb kept watch over the school, riding with Rose and Phoebe back and forth from the plantation. Jeb was not merely their driver, he had also become a close friend.

Jeb rumbled away toward the barn, where he would unhook the horses and give them their feed.

"How was your Bregdan Women meeting?" Moses asked in his deep voice.

"The children are all in bed," Anthony added.

Carrie sank down in a rocking chair next to Anthony, waiting until Rose and Abby had claimed their seats. She pulled a blanket around her shoulders to ward off the chill that had settled over the night. Spring had arrived, but the nights would be nippy for a while.

"It was wonderful!" Abby answered. "Every single one of the women agreed to donate a percentage of their earnings from the quilts to the orphanage."

"*All* of them?" Anthony asked, the surprise evident in his voice.

Abby smiled. "You wondered if the white women would want to donate to an orphanage for black children?"

"Well, yes," Anthony admitted. "Now I feel bad for even thinking it."

"I wondered the same thing," Moses said.

"I was very proud of them," Abby replied. "The white women merely said that children are children, and they need to be taken care of. They realize how much making the quilts has created a different life for their own children."

"Abby very wisely told every woman that they could decide on the percentage they gave away," Rose added. "Every time we sell quilts, we'll put out a box for donations and each woman will give what she wants. No one will ever know but them."

"Smart," Thomas said admiringly. "Of course, I've always known I have a brilliant wife."

Abby smiled at him lovingly. "We're sending a new shipment of quilts up to Nancy in New York in two weeks. She has buyers for all of them, and eager women waiting for the next shipment. We'll be able to send help to the orphanage soon."

"Like I said," Thomas replied as he reached over to take his wife's hand. "I have a brilliant wife."

"What was the decision about the children?" Anthony asked. "I've thought about that a lot tonight."

Rose answered the question. "Annie gave them a lot to think about. My mother-in-law was quite persuasive. No one could make a decision, of course, because many of them have to go home and talk to their husbands, but we're going to have a meeting where everyone can come and ask questions." She paused. "One of the women made an excellent point. She said that the reason she was seriously considering taking a child in was because of the community we've created here. She knew they wouldn't be alone in raising another child because everyone would help."

"Amen to that," Thomas replied.

Anthony stood and reached for Carrie's hand. "It's been a long day. If I'm going back to Richmond tomorrow, I need some sleep."

"Are you riding or taking the carriage?" Abby asked.

"The carriage," Anthony said promptly. "How else will I be able to bring your new grandson back?"

Carrie smiled up at him and turned toward the house. She prayed he was right. Somehow, in all the discussion about Russell, he had already become her son in her mind.

She knew she would be on pins and needles until her husband returned.

## Chapter Four

Willard looked up with surprise when Anthony strode into River City Carriages late the next morning. "What are you doing here?"

Anthony grinned but didn't answer the question. "Where is Russell?"

A knowing look appeared in Willard's eyes. "He's cleaning out the stalls down at the south end of the stables."

"How's he doing?" Anthony asked.

Willard smiled. "He's a good worker, as far as I can tell in twenty-four hours. He didn't even flinch when I showed him all the stalls. He got his room cleaned out last night." He paused and held Anthony's gaze. "But I suspect he might not be needing it anymore?"

Anthony allowed himself another grin. "Russell and I will be in my office for a while if you need anything."

"Sure thing, boss," Willard said with a grin of his own. He turned and headed the other direction, whistling as he went.

Anthony found Russell in the fourth stall from the end, shoveling manure into a wheelbarrow that was close to full. "Good morning, Russell."

Russell dropped the forkful of manure he was holding and jumped back with surprise. "Mr. Wallington! I thought you was gone."

"I was," Anthony said, not able to control the smile twitching his lips. "I came back."

"Oh," Russell replied uncertainly. He looked around the stall. "Am I doing this wrong?"

"Not at all. As far as I can see, you're doing a fine job. How are things going here?"

Russell eyed him, clearly confused by his sudden appearance. "Alright I guess. I had a place to sleep last night. I had food for dinner and breakfast. I'm not hungry. I'm real grateful."

Anthony flinched at the vision of the little boy sleeping outside, cold and hungry during a long winter. "Can I talk with you?"

"Sure," Russell said readily, leaning on his pitchfork. "You need me to do something else?"

"No," Anthony assured him. "I would just like to talk to you. Will you come to my office with me?"

"Your office?"

Anthony understood the wary look that shone in the boy's eyes. "You haven't done anything wrong," he assured him. "I merely want to talk."

"Okay," Russell answered uncertainly. He leaned the pitchfork against the side of the stall and walked out to join him.

Anthony looked down at the thin figure walking bravely beside him. The affection he felt for the boy was growing deeper by the moment. When they entered his office, he pulled up a chair so he and Russell didn't have the desk between them.

"You sure I ain't done nothing wrong?" Russell asked. He swallowed deeply. "I don't figure I been here long enough to get in trouble."

"You're not in trouble," Anthony told him again, knowing his silence was making the boy uncomfortable. "My wife and daughters asked me to come back to Richmond to talk to you."

"Huh?" Russell's eyes squinted with confusion. "They know about me?" His look grew more uncertain. "I reckon they sent you back here to do something more to me since I was stealing from you."

Anthony shook his head. "You're not in trouble, remember?"

Russell eyed him for a long moment. "I don't get it," he said finally. "If I ain't in more trouble, why did you come back here today?"

Anthony leaned forward. "Because I have a question for you." During the long ride from the plantation, he had thought long and hard about the approach he would take. "We're wondering if you would like to come live with us at Cromwell Plantation. It's our home."

Russell stared at him. "What?" His voice and eyes were more confused than ever.

"Cromwell Plantation is where I live with my family," Anthony replied. "My wife grew up there. When we got married, I moved there, too. Now we have two daughters that we adopted."

Russell cocked his head. "Adopted?" The interest was obvious in his voice.

Anthony nodded. "Frances is my oldest daughter. We adopted her after her family died in one of the flu epidemics. Minnie, our youngest, lost her family to a fire in Philadelphia. She came to live with us two years ago."

Russell listened intently. "You aiming to adopt me, Mr. Wallington?" he asked bluntly.

Anthony had prepared for the question. He couldn't tell from Russell's voice how he felt about the idea. "Only if you want us to, Russell. I figure that isn't a question I can ask you right now. You don't know me. You don't know my wife and daughters, and you don't know anything about Cromwell Plantation. I'm simply asking if you want to come live out there for a while. You can decide more about what you want when you see what everything is like."

Russell stared at him, his eyes wide with bewilderment and surprise.

Anthony thought he detected a bit of longing, but he couldn't be sure. He waited for the boy's reply, trying not to show how anxious he was for Russell to agree.

Russell was silent for a long moment before he replied. "That's a real nice offer, but I really like being here with the horses, Mr. Wallington. I know I ain't been here long, but I like it a lot."

"I know you do," Anthony replied, deciding he would use what Jed had suggested the day before. "But we have even more horses at Cromwell Plantation." He hid his smile as Russell's eyes widened even more.

"*More* horses than here?"

"Yes. Except you can ride the horses on the plantation."

Russell gasped. "I could *ride* horses on the plantation?"

"You could," Anthony said gravely.

"When I'm not working?"

Anthony's heart swelled. "I'm not asking you to come out there and work, Russell. I want you to come live with me and my family. You'll go to school, and you'll have other children on the plantation to play with. And ride horses with," he added, knowing that was a key component to getting Russell to agree. He had decided on the trip in that he wasn't above bribery.

Russell sat silently for several moments, obviously trying to absorb this startling turn of events. Finally, he looked up and met Anthony's eyes. "Why are you doing this?"

"Because I like you," Anthony said promptly. "And because I would like you to have a family. If you decide you want one," he added quickly. In the short time they'd had together, he sensed Russell was a boy who would resist if he felt he was being pushed. He had to be strong to have endured what he had lived through in life. He was a young boy, but he was strong.

Russell looked away again briefly. "You said there are other children?"

"My daughter Frances is fifteen. Minnie is ten. There are three other children who live in the same house. John is nine. Jed is ten. Hope is six, but will soon be seven."

Russell's eyes narrowed. "There's enough room in this house for everybody who lives there?" His voice was skeptical.

Anthony was positive Russell had never experienced anything like Cromwell Plantation. "There's enough room," was all he said. He could tell Russell's brain was working furiously.

"Do I really got to go to school?"

"Yes," Anthony said firmly. "Everyone there goes to school." He paused. "Do you think your mama would be happy for you to go to school?"

Russell considered the question. "I reckon she would," he admitted half-heartedly. "She used to talk a whole lot about me going to school, but I never got to." He frowned suddenly. "I don't know how to read and write. What if I'm dumb?"

Anthony reached forward and put a hand on the boy's shoulder. "I promise you're not dumb. Anyone who could survive the way you have is smart and resourceful. It's one of the things I like about you."

A sudden glow appeared in Russell's eyes. "Really?"

"Really." Anthony tried to appear relaxed, but the longer he talked with the little boy, the more he wanted him to take him home. It was too soon to talk about adopting him, but he felt Russell was his son. "What do you say? Will you come home with me?"

Russell took a slow, deep breath and nodded his head. A nervous smile twisted his lips. "I reckon I would like that, Mr. Wallington."

Anthony allowed a grin to spread across his face. "I'm glad!"

Russell suddenly frowned and looked around with concern. "What about the work here? You told me I needed to work so I could make life easier for the drivers."

"The drivers will be fine," Anthony assured him. "I decided on the way back today that I was going to hire someone else to do the work. I'd never really thought about it before, but my drivers work very hard. It will be nice for them to not have to care for their horses."

Russell brightened. "Paxton!"

It was Anthony's turn to be confused. "Paxton? Who is that?"

"He's a boy I live on the streets with. He's older than me," Russell explained earnestly. "I think he's sixteen. I know he's wondering where I am." He turned beseeching eyes to Anthony. "He helped me a lot this winter when things were real hard. He sure could use a job and a place to sleep." The boy's eyes grew thoughtful. "I'll come home with you"—he paused—"if you'll give Paxton a job." His voice was firm and his eyes met Anthony's squarely.

Anthony couldn't stop the laugh that erupted from him. "You are quite the negotiator, aren't you?"

"He needs help, Mr. Wallington." Russell looked suddenly nervous, as if he was afraid he had pushed too hard and now Anthony would retract his offer.

Anthony knew he was going to say yes, but he let the silence stretch out before he nodded. "How do we find him?"

Russell relaxed. "He usually hangs out under one of the bridges across the river. Can we go find him now?"

Anthony's heart tightened as he thought of another boy in such need. He suspected he shouldn't show up at home with *two* boys, but he could give Paxton a safe place to live. Perhaps one of the families around the plantation would consider taking him in. Anthony stood and held out a hand. "Let's go find him."

Russell promptly took his hand.

Anthony felt his love for the boy deepen as they walked out of the stables and climbed into the carriage.

It took close to an hour for Anthony to wind his way through the Richmond roads. Throngs of carriages, wagons, and pedestrians often brought things to a standstill. It would have been faster on horseback, but he had no idea of Russell's riding ability. As he watched Russell's head swivel to take in all the activity, he suspected the boy had never seen the city from the vantage point of a carriage seat.

Spring was rapidly swallowing the winter dullness of the capital city. Most trees were beginning to leaf out. Oaks, maples, and poplars fought to give the most brilliant green foliage. Daffodils lent bright splashes of yellow everywhere he looked. Women, eager to shed their winter coats, had adorned themselves in brightly colored dresses, their parasols raised for protection from the sun. Groups of men wearing suits and top hats, thronged every street corner.

Seven years had created a vast difference in the city that had been horribly destroyed by four years of war. The final fire that had devoured the majority of the downtown district was now a thing of the past. New buildings had concealed all evidence that such a catastrophe had ever happened. New banks and businesses were working hard to restore the prosperity and opulence that had once made Richmond the jewel of the South. There was much work to be done, but the progress was impressive. Every time Anthony returned to the city, something had changed.

"You like it here, Mr. Wallington?" Russell's eyes shone as he took in the activity.

"I do," Anthony answered. "But not as much as I love the plantation."

Russell looked at him dubiously. "Ain't it boring to have to live out in the country?"

Anthony shrugged, certain once again that Russell had no idea what he was about to experience. "I've certainly never been bored on Cromwell Plantation. We'll see how you feel about it once you get there." He turned the carriage right at the next road and pulled to a stop near Railroad Bridge.

Russell leaned forward in his seat, his body tense with anticipation. "I'll run go find Paxton."

"I'll come with you," Anthony said. He knew the boy was capable of taking care of himself, but it was important for him to understand what Russell had lived through for the last year.

Russell shook his head decisively. "Under the bridge ain't no place for a man like you," he said firmly. "I'll go get Paxton and bring him out to the carriage."

Anthony swung down from the seat. "I appreciate that, but I'm coming with you." His voice was calm but left no room for dispute.

Russell shook his head. "Don't say I didn't warn you," he muttered.

Anthony, despite Russell's words, wasn't prepared for what he saw when they ducked under the shadow of the bridge. Dozens of children, both boys and girls, stared up at him. He cringed when he realized some of them were even younger than Russell. Most of them had dazed expressions; all of them looked hungry. Tattered clothes hung from thin, dirty bodies. Shoddy stick structures, covered with reclaimed pieces of canvas, were their shelters. One small fire, surrounded by rocks, seemed to be their sole source of warmth.

Anthony's heart sank as he stared around him. He had known children were suffering but seeing it for himself was another matter. He could only imagine what they had been through in the cold winter months.

"Is this where you've been living, Russell?"

Russell shrugged. "It's been alright," he mumbled. "Where's Paxton?" he yelled, darting toward a canvas shelter far up under the bridge.

A tall, lanky boy of about sixteen stepped out moments before Russell reached it. "What you yelling for, Russell? And where you been? I figured you must be locked up or something." His eyes caught sight of Anthony. He jolted to a stop and looked around as if searching for an escape. "Who is that? What you bring him here for?"

"It's alright," Russell assured him. "This is Mr. Wallington. He owns River City Carriages."

Paxton's eyes widened. "The place you been...?" He snapped his lips closed.

"Yes, the place he's been stealing from," Anthony finished wryly.

Paxton turned questioning eyes back to Russell.

"He caught me two nights ago," Russell admitted.

"Why ain't you in jail?" Paxton demanded.

Russell smiled slightly. "Cause he gave me a job and a place to live."

Paxton snorted his disbelief. "You're lying to me."

"He's not," Anthony assured him.

Paxton turned his head toward Anthony, his eyes hard and disillusioned. "Why'd you do that? What do you want from him?"

Anthony didn't know how long the older boy had been on his own, but life had obviously dealt him many hard blows. "I wanted to help."

Paxton's look said he clearly wasn't falling for what he was hearing. He turned back to Russell. "What you doing here? What'd you come back for?"

"'Cause I'm leaving. Mr. Wallington lives on a plantation outside the city. He asked me to come live there for a while with him and his family."

"So you can be his slave?" Paxton asked derisively. He turned a look of scorn on Anthony. "You telling me you weren't smart enough to tell him to get lost?" He shook his head. "I thought I taught you better than that."

Russell suddenly looked doubtful.

Anthony took a step closer. "Everything I told you is true, Russell."

Russell locked eyes with him for several moments before he shrugged. "Can't nothing be worse than the life I'm livin' now. I'll take my chances." He turned back to Paxton. "We came to look for you because Mr. Wallington said you can have my job at the stables if you want it."

Paxton's eyes narrowed. "What do I have to do?"

"Clean out stalls and oil tack," Russell said. "There's even a room you can live in. I cleaned it out yesterday. It has a bed."

"How many horses?"

"Forty," Russell replied. "They're real nice horses."

Paxton shook his head. "I'm going to take care of forty horses? Just for a place to sleep?" His lips curled back. "I told you he wants a slave."

"It ain't like that," Russell replied. "You're gonna get paid."

"How much?"

"Twenty-five dollars a month."

Anthony watched the teen's reaction carefully.

Paxton's mouth dropped open. "Twenty-five dollars a month?" He turned to Anthony. "Is he telling the truth?"

Anthony held the boy's eyes. "He's telling the truth, but you'll have to work hard. We require the best of care for our horses. If I find out you're not working hard, you'll have to leave."

There was a glimmer of hope in Paxton's eyes, but he maintained his defiant expression. "I reckon that sounds alright to me."

Anthony was beginning to have his own doubts. Perhaps the boy had been on his own too long. He might be too hard and cynical to fit in at River City Carriages. Then he thought of all the drivers working for him that had spent most of their lives in slavery. They had every right to be hard and cynical, but they were some of the finest men and workers he had ever known.

"This is a chance for you to have a new start, Paxton," Anthony said. "I know life has been very hard for you, but it doesn't mean it always has to be like that."

Paxton looked doubtful, but the hope was shining brighter. He didn't look away from Anthony. "When would I start, Mr. Wallington?"

"Unless you have a strong attachment to that canvas you're sleeping under, you can come with us now," Anthony replied.

Paxton's eyes widened. "Now?"

"Or when you're ready."

"I'm ready now," he blurted. "I got to gather up a few things." Suddenly he stopped and looked around him. All the children were watching the exchange, alarmed expressions appearing on their faces as they understood what they were hearing.

Paxton turned back to Anthony. "I'd sure like to work for you, Mr. Wallington, but I ain't gonna be sleeping in the stables."

Anthony knew the reason, but he asked anyway. "Why is that?"

"They need me here," Paxton replied. "I'm the oldest one here. Most of the children be lots younger than me. I help take care of them. The money will come in handy, but I got to be here every night." He shook his head. "Bad things happen to children out here, Mr. Wallington."

Anthony took a deep breath, his imagination filling in what some of those bad things might be. "I understand. I'm happy to give you a job."

Paxton's eyes filled with relief. "I'm gonna talk to everyone for a minute. I'll be out soon." He hesitated. "If that be alright with you."

"Go ahead," Anthony said. "We'll be over in the carriage."

"I'm gonna stay here with him," Russell said. "If that's alright."

"Of course it is," Anthony answered. Besides the need to talk to the children, he also knew the boys wanted a few minutes to speak alone.

Anthony walked out into the sunshine, but not until after he had taken time to look at each of the children. He smiled into each set of eyes. A few returned his smile. Most of them stared blankly or looked away. He wanted to gather up each of them and take them out to the plantation. Each of them deserved the opportunity to laugh and play; the chance to not be hungry, or cold, or afraid. They'd had nothing to do with the war that had torn their lives apart, but they were paying the price for it.

He knew he couldn't rescue all of them, at least not today. He was going to meet with the Bregdan Women's group when they came with their husbands to talk about what Annie had proposed the night before. Surely, once they heard the conditions these children were living under, they would want to help. In the meantime, he would do what he could.

## *Chapter Five*

Anthony gathered up the reins when Paxton and Russell returned to the carriage. "Ready?"

"We're ready," Russell announced.

"Ready," Paxton said firmly.

Anthony hid his smile, but it was obvious that whatever Russell said in the short amount of time the boys talked had made a difference.

When he was close to the stables, he pulled to a stop in front of a grocery store and turned to Paxton. "How many children live under the bridge?"

Paxton gazed at him and then looked back at the grocery store. "Twenty-seven, sir."

Anthony nodded. "I'd like both of you to come inside with me to pick out some food."

"Food?" Russell echoed. "For who?"

"For your friends under the bridge. I can't provide a home for all of them, but I can make sure they don't go hungry."

"How you gonna get the food to them, Mr. Wallington?" Paxton asked doubtfully.

"My drivers are going to take turns delivering it. You're going to show them how to get there, Paxton. You'll also make sure your friends aren't afraid to take the food." Anthony took a deep breath. "Can you do that?"

"Yes, sir!" Paxton said eagerly.

Anthony set the brake on the wagon, and vaulted off the seat. "Let's go, boys."

Once inside the store, he approached the man behind the counter. "Are you the owner?"

A portly man with a shiny bald head gave him a gentle smile. "Yes. How can I help you?" He looked askance at the two boys, dirty and in ragged clothes, but turned his gaze back to Anthony with respect.

Anthony turned to Paxton and Russell, suspecting they received treatment like this from everyone they met in the city. Little did the store owner know the resilience and courage these two children had. "Will you help me pick out food your friends will like?"

The boys' eyes widened, and they nodded their heads vigorously.

Thirty minutes later, they laid a mountain of cloth sacks on the counter loaded with vegetables, loaves of bread, fresh fruits, and thick cookies. Anthony had wanted to include milk, butter, and meat, but without refrigeration the food would go bad. At least the food was healthy and would fill them up. He suspected many of the children suffered from malnutrition. Once the drivers had their schedule for deliveries, those things could be added. For at least a few meals a week, they would have meat, butter, and milk.

The owner's eyes brightened as he watched the food pile up. "All of this, sir?"

"Yes. My name is Anthony Wallington. Who are you?"

"Michael Saul, sir."

"It's nice to meet you, Mr. Saul. I own River City Carriages. Every two days, one of my managers will be in to purchase more food. Will you be able to handle the demand?"

"Certainly." Mr. Saul hesitated. "Do you mind me asking who all this food is for? It's not often that I have anyone buy so much at one time."

Anthony smiled. "This food is for some very special children." He saw no reason to add more. He had caught on to the fact that having food could make the children targets. "Please make sure that they always receive the very best quality you have."

"Yes, sir!"

Anthony turned to Paxton and Russell. "Please carry this out to the carriage."

The boys sprang to do his bidding, wide smiles splitting their faces.

Anthony paid for the food and then joined the boys in the carriage.

"Mr. Wallington?"

"Yes, Russell?"

"Would it be asking too much if we could take the food back to the bridge now? I sure would like to see all my friends eating a real meal." Russell's eyes glimmered with joy. "It would be the first time."

Anthony adjusted his thinking quickly. Instead of heading back to the plantation, they would stay at the Cromwell house on Church Hill that night. "That sounds like a wonderful idea," he said enthusiastically.

He picked up the reins but paused. "If we're going back now, there are a few things I want to add. Wait here." He leapt out of the carriage, returning a few minutes later with a sack full of butter and a crate full of glass bottles of milk. "I say we should make this a real feast!"

Russell and Paxton laughed as they eagerly nodded their heads.

Anthony would never forget the sight of the children's faces when they saw the amount of food

Paxton and Russell unloaded from the carriage, nor would he forget the looks of disbelief when they learned more would arrive every two or three days.

"All this food is for us?" one little boy demanded. His brown eyes, peering from beneath a grimy thatch of shaggy red hair, shone with a combination of disbelief and delight.

"Just for you, Tommy," Russell said firmly. The look he gave Anthony was full of gratitude.

Anthony was quite sure the moment was one of the highlights of his life.

Paxton waved his arms and told the children to sit. It was clear he was the leader of the motley group. "You can't go around telling people you got all this food," he said. "They'll come steal it from us. You got to keep it hidden under your canvas, and you can't run your mouth about it. Understand?"

The children nodded silently, their expressions revealing they were aware of the danger they faced every day.

Paxton turned to Anthony. "Everybody who lives under this bridge is young. We learned early on that we had to stick together. It ain't safe to be with the older people."

Anthony gulped at the look in Paxton's eyes. Clearly, the boy had seen far too much. "It will help to have my drivers coming around every few days. I'll make sure they come at different times. That way, no one will know when to expect them. I'll also make sure the food is hidden under blankets, so it won't be obvious."

Paxton nodded, his dark eyes serious. "That's a real good idea."

Paxton turned back to the children. "I'm going to work at River City Carriages," he explained, holding up his hands when the children erupted in protests. "I told you this already. Don't worry. I promised I'll be back every evening. I ain't leaving you alone. The money will come in handy to take care of things around here." He turned toward another boy perched on a splintered crate. "Willy, like I said before, you're going to be in charge while I'm gone during the day. You're the next oldest, so you got to take care of things. You certain you can do that?"

Willy, a slight boy as food deprived as the rest, nodded solemnly. It was hard to tell his age, but Anthony guessed him to be about thirteen. "I reckon I can do that, Paxton."

"You know where River City Carriages is, don't you?" Paxton asked.

"Sure do."

"If you need anything, you come there and get me. Things gonna be better now that we got food, but I'll still be watching over you. Don't you worry about me going away." He gazed around him. "I'll be back every single night," he promised.

Anthony's throat tightened even more as he watched the exchange. Left on their own, these destitute children had formed their own community. His thoughts turned once again to the upcoming Bregdan Women's meeting. Whatever it took, he would find a way to help these orphans.

Frances raced into the clinic, her face glowing with excitement. "Are there patients coming in this afternoon?"

Carrie smiled, exchanging a knowing look with Janie. "Unfortunately, yes." She loved her daughter's enthusiasm for medicine, but her heart ached for the patient who would soon arrive. "First, how was school?" Frances was an excellent student, but only because she knew it was necessary to reach her goal of being a doctor.

Frances waved a hand through the air. "It was fine," she said impatiently. "The best part is that it's over." She frowned with concern. "What happened?"

"Do you remember Sarah Lee Trident?"

Frances nodded. "Yes, she's part of the Bregdan Women group. Her daughter Caroline is in the same class as Minnie."

Carrie sighed. "She has been badly burned. A neighbor was here just before you arrived to let me know. Her husband Matt is bringing her in."

"How did she burn herself?" Frances' eyes were bright with sympathy.

"Her son was playing in the house when she was lifting a kettle of boiling water off the stove. He accidentally knocked into Sarah, and to protect him, she grabbed the kettle with both hands. It spilled all down her front."

"Her arms and hands got the worst of it?" Frances guessed.

"I'm afraid so," Carrie replied.

"Why aren't we going to her house?" Frances asked. "Wouldn't it be better if we treated her there?"

Carrie smiled, impressed by her daughter's grasp of the situation. "Normally, I would say yes. However, if the burns are as extensive as her neighbor says, Sarah Lee is going to need to stay here for a few days."

"You're afraid of infection," Frances murmured.

"You are just like your mama," Janie said with a chuckle.

"That's a good thing," Frances said staunchly. "I think the best thing in the world would be to be just like Mama. I hope someday I will be as good a doctor as she is."

"Oh, you will be," Carrie assured her. "In fact, I believe you will be even better."

"Why?" Frances asked.

"Because you will have even more time than I will to learn everything you possibly can. Medicine is changing every day," Carrie said. "It takes constant study to keep up. By the time you get to medical school, you'll be learning about things I never could have dreamed of."

"Nice try, Mama," Frances chided. "We both know that isn't true, though."

Carrie raised a brow. "Excuse me?"

"I appreciate that you're trying to encourage me, but the reason I study hard now is because you've taught me I can never stop learning, no matter how old I get." She pointed at the bookcase against the far wall. "There are new books and magazines every week.

I figure it's going to take all I can do to keep up with you."

Janie laughed loudly. "Your daughter makes a very good point."

Carrie felt a warm glow of pride. Frances insisted she wanted to return to the plantation after medical school and go into practice with her and Janie. Carrie, more than anyone, knew how quickly the reality of life could change plans, but the knowledge that her daughter dreamed of doing it was enough for now.

"Mama, will Daddy be home today?"

"I hope so," Carrie replied. "Since he didn't come home last night, I imagine he had things that kept him in Richmond. I know, though, that he's eager to return."

"And he'll have Russell with him?"

Carrie shook her head. "I don't know, honey. I know he's going to try to convince him to return with him, but the decision will be up to Russell."

"Stealing and living outside in the cold can't be more appealing than coming to the plantation!" Frances exclaimed.

Carrie raised a brow but remained silent.

Frances flushed. "I wasn't asleep the other night when Daddy was talking about Russell to everyone," she admitted. "Your voices were loud enough to hear through the window."

"I see," Carrie answered.

"Minnie didn't hear," Frances hastened to add. "But neither of us would care, Mama."

"You wouldn't?" Carrie asked carefully. She and Anthony hadn't wanted the girls to know Russell's story until they had a chance to get to know him.

"Why would we?" Frances asked. Her eyes glowed with compassion. "If there hadn't been an orphanage for me after my family died, I could have ended up the same way. Even in the orphanage, I was never happy. The best day of my life was when you came to get me." Tears glistened in her eyes as she continued. "Minnie knows that if you and Daddy hadn't adopted her, she could have ended up in the streets like so many other children in Philadelphia." She paused. "Russell must be very brave. I can't imagine having lived outside during the winter we just had. I suppose I would have stolen to eat, too!"

Carrie gazed at her daughter, catching the admiration on Janie's face from over her shoulder. "You're quite remarkable," she said quietly. "Do you know that?" Frances, fifteen years old, showed a compassion and maturity that many adults didn't have.

Frances smiled. "I'm lucky," she said firmly. "I've been reading about how many war orphans there are. No one really knows the number for sure, but they believe it's hundreds of thousands."

Carrie knew the number was true, but the war wasn't the sole cause. The war had produced most of the orphans, but the numbers had increased during the cholera and flu epidemics that had followed the war.

"People are doing all they can to help," Janie said. "Orphanages are being set up all over the country."

Frances scowled. "Orphanages are better than living on the streets and going hungry, but they aren't like having a real family." Her scowl deepened. "And there obviously aren't enough, or Russell wouldn't be living like he does."

The clatter of wagon wheels outside the door ended the conversation.

Carrie opened the door quickly, and stepped outside onto the stairs. "Please bring Sarah right inside," she called.

Sarah's husband, Matt, helped her out of the wagon. Two young boys, both of their faces tight with fear, peered over the side.

"I'm real sorry, Mama!" the youngest called shrilly. "I'm real sorry!"

Sarah, her normally attractive face twisted with pain, attempted a smile. "I'll be fine, Terrence. Don't you worry."

Carrie stepped down and wrapped her arm lightly around Sarah's waist, being careful not to touch her arms. "She's right, Terrence. We'll take good care of your mama." She kept her voice calm, but her heart twisted at the sight of the burned skin that was visible.

Janie turned to Matt. "We've got her. You can take the children home. We'll send word when we know more."

Matt nodded solemnly, obviously understanding what she wasn't saying. It would be best for the children not to hear the screams of pain that would surely come when they had to peel back her shirtsleeves from the hidden burns. His face rigid with concern for his wife, he climbed back into the wagon and clucked for the horse to move out.

Sarah watched the wagon disappear before she turned to Carrie. No longer needing to be strong for her children, her face crumpled with pain and fear. "It hurts, Dr. Carrie," she whispered.

Carrie smiled gently. "I know it does. Let's get you inside where we can take care of it."

Sarah followed her in, lying down on the table Janie had covered with soft blankets and a pillow. "Terrence feels real bad."

"It was an accident," Janie said soothingly. "Things happen."

"What are you going to do?" Sarah asked, her voice catching with the pain. She stared at them, resolutely refusing to look at her marred hands.

Carrie exchanged a look with Janie, her mind racing. The burns were worse than she had first thought. They ranged from second-degree to third-degree. While the second-degree burns were painful and would cause scarring, the third-degree burns caused the most concern.

"You gave Matt some herbs when he cut himself real bad last year," Sarah said. "Is that what you're going to do?"

Carrie shook her head. "I'm afraid your burns are too bad for an herbal remedy, Sarah. But," she hastened to add when Sarah's eyes widened with alarm, "there are homeopathic remedies that will help." She laid a hand on the woman's shoulder. "First, though, I would like to ease your pain and make this procedure simpler."

Janie stepped forward, immediately understanding the plan. "We would like to put you to sleep with chloroform," she said gently.

Sarah's face whitened even more. "Put me to sleep?"

"We don't have to," Janie replied, "but the pain of cutting your sleeves away from the burns is going to be intense. We can do it without a sedative, but I wouldn't suggest it."

"The choice is yours," Carrie assured her.

Sarah stared at them and nodded slowly. "I've been hurting real bad ever since it happened. I suppose if I don't have to feel more pain, that would be good." Her eyes glimmered with a mixture of fear and relief.

Janie nodded. "You won't feel anything, Sarah."

Carrie sat with Sarah while Janie went to the supply closet to get the chloroform. She used it as little as possible, but it was the best choice for surgery. Skill and care were necessary to differentiate between an effective dose that would put Sarah to sleep, and one that would paralyze the lungs, causing death. She was confident in Janie's ability to give it to her correctly.

Janie returned quickly, doused a cloth with the chloroform, and skillfully administered it.

They sat quietly together while Sarah slipped into a deep sleep.

"We can't use herbs?" Frances asked when Sarah was unconscious.

"No," Carrie replied. "It's not that they'll hurt her, but it won't provide the healing needed for these kinds of burns." She decided to take a moment to teach her daughter, giving Sarah more time to lapse into an even deeper sleep.

"If the only symptoms were pain and redness to the skin, Sarah would have first-degree burns. That means just the top layer of skin, the epidermis, is burned." She pointed to the blistered skin covering their patient's right hand. "These blisters show the burns here are second-degree burns that have damaged the top layer and some underlying areas of skin. They're very painful and will produce scarring but are more easily treated." Then she indicated the left hand. "Most of the boiling water must have poured onto this hand."

"The skin is almost black," Frances observed.

"Yes," Carrie said grimly. "These are third-degree burns. All the layers of the skin have been burned through. It's possible that the underlying fat, muscle, or bone have also been injured. Though these are the most serious burns, it's possible that Sarah's pain came solely from the second-degree burns. Burns this severe can destroy the nerve endings under the skin. They produce less pain in the beginning, but they're the most dangerous."

"They also have a higher risk of infection," Janie added with a frown. "They can take months to heal."

Carrie knew her friend was thinking of the soldiers they had treated during the war who had come in with massive burns on their bodies. Most of them had died.

"What are we going to do?" Frances asked, her eyes soft with sympathy.

"First, we're going to cut away her sleeves. We need to discover how far the burns are up her arms." Carrie paused. "Please get a bucket of water, Frances. We have to soften the cloth so it will release from her skin."

Frances grimaced. "That's why you had to use the chloroform."

Janie nodded. "The pain would be unbearable without it. In order to treat the burns and prevent infection, the cloth has to go. Unfortunately..."

"Removing the cloth is going to take the skin with it," Frances finished grimly.

"Right," Janie replied. "The water to soften the cloth will make it a little easier."

Frances grabbed a pan and dashed outside to fill it with water.

Carrie and Janie exchanged a long look.

"She's going to scar," Carrie said. "But infection is our biggest concern."

"We treated many wounds like this during the war," Janie answered. "The conditions here are far better than we had in the hospital."

"Yes," Carrie agreed. "We can be grateful for that."

Frances returned with the pan of water. "Mama, won't her sleeves have protected her from the boiling water? Perhaps the burns won't be as bad," she said hopefully.

Carrie shook her head. "I'm afraid it doesn't work that way. Her sleeves actually retained the heat from the boiling water. It usually increases the severity of the burn. Matt had no reason to know this, but he could have cut the sleeves away from Sarah's arms as soon as it happened in order to reduce the burns. As it is..."

Frances scowled and set her lips. "How can I best help?"

"I want you to work on the right arm," Carrie replied. "First, you have to soak her sleeves for twenty minutes. Dip some towels in the water basin until they're soaked. Lay them gently on her arm, but only on the cloth. We don't want to break the blisters that have formed, because they're providing protection for the skin below."

Frances sprang into action.

Janie laid wet towels on Sarah's left arm and joined Carrie at the medicine cabinet. "Do you want me to ride over to the greenhouse to get some aloe vera?"

"Yes, please. I'm relieved we have an environment to grow it in. There are many reasons I'm grateful for the greenhouses that Felicia insisted we build, but at this moment, having aloe vera is at the top of my list."

Janie nodded and left. The sound of galloping hoofbeats said she would return as quickly as possible.

Carrie could have sent Frances, but she wanted her to have this experience. She and Janie had treated many burn victims. This would be her daughter's first.

While Carrie waited for the towels to soften the cloth, she gathered other supplies.

Frances appeared at her side. "What are we going to use, Mama?"

"Janie has gone to get aloe vera from the greenhouse. We'll squeeze the gel out of the leaves and apply it directly to the second-degree burns. It has amazing healing qualities. It will reduce the swelling, promote circulation, and inhibit the growth of bacteria. I'm also using Hypericum."

Frances eyed her quizzically. "The same homeopathic treatment you give the veterans with amputated limbs?"

Carrie thought about the dozen veterans who had regained their lives after phantom pain from amputated limbs had left them hopeless and in agony. "Yes. The wonder of Hypericum is its ability to restore nerve loss. It's the best treatment for Sarah." She reached into the cabinet. "For the second-degree burns, we're going to use a diluted tincture of Hypericum—one part tincture to three parts water—before the blisters break. You'll use a dropper directly over the burn, letting the liquid run over the entire burned area. Then we'll cover it with the aloe vera."

Frances listened carefully. "What will go on the third-degree burns?"

"Nothing," Carrie replied. "I will give her three to five drops of Cantharis tincture in a half-cup of water three times a day when she wakes up. Burns this severe have to begin to heal from the inside. When the burns have started to heal, I will apply either a Calendula or Hypericum tincture to promote faster healing."

Frances shook her head. "How do you hold so much information in your brain?"

Carrie chuckled. "It's not about holding it in my brain. It's about having access to the information when I need it." She waved her hand toward the bookshelf. "When I received news of Sarah's accident, I researched burn care. You'll never be able to remember everything you learn about medicine, Frances. What's most important is to remember where you learned it, so you can access it again."

"How are we going to keep the infection away?" Frances asked.

"By keeping it as clean as possible," Carrie said promptly. "We'll also have Sarah drink garlic and honey tea. I've never seen anything more impressive than garlic at keeping infection at bay. Thankfully, we're treating this before the infection has set in. We'll have her stay here for four or five days before we let her go home. She'll have to come back to have her bandages changed, but the major danger of infection should have passed."

"Sarah is lucky to have you and Janie as her doctors," Frances said fervently.

Carrie knew her daughter was right. Though choosing to close the Bregdan Clinic in Richmond had been painful, she was grateful every single day that the plantation clinic was available to everyone in the area. She was also grateful that her profits from the Cromwell Stables assured that every patient, regardless of their ability to pay, was provided care.

"The cloth should be wet enough to remove," Carrie said as she picked up two narrow forceps. "I'll show you how to do it."

Frances didn't reach for the forceps Carrie held out to her. "Do you really believe I can do this, Mama?" she asked nervously. "What if I make a mistake?"

Carrie smiled. "You'll probably make a mistake every day for the rest of your life, Frances. I learned a long time ago that I can't let my fear of mistakes keep me from doing what needs to be done. I will learn from every experience, and what I learn will make me a better doctor for my next patient." She pressed the forceps into her daughter's hand. "If I didn't believe you could do this, I wouldn't let you work on Sarah. Watch what I do very carefully. It's not hard, but it does require careful attention."

"Won't I be taking off skin?" Frances looked slightly ill.

"You will be," Carrie said gravely. "There's no way to avoid that. It's also the only way to make certain Sarah gets well. Just remember, she can't feel anything right now."

Frances looked uncertain. "And afterwards?"

"It will be painful," Carrie said honestly. "But we'll give her willow bark tea to ease her discomfort." She moved to Sarah's left side. She knew action was the best way for Frances to conquer her fear. "Let's get started."

Frances took a deep breath and nodded.

Carrie spent several minutes showing Frances how to cut the sleeve cloth away and pick out the remaining material from the burns. "Are you alright?" she asked.

Frances, her lips set in a tight line, nodded. "Yes."

Carrie felt a moment of admiration for her strong daughter, and then blocked everything from her mind but the task before her. Thankfully, the wounds uncovered on Sarah's right arm were also second-degree burns. As she pulled away the cloth on her left arm, however, she realized at least half of the burns were third-degree. She winced as she gazed at the raw, leathery flesh, and carefully picked out every fiber of cloth, knowing anything left behind could cause an infection.

When she completed her task, she straightened and stretched her back before she looked over at Frances.

"I'm finished," Frances announced. Her face was ashen, but her voice was calm.

"I'm proud of you," Carrie said warmly. A glance down at Sarah's right arm told her Frances had done a perfect job.

Frances smiled wanly, but gratitude glowed in her eyes.

The sound of hoofbeats alerted them to Janie's return.

Moments later, Janie opened the door, holding a bag full of aloe vera. "How are things here?"

"As good as can be expected," Carrie replied. "We've finished removing the cloth. We'll apply the tinctures next and put aloe vera on the second-degree burns." She was grateful for the sticky, transparent and tasteless substance obtained from the inner pulp of the aloe vera leaves.

"How long before she wakes up?" Frances asked.

"About an hour," Carrie replied. "We'll wrap her arms lightly with a sheet and cover her with a blanket until she wakes up." She turned toward the stove in the corner. "I'll make the teas while you and Janie apply the aloe vera."

Before she reached the stove, the clinic door opened again. Polly, her ebony face set with determination, strode in. "I heard about what happened to Sarah. She be a real good friend of mine. What can I do to help?"

Carrie smiled. "You're not supposed to be working today, Polly." The clinic's assistant was also a good friend. "You weren't feeling well when you left last night."

"I'm feeling a lot better than Sarah is," Polly retorted, before she repeated, "What can I do to help? Amber will be at the barn until late tonight 'cause there are supposed to be some new foals coming. Gabe had to go to Richmond to pick up a wagon of supplies for Moses. He won't be back until tomorrow." She stalked over to look at Sarah, her tiny form standing tall with determination.

"She's burnt badly," Carrie said quietly.

Polly's face tightened with distress. "I see that." She bent over to examine the burns. "When is she gonna wake up?"

"Less than an hour," Janie said.

"She's gonna be in a heap of pain," Polly said. "I reckon you want her to have some willow bark tea, and follow that with some garlic and honey tea for the infection. She's also gonna stay here a few days."

"That's right." Carrie wasn't surprised Polly knew their treatment plan.

"Y'all finish up what you doing," Polly said. "Then y'all just go on home. I'll take care of Sarah for the night. I'll be here if she needs anything." She paused and glared at Carrie. "Don't even be thinking of trying to tell me I ain't gonna do it. Sarah is a good friend. We been making quilts together all winter. She was a big help to me when Amber was sick with the flu last winter. I ain't leaving here until I know she's alright."

"Thank you," Carrie said simply. "You're what Sarah will need when she wakes up. She'll need the tea every couple of hours. I'll leave the Hypericum tincture. You'll want to squeeze a dropper full over the wound at least two times tonight. She'll need the Cantharis tincture in a tea every three hours. I want you to keep her drinking as much as possible. Burns can cause dehydration. I'll have Jeb swing by this evening to see if you need anything, and I'll be in early tomorrow morning to check on her."

Polly listened intently. "I'll do all that," she promised. "Now, I know Anthony is coming home tonight with that little boy. Amber told me about it."

"His name is Russell," Frances said eagerly.

"Russell," Polly added. "I know you want to be there when he gets back. Me and Janie will finish up here. You go on now."

Carrie hesitated, but Janie nodded her agreement.

"Go," Janie urged.

Carrie felt a twinge of guilt for leaving, but she knew Sarah was in good hands. Still, she hesitated.

"Can we, Mama?" Frances asked. "It sure would be nice to meet Russell when he first gets here."

Carrie looked into her daughter's pleading eyes and knew she wanted the exact same thing. She pulled off her apron. "Let's go."

## Chapter Six

Russell's eyes widened as the carriage pulled between the towering brick pillars that announced the entrance to Cromwell Plantation. "Is this it? The plantation?"

"It is," Anthony replied, anticipating the boy's reaction when they reached the house.

"How long is the driveway?"

"About a mile."

Russell's mouth dropped open. "A whole mile before we reach the house?"

Anthony nodded, knowing the boy must be feeling completely overwhelmed. Russell had peppered him with questions during the long ride out. He'd been amazed to discover Carrie was a doctor. He'd asked many questions about Frances and Minnie. Anthony had told him about Thomas and Abby.

Russell had absorbed it all eagerly, until Anthony got to the part about Moses, Rose, and their children.

Russell had stiffened when Anthony told him they were black. "You mean, there are niggers living in the house?"

Anthony fought to keep his voice calm. "We don't use that word on the plantation, Russell. The true meaning of nigger is ignorant. I can assure you there are no ignorant black people on the plantation. As a matter of fact," he continued, "we don't use that word to describe *any* black people. We consider it insulting."

The scowl on Russell's face didn't diminish.

Anthony knew the boy had lost his father during the war. Though he was quite sure Russell's family had never been wealthy enough to own slaves, the belief in white supremacy was strong among every part of the Southern population.

Anthony thought quickly. "Do you like being called a ratbag?"

Russell jerked his head around to glare at him. "I ain't a ratbag!"

"I know that, but isn't that what people in Richmond called you?"

Russell flushed. "They called me a dirty ratbag just 'cause I had to live under that bridge."

"That wasn't very fair," Anthony said quietly. "Do you think it's fair that black people are called niggers merely because of their skin?" Russell didn't reply, but Anthony could tell he was thinking.

"My mama told me ni... I mean, black people, are meant to be slaves because they're dumber than white people."

Anthony began to wonder if he'd made a mistake in bringing the boy to the plantation. On the other hand, Russell was only ten. All he knew was what he'd been taught. The only thing that would change his thinking was to discover his thinking was wrong. Everything he believed was about to be challenged.

"Don't you think they're dumber than white people?" Russell demanded.

"No," Anthony said simply. "But I'll let you make that decision for yourself."

"What does this Moses do, anyway?"

"He's half owner of the plantation," Anthony said casually. He swallowed his chuckle when the boy's mouth gaped open again. What he was hearing would be virtually impossible to comprehend.

"*Half owner*? Is that really true?"

"That's really true," Anthony assured him. He leaned forward eagerly. "We're almost there. This is the last curve before you can see everything."

Russell stopped talking and leaned forward as far as he could, as if hoping he would reach it sooner if he did.

Anthony watched his face as they rounded the last corner. He tried to see it through the boy's eyes. The three-story plantation house gleamed gold in the distance, the white paint colored by the setting sun. Verdant green fields stretched out all around, with an ocean of brown fields waiting for the growth of tobacco behind that, but a quick glance told him Russell's attention was fixated on one thing - the horses.

"Look at them..." Russell breathed. "They're the most beautiful things I done ever seen."

Anthony agreed with him. Cromwell horses revealed their breeding and care. Every coat gleamed. Every horse stood with their head held proudly, as they watched the carriage approach. Suddenly, a tiny form darted out from the tangle of horses.

"A foal!" Russell cried with delight.

"Evidently born just last night," Anthony replied. "The next few weeks will mean a lot of new foals."

Russell looked like he was in heaven, until he glanced toward the house. "Who are all those people?" His voice was tense, bordering on frightened.

Anthony had known the sound of the carriage would bring everyone outside. "That's my wife, Frances, Minnie, Mr. and Mrs. Cromwell, the Samuels family, and Annie."

"Why are they all out there?"

"They're eager to meet you," Anthony replied.

"How did they know I would be coming?" Russell demanded. "I might have said no."

"Yes," Anthony agreed calmly. "They would still be out there to greet me. It just so happens they're getting a bonus with you coming. They can see you sitting in the carriage, so they know you came with me."

Russell remained silent, but his tension didn't dissipate.

"You don't have to be nervous," Anthony said reassuringly. "They're going to love you."

Russell turned to stare at him. "Why? Do they know about me stealing from you? Do they know I live under the bridge?" He glanced down at the new clothing Anthony had bought for him the day before. "At least I'm clean," he muttered.

Anthony thought about the long bath Russell had taken the night before at the Church Hill house. He'd fallen asleep almost as soon as he had crawled out of the clawfoot bathtub. Anthony had pulled the covers over him, quite sure it was the first time in a very long time that Russell was both clean and warm.

"They're going to love you because I love you," Anthony said quietly.

Russell turned startled eyes to him, but before he could say anything, they pulled up to the porch.

"You're home!" Minnie cried.

"I thought you would never get here!" Frances called as she ran down the stairs with her sister. She slowed when she reached the carriage and smiled. "You must be Russell. Welcome to Cromwell Plantation!"

Russell gazed at her, seemingly struck dumb. "Thanks," he managed as his gaze swept the crowd of people on the porch.

John, Hope, and Jed broke free from the group and ran down to join the girls.

"Hello," John called. "I'm John. We're glad you're here. We've been waiting all day to see if you would come."

"I'm Jed! I'm the same age as you," Jed said, his face split by a wide grin.

"I'm Hope! I'm very glad you're here. Do you want to go see the horses? I have my own pony. Her name is Patches. She used to belong to John, but now she's mine because he has a bigger horse." Hope took a quick breath, her black eyes shining from her lovely face. "Are you hungry? Annie made fried chicken because she says everyone loves fried chicken. Do you love fried chicken?"

Russell gazed down at the little girl, his expression one of stunned amazement.

Anthony chuckled, knowing the boy must be overwhelmed.

Carrie came to Russell's rescue. "Enough everyone," she called as she swept down the steps. Her green eyes shone with amusement and welcome. "Let's not terrify Russell before he's even had time to eat a meal. He's had a long ride from town. Let's get some food into him and y'all can play outside after dinner." She smiled warmly up at the boy. "Hello, Russell. I'm Mrs. Wallington. You can call me Doctor Carrie if you'd like. I'm very glad you've come to stay with us."

"Hello," Russell managed. "You have a real nice place."

"Thank you," Carrie replied. "We all love it. We hope you will, too."

Russell's eyes turned toward the pasture as if drawn by a power he couldn't resist.

"I understand you like horses?" Carrie asked.

"Yes, ma'am!" Russell said eagerly. "I reckon I like horses more than anything."

Carrie chuckled. "You're going to fit right in, Russell." She glanced up at the porch. "Are you hungry?"

"Yes, ma'am!"

Anthony laughed. "You've been eating practically all the way out here. May put together more food than I've ever seen in that basket. How can you be hungry?"

Russell shrugged, looking slightly embarrassed.

Annie scoffed and walked to the edge of the porch. "May don't know how to make fried chicken like I do."

She cast an appraising look over Russell's bone-thin frame. "I reckon it will take a while to get you fattened up, but I sure 'nuff know how to do it."

Russell stared up at her, obviously mesmerized by her stout frame and kind face. "Thank you, ma'am."

"You come down out of that carriage, boy," Annie demanded. "Can't do nothing from that carriage seat, now can you? How you feel about Irish oatmeal cookies? I got a few set aside just for you. To hold you until dinner is ready."

"I ain't never had an Irish oatmeal cookie," Russell admitted as he eased down from the carriage seat, most of his tension gone.

"They're the best thing in the world!" Hope cried. "Grandma, can I bring the cookies to him?"

"Of course you can," Annie answered.

John rolled his eyes. "Hope believes anything Grandma makes is the *best thing in the world*," he said dramatically.

"And she would be right," Annie said sternly. "If you don't agree with her, I reckon you don't need any more of them cookies. I'll give yours to Russell."

John shook his head quickly. "I was just kidding, Grandma. Everything you make is the *best thing in the world*."

"Everybody knows *that*, Grandma," Jed said solemnly.

"You just keep knowin' that," Annie replied tartly. "You might just keep getting' to eat."

Everyone but Russell giggled. He continued to stare up at Annie with something like awe.

Anthony watched with the same kind of awe as Annie smiled down at the boy and wrapped her arm around his shoulder.

"You come on up here with me, Russell. You gotta meet Mr. and Mrs. Cromwell. And Mr. and Mrs. Samuels, though truth be known that still sounds strange to me. That giant of a man right there be my son, Moses. That pretty little thing is his wife, Rose."

Russell bobbed his head. "Pleased to meet you, Mr. Samuels. You too, Mrs. Samuels."

Anthony was impressed with his manners. His mother had taught him well before she died.

"And this is Mr. and Mrs. Cromwell. They be Doctor Carrie's folks."

Abby smiled warmly but stayed where she was, evidently sensing Russell was close to being completely overwhelmed. "Welcome, Russell. We're glad to have you come stay with us."

Anthony sagged against the carriage seat with relief. No one was saying a word about his and Carrie's desire to adopt Russell. They were simply welcoming him to the plantation as a guest.

Thomas reached out his hand. "Welcome to Cromwell Plantation, Russell."

Russell gazed at him intently before he reached out to shake his hand. "You're Mr. Cromwell?"

"That's right."

"This be your place?" Russell asked.

"Well, it started out as my place. My great-grandparents came over from England and created the plantation. This is where I grew up. Doctor Carrie, too." Thomas paused. "Things have changed some, though. Mr. Samuels is now co-owner of the plantation. He does all the hard work around here."

Moses chuckled. "Don't let him fool you, Russell. He helps me figure out all the finances around running a place like this, and he has decades of experience that I draw on. I mostly just ride the fields anyway. We have dozens of men who do all the truly hard work."

Russell's eyes swung from Thomas to Moses.

Anthony could tell he was trying to make sense out of dynamics he'd never experienced. He was doing it respectfully, however, and Anthony couldn't ask for more than that. He'd asked Russell to come experience the plantation so that he could decide whether he wanted to stay, and that's what the boy was doing.

"Is the tobacco going in soon?" Russell asked Moses.

"It is. Do you know something about tobacco?"

Russell shrugged. "My uncle raised tobacco until he died. My mama and I moved into town after that. Then she died. I don't reckon I remember too much about the tobacco, just that he grew it."

"I'm sorry about your mama," Moses said gently. "We're planting the tobacco next week. Would you like to ride with me to watch it go in?"

Russell's eyes widened. "Ride a horse? Through the tobacco fields?"

"That's right. Would you like to do that?"

Russell hesitated. "It's been a while since I been on a horse. I ain't never ridden a whole lot, but I sure do like it."

Moses nodded solemnly. "I guess we better get you on a horse as much as we can then, before we ride the fields." He motioned to John and Jed. "Do you two think you can get Russell comfortable on a horse before the tobacco goes in?"

Miles approached the porch as Moses called out the question. "I reckon we'll make that happen. I got just the horse for Russell to ride. I'll go out with all the boys for the first few times."

Russell's head swiveled to Miles. "Who are you?" he blurted.

Miles smiled easily. "Name is Miles. I happen to be married to Annie, so that makes me Grandpa to these three rascals here. I also work in the stables."

"The stables?" Russell asked eagerly. "Do you know a lot about horses?"

"I reckon I know a little bit," Miles said casually.

Anthony laughed loudly as he stepped onto the porch. "Don't let him fool you. This man knows more about horses than all of us put together."

"He's right," Carrie chimed in. "Miles taught me everything I know about horses. He taught me how to ride when I was a little girl."

Anthony could see the wheels turning in Russell's head.

"You been on the plantation a long time," Russell said as he looked back at Miles.

"Reckon I have," Miles agreed. "I started out here as a slave, but I escaped before the war and headed up to Canada. Freedom done be calling my name. Once the war was done and everyone be free, I came back down here and got me a job."

Russell stared. "You were a slave here?"

"That's right."

Russell looked deep in thought before turning to Thomas. "You owned slaves, Mr. Cromwell?"

"I did," Thomas replied. "I hate to admit that, but it's true." He seemed to sense that Russell was struggling. "I changed my thinking during the war. I used to think blacks were inferior to whites."

"You don't anymore?" Russell demanded.

"I don't," Thomas said firmly. "Blacks are exactly like you and I, Russell. They just have darker skin. They're every bit as smart as any white person I know. They're strong and courageous. Slavery was a terrible thing, but it's over. Now we have to rebuild a country based on equality and respect."

Russell remained silent.

Annie stepped into the sudden quiet. "That be plenty 'nuff talk for now. Y'all done enough jabbering to allow the biscuits to finish cookin'. I reckon it be time for dinner."

Hope stepped through the door with a platter of cookies. "But Grandma, I thought Russell was going to eat some Irish oatmeal cookies first!"

Annie bent down and kissed Hope's head. "That be real sweet of you to bring them out, but I reckon it's time for a real meal. There be lots of time for Russell to have my cookies."

Annie stepped over and wrapped an arm around Russell's shoulders. "This boy be hungry. I reckon it's time we show him what it's like to eat a Cromwell meal." She smiled down at him. "You ready for that?"

"Yes, ma'am," Russell said eagerly.

Anthony didn't know if Russell was hungry or simply eager to end the conversation he was having, but it didn't matter. The boy had more than enough to ponder.

Russell sat back in his chair and swallowed a groan. He'd never been so full in his life. Annie had insisted he should eat whatever he wanted, so he did. Now his stomach was stuffed with fried chicken, potato salad, hot biscuits with butter and jam, pickles, carrots, and three slices of fresh rhubarb pie.

"Full?" Anthony teased.

"Can you die from eating too much?" Russell managed.

Anthony chuckled. "I suppose it's possible, but I don't think you're there quite yet."

Carrie smiled. "Would you like the last piece of pie?"

The best response Russell could offer was a moan of denial.

Everyone around the table laughed.

"Hey, Russell! You want to go play tag on the lawn?"

Russell looked at Jed with disbelief. "How can you think about running? I don't reckon I can even move right now."

Jed laughed loudly. "I used to eat like that when I first got here. I'd never seen so much food in my life. I pretty much decided I was going to eat all I could because I was afraid it would disappear."

Russell cocked his head. "How long you been here?"

The table fell silent as the boys talked.

"Just since last summer," Jed replied.

"Why?" Russell asked. "I thought Mr. and Mrs. Samuels be your folks."

"They are now," Jed answered. "Weren't always like that. My parents died last year. My mother got killed by the KKK when they busted into our house one night. They took my daddy out and beat him real bad. He lived long enough to get me up here to Cromwell Plantation, but he died, too." His voice quivered and then strengthened. "The Samuels adopted me. Now I'm their son."

Russell stared at him. "Your folks got killed?"

"Yep," Jed said matter-of-factly. "Felicia's folks did, too."

Russell was confused. "Who is Felicia?"

"She's my older sister," Jed replied. "John and Hope were born to my mama and daddy, but not me and Felicia. Felicia is almost seventeen. She's in Ohio going to school at Oberlin College. She was twelve when her parents got killed in Memphis by some white policemen. Daddy brought her home so she could live here and be their daughter. She's real smart," he said proudly. "I'm going to be as smart as her some day!"

Russell gazed at him. "Felicia is in college?" He had registered the fact that both Jed and Felicia had been adopted, but what surprised him the most was that Felicia was in college. He didn't know that much about college, but he was sure you had to be very smart. He didn't know black people went to college.

"Yep. My mama and daddy also went to college," Jed answered. "Did you know my mama is the teacher here at the school? She started the school all by herself!"

Russell's brain was having trouble absorbing everything he was hearing. He turned to stare at Rose. "You're a teacher?"

"I am," Rose answered with a smile. "We'll give you a week to get settled in before you start school."

Russell wanted to scowl, but there was something in the warm compassion in her eyes prevented it.

"The stupid Virginia School Board keeps us all from being in the same class, though," Minnie said, jumping into the conversation. "They said white and black students can't be in the same school anymore, so now we have two different schools. They're right beside each other, but it's dumb."

"Oh," was all Russell could manage. "I ain't never been to school."

Minnie nodded with understanding. "I hadn't either," she confided. "Until I came here."

Russell's head started spinning again. "What do you mean?"

"Mama and Daddy adopted me. After my family was killed in a fire in Philadelphia. I knew how to read, but just barely. My mama couldn't send me to school, so I didn't go." She glanced over at her sister. "Frances taught me how to read," she revealed. "We were just friends then. It was before we became sisters."

Russell turned his eyes toward Frances. "Are *you* adopted, too?" He vaguely remembered Anthony talking about the adoptions but it hadn't truly sunk in.

Frances grinned. "Yes. I met Mama on a wagon train trip to New Mexico with my family, when she saved my life. When my folks died from the flu up in Illinois, I got put in an orphanage. Mama came and found me three years ago. I'm going to be a doctor now!"

Russell wasn't sure which was harder, absorbing the fact that Doctor Carrie had been on a wagon train to New Mexico, or the fact that Frances was adopted too. He decided to focus on the fact that Frances was adopted, because he had no idea where New Mexico was.

He swung his gaze to John and Hope. "Are y'all adopted?"

"Nope," John answered. "Mama had both of us, but she loves all her children the same. I'm glad she and Daddy had me, though, because some day I'm going to be as big as my daddy!"

"How old are you?" Russell asked.

"I'm nine."

Russell could feel his eyes widen. "You're younger than me, but you're a lot bigger."

"Yep," John said proudly. "That's because I'm Daddy's son. I can eat almost as much as him. Grandma tells me I'll be as big."

"Guaranteed," Annie declared. "Bigger, most likely."

Russell gazed up at Moses, who stood towering above the table. He'd never seen such a big man. He wasn't scary big, though. Russell had always felt scared around black people because his mama told him they hated white people and wanted to hurt them. He didn't feel that way right now. Moses made him feel safe for some reason; like nothing could ever hurt him if he was around.

Suddenly, his brain was simply too full, even fuller than his stomach. "Let's go play tag," he announced.

"Yes!" John and Jed yelled simultaneously.

"Let's play!" Hope cried.

"You're it first!" Minnie told her sister, reaching over to punch her arm.

Frances shook her head. "Not tonight. I'm tired. I'm not going to play."

"That's good," Hope answered. She reached over and punched Russell's arm. "You're it! I bet you can't catch me!" Turning, she dashed toward the front door.

Before Russell could register what had happened, he heard the front door slam, and the clatter of feet on the porch stairs.

All the adults laughed.

Anthony grinned at him. "I guarantee you'll run off that dinner by the end of the night. Have fun."

Russell looked around. Was it really alright to leave the table like that?

Carrie smiled warmly. "Go on, Russell. All the children play every night after dinner. You don't need to stay inside."

Russell nodded, trying to remember what his mama had taught him. "Thank you for dinner, Annie. It was real good."

Annie reached over and took his hand. "You be real welcome, Russell. Now get on out there and catch that granddaughter of mine."

Russell laughed, jumped up, and ran out the door. He could think about everything later. Right now, all he wanted to do was play.

Anthony watched Russell run out the front door. "I think he likes it here."

"Wait until he goes riding," Moses said. "He'll be in love."

"He's just out here to see how he likes it. I decided to not mention adoption to him. Not yet. I was afraid it would be too much."

"I think that was wise, dear," Carrie said. "I know all of this is a lot to take in."

"He has a lot to experience and think about," Anthony agreed.

"He's having trouble with black people living here in the house," Rose said calmly.

Anthony wasn't surprised that she'd picked up on that. "It's a different world for him. We talked about it on the way out here, but he'll need time to change his beliefs and feelings."

"He's ten," Thomas said. "At least he doesn't have five decades of thinking and beliefs to undo like I did. He'll be fine." He nodded toward the window.

Anthony turned his head and watched Russell running around the front yard, his face alight with laughter. It did his heart good to see all the children playing together, until he remembered the others he had left behind in Richmond.

"Why the frown?" Abby asked.

Anthony took a deep breath. "You have to see it to truly understand how terrible it is."

"Where Russell lived?" Carrie asked keenly.

"Yes. All he told me in the beginning was that he found different places to sleep at night. The truth is that he's been living under Railroad Bridge, next to the river. The conditions are appalling. There are twenty-seven children who live under that bridge. Paxton, the oldest, is sixteen. The youngest looks to be about seven."

"*Seven?*" Carrie looked horrified. "Living under a *bridge*? How is that possible?"

"They've formed an odd kind of community," Anthony replied. "Russell explained more to me on the way here. The older ones like him—"

"He's ten!" Abby exclaimed.

"I know," Anthony said grimly. "The older ones like him do the stealing. They sell what they steal so all the children can eat. Not that they eat very much." He explained about setting up deliveries from the grocery store. "At least they'll have food now."

"That's wonderful, Anthony! But what about clothes and medicine?" Carrie demanded. "Do they get any kind of medical care?"

"I'm sure they don't," Anthony answered. "As far as clothing, everything is tattered and filthy. I shudder to think how cold they were this winter."

Silence settled around the table for a long moment.

"Twenty-seven children?" Annie's voice was hoarse with emotion.

"Yes."

"What color they be?"

Anthony thought carefully, sure of where she was going with her question. At least, he hoped he was sure. "I'm not positive. I'd say most are white, but perhaps eight or so are black. I was too stunned by what I was seeing to register everything."

Annie nodded thoughtfully. "We got to find a way to take care of them babies." She turned to stare out the window. "I daresay it's been a right long time since that boy had a full stomach and something to laugh about."

"Do you think the Bregdan Women families would take them in?" Anthony asked hopefully.

"Ain't but one way to find out," Annie answered. "If I got anything to do about it, all of them babies gonna have full bellies and somethin' to laugh about!"

## Chapter Seven

April had arrived when Carrie settled back against a log and gazed out over the James River. The tide was completely in, the water lapping against the rocks inches from her feet. She watched a great blue heron glide in, landing with a splash only yards away. A bevy of purple martins darted and soared over the water, catching the dusk bugs that had begun to emerge. An osprey caught her attention as it halted its flight, flapped its wings to hover in place, and dove straight down to plunge into the water, emerging with a trout dangling from its hooked beak.

"Well done!" Carrie called. She breathed deeply, relishing the warm spring air. No Regrets and Granite grazed in the field behind her, their gleaming coats catching the last rays of sunshine.

Rose approached, a basket dangling from her hands.

Carrie smiled. "Was Annie concerned we would starve?"

Rose grinned. "My mother-in-law lives to feed people. When she discovered we were going to miss dinner, she insisted on sending some ham biscuits and cookies. Not her regular feast, but I assured her it was all we needed."

Carrie grabbed the basket. "I was actually wondering if I would starve before I got back to the house. I haven't eaten since breakfast." She opened the basket, pulled out a large cloth bundle, and extracted a thick biscuit.

Rose frowned. "Hard day at the clinic?"

"A long day," Carrie corrected. "Patients were waiting for us when we arrived. Neither Janie nor I had a break all day. Polly was our salvation. Without her, we never could have treated everyone. None of it was serious, but it was constant." She took a big bite of her ham biscuit. "It's so good..." she groaned. "I'm grateful I don't have to be worried about manners with you," she mumbled around a full mouth.

"Your children would be appalled," Rose admonished her with a laugh.

"What they don't know can't hurt them!" Carrie retorted before she took another bite.

Rose chuckled and leaned back against the log. "I received a letter from Felicia today."

Carrie eyed her for a moment, swallowed her bite, and took her best friend's hand. "It doesn't sound like it was good news."

Rose shrugged. "It wasn't *bad* news," she said slowly. "Felicia is nervous about the summer speaking tour with Sojourner Truth."

"I'm not sure she would be human if she wasn't nervous," Carrie said wryly. "Sojourner Truth is quite a woman. I imagine both of us would be awestruck to take the stage with her. She has made a massive difference for both blacks and women."

"She has," Rose agreed. "I'm sure I would be every bit as nervous as Felicia, perhaps more." She chuckled and asked, "Have you read *The Narrative of Sojourner Truth* that was published in 1850?"

"Not yet," Carrie admitted. "I have a copy of it, but I've not had time to read it."

"I finished it yesterday," Rose said. "It's quite intriguing. Sojourner can neither read nor write, so the book was written as told to her neighbor, Olive Gilbert. In all this time, she hasn't learned to read or write. She relies on her powerful speaking ability to communicate."

"Which obviously has worked well for her. What did you find most intriguing?" Carrie knew Rose was both excited and scared for Felicia to join the famous abolitionist and women's rights activist. She wasn't surprised her friend was learning everything she could about Sojourner.

"It's made me rethink how I view the North in regard to slavery," Rose said thoughtfully. "I think most Americans, including myself, believe slavery has existed almost exclusively in the South, but that isn't true. Sojourner was born in 1797 with the name Isabella in Ulster County, New York. There were tens of thousands of black slaves in New York. A large percentage of them grew up speaking Dutch because they were enslaved by Huguenot settlers."

Carrie was surprised. "Tens of thousands of slaves? In New York? I had no idea."

"Most people don't," Rose replied. "Slavery was a very important part of Northern life in the early part of this century. New York seemed to have had the most, but there were also slaves in all the other Northern states for many decades."

Carrie shook her head. "I've read so much about the open-minded, progressive, free North, contrasted with the closed-minded, backward, slave-owning South. I guess I never thought about what it was like in the past."

"The South is definitely closed-minded and backward," Rose said ruefully, "but the North wasn't a paragon of virtue. New York emancipated their slaves in 1827 – just forty-five years ago. By 1835, Northern slave states had emancipated all their slaves, shed the stigma of slavery, and emerged as the rhetorical home of freedom."

"Just thirty-seven years ago," Carrie mused. "In the big scope of time, that's nothing. Obviously, I need to learn more about the history of my country."

"The thing I found most intriguing," Rose continued, "was how differently Sojourner grew up. She was raised with her parents until she was nine, but then was sold, just like her ten siblings. She was separated from everyone."

Carrie gasped, feeling tears come to her eyes. "*All* of their children? That's horrible!"

"It gets worse," Rose said grimly. "Her new owners spoke no Dutch. She spoke no English. The result of the miscommunication was severe beatings. Now," she said matter-of-factly, "that was no different than the reality of many Southern slaves—neither the selling at slave auctions nor the beatings. What was different is that most Northern slaves worked and lived mostly alone among white people. Most Northerners could only afford one or two slaves, so there was no plantation slave quarters to take refuge in. There was no one to give her support."

Carrie thought through what she was hearing. "Not only was she sentenced to unremitting labor for the benefit of others, she was also severed from any psychological support of friends and family."

"That's right," Rose agreed. "When she was beaten or raped, or denigrated for being black, she was completely alone. As I was reading, I was thinking about how the slave quarters here at Cromwell enabled many of us to survive those years."

"Totally alone... That reality would either make you incredibly strong, or it would destroy you," Carrie said sadly. She had vivid memories of the laughter and singing that had filled the slave quarters here on the plantation. She knew it had concealed great pain, but the strong relationships among the slaves had been authentic and vital.

"True," Rose said. "In Sojourner's case, it made her strong. I won't go into everything the book says because it would ruin the reading for you."

"The book was published twenty-two years ago," Carrie said. "Has she spent all those years speaking?"

"Not all of them," Rose replied. "Her religion is very important to her. There have been years when she was part of a religious community, but her passion for abolition and women's rights has never waned."

"She's seventy-five," Carrie mused. "I wonder how long she'll continue to speak and tour."

"My guess is for as long as she's physically capable," Rose responded. "I can understand, though, why she wants Felicia to join her. The two of them speaking together will reach many more listeners because it will span generations." She paused. "The good thing about her being old is that she's well cared for when she's on tour."

"Which means Felicia will be too."

Rose smiled. "I'm counting on it."

The two friends fell silent, letting the peace of the waning afternoon wrap around them.

A flash of red caught Carrie's attention. "Oh my," she breathed.

"A cardinal?" Rose asked as she looked toward the maple tree that guarded a portion of the shoreline.

"No," Carrie said, leaning forward so she had full view of the oak tree to her right. "That is a scarlet tanager. They're just migrating back from South America. They're magnificent! The male is a bright red, but the female is yellow."

Rose cocked a brow. "Since when did you become a bird expert?"

Carrie grinned. "Since Frances decided she wants to know everything she can. She had my father bring her some bird books back from his last trip to Richmond. She's been devouring them, trying to identify as many birds as possible. Whenever we come to the river or roam through the fields, she teaches me about them."

Rose watched as three birds flew overhead. "What are those?"

Carrie looked up and grinned. "Loggerhead shrikes."

"Come again?"

Carrie laughed. "I learned these last week. You don't often see them over water. Those are probably headed to the closest open field where they can forage in a red cedar."

A blast of squeaky whistles split the quiet dusk.

Rose looked bemused. "Is that the birds?"

"It is. Loggerhead shrikes aren't known for their songs and calls. I'll admit they're rather harsh and jarring."

"A pity," Rose commented. "They looked pretty, until they made noise."

Carrie smiled. "I like them. They aren't as beautiful as the tanager, but I like the black mask that extends across their eyes to their bill. The wings are black, but they have a distinct white patch that makes them stand out."

Rose shook her head. "You're learning a lot about birds," she said teasingly.

"Frances loves them so much," Carrie replied. "Her passion is rubbing off on me."

"I suppose I should let her teach about birds in school," Rose replied thoughtfully. "It would be fun to see if her passion will rub off on the other students. Felicia gave many of my students a love for astronomy after she taught about meteor showers. Perhaps there are others that would fall in love with birds."

"I know Frances would enjoy it," Carrie said enthusiastically. "Everyone knows her passion for medicine, but this would give her something less intense to focus on."

"Is she still excited to learn all the herbs my mama taught you about?"

"Where do you think we see all the birds?" Carrie asked. "Every time we go out to identify the herbs we use for medicine, we see new birds. Frances decided she needs to know about them." She paused. "Frances loves the plantation as much as I did at her age. She wants to learn everything she can, about everything."

"What about Minnie?"

Carrie shrugged. "She loves the plantation, but she isn't hungry for the same kind of knowledge Frances is. She wants to ride and play. And cook with Annie. She seems to love cooking as much as Frances loves birds. After everything she's been through, that's perfectly fine with Anthony and me."

"She's ten," Rose observed blandly. "It's so wonderful to see her playing and cooking with Annie." She paused and looked out over the water. "It brings me so much joy to see John, Jed, and Hope riding and playing and going to school."

Carrie knew where her thoughts were. "You were already working in the house at that age. All the other plantation children that age were out in the fields." The memories made Carrie sad.

Rose changed the subject. "How's Russell doing? He seems happy at school, but other than meals, I don't see him much."

Carrie felt the familiar surge of joy when she thought of the young boy. "He's happy. He and Anthony ride out to join Moses and your children in the fields every day. He's only been here a few weeks, but he looks like he was born on a horse, and he's determined to know as much about tobacco as Moses does. Anthony says he never stops asking questions. He seems to love everything about it." She and Anthony had decided it was too soon to talk to him about adoption, but there was no doubt he loved being on the plantation.

"He's smart," Rose said. "I'm surprised how fast he's progressing at school. He was nervous and intimidated when he first arrived, but he seems more comfortable every day."

Carrie nodded. "Frances and Minnie work with him on his reading every single night. At first, he seemed disgruntled to have girls teaching him, but now I can hear the three of them laughing long after they're supposed to be asleep. I have to go in and send him off to bed every single night."

"John and Jed seem to like him." Rose pulled her head back and gazed up into the sky just as a flock of geese flew overhead. "Hope is in love. She wants to follow Russell everywhere. The most amazing part is that Russell seems alright with that."

Carrie nodded, a catch tightening her throat. "Russell told me last night that Hope reminds him of one of the children under the bridge."

Rose's face grew serious. "The meeting with the Bregdan Women is tomorrow night. Is Russell still going to talk to them?"

"He is," Carrie assured her. "He's nervous about speaking, but he knows how important it is for all his friends."

Rose turned to gaze at her. "You haven't talked to him about staying? About letting you adopt him?" Her eyes narrowed. "Are you and Anthony having second thoughts about keeping him?"

"No!" Carrie said quickly. "We're just afraid of pushing him too fast. We talk about adopting him every night, but it never seems to be quite the right moment." She sighed. "I wish we could be sure."

Rose continued to gaze at her. "You're going to have him talk to the Bregdan Women about adopting all his friends, but you haven't said anything to him about being adopted? Why not? Surely he must be wondering." She held up a hand. "I don't believe it's about not pushing him. Would you like to try again?"

Carrie flushed, both grateful and annoyed that her friend knew her so well. She hesitated before opting for honesty. "Anthony suggested we wait."

Rose looked surprised. "Why? He genuinely seems to love that little boy. Am I missing something?"

Carrie shrugged. "I wish I could tell you. I've asked Anthony if there's a problem, but he avoids answering. I don't want to push him, either. He loves our daughters, but I know he also wants a son. Since he's the one who caught Russell stealing, and wanted to bring him here, I've got to let him take the lead on this one."

Rose chuckled. "That has to be a challenge."

Carrie laughed but knew Rose could see the struggle in her eyes. "It's not part of my nature," she admitted. "I'm trying to be patient."

"How will you feel if Anthony doesn't want to keep Russell?" Rose pressed.

Carrie took a deep breath. "I'm not letting my thoughts go there. It's been less than three weeks. As far as I'm concerned, Russell is part of the family."

Rose didn't say anything more, but Carrie's heart was troubled. She would find out tonight why Anthony wasn't ready to talk to Russell. There was no way she was going to let that boy return to living in the stables, or under a bridge.

"You ready to talk about it?"

Anthony turned to Moses as they jogged lightly between tobacco fields newly planted with green seedlings that were beginning to stretch toward the sky. Warm days and brilliant sunshine were working their magic. He decided pretending ignorance was his best approach. "Talk about it?"

Moses rolled his eyes and cast a pointed glance to where Russell rode, side by side with John and Jed, ahead of them. "You ready to talk about it?"

Anthony sighed, knowing Moses wouldn't let him off the hook. While close before Russell had arrived, the hours the two men spent riding in the fields had brought them closer. "I don't know what to do," he confessed.

"About adopting Russell?"

Anthony nodded, truly not understanding the conflicted feelings he was having. "He's a wonderful boy. He loves the plantation, and he seems to be fitting in well."

"*Seems* to be?" Moses asked with a snort. "Everyone loves him. He even has my mama wrapped around his finger. Do you know she hid cinnamon rolls from John and me this morning to make sure Russell would have some?"

Anthony whistled. "That's big. The rest of us have to hustle to the kitchen early each morning to get our share before you and John come down to demolish them."

"You're right about that," Moses replied with a grin. "Mama told me that boy has had enough suffering in his life. She aims to make sure he feels spoiled out here on the plantation."

"I'd say she's accomplishing that!" Anthony replied with a laugh. "I swear that boy has gained ten pounds and grown an inch in less than three weeks."

"Then what's the problem?" Moses demanded.

Anthony took a deep breath and knew he had to face what was bothering him. He lifted his gaze to the horizon, taking in the varying shades of green coming to life from the border of trees lining the fields. The truth pounded into his heart like the strike of a hammer on an anvil. He looked back at Moses. "Tim."

Moses stared at him and shook his head. "Tim?" he asked with confusion. "Who's that?"

Anthony remained silent for a long moment before he answered. "My son." Merely saying the words made a fresh wave of pain roll over him. "He died shortly after birth. Seven years ago."

"Right after your wife died," Moses said quietly. "I'm sorry."

Anthony nodded, struggling with the emotions rampaging through him. Unable to say anything else, he gazed around the plantation as they rode. He waved to a number of the men who greeted them.

Moses waited for several minutes before he spoke again. "Help me understand what you're feeling."

Anthony sighed, wishing he could turn around and ride back to the house. Anything to avoid this conversation. He supposed he couldn't avoid it forever, though. "I couldn't protect Victoria and Tim." Moses was watching him carefully, but Anthony could tell he didn't understand. "I know it doesn't make any sense."

"It doesn't seem to," Moses answered honestly. "What does that have to do with Russell? You didn't seem to have a problem adopting Frances and Minnie."

Anthony fought to communicate his feelings. "Carrie adopted Frances before we married. Minnie was part of the family in Philadelphia because she was usually with Deirdre when she came to cook for us. I was with Minnie when she watched her family burn. She needed us." He fell silent, not sure how to continue.

"You don't think Russell needs you?" Moses asked, his eyes locked on the slight figure of the boy ahead of them.

Anthony shook his head. "That's the problem. I know he needs us. I know he needs *me*."

Moses said nothing, his dark eyes urging Anthony to continue.

Anthony felt a wave of helplessness roll over him; the same helplessness he'd felt when he watched his young son die seven years earlier. "What if I can't protect him? What if I adopt this boy, and I can't give him what he needs?"

Moses' eyes softened with understanding. "Did you watch Tim die?"

Anthony swallowed hard, blinking to rid himself of the memory of watching his tiny son struggle for breath, eventually relaxing into stillness when death claimed him. "Yes," he managed. "He was six hours old." He didn't need to add that he was also wrapped in grief, because his wife had died during childbirth a few hours earlier.

"Then you're the best father possible for Russell," Moses said firmly.

"What?" Anthony was startled. "I couldn't save my son." The image of Tim's death had been haunting him ever since Russell had arrived.

"You know the value of life," Moses replied. "You *already* love Russell. You have *already* saved him. You could have called the police on him, but instead you gave him another chance, and decided you wanted to give him a new life." He gazed ahead of them. "I've seen the way Russell looks at you. He adores you. You're his idol."

"But..."

Moses held up a hand. "We can't always protect them, Anthony. I worry about my children every single day. With the exception of John almost dying in the flood, I'm fairly confident my children are safe here on the plantation. It's what is waiting for them out in the world that terrifies me. America is not a good place to be black. All Rose and I can do is love them and prepare them the best we can."

Anthony felt a surge of sympathy. He knew his friend's children would face challenges his never would.

"Adopt that boy," Moses said firmly. "You love each other. Letting your fear stop you is nothing but a waste of time and love."

Anthony let the words seep into his heart, feeling the truth wash away the fear. Suddenly, he grinned, certain of his next step. "Thank you." He looked over his shoulder. "Carrie is down by the river with Rose. I want to go talk to her."

"Go," Moses said instantly. "I've got the boys."

Anthony, needing no more urging, turned his gelding and took off at a rapid canter.

Carrie and Rose exchanged startled glances when the sound of rapid hoofbeats interrupted their walk back down the trail. Carrie hated that her first thought was of trouble on the plantation. It had been a long time since anything bad had happened, but everyone knew better than to let down their guard. She tightened the hold on No Regrets' lead line and called Granite to her side. The colt trotted to her instantly, pressing close to her body.

As the rider rounded the curve in the woods, Carrie recognized her husband, his slim, wiry body moving in perfect rhythm with his horse. The sun glimmered off his blond hair as Anthony pulled his horse to a stop.

"What's wrong?" Carrie asked anxiously. "Has something happened?"

"Everything is fine," Anthony assured her. "I'm sorry I scared you." He smiled as he vaulted off his horse and pulled her into a warm embrace.

Carrie melted into his arms. "To what do I owe this pleasure?"

Anthony glanced at Rose. "Do you mind if I talk to my wife for a moment before we head back?"

"Not at all," Rose said easily. "I'll walk on ahead, but I can tell you she's going to say yes."

Carrie stared at her and then looked back at Anthony. Her husband was gazing at Rose with a bemused expression.

"You know, don't you?" Anthony asked.

"Doesn't matter what I know," Rose replied with a smile. "Carrie needs to know."

Suddenly, Carrie was certain what was about to happen. She grinned. "Is this about Russell?"

Anthony couldn't help but laugh. "So, the two of you have been talking about Russell?"

Carrie nodded but remained silent. Though she was certain what was coming, it wasn't up to her to say it.

"About why I haven't said anything about adopting him?" Anthony pressed.

"It's possible," Carrie said, gazing steadily into the green eyes she loved so much.

Anthony took a deep breath. "Since you both have been talking about it, and since Moses knows, I suppose it's only fair that Rose knows as well."

Carrie took a deep breath. "We're going to adopt Russell?"

Anthony could barely contain his excitement. "If he wants us to." His eyes danced with delight and anticipation.

Rose chuckled. "As my mama would say, *it don't take no brains to know what that boy done want.*"

Carrie nodded eagerly. "That's exactly right." She threw her arms around Anthony. "I can hardly wait to talk to him." She paused. "What made you decide?"

Anthony turned toward the river for a moment, his eyes skimming over the glistening surface before lifting to take in the bank of clouds aglow with the golden rays of the setting sun. "Moses helped me understand that I can't let fear stop me." He turned his eyes back to Carrie. "I've been thinking about Victoria and Tim."

Carrie understood perfectly. "You were afraid you couldn't protect Russell."

Anthony nodded. "I know it's silly but…"

Carrie reached up and laid a hand tenderly on his cheek. "It's not silly, my dear. You loved both of them so much. Watching Tim die is something you could never forget." She would never forget Robert dying in her arms, and she would always carry the trauma of waking up to discover her little girl had died while in her womb.

"You're not afraid anymore?" Rose asked quietly.

Anthony turned to her. "Moses and I agreed we'll always be afraid for our children, but he convinced me I can't let that fear stop me from adding them to our family." He wrapped his reins around his arm and turned in the direction of the house. "How about if we go find Russell and talk to him?"

## *Chapter Eight*

The children were playing a rowdy game of tag on the lawn when they returned to the house. On the way home, Anthony and Carrie had agreed they needed to talk with Frances and Minnie before they asked Russell to be their son. They were confident of the girls' answers, but they wanted them to feel part of it.

The three friends climbed the stairs and settled down into empty rocking chairs. The other chairs were occupied by Thomas, Abby, Moses, Annie, and Miles.

Moses watched them keenly, taking Rose's hand when she settled down in the rocker next to him.

Anthony allowed his eyes to settle on Russell, delighting in the boy's laughter as he ran around the yard with the other children.

"You going to put him out of his misery?" Moses asked after the silence had stretched out.

Anthony grinned but didn't look away from the boy. It was true that Russell had gained weight, but it was his flushed cheeks and the shine of happiness in his eyes that confirmed he belonged with them as their son.

Thomas leaned forward in his chair. "You mean you're going to let that boy finally know he's our grandson?"

Carrie smiled. "You agree with us adopting him?"

"More like we were going to never forgive you and Anthony if you let him leave," Abby retorted. "Russell is special. We've never had a grandson. It's about time!"

"Not to mention there weren't no way I was gonna let you take that boy away from here," Annie added. "He's part of this family. I reckon I was gonna have to knock some sense into y'all's heads. Glad to know I don't gotta do that!"

Everyone laughed.

Frances and Minnie were snuggled in their beds when Carrie and Anthony went in to talk to them.

Frances gazed up at them sleepily. "Good night," she murmured.

Minnie was struggling to keep her eyes open, yet Carrie wasn't ready to let them sleep. She was too eager for an answer.

"Girls, can we talk to you for a minute?" Anthony asked, perching on the side of Frances' bed.

Carrie settled next to Minnie. "We know you're tired, but..."

Minnie peered up at them groggily before bolting upright. "Are you finally going to ask us the question?" Her blue eyes were instantly awake and alert. She looked over at her sister. "Frances, they're going to ask us the question!"

"The question?" Carrie asked. "What are you talking about?"

Frances inched up to lean against her oak headboard, her brown hair gleaming in the lantern light. "John told us about it," she explained. "He said his folks came in to ask him and Hope *the question* before they adopted Jed."

Minnie pushed aside her covers, leapt up, and settled down on her knees, bouncing excitedly. "Are you going to ask us the question about Russell, Mama?" She reached out to grab Anthony's hand. "Daddy?"

Carrie chuckled and looked toward her husband.

Anthony laughed as well, and then grew serious. "I suppose we are, girls. How would you feel if we adopted Russell?"

"Yes!" Minnie cried. "I think it's really fun that I'll have a brother almost my same age. It's kind of like having a twin!" She clapped her hands joyfully. "He's already like a brother, even though I wish he didn't catch me in tag so much."

Carrie cupped her daughter's glowing face in her hands. "You really are quite extraordinary."

Minnie's smile disappeared as a serious expression filled her face. "Mama, Russell needs us. He doesn't have anyone. Just like I didn't. He doesn't say a whole lot, but he told me how scary it was to live under the bridge." She turned her eyes to Anthony. "He hated stealing things, but he said he had to make sure the younger children didn't go hungry."

Carrie's heart caught in her throat. She turned to Frances. "How do you feel about it, honey?"

"Well, of course we're going to adopt Russell," Frances replied calmly. "I already told him it was just a matter of time."

Carrie gasped. "You did? When did you do that?" She exchanged a look with Anthony. How long had Russell been waiting for them to ask?

Frances shrugged. "A few days after he got here. Anyone with a brain could tell what was going to happen."

Anthony took his daughter's hand. "You haven't told us how you feel about it, though. That's important to us."

"I'm excited," Frances replied instantly. "I haven't had a brother since Danny died on the wagon train."

Carrie held a hand to her throat, swamped by the memory of Frances' brother, frozen to death during the snowstorm four years ago. Though she'd been able to save Frances, her parents, and her two sisters during the blizzard, her entire family had died during the flu epidemic a year later.

Frances sought Carrie's eyes. "I think Danny would be happy for me to have another brother. He was always the favorite of my siblings."

Carrie managed to smile and nod. "I think you're right."

Frances turned to gaze at Anthony. "That was the day I knew I wanted to be a doctor," she said earnestly. "When I watched Mama save me and the rest of my family, I knew I wanted to be exactly like her." She smiled. "Of course, I had no idea how I could ever *become* a doctor, but I knew I wanted to be one." She shook her head. "It's a miracle to me that I have a life now that allows me to become what I want to be." Her voice grew serious. "I want Russell to have a chance to become what he wants, too. Adopting him will make that possible."

Carrie felt tears welling in her eyes. "You are quite a remarkable young woman, Frances." She squeezed her hand and then grasped Minnie's. "Both my girls are so special."

Minnie squeezed her hand tightly. "What are you waiting for, Mama and Daddy? You have our answer. It's time to go tell Russell!"

Anthony stood and reached for Carrie's hand. "I believe you're right, honey."

"What if he's asleep?" Carrie asked.

"Wake him up!" Minnie answered promptly. "He'll want you to!" She laid back down and pulled the covers up to her chin. "I'm ready to go to sleep now. Our job is done."

Anthony and Carrie laughed, kissed both the girls, told them goodnight, and started down the hallway toward the room Russell shared with John and Jed.

"Do we really wake him?" Carrie whispered.

"I agree with Minnie," Anthony said with a chuckle. "He'll want us to wake him."

Anthony opened the door quietly. Carrie smiled when she looked in. John and Jed were sound asleep, but Russell was perched on the windowsill, gazing out at the night sky. She thought of all the nights, growing up, when she had done the same thing – staring into the sky for answers to the serious questions of her young life.

"Russell?" Anthony whispered.

Russell spun around, clearly surprised to see them, but came when Anthony beckoned him to the door. "Yes, sir?" he whispered. His eyes widened more when he saw Carrie.

"Can we talk to you?" Anthony asked quietly, holding the door open so Russell could slip through.

Russell looked uncertain but followed them.

Nothing was said until they reached the porch. Everyone had gone to bed, so they had it to themselves. Anthony waved Russell to a chair, then took one next to him. Carrie settled down in the rocker on the other side of the little boy.

Russell swiveled his head to look at them both. "Am I in trouble?"

"Definitely not," Anthony said. He took a deep breath. "We want to ask you something."

Russell stared at him, his eyes uncertain, and his body tight with tension. "Alright."

Carrie watched him closely. She was certain she saw flickers of hope mixed with the obvious concern. When Anthony began to speak, she could tell he was choosing his words carefully.

"When I came to Richmond to get you, I asked you if you would come to the plantation and see if you liked it. You've been here almost a month. How do you feel about it?"

Russell smiled, but the serious look didn't leave his eyes. "The plantation is wonderful. I like it out here just fine." Then he frowned. "Is it time to go back to Richmond? Is that what you came to tell me?"

"No," Anthony said quickly. "It's quite the opposite, actually. Carrie and I love having you here on the plantation. In fact, we have fallen in love with *you*." He took a deep breath before he continued. "We would like to adopt you and keep you here forever as our son, Russell. What do you think of that?"

Carrie held her breath as they waited for Russell's answer. Thankfully, they didn't have long to wait.

"Really?" Russell breathed. "You want to adopt me?" He gazed at both of them and then frowned slightly. "Why?" he asked bluntly. "I mean, why would you want to do that? I stole from you!"

"In order to eat and help care for the younger children under the bridge," Anthony replied. "Stealing is wrong, but if I had been in your situation, I would have done the same thing. I'm counting on the fact that you'll never have to do that again."

Carrie reached out and took Russell's hand. "You're a wonderful boy," she said warmly. "We love you because you're courageous and caring. We love you because you're smart. Mostly though, we love you because you're very special. We will be honored if you agree to be our son, Russell."

Russell gazed at her. After a long moment, two tears slipped down his cheek. "I didn't reckon I would ever have a family again," he said hoarsely. He turned and stared out into the darkness, smiling slightly when a horse whinny split the quiet. "I think my mama would be real glad to have me out here. She hated moving into Richmond when my uncle died, but she didn't have no choice. The last thing she said to me before she died was, *I'm sorry*. She didn't want to leave me all alone."

"I know she didn't," Anthony said, taking Russell's other hand in his. "We promise to take good care of you. Will you be our son?"

Russell nodded slowly. "I reckon I would like that a lot." A smile broke through his tears. "Thank you," he whispered.

Carrie laughed loudly. "No, Russell. Thank *you*!" She released his hand and wrapped her arms around him. "Welcome to the family. We love you."

Anthony knelt in front of them, wrapping both of them in his long arms. "Welcome to the family, Russell. You've made both of us incredibly happy tonight."

"Not just them," Minnie said excitedly. Her voice floated from above them.

Carrie chuckled. She had forgotten the girls' window had been left open to enjoy the fresh spring air. Evidently, they had decided listening in on the conversation was much more appealing than sleeping.

"I'm real glad you're going to be my brother, Russell!" Minnie called.

"Me too!" Frances said.

Russell looked up, his eyes glowing with wonder and delight. "Thank you," he managed. Suddenly, he threw back his head with a loud laugh. "I'm going to be a Wallington, and I live on Cromwell Plantation!"

Breakfast the next morning was a boisterous affair, with lots of laughter, congratulations, and welcome flowing around the table. Russell sat quietly, absorbing all of it with a huge grin.

"So," Minnie cried, "does this mean we can talk about our trip to Boston and New York City now? Now that Russell will be coming with us?"

"Huh?" Russell asked, the confusion evident on his face. "What are you talking about?"

"We're going to Boston for Dr. Elizabeth's wedding," Minnie said importantly. "She's getting married at the end of May. We've all been invited. Now that you're our brother, that means you too! Have you been to Boston before?"

Russell shook his head, clearly puzzled. "I ain't been much of anywhere. Where is Boston?"

Frances smiled. "Just a minute." She disappeared into the library and quickly returned with a rolled-up piece of paper. "Let me show you on this map."

Russell's eyes widened when she unrolled the thick parchment. "I ain't never seen a map like this before." He hunched over it when she laid it on the table in front of him.

Frances pointed at things as Russell studied the map. "This is where we live. We're in Virginia." She outlined the state with her finger. "This is Washington, DC. It's the capital of our country. It's where the president lives."

Russell listened closely, following her finger as she moved it.

"This is Philadelphia. It's in a state called Pennsylvania. Minnie was born there, and I've been there several times. Grandpa and Grandma own a factory there. Rose's brother, we call him Uncle

Jeremy, lives there and runs the factory. It's also where Mama went to medical school. I'll live there someday, when I'm in medical school," Frances told him.

"Is Boston in Philadelphia?" Russell asked.

"No." Minnie jumped in. "Boston is in Massachusetts." She ran her finger up the map. "Boston is way up here. I haven't been there either. I'm real excited to go." She lowered her finger. "Then we're going to New York City! I've never been there either! It's the biggest city in the whole country."

Russell stared down at the map, his face tight with concentration.

Anthony could tell he was feeling overwhelmed. How could he not? His whole world was changing dramatically.

"How we gonna get there?" Russell asked. "Are we gonna take the wagon?"

"No," Minnie giggled. "It's way too far for that. We're going to take the train." She paused. "Have you ever been on a train?"

Anthony understood when Russell flushed with embarrassment. There was much he had no way of understanding. That would change in time, but for a while he was going to feel at a disadvantage among these children who had done much more than he had.

Jed came to Russell's rescue. "I ain't never been to Boston or New York City either. I've never even been to Philadelphia. I hadn't ever been anywhere until my mama got killed and my daddy brought me here."

Russell turned to his friend with relief. "Are you going to the wedding?"

"No," Jed told him. "John and Hope are going with Mama, but I'm going to stay here and help Daddy in the fields. He can't leave in the middle of tobacco season. I'll go to those places someday, but I'd rather be here."

Russell looked hopeful. "Maybe I'll stay here too. I can help with the tobacco crop."

Anthony thought quickly. He didn't want to pressure Russell to do something he wasn't ready for, but he wanted him to join them. "You can do that if you want to, but I would love it if you would come with us."

Russell turned his eyes on him. "Why?"

"Because I want to show off my new son," Anthony said promptly, glad Russell felt comfortable enough to ask questions. "I'm proud of you. It will make it more special if you're with us. I also want to show you all these places."

Russell gazed at him, and looked back down at the map, unable to hide his longing. "You been to all these places?"

"I have," Anthony assured him. "I think you'll love all of them."

Russell slowly nodded. "Alright." His agreement was followed by a frown. "I ain't got no real nice clothes, though. I got the new clothes you got me for out here, but I don't reckon they're meant for something fancy."

"You don't have to worry about that," Minnie piped in. "We're all going to Richmond to go shopping."

Russell looked up alertly. "You're going to Richmond? When?"

Minnie looked to Carrie for help.

"In two weeks," Carrie said. "You'll get new clothes too."

Anthony could tell Russell wasn't thinking about clothes. At least not clothes for him. He could practically hear the wheels turning in the little boy's head.

"Can I see my friends while we're there?" Russell asked.

"Of course," Anthony replied. "We had planned on that."

Russell hesitated and took a deep breath. "You reckon we could get some new clothes for them, too? I don't need much. Whatever you're gonna spend on me, you can spend on them instead."

Anthony's heart swelled at more proof of Russell's generosity.

Abby entered the conversation. "That won't be necessary, Russell. We've been collecting clothes from people ever since we heard about your friends. We've got two crates full. Some of the women have been sewing clothes for them. We're going to make sure they have what they need. If there isn't enough, we'll buy what is needed."

Russell's mouth dropped open. "You've been doing that for them, Mrs. Cromwell?"

"We have," Abby assured him.

Anthony knew it would take some time before Russell would be ready to call them anything other than their given names. Fortunately, they were willing to be patient.

Carrie reached for his hand. "Dr. Justin is going with us as well. She, Frances, and I are going to check everyone out and see who needs medical care."

"You are?" Russell breathed.

Anthony answered before Russell could ask the question he knew was coming. "We're doing it because we love you. That means we love the people who are important to you. Especially the children you lived with under the bridge. We're going to do everything we can for them."

Russell smiled brightly. "And tonight I talk to that group you call the Bregdan Women. About adopting some of my friends. Right?"

"Right," Abby answered. "They're looking forward to hearing from you. There will be a lot of people there tonight, but you don't have to be nervous. They're all coming because they want to know how they can help."

Russell turned to her, his face grave. "And all I've got to do is tell stories about my friends?"

"That's right," Abby assured him. "Someone's name is simply a word until you know their story. Then those names become real people. I want you to tell everyone what you know about your friends."

"And how they ended up under the bridge?" Russell asked.

"Yes." Abby paused. "If you'd like, you could tell me some of the stories before tonight. Sometimes, when I talk to a group of people, it helps if I practice first. Would you like that?"

Russell considered the question. "I reckon that sounds like a good idea. I know it's real important for me to tell good stories." He frowned. "I don't want to be the reason my friends don't get a good home like I have."

Anthony hid his own frown. He didn't want a ten-year-old to have to carry that kind of responsibility. He opened his mouth to reply, but Annie beat him to it.

"You ain't got nothin' to worry 'bout, Russell," Annie said firmly. "I been talkin' to these women ever since you got here. Your stories will make these chillun feel more real to them, but I know they already plannin' on helping out."

Russell turned to Anthony, accusation flaring in his eyes. "Is that what you're doing? Helping me out?"

Anthony understood why the idea was distasteful. "No," he said resolutely. "I fell in love with you that night when I caught you stealing. I knew you were special, and I wanted you as my son from that moment. I didn't tell at that moment because I thought it would be too much for you to believe. I wanted you to decide you *wanted* to be our son."

Russell pondered his answer, his eyes soft with emotion. "You reckon some of these families will love my friends, too?" His lower lip quivered. "It's kinda nice to feel love again."

Anthony knew without looking that there wasn't a dry eye around the table. "I reckon these families will fall in love with your friends," he assured him. "We'll make sure of it." He suddenly knew what Russell was really asking. "I promise you that we won't let a single one of your friends go to a family that won't love them like we love you."

Russell smiled brightly and turned to Abby. "Can we start practicing after breakfast?" He turned to Rose. "If it's alright with you, Mrs. Samuels, I would like to miss school today. I reckon being ready for tonight is more important."

"I agree," Rose replied. "I know you're going to do a great job, Russell."

"I hope so," Russell said doubtfully, his expression revealing he knew how important it was.

Anthony also knew how important it was. The fate of twenty-seven children huddled under a bridge depended on what the families decided tonight.

## Chapter Nine

The schoolhouse was packed when the meeting started. Every chair was full, with people standing along the walls.

Abby watched, examining each face as people filed in. Their expressions were a mixture of hope, determination, and compassion. She knew each family had their own reason for attending. Some simply wanted to extend the blessings of their family to a child in need. Others desperately wanted more children. Some wanted their first child. Several women who had lost their husbands during the war, had never had a chance to bear children. They were hoping to start their family. The stigma of being a single mother had eased as the reality of how many men never returned to their families grew clearer.

Thomas checked his watch and nodded.

Abby stepped to the front of the room. She waited for quiet, filled with gratitude for the people who had come. When she started Bregdan Women on Cromwell Plantation, she'd really had no idea what to expect - certainly not that seventy-five women would join her and create a unique community.

She'd been constantly amazed as she watched the women, both white and black, form deep friendships. Families that had been in dire straits were now comfortable, thanks to the income from the quilts that were regularly shipped north to New York City to be sold by her friend Nancy Stratford.

Women who had come in frightened and timid had become confident. They eagerly absorbed the business skills she taught them. Their children had also developed skills and were now planning more ventures to create income.

Now they were ready to give back.

"Welcome, everyone," Abby said warmly. "I'm not going to spend a lot of time talking, because we know why we're here. There are twenty-seven beautiful children living under a bridge in Richmond. We're going to change that reality for as many as we can." She looked around. "Some of you will decide it's not the right time for your family to make a lifetime commitment. There will be no judgement. The fact you're here says you care. Only you know what is right. Children need aunts and uncles too! Not just moms and dads!"

The faces looking back at her were both serious and hopeful.

"Actually, there *used* to be twenty-seven children under that bridge," Abby continued. "One of them will now become a Wallington." She smiled at Russell.

"Russell has agreed to be adopted by Carrie and Anthony. Thomas and I are thrilled to have such a special boy as our grandson."

Clapping and smiles broke out around the room.

Russell blushed but smiled broadly.

"And now," Abby continued, "Russell is going to do something that many of us would be too frightened to do. He's going to stand in front of you and tell you about his friends. For the last year and a half, Russell lived under that bridge. His father was killed during the war. His mother passed away during childbirth after they moved to Richmond. He's been alone in the world until now. There's no one better to tell you about the children you're considering inviting into your family."

Abby reached out a hand to Russell. "Thank you for doing this, Russell."

Russell gulped, took her hand, and moved to stand next to her, his eyes darting nervously around the schoolhouse.

"Russell, I know you're anxious," Abby said, "but you don't have to be. Everyone here is a friend. They want to hear you tell them about your friends." She had listened to him tell his stories several times today, impressed with the improvement that came with each recitation. He was determined to do the best he could to help his friends. He may be ten years old in actual living, but he was much older in experience.

Her heart swelled as she saw Russell's fear morph into determination. He took a deep breath and stood straight.

"Hello, everyone," Russell began, his voice ringing through the room. "I'm here to tell you about my friends under that bridge. First thing you oughta know is that not one of us wanted to be there. We were there 'cause we didn't have nowhere else to go. I ended up there because of Paxton. Paxton is the oldest of us. He's sixteen."

Abby thought about what Anthony had told her about Paxton. He had received word from Willard and Marcus that Paxton was working hard and doing a fine job at the stables. As he had promised the children, he walked away from the comfort of his own room in the stables and returned to the bridge every night to sleep with the other orphans. He helped with delivering the food, and made sure meals were cooked at night.

"Anyway," Russell continued, "Paxton saw me on the streets not too long after my mama died. She died owing money for the room we lived in, so I got kicked out."

A murmur of outrage that an eight-year-old child had been cast out on the streets rose in the room.

"Paxton found me. I guess I looked real hungry and lost, 'cause he asked me where I lived. I told him about my mama. He took me back to the bridge that night. I been there ever since. He helped me find a piece of canvas to make a shelter and did his best to make sure we all ate every night." Russell frowned. "It's hard to feed that many children, though. There were lots of nights we went to bed hungry." He closed his eyes for a moment. "Emma and Clara used to cry the loudest. They probably still do."

He opened his eyes, looked at the crowd, and took a deep breath. "Emma ain't but seven. She's real cute. Her daddy died during the war. Her mother died when cholera went through 'bout seven years ago. Emma was only a baby. Her grandma took her in when her folks died. Her grandma didn't have much, but I reckon they did okay. Emma weren't that skinny when she first came. She woke up one morning and found her grandma dead in bed. She didn't have no idea what to do. She told me she stayed there in that room for a few days with her grandma, but then she got real hungry."

Russell frowned. "I don't reckon it was smelling too good by that time, either."

Abby flinched when she realized how familiar he must be with the stench of death.

"Anyway, I was the one who found Emma. I saw her digging through some trash looking for food. I asked why she was doing that. She was scared, but she finally told me." Russell frowned. "I know what can happen to children on the streets..." His voice trailed off.

Abby flinched again, her mind filling in the blanks of what he wasn't saying. He'd been unwilling to talk about it earlier that day, so she knew it had to be bad.

"I brought Emma back with me, and I been looking out for her ever since." He took a deep breath and stared straight at the crowd. "I stole things so we could eat. I ain't proud of it, but hearing Emma and Clara cry at night was worse than stealing, so I did it. That's how Mr. Wallington found me. I was stealing from River City Carriages when he caught me." He flushed bright red. "I reckon getting caught was the best thing that ever happened to me. My life has sure changed a lot, but I can't stop thinking about my friends. I want them to be as lucky as me."

Abby watched the room as Russell made his confession. She saw nothing but compassion on every face. These were people and families who knew and understood desperation.

"Then there's Clara," Russell continued. "She's nine. Her daddy died during the first battle of the war. At least, that's what her mama figured. She never really knew for sure. He went off to fight right when the war started, and her mama never saw him again. Ain't heard from him after that, either." He hesitated for a moment. "Clara's mama didn't die. Least not that she knows. She just up and disappeared one day. Clara reckons she didn't want to take care of her anymore. She stayed in the little room they had together until she decided her mama weren't coming back. She was real hungry, but she didn't know what to do, so she just went out walking one day. Paxton found her and brought her back to the bridge."

"What about an orphanage?" one lady interrupted to ask, her face a mask of kind concern.

Russell met her eyes. "There don't be enough of them, ma'am," he said earnestly. He met Abby's eyes for a moment.

Abby nodded her encouragement. She'd told Russell to be completely honest.

"And," Russell added, "they aren't all good places. I seen kids in some of those places that don't eat no better than we did. I reckon people started them because they wanted to help, but maybe they ran out of money. At least, if we stole enough, we had some nights when everyone ate well. Those kids in the orphanages didn't have no say. I know some of the orphanages are good, 'cause I used to watch the children through the gates, but those of us under the bridge weren't willing to take a chance."

Abby decided to chime in. "The children under the bridge have formed a very unusual family. They suffer, but they care for each other. That's why Russell has enough courage to tell you about them. They're not merely his friends, they're his family." She smiled at Russell. "You're doing wonderfully. Keep going."

Russell gave her a grateful look and continued. "Bertha and Lizzie are sisters. Bertha is eleven. I think Lizzie be twelve. When they were babies, they were slaves on a plantation with their folks. After the war, they came to Richmond. They were still babies. Their folks said they were looking for a good opportunity." He spoke the word carefully and then frowned. "I don't reckon they found it. They got caught up in one of them riots a few years back. Her daddy was shot by some policemen. Her mother got trampled by people running away."

Russell stopped for a moment and once again looked into the faces of the crowd. "Now, when I first got out here to the plantation, I figured I was better than black people." His voice was earnest with honesty. "Mr. Wallington set me straight real quick, but that didn't mean I believed any different. Then I met Mr. and Mrs. Samuels. I started going to school. I rode out in the tobacco fields with Mr. Samuels. I played and rode horses with John and Jed. And Hope," he added. "I realized all that stuff I been taught weren't right. Not at all." He smiled at his audience. "Bertha and Lizzie deserve to have a real good home. I hope somebody here wants to give them that. It's been real hard for them under the bridge. Lizzie got real sick this winter. We all figured she was gonna die, but somehow she didn't. She's a little better now that the weather ain't so cold, but I'm real glad Doctor Wallington is gonna see her soon." He glanced toward Anthony. "I know they're doing better 'cause of the food they're getting now. Mr. Wallington made sure no one would be hungry anymore."

Abby was quite sure Carrie, as she listened, was making plans for them to go to sooner than they'd initially planned. Those children needed her and Janie *now*. A quick glance at her daughter's concerned face confirmed her suspicion.

"Then there's Willy," Russell said. "He's the next oldest. He's thirteen. Willy's in charge when Paxton ain't there, which is during the day now since Paxton is working for Mr. Wallington. His daddy made it through the war. He moved to Richmond with his folks when his daddy got a job working at Tredegar Ironworks. He told me things were going pretty good for a while. He even got to go to school." He paused and glanced around the schoolhouse. "This is the first time I ever been to a school. I know how to read now, and my new sisters are trying to get me to talk better." He grinned. "I reckon it's gonna take a while, though."

A ripple of laughter rolled over the room.

Russell grew serious again. "Willy's folks died of yellow fever two years ago. They made him leave the house so he wouldn't get sick. He stayed with a neighbor for a few days. When he went back to check on his folks, they were both dead," he said sadly. "The neighbor didn't want him no more 'cause they was afraid of getting the fever. He was out on the streets for a few days." He looked straight into the crowd. "Paxton found him just as a few men were coming after him." He cleared his throat. "I guess Paxton saved him from something real bad. Anyway, he's been under the bridge ever since. He's taking care of everybody now. Willy is real brave."

Russell spent another twenty minutes telling about his friends. The audience listened with rapt attention, their faces expressing the whole gamut of emotions as he revealed the reality of the children's lives.

Abby thought he was done, until Russell turned around and met her eyes. "There's somebody I ain't told you about. I wasn't sure I oughta."

Abby's heart caught at the hesitant, yearning look in his eyes. "Do you want to tell us now?"

Russell nodded slowly, his eyes never leaving hers. "I reckon I oughta. She needs a home real bad."

"Who is she?" Abby asked gently, knowing he was looking to her for courage to tell the rest of the story.

"She's just a baby," Russell admitted. He turned to look at Anthony. "You didn't see her that day under the bridge 'cause we keep her hid real good. So nobody will hurt her."

"How old is she?" Abby pressed, her instincts telling her this information was important.

Russell shrugged. "I reckon she be about eight months old now."

A gasp sounded through the room.

"Eight months?" She tried to keep her voice calm, but her head was spinning. *How was that possible?*

Russell continued. "Willy was out stealing some things one night so we could eat. It was real cold out that night, and he heard a sound coming from a trash bin. When he looked inside, he saw a baby. There weren't nobody else around. The poor little thing was wrapped up in a real thin blanket. Willy didn't know what to do, so he took her and brought her back to the bridge. Paxton said she didn't look like a brand new baby. Maybe a few months old. That's why we don't know for sure how old she is.

Russell took a deep breath. "We didn't know what to do, but we been taking care of her ever since. She always gets the first food, and we made sure she gets milk. A few of us gave up our blankets so she would be warm. A couple of the girls wash her diapers in the river the best they can. They know more about taking care of babies than I do." He shrugged. "She don't eat a whole lot, mostly mush and milk. She cries some, but mostly she smiles a lot," he said proudly. "I don't know much about babies, but I reckon she should be bigger than she is. Bridget needs a real good home."

Abby knew instantly the source of the gasp that sounded through the schoolhouse.

"Her name is Bridget?" she asked softly.

"Yes, ma'am."

Abby felt the tears well in her eyes as she envisioned holding Carrie's baby girl. Bridget was stillborn with a perfect cap of black curls and rosebud lips. Carrie had been so sick that she'd not regained consciousness until both Robert and Bridget were buried.

She turned toward Carrie, expecting the ashen look she found. She also saw the look of determination and purpose shining in her eyes.

"I reckon that's all I got to say," Russell said.

Abby gathered her composure, smiled, and wrapped an arm around his thin shoulders. "Thank you, Russell. You did a wonderful job!"

"Thank you, son!"

"Thank you, Russell."

"We so appreciate everything you've told us."

A chorus of thanks rose around the room.

Russell grinned broadly, pride shining in his eyes.

Abby leaned down to whisper in his ear. "I'm so proud of you, Grandson."

Russell's grin grew wider. "Thanks, Grandma," he whispered back.

Abby made no attempt to hide the tears in her eyes. She gathered the boy into a warm hug and kissed his cheek.

"What's next?" someone called. "When do we get to meet the children?"

Abby identified the speaker. "That's a good question, Bertha."

Bertha stood up, her slender black body held erect. "I'm hoping to give Bertha and Lizzie a home. I figure it's a sign that me and the youngest share the same name, and I don't aim for two sisters to be separated. I got sold away from all my siblings when I was little. I still miss them." She cleared her throat. "When do I get to meet them?"

"Yes. When do we get to meet them?"

"Are they coming soon?"

The calls came from all over the room.

Anthony was the one who answered the question. "We had originally planned to go into Richmond in a couple weeks to bring the children back." He locked eyes with Carrie. "I imagine we're leaving tomorrow, though?"

Carrie's eyes filled with tears. "Yes," she said loudly. "We're going tomorrow."

Abby looked at Thomas. He nodded, proving he was thinking the same thing. They would all go together, driving enough wagons to bring the children back. All the children were precious, but she knew Carrie was going to save a little girl named Bridget.

Carrie's heart was pounding so loudly she could hear it over the rumble of the wheels on the cobblestone as the wagon approached the bridge spanning the glistening water of the James River. The waters ran broad and placid near the plantation, but here they rushed and tumbled over rocks, forming a myriad of waterfalls and rapids as the river rushed toward the sea.

The riotous waters reflected the state of her emotions. Ever since Russell had uttered the baby's name—*Bridget*—she had been able to think of nothing but that innocent child surviving under a bridge.

Russell stood up as they neared the bridge. "We're almost there!" he called excitedly.

Paxton joined him as they leaned against the carriage seat to peer over Carrie and Anthony's shoulders.

Thomas and Abby had agreed to stay back at the Church Hill house with Frances and Minnie. Frances would join them the next day to help provide medical care for the children, but Carrie wanted to check things out first.

Janie was in the back of the wagon surrounded by medical supplies and clothes. Willard was seated next to her. He had joined them to make sure the wagon was secure when they weren't with it. Poverty was rampant in Richmond as the city fought to recover from the war years. Theft was commonplace.

Russell and Paxton leapt from the wagon as soon as it drew to a stop. "We'll let everyone know you're coming," they yelled as they dashed under the bridge.

Anthony turned to Carrie and Janie as they stepped down. "It's bad," he said quietly.

Carrie shrugged. "You've warned us about a dozen times now. We know it's going to be bad, but I can guarantee you we saw worse during the war."

"Not with children," Anthony reminded her.

Carrie knew that was true, but from everything she'd heard, these children weren't missing limbs and riddled with bullets. Hunger and misery weren't deadly. Anthony had never seen what she and Janie had experienced, so she couldn't expect him to understand. Quite honestly, she was glad that he couldn't.

"Let's go," Carrie said firmly. "We'll know what we need after we've seen the children."

"I'll keep an eye on things," Willard assured her. "Nobody will mess with the supplies."

The shadow of the bridge swallowed the bright spring sunshine when they walked under the overhang. Carrie blinked her eyes rapidly to adjust to the change.

Anthony whistled. "Things don't look as bad as they did." He turned to Paxton. "What happened?"

"You happened," Paxton said promptly. "You and the drivers from River City Carriages. They been bringing food ever since you and Russell left, but they also been bringing other things. Wood. Canvas. Blankets. They been helping us build better shelters to keep everyone dry and warm."

Carrie gazed around her. If what she was seeing was a huge improvement, she could imagine how bad it had been before. She winced at the sound of hoarse coughs coming from several of the shelters. Her heart began to pound when she heard the thin cry of a baby rising above the coughing.

Paxton frowned. "Some of the children have gotten sick in the last week. I used some of my money to buy some medicine, but I don't know if it's really working."

Russell pointed toward the largest shelter. "How is Bridget? Why is she crying?"

Paxton shrugged as he looked around. "Willy? What's wrong with Bridget? She weren't crying this morning when I left. She seemed alright last night."

"I don't know," Willy replied, his eyebrows knit together with worry. "Lizzie and Bertha are looking after her. They said she woke up with a fever this morning. They don't know what to do."

Carrie's heart tightened. "May we look at her, Willy?"

Willy cocked his head and examined her shrewdly. "You the doctor?"

"Yes. My name is Dr. Wallington, and this is Dr. Justin. We're here to take care of all of you."

Willy sagged with relief. "I reckon it be alright then." He walked over to the shelter and pulled back a flap of canvas. "Bertha. Lizzie. We got a doctor here to check on Bridget." He motioned to Carrie and Janie. "You can go on in."

Carrie pulled back the flap, laying it over the top of the shelter so more light could come in. It was dim, but light enough to see two thin girls crouched next to a small bundle on the ground. They had laid several blankets under the baby, but Carrie knew it wasn't enough to truly protect the infant from the cold ground. Spring warmth hadn't reached under the bridge. "Hello girls. I'm Dr. Carrie. This is Dr. Janie."

"How do," the oldest one said in a worried voice. "I'm Lizzie." She pointed to the younger girl. "This is my sister, Bertha." Then she pointed down. "This is Bridget. She's sick. Can you help her?"

Carrie moved closer. "We're going to do our best," she said gently. Remembering what Russell had said about Lizzie being sick through the winter, she looked closely at the girl. Lizzie erupted into coughing, her thin shoulders heaving with the effort.

Janie laid a hand on Carrie's arm. "Go on. I'll take care of Lizzie and Bertha."

Leaning down, Carrie scooped the crying baby into her arms, shocked by how tiny she was. If she was truly eight months old, she should be bigger. Carrie's lips tightened when she felt the fever radiating through the thin blanket. "The first thing I'm going to do is take Bridget out to our wagon, girls. We'll need more light to treat her."

Lizzie regained her breath enough to answer. "Alright. If Paxton brought you here, I reckon we can trust you."

Janie took the girl's hand. "Sit down here. I know you've been sick. We want to help you, too."

Lizzie blinked her eyes. "Thank you, ma'am. I sure appreciate it."

Carrie, knowing both girls were in good hands, carried the baby out of the shelter.

Anthony appeared at her side. "How is Bridget?"

Carrie frowned. "She's sick and malnourished. I hope we got here in time." She hurried from under the bridge, sighing when the bright sunlight immediately warmed the air. The sound of coughing told her many of the children needed treatment, but the baby would be the most fragile.

Climbing into the back of the wagon, she smiled her thanks to Willard, who had hastily put together a thick pile of blankets when he saw her emerge from beneath the bridge.

Both Anthony and Willard remained silent, letting her work.

Carrie sucked in her breath when she pulled the blanket back from the baby's face. "Bridget," she breathed. Having never seen or held her daughter, she had only what Abby told her to know how she had looked. This Bridget was eight months old, and she was thinner than she should be, but the cap of black curls topping green eyes made Carrie gasp with delight.

Bridget gazed up at her, fear sparkling in her eyes, and began to cry harder.

'It's alright, little girl," Carrie crooned. "I know you feel terrible, but you're going to be fine." She prayed she was right. She held Bridget closely until the baby began to relax, and then laid her down gently on the blanket.

Fever wasn't necessarily a bad thing. She knew it could actually be beneficial. It wasn't only a valuable warning that Bridget's body was fighting an infection, it was also part of the body's defense against that infection. Ancient physicians, like Hippocrates, considered fever to be a means by which the body cooked and eliminated the disease.

Bridget was quite hot. A practiced hand on the baby's forehead told Carrie the fever wasn't high enough to be dangerous, but there was risk of dehydration. Bridget's face was flushed, and it was obvious she was fearful and anxious.

Carrie reached into her bag and took out some Belladonna. There were other homeopathic remedies for fever, but this was the one she always chose first when there was a sudden onset. Paxton had said the baby was fine when he left that morning, so she would use it first.

She stirred the Belladonna into a small cup of water from one of the canteens in the wagon, holding the baby's head while she gently raised the cup to her lips. It took some time, but she gradually got the fluid into the little girl.

What Bridget needed now was a bath to bring down the fever, more liquid, and a soft bed—none of which could happen under the bridge.

Janie appeared and hurried to the side of the wagon. "Six of the children are sick. I don't think it's serious. *Yet*," she hastened to add. "But all of them have sore throat, fever, and coughs."

Carrie frowned as she thought of the dampness under the bridge. "Which could turn into pneumonia if we don't treat them quickly."

Janie nodded. "I suspect Lizzie had pneumonia this winter. Her lungs have been damaged. It's a miracle that she recovered, but she's still very weak." She gazed down at Bridget, her face softening with compassion. "How is she?"

"I believe she'll recover, but not here..." Carrie replied.

Carrie thought quickly and then turned to Anthony. "You stay here with Russell and Paxton. Help them explain to the children what's going to happen in the next few days. Willard, I need you to drive us back to the house, and then return for the others. Janie and I are going to take Bridget and the other children home to the house on Church Hill. They will get well much quicker there." She turned to Janie. "Make sure Lizzie is part of the group. She's not going to spend another night under that bridge."

Anthony kissed her quickly and then stepped back.

Carrie watched as he and Janie disappeared under the bridge. She gathered Bridget into her arms, speaking to her soothingly as she waited for the other children. She smiled when the baby relaxed and fell asleep, her long, dark eyelashes fanning her cheeks. Carrie rocked her gently, knowing sleep was the best medicine.

Ten minutes later, seven children, including Lizzie, emerged from beneath the bridge, blinking in the bright sunshine. Carrie watched them, wondering how often they came out from under the protection of their refuge. She doubted it was often. Her lips tightened. That was about to change.

"Hello, everyone," Carrie called brightly. "Climb into the back of the wagon."

Lizzie looked frightened. "Where we going?" She looked back toward the bridge. "I'm not going to any orphanage. I won't leave Bertha," she added.

"You're safe now, Lizzie." Janie wrapped an arm around her waist. "You're not going to an orphanage. We're bringing you to a house where we can take care of you better. You, and your friends."

The rest of the children, looking to be between eight and twelve, gazed around them with bewildered expressions.

Carrie stood in the back of the wagon, holding Bridget as she beckoned them forward. "We're all going to a house that my father owns. You'll be safe there. You'll each have a bed and a bath tonight."

The children exchanged doubtful looks; some just looked confused. Carrie's heart constricted with pain when she realized some of these children may never have experienced anything like a bath and bed.

Russell appeared suddenly. "It's alright," he told them earnestly. "Dr. Carrie is my new mama. She done adopted me. I've been treated real good. You can trust her."

The children listened, their faces solemn, and then slowly climbed into the wagon.

Carrie realized the children needed the assurance of a familiar face. "Russell, please go tell Mr. Wallington that you're coming with us. I want everyone to feel comfortable. We need you to make sure that happens."

Russell straightened with importance. "Yes, ma'am," he said promptly. Turning, he dashed back beneath the bridge. He returned moments later and leapt into the back of the wagon. "Let's go."

It was early evening by the time the children had been bathed, fed, and given cups of hot tea with honey and lemon to soothe their throats. They'd been given clean nightclothes when they emerged from the tub, and then tucked into bed. Exhausted, and awed by their rapid shift in accommodations, they'd fallen asleep quickly.

May and Micah, Carrie's father's long-time servants, had worked hard to heat and carry water.

Russell, Frances, and Minnie had helped them every moment. When Spencer, May's husband, had arrived home, he had joined in hauling the bath water, his good cheer making the children laugh.

A huge pot of chicken soup, accompanied by hot biscuits with slathered butter, had disappeared quickly.

Carrie knew that being clean, hydrated, and full of healing soup was what the children needed more than anything. A good night's sleep would do them a world of good. She believed they would be ready to travel in three to four days.

Abby appeared at the door to her and Anthony's bedroom. "How is she?"

Carrie beckoned her in. "She's sleeping," she whispered, pulling back the light blanket Bridget was swaddled in so her mother could see the baby's face.

"She's beautiful," Abby whispered back, tears flooding her eyes. "Carrie, she…"

"Looks like my Bridget," Carrie said softly. "I know. It's wonderful, but it wouldn't really matter to me what she looked like. She needs a family."

"Which you and Anthony are going to give her," Abby replied with a knowing smile.

Carrie nodded. She was slightly overwhelmed that they were adopting two children at one time, but she didn't doubt for an instant that it was meant to be. "The moment Russell talked about her, I knew," Carrie admitted. "Even before he said her name, I knew this baby was going to be part of our family." She smiled down into the content little face.

After Bridget had been immersed in a lukewarm bath to bring her fever down, patted dry with a towel, and given warm milk, she'd fallen into a deep sleep. Carrie hadn't been willing to let her out of her arms since. Several times the baby had stirred, but only to press closer to the warm body that cuddled her. Carrie's heart had swelled with love throughout the day.

"The children did a remarkable job keeping her alive," Abby said.

"It really is something of a miracle," Carrie agreed. "The fact that she didn't get sick until now..." Her voice trailed off. She imagined what could have happened if they'd come to Richmond two weeks from now, as they'd planned. She doubted Bridget would have survived.

"Anthony arrived a few minutes ago," Abby informed her. "He stayed with Paxton at the bridge so the children could get to know him. He wants them to feel comfortable about coming out to the plantation with us. He'll go back each day until the other children are well enough to leave."

"Is he eating?"

Abby nodded. "May is plying him with chicken soup, biscuits, and strawberry pie."

Carrie raised a brow. "Strawberry pie? The rest of us didn't get that," she protested. May's strawberry pie was legendary, though she would never tell Annie that. The ongoing competition between the two cooks was as legendary as their cooking.

"You know May spoils that charming husband of yours. He spends a lot of time here at the house when he's working in town. She's quite fallen in love with him," Abby said with a laugh. "The children will all have strawberry pie tomorrow. Spencer has been picking berries since they went to bed, and May is rolling out crust at this very moment. She's determined to make enough pies to send to all the children remaining under the bridge."

Carrie smiled. "Where is Russell?"

"Sound asleep," Abby assured her. "He was exhausted from the long day and hauling so much water. He's a special young man. He wanted to make sure his friends were taken care of."

"He was extraordinary," Carrie agreed, stifling a yawn. She was determined to stay awake until Anthony came upstairs, but she was fighting to keep her eyes open.

"So," Abby said, "how does it feel to be the mother of four children?"

Carrie laughed. "Completely surreal." Then she sobered. "When Robert and Bridget died, I thought I would never have another husband *or* a family." She gazed down into Bridget's face. "To have three beautiful daughters and a son is more than I can comprehend." She looked up at Abby. "How does it feel to be the *grandmother* of four children?"

"Absolutely wonderful," Abby replied immediately. "Like you, I never dreamed of a new husband and a new family. Thomas...you...Anthony...the children." She threw back her head with a joyful laugh, her gray eyes glowing in the lantern light that reflected back the silver in her brown hair. "I feel so incredibly lucky every day. I would have been happy with just Frances and Minnie, but to add Russell and Bridget so quickly has made me deliriously happy."

"And Father?"

"If possible, he feels it even more than I do," Abby said. "I never told you how shattered he was when Bridget died. You had enough of your own grief. He loves all his grandchildren, but he has always longed for a baby that he could completely spoil."

"Something he is extremely good at," Carrie replied. "Even with my mother trying to keep it from happening, he found ways to spoil me." She looked down at the baby. "You're going to be a very lucky little girl," she whispered.

"Frances and Minnie are just as excited," Abby revealed. "When I went to tuck them in for the night, they couldn't stop talking about their new little sister."

Carrie's heart glowed with happiness. She could hardly wait to get home, so Rose could meet Bridget.

Just at that moment, Anthony appeared in the doorway, his tall body outlined in the lantern light.

"How is she?" he whispered.

"Sleeping," Carrie replied. She pulled the blanket back so Anthony could get his first truly good look at her. "Isn't she beautiful?"

Anthony smiled. "As beautiful as her mother," he said tenderly.

Carrie gazed up at him. "So…"

"So, of course, she's ours. We both knew it the moment Russell said her name." He reached down to touch one of Bridget's black curls. "God gave us a baby," he whispered. "I imagine she's going to stay right there in your arms tonight?"

Carrie smiled brightly. She had propped herself up with several pillows so she could lean back against the massive headboard and cradle Bridget against her chest. "You would be correct, Mr. Wallington."

Four days later, three wagonloads of children pulled out of Richmond, their excited squeals heard above the noise of the city. Upon Paxton's insistence, the pieces of their bridge encampment had been carefully collected and were now stored in an empty stall at River City Carriages. Though the older boy hoped none of the children would return to live under the bridge, he wasn't going to take any chances that he couldn't provide for them.

Carrie glanced over her shoulder as they left the city limits. "Do you really think it's best for Paxton to stay in Richmond?"

"He's sixteen," Anthony answered. "Paxton says the carriage drivers have become his family. He's earning good money and is planning on being a driver someday." He chuckled. "Actually, I believe he plans on taking over from Willard or Marcus as manager. That boy certainly has ambition." He shook his head with amusement, before he sobered. "He also says there are more children who may need his help." He glanced back over his shoulder at the wagons full of children that Paxton had saved. "We'll make sure he has everything he needs. Willard has agreed to help him with his reading, and we'll send back books for him. He's eager to learn all he can."

Carrie snuggled Bridget against her chest. The jostling wagon had bounced the infant to sleep before they'd driven even a few blocks from the Church Hill house. "More children to help? Under the bridge?" she asked skeptically.

Anthony shrugged as he looked pointedly at the children who filled the wagons. "Paxton saved these children," he reminded her. "We'll let the future unfold as it unfolds. If you had told me six weeks ago that we would have a new son and daughter, and that we would be providing homes for twenty-five other children, I would have said you were crazy."

Carrie laughed. She agreed with him completely. "And now look at us!"

Their three-wagon caravan represented hope and new life for more than two dozen children and the families that eagerly awaited them. Anthony had sent one of his drivers to the plantation the day before to let them know they would be arriving today. All the families who had decided to meet the children would be waiting at the schoolhouse.

Carrie knew things could go wrong. She knew some of the children might not be adopted into families. She had no idea how they would handle that if it happened, but they would just have to cross that bridge if they came to it. The one solitary thing Carrie knew for sure was that not one of these precious children would be sent back to Richmond.

## Chapter Ten

Halfway through the return trip to the plantation, Carrie switched places with Willard. She was more than capable of driving the wagon, and she wanted time to talk to Janie. He moved up to ride with Anthony.

Janie reached for Bridget eagerly. "Give me that little girl," she demanded. "Just because you're her new mama doesn't mean you get to be greedy with her."

Carrie chuckled and passed the precious bundle to Janie.

Bridget gazed up into Janie's face and gurgled happily.

Janie smiled tenderly. "She looks like she's gaining weight!" she exclaimed. "Her eyes look so much better and there's actually color in her cheeks."

"Color that isn't from a fever," Carrie said with relief. She picked up the reins and clucked to move the horse forward. A quick glance told her the children were comfortable leaning against the side of the wagon and eagerly watching the countryside. "May kept a steady supply of mashed carrots, beans, potatoes, and fruit coming to me. Bridget ate almost every bite of it, along with all the milk she would drink."

Janie watched her carefully. "You look concerned, though."

Carrie smiled. "I've missed talking to you." Though they had been in the same house for the last few days, the children kept them so busy that they'd barely spoken. Carrie lowered her voice so the other children couldn't hear. "Bridget is much smaller than she should be. The children did their best, but she is badly malnourished. I'm afraid she'll be impacted for the rest of her life."

Janie peered down into the baby's face again. "Nonsense!" she said crisply. "I agree that she's underweight, but she's alert, and her eyes are bright. It will take her time to grow and catch up, but she will. She might be smaller than she could have been, but we have no way of knowing that. You know she's going to be spoiled by every single person on the plantation. Love has a way of working miracles."

Carrie took a deep breath, absorbing Janie's certainty with gratitude. "Thank you," she said softly. Getting Bridget had made her understand Anthony's reluctance to adopt Russell. Her husband had been afraid he couldn't protect the little boy because he hadn't been able to save his own newborn son. Adopting Bridget was wonderful, but it also awakened the fears she had after losing her own baby girl five years earlier.

Janie understood what she was feeling without her having to say a word. "You're the best mother possible for Bridget," she said. "It's going to be fine."

Carrie smiled her gratitude. "I've been thinking about what Bridget needs. We don't know how old she is, but it's obvious she never had much breast milk. We don't know that she ever had any. She's eating some soft foods, but breast milk is so much better for her than cow's milk."

"True," Janie agreed. "She's tiny because her little body can't digest the cow's milk the children have been giving her. It was better than nothing, but what she needs is breast milk."

Carrie frowned, deciding to voice what she'd been thinking. "Is there anyone around the plantation who has recently given birth?"

Janie immediately grasped her thoughts. "A wet nurse! Carrie, that's the perfect idea." She knit her brows together in deep thought. "We have several new mothers. Patty has a three-month-old. Brenda's baby is only two months. And Sally's son was born just a few weeks ago. As far as I know, all of them are doing well. We've also got some mothers with their children nearing one-year-old. They will still be producing plenty of milk."

Carrie listened closely, feeling a spark of hope. "Do you think...?"

Janie interrupted her before she could finish the sentence. "Any one of them would be a wet nurse for Bridget. In fact, *all* of them would. They'd do anything in the world for you because you've done so much for everyone else. I'm sure they would appreciate a chance to do something for you."

Carrie's brain was spinning. "We don't know how old she is. Can she really learn how to breastfeed now?"

Janie nodded firmly. "I've studied so much about newborns. While you were learning how to do surgery and help veterans with amputations, I was learning about infants. Babies are born with the instinct to nurse. Even if they haven't been doing it, they want to. You just have to teach them."

"How?" Carrie demanded, eager for Bridget to get the nutrition she needed.

Janie shrugged. "There are tricks. Lying Bridget tummy down on a wet nurse's chest releases the feeding reflexes that will spur her to nurse. Another way to introduce her to nursing is to wait until she's in a light sleep. Any natural resistance is overcome by instinct. Plan the nursing around Bridget's nap time. Once she starts, it will be easier for her to nurse when she's awake." She looked down into Bridget's face. The little girl was listening intently, as if she understood. "Polly will have some ideas too. She's been a midwife for as long as you and I have been alive. She'll have seen everything."

Carrie nodded thoughtfully. "That's true." She thought through the possibilities. "If her wet nurse could come to the clinic, that would be optimal."

"Patty lives the closest to the clinic," Janie replied. "And her baby is the oldest, so her life should be a little more settled by now. We'll talk to her when we get back."

Carrie felt a measure of relief, but now she was more anxious than ever to be back on the plantation, so Bridget could have everything she needed.

She changed the subject. "Will Matthew be home by the time we get there? I know he and Harold went off on an assignment, but I don't know anything about it. Was I imagining that he was acting quite mysterious?"

Janie sighed, her expression troubled. "You weren't imagining it. Susan and I don't know anything about it either. We've talked about it and decided the twin brothers have probably done things like this their entire lives," she said ruefully. "They make quite the team."

"Do you even know where they went?"

"Alabama," Janie answered with a shrug. "That's all either of us knows. We both asked, but were told if they learned what they thought they would learn, then they would tell us when they got back." She snuggled Bridget closer when the baby began to fuss. After several moments, the little girl lapsed back into sleep. "He might be there when I get home. I was expecting him to be back before we left for Richmond, but he said nothing was certain."

"I thought Matthew was done with reporting," Carrie said. "His books are selling so well. I didn't think he wanted to go back to that life."

Janie shrugged again. "He didn't, but whatever Harold talked to him about made him change his mind. Not knowing where he is or what he's doing is hard," she admitted. "He's gone through so many terrible experiences in his reporting. I had hoped he was done with that life, but obviously he felt this was important. I have to respect that, but I don't have to like it."

Carrie nodded, thinking about the plethora of difficult experiences Matthew had been through. She also acknowledged her gratitude that Anthony only worked in Richmond. There were times she struggled with his absences when he went to town to oversee the business operations of River City Carriages, but she never worried like Janie must be now. "I know you'll be happy to see Robert and Annabelle," she said to get her friend's mind off her husband.

"My babies," Janie said softly. "I know they're being well cared for by Rose and Annie, but I've missed them."

Carrie loved three-year-old Robert and eighteen-month-old Annabelle. Robert, with his red hair and bright blue eyes, was the spitting image of his father. Annabelle was growing into a tiny replica of Janie, with the same brown hair and soft blue eyes. "They'll be ecstatic to have you home."

"Hey, Dr. Carrie?"

Carrie glanced over her shoulder at Clara. The inquisitive nine-year-old, abandoned by her mother, waved a hand. "Yes, Clara?"

"How long till we get there?"

"A couple more hours," Carrie replied. "Are you hungry?"

Clara shook her head emphatically. "I reckon May sent enough food to feed us for days!"

Carrie chuckled. She'd seen May overdo it before, but never quite like this. There was enough food in each wagon for thirty children, not the nine who were riding out to the plantation.

Clara leaned closer to her shoulder. "I got to go," she whispered. Her brown eyes gleamed beneath clean blond hair platted into long braids.

Carrie looked down the road. They were drawing close to the clearing they often stopped at on their long trips to or from the plantation. "Can you wait just a few more minutes?"

Clara pursed her lips and considered the question. "I reckon so," she said seriously.

Carrie swallowed her laugh and concentrated on the rutted road before them. As they neared the clearing, Anthony glanced over his shoulder. Carrie nodded to indicate they should stop. She was sure the children were ready for a break and would appreciate the chance to stretch their legs.

She also knew each one was wondering whether they would have a family by the end of the day.

Anthony leaned back in his rocking chair on the porch, one arm cuddling little Bridget, as he used his free hand to guzzle the lemonade Annie had brought out to everyone. The older children ran wild around the yard, while the first fireflies of the season danced in the trees. The late evening was warm, but a soft breeze made it comfortable. After six days in Richmond, he was more than ready to be home.

"You look like a happy father."

Anthony looked up when Thomas walked out onto the porch. "Happier than I ever dreamed," he admitted. "Carrie and I were so glad to adopt the older children who have joined our family. I never imagined we would have a baby."

"Especially one you found under a bridge?" Thomas asked. His blue eyes glinted with amusement under his thick thatch of gray hair.

Anthony chuckled. "Especially that." Thomas settled down into the chair next to him. Without being asked, Anthony handed Bridget to her grandfather.

Thomas smiled with delight and gathered her into his arms. "I never imagined a baby either." He gazed down at Bridget, who chose that moment to wake and smile up into his face.

Anthony watched the two for a moment, thrilled as much for Thomas and Abby as he was for him and Carrie. He hadn't been a part of their life when Carrie's first husband, Robert, and her baby daughter had died, but he knew the pain it had caused. Carrie had often talked wistfully about trying to have another child, but both of them knew it was too dangerous.

Thomas looked up. "I'm so glad all the children are with families for the next month."

Anthony nodded. "I think the couples who took them were as happy as the children." Everyone had agreed that one month would give each family time to decide if they wanted to keep the children, as well as giving the children time to decide if they wanted to become part of the family they'd been placed with. He thought about his promise to Russell. He wouldn't allow any child to stay in a family that wouldn't love them like he and Carrie loved Russell.

He, Carrie, Thomas, Abby, Moses, and Rose had stayed at the schoolhouse until the children had ridden off with families. Every face was bright with hope, though he would admit some of the children looked anxious. Anthony knew each of them was experiencing so much change in a short period of time. He prayed the change would be positive for everyone.

Thomas spoke what Anthony was thinking. "It will help immensely that they will see each other at school."

"I agree. Separating them, after how closely they've lived together, has be traumatizing. This way, they can ease into their families but still have each other."

Silence fell on the porch as laughter floated down from the window.

Anthony glanced up and smiled. "Carrie, Rose, and Abby are talking. I know they're answering Rose's many questions, and she's celebrating our return with a baby. You should have seen the delight on her face when she held Bridget."

Thomas grinned but changed the subject. "Who was the woman I saw coming to the clinic with a baby? She didn't stay long, but Carrie had a bright smile when they came back outside."

"That was our new wet nurse, Patty Loving. She lives less than a mile from the clinic. Her son is three months old. She's agreed to nurse Bridget two times a day for the next few months. Carrie says that's the best way to address how malnourished Bridget is. She needs breastmilk to recover from the first months of her life."

"That's wonderful!" Thomas said enthusiastically. "When Carrie was born, her mother nearly died in childbirth. By the time she recovered, she wasn't able to feed her daughter. Carrie was fed by a wet nurse from the very beginning. One of our people had recently given birth."

Anthony was surprised. "Really? Does Carrie know that? She's never said anything."

Thomas shook his head. "Probably not. It made her mother uncomfortable, because not being able to feed her daughter made her feel like a failure. Besides, until I ended up with a doctor for a daughter, that wasn't something you really discussed," he said wryly. "It was considered private."

Anthony chuckled. "And now, with two doctors on the plantation, not to mention Frances, nothing seems to be private."

Thomas laughed with him. "That's true. I hear conversations I never dreamed would happen on this porch."

"I'm afraid you're about to hear another one."

Anthony jumped when a voice sounded from the deepening dusk. "Matthew? Is that you?"

"Yes," Matthew said as he wearily climbed the porch steps. "I have Harold and Logan with me. Janie is putting the children to bed."

Annie appeared on the porch and called out. "Chillun, it's time to get your bodies inside. I told your mamas I would get you into bed, so I don't want no dillydallying out there," she said sternly.

As she waited for the children to join her, she looked over. "Welcome home, Matthew. You too, Harold," she said brightly. "Neither one of y'all looking too good right now, but it's real good to have you back." Her smile faded when she saw the third man. She appraised him slowly, her eyes deepening with sadness. "You done seen a world of trouble, ain't ya, boy?"

Logan, who looked to be in his twenties, was a short black man with somber, dark eyes. "I reckon that's so," he said simply.

Anthony knew that whatever was going to be revealed shouldn't be heard by children, of any age. "I'm going to take Bridget up to bed. I'll be back quickly."

Annie reached out and put a hand on Logan's shoulder. "I'm gonna bring out some hot tea and cookies. You need more than that?"

"No, ma'am. Mr. Matthew and Mr. Harold been feeding me real fine."

"That's good," Annie said gruffly, and then turned to the children running up the porch steps. "Go on in and get ready for bed, y'all. I'll be up with some milk and a cookie for each of you."

The children, laughing and playfully pushing, disappeared inside the house.

Jed was the only one who didn't follow. He stopped and looked over at Logan, his face creased with concern and sympathy. "You okay, mister?"

Anthony stopped, knowing Jed recognized the same pain on Logan's face that his father had carried when he had come to the plantation the summer before, after he was beaten and left to die.

"I be alright," Logan answered. "I reckon you better go up for your milk and cookie."

Jed hesitated a moment before he nodded solemnly and traipsed inside.

Anthony looked at their guests. "I'll have Carrie, Abby, and Rose come out to join us."

Just then, a deep voice sounded from out in the yard. "I'm here too," Moses said wearily as he clomped up the stairs.

"Are you just getting back from the fields?" Matthew asked with surprise.

"Yes," Moses admitted. "I was at the school most of the afternoon with the children. I wanted to check everything before I ended the day."

Thomas frowned. "Were you anticipating trouble?"

Moses eased himself down into the chair, resting his head against the back of the white rocker, "No. But I intend for this to be the best crop we've ever had. That means I want to know everything that's going on." When his eyes found Logan in the shadows, they became instantly alert.

As Anthony disappeared into the house, he heard Annie's voice.

"I'll bring you some food once I get these chillun to bed."

"I'm fine, Mama," Moses said, his eyes never leaving Logan.

"Ain't never seen a time you wouldn't eat what I put in front of you," Annie scoffed.

Moses smiled. "It won't happen tonight, either."

Moses wasn't in the mood to hear about trouble, but he knew that's what he was about to hear. He would hold on to the memory of the joy he had witnessed on the faces of the children from under the bridge. Sometimes, holding on to the joy you found was the only way to get through the rest of the things life threw at you.

He leaned forward and reached out to grasp the other man's hand. "Hello. I'm Moses Samuels. Welcome to Cromwell Plantation."

The younger man, his hand rough, callused, and scarred, returned his handshake. "Howdy. I'm Logan."

Moses watched Logan carefully. His voice was strong, but his eyes were haunted. Moses had seen many traumatized black men make their way through Cromwell, some staying to work, but his instincts told him this was something different. A quick glance at Matthew and Harold's faces confirmed his suspicions. He wasn't sure he had ever seen them so troubled and grave.

He opened his mouth to ask a question, but Matthew interrupted him.

"We're going to wait for Abby, Rose, Carrie, and your mama."

Moses nodded and sat back. "Alright."

Silence filled the porch while the men waited.

Moses focused his thoughts on the tobacco crop. The fields were in wonderful shape, the new seedlings more than a foot tall. The combination of the oyster marl and the crop of rye grass that had been tilled back in before planting, had deeply enriched the soil. The men had worked hard over the winter to clear another large field, cutting the trees to provide firewood for everyone. It had been backbreaking work, but if this year's crop was a good one, it would be well worth it. Their workers would earn more from their bonus, and he and Thomas would completely replenish the reserves they'd spent after the flood two years earlier. It was worth the extra effort to make sure everything ran smoothly.

Turning his attention from the crop, he watched as night claimed the plantation. The deep blue of dusk was swallowed by the night sky. Fireflies competed with the glow of stars, the new moon a mere sliver in the sky. He could hear whinnies from the barn. He knew the lantern light glowing from inside meant Miles and Susan were expecting more foals to be born that night. If possible, they attended every birth. Most births went without a hitch, but Cromwell Stables' horses were so valuable no one was willing to take a chance.

He willed himself to relax, but his mind knew any relaxation would be short-lived. He was quite certain trouble had returned once again to the plantation.

Annie was the first to appear on the porch. "The rest will be here in a minute." She laid a plate on Moses' lap full of roast beef, potatoes, carrots, and green beans. Three biscuits were perched on top of the mountainous heap.

Despite the tense atmosphere on the porch, Moses laughed at the expression on Logan's face. "When you're as big as me, you eat a lot."

"I guess," Logan agreed, his wide eyes fixed on the plate.

Moses ate quickly, knowing that whatever he was about to hear would probably destroy his appetite. Just as he took his last bite, the door opened. All the women walked out and settled into chairs. Anthony was right behind them.

Moses glanced up. "Is the window closed?" He didn't want any of the children to overhear the conversation that was about to happen.

"It is," Anthony said gravely.

Carrie looked around with concern. "What's going on?" She spotted Logan at the same time she was speaking. Her face immediately softened with sympathy. "Hello. Who are you?"

"Name is Logan."

"Welcome to Cromwell Plantation," Carrie said warmly. "Are you staying with us for a while?"

Logan looked taken aback at the question but shook his head quickly. "No ma'am. I be passing through."

"Matthew, do you and Harold want to tell us what's going on?" Moses asked quietly.

"No," Matthew replied. "I'm going to, but I wish more than anything that I didn't have to."

## Chapter Eleven

Matthew took a deep breath. He wished he didn't have to reveal the truth of what he was about to say. Everyone would be disgusted, but he was also about to ignite fear in some of his listeners. He locked eyes with his twin, hoping for the strength to continue.

Harold reached out to briefly grip his hand. "We'll do it together."

Alarm showed on every face.

"What is going on?" Thomas demanded. "Just tell us what it is."

Matthew nodded. "I'm trying to find the right words."

Annie spoke sharply. "We already done figured out that words ain't gonna make what you got to say any easier, but it be better than not knowing. I reckon you and Harold had a real hard trip. You might as well get the tellin' over with."

Matthew sighed. "Yes." He turned to their guest. "This is Logan. He's on his way north, although we convinced him to spend a few days with us on the plantation before he leaves."

"So I can feed him?" Annie asked.

"No," Matthew said somberly. "He's here to tell his story. Harold and I didn't figure you would believe it if you didn't hear it from him."

Silence met his statement. Matthew knew they were waiting to hear more. "Harold, when he was down in South Carolina last year doing research on the KKK, heard something that he didn't want to believe was true. He came back and told me about it. We talked and decided we needed to find out the truth for ourselves before we said anything."

A chorus of tree frogs split the silence that followed his words.

Matthew listened for a moment, relishing the peace of being home again on the plantation before he continued. "Logan is from Alabama. That's where we've been. What I'm about to tell you is happening in many places in the South, but it's happening in greater numbers in Alabama. That's why we went there. Alabama has fought against the freeing of the slaves ever since the end of the war. The last seven years have done nothing but intensify their effort."

"Four years ago," Harold said, "more than a thousand former slaves filed suit against white landowners. They demanded that the former slave masters be compelled to pay wages earned during the prior season's work."

"But they weren't slaves then," Carrie protested. "They should have been paid."

"True," Harold agreed, "but that isn't how it's worked in most of Alabama since the end of the war. They offered the former slaves the opportunity to be sharecroppers yet made sure none of them would actually make any money. They were slaves in all but name. When their black workers dared to demand pay, the landowners responded by burning down the courthouse. The courthouse that contained the entire eighteen hundred lawsuits that had been filed."

Moses was the first to speak. "That's terrible, but it's not anything that isn't happening all over the South," he said flatly.

"You're right," Matthew said. "But what's happening now is far worse." He took a deep breath. "I don't know if you're aware, but slaves have long been used for more than plantation work. Before the war, and especially during the war, hundreds of thousands of slaves were sent to iron and coal furnaces all over the South. Since most Southern men were fighting, they needed workers to make sure they had the materials needed to create more guns and munitions."

"And," Harold added, "they needed slaves to dig coal. If slave owners were willing to transport their slaves to the new mining regions of Alabama to dig coal, they wouldn't be conscripted into the army to fight." He scowled. "They were more than willing to have poor whites fight the battles for them."

"The centerpiece of Alabama's military enterprises was a massive and heavily fortified arsenal, naval foundry, ironworks, and gunpowder mill located in the city of Selma," Matthew explained. "They relied on enormous amounts of coal and iron ore that were mined in nearby counties."

"Which meant they relied on a huge number of slaves to run everything," Harold added.

Matthew could tell his listeners were confused. They were familiar with what had happened with slaves before and during the war, but the end of slavery had changed everything. Or so they thought. What he was telling them was important, but they didn't have a point of reference to understand *how* important. He wasn't sure he was doing a good job communicating, because he was struggling himself with just how to do it.

"In March of 1865, at the end of the war, the North sent down troops that decimated the entire Alabama industrial infrastructure. They burned and wrecked iron forges, mills, and massive stockpiles of cotton and coal. They completely destroyed the machinery at the major ironworks and freed the slaves working there."

"Like the destruction in the Shenandoah Valley during the last year of the war," Thomas observed. "The North was determined to break the will of the South."

Matthew listened carefully for any resentment in Thomas' voice but heard a simple matter-of-fact statement. "Yes, Alabama was almost totally destroyed. Our research shows the state suffered losses totaling five hundred million. Farm value became almost nothing. Every bank in the state collapsed. Agricultural production won't be the same for decades."

"Look," Harold said. "I know this information might not seem vitally important, but it is. It explains what we're getting ready to tell you. Without understanding it, there's no way to fight it."

"Fight what?" Rose asked. "I understand you're trying to tell us something. Can we get to the point?"

Matthew sighed. She was right. They could come back and explain more in detail once everyone truly understood what was going on. "The citizens of Alabama have responded to their destruction with a vicious white insurgency against the Union occupation and the freed slaves that they blame for their situation. Violence is bad through the entire South right now, but it's far worse in Alabama."

"How does that help them rebuild their state?" Abby asked. "What they're doing is making things worse."

"You're right," Matthew agreed. "But desperate men don't usually think clearly. They hate the blacks, but they also realize the South won't survive without them. The white men who owned the plantations that produced most of Alabama's crops don't know how to do what's needed. The same is true in the factories and coal mines fighting to recover. The actual work was done by the slaves, but there isn't enough money to pay them wages to do the work now."

"So, they decided to turn us into slaves again," Logan said harshly, his eyes flashing with pain and anger.

Matthew decided to let Logan tell his story. He could go back and provide information later. A quick look at Harold confirmed his agreement.

"Slaves?" Moses asked sharply. "What are you talking about?"

"Just what I said," Logan stated. "There be thousands of black men working in the mines down in Alabama. That Emancipation Proclamation don't mean nothing down there. We all be just as much slaves as we were before." His face tightened. "I reckon it's even worse for most of us."

"I don't understand!" Carrie exclaimed. "How is that possible?"

"We'll explain," Matthew replied, "but I think it's important that you hear Logan's story." He turned to their guest. "Logan, tell them what happened to you."

"I fought with the Union during the war," Logan began. "I escaped my plantation during the second year of the war and signed up to fight. I should have stayed up North when the war be done, but my family be down in Alabama, so I went back." He shook his head, his eyes heavy with sorrow. "I didn't aim to work on the plantation no more, but I couldn't find work, so I found myself back in the fields. Weren't no different than being a slave, 'cause all we did was work. If we didn't work hard enough, they came at us with the lash, just like before," he said bitterly. "But even that was better than where I ended up."

Silence fell on the porch as they watched Logan struggle to continue speaking.

"You be with friends," Annie finally said. "You take all the time you need, Logan."

Logan locked eyes with her, obviously taking strength from the empathy he saw shining in her eyes. He took a long, deep breath and regained his composure. "The day came when I got enough of being back on the plantation and decided to move north. I was a free man, so I left one day. Didn't get far though. I had to go through Selma to try and catch a train up north. I didn't have no money for train fare, so I was gonna hop on one of them freight trains when it came through town." He sighed. "There was a bunch of us down by the tracks. We didn't want nothing but to get outta there. We waited till night to hop on one of them trains, but there be police in the woods, just waitin' for us to make our move."

Another silence fell on the porch. Everyone had leaned forward in their chairs, but no one spoke.

"They took us all," Logan said, his voice one of deep resignation. "They hauled us off to the jail, booked us, and told us what our fine would be." He shook his head. "Not a one of us could pay it 'cause we ain't got no money. Then they took us into court. By the time we done left that day to go back to jail, the fines done gone up a bunch. They said we gotta pay court fees, something called bailiff fees, and some other stuff I don't remember. Course, none of us could pay that neither."

Logan stopped talking again, his voice trembling as he remembered.

Matthew reached over a hand and laid it on his shoulder. He knew this story by heart, but it made his stomach clench every time he heard it.

Logan gave him a grateful look and straightened. "The next day, Selma sold us to the mine."

A collective gasp rose around the porch.

"What?" Abby asked, her words dripping with horror. "They *sold* you? That isn't possible!"

Logan looked to Matthew to explain.

"Turns out it *is* possible," Matthew said grimly. "I know about agricultural slavery before the war, but I've only recently learned about industrial slavery. Especially in Alabama. Tens of thousands of slaves built the state's industrial locations and mined the iron ore and coal. Southern railroads, before the war started, owned about twenty thousand slaves."

"But that was *before* the war!" Carrie protested.

Matthew held up a hand. "They found a way to make sure that didn't end when the war was over. And it's legal," he snapped angrily. "I think that's what makes me the sickest."

Thomas took a deep breath. "Logan, I want to hear the rest of your story, but Matthew, I need to know what you mean."

"The Thirteenth Amendment makes it legal," Matthew stated.

"That's the amendment that abolished slavery," Thomas protested.

Matthew gripped the arms of his rocking chair tightly. "Yes. It also specifically permits involuntary servitude as a punishment for *duly convicted* criminals." His words dripped with sarcastic anger.

"Our *fine friends* down in Alabama quickly figured out how to make this work," Harold continued. "Since their economy was in ruins, they seized on the concept of reintroducing the forced labor of blacks to rebuild their state. They told their white citizens that it was the only practical way of eliminating the cost of building prisons, and that it was the solution to returning blacks to their *appropriate position* in society." His eyes flashed.

"As soon as the war ended," Matthew explained, "every Southern state began to enact an array of laws that were intended to criminalize black life. Many of the laws were struck down in court, but they kept creating new ones. It's never been said that they were meant explicitly for blacks, but it was understood they would rarely, if ever, be enforced on whites."

Harold pulled a sheet of paper out of his pocket. He unfolded it and held it close to the lantern so he could read. "Every time you hear the word leased, please know that it means they *sold* the convicts," he said, and then he began to read. "In 1866, Texas leased two hundred and fifty convicts to two railroad companies for twelve dollars and fifty cents a month. Two years later, Georgia signed over a total of three hundred and forty-three convicts to railroad companies. Arkansas followed their example. As did Mississippi. In 1868, Georgia turned over two hundred and forty-one prisoners to the state's largest cotton planter." His lips tightened. "Last year, those same convicts were transferred to Nathan Bedford Forrest." He stopped speaking to let the meaning of his last words sink in.

Thomas raised a hand. "Wait a minute. Nathan Bedford Forrest? The Confederate general? One of the founders of the Ku Klux Klan?"

"The same," Matthew replied. "Forrest is now a major planter and railroad developer. He found a way to make sure he would continue to have slaves."

Angry mutterings rose on the porch.

"North Carolina recently began selling their convicts," Harold continued, holding the paper back to the light. "Last year, Tennessee sold eight hundred prisoners to Thomas O'Conner, a founding partner of the Tennessee Coal, Iron and Railroad Company."

Thomas shook his head, his face a mask of disbelief and anger. "Enough." He turned to Logan. "Please finish telling us your story."

"Me and the rest of the men trying to catch that freight train got shipped off to the mines, but it weren't only us. Men who didn't have no work got pulled in for vagrancy. They couldn't pay the fines neither, 'cause they didn't have no money. A couple fellas got hauled in 'cause they said a cuss word where some white folk could hear them. Another man ended up in the mines 'cause some white woman smiled at him."

"So basically, they were thrown in jail for nothing!" Abby sputtered.

Logan looked at her. "That be the truth, ma'am. Them mines needed more slaves, so the police went out and found some. Then they made money off of selling us. Lots of towns in Alabama be making their money that way now. When I first got pulled in, they tole me my fine was five dollars. By the time I got out of court that next day, the fines done gone up to over a hundred dollars. It be the same for all of us." He shook his head. "Ain't no way any of us could pay. We got told it would take two years of labor in the mines to pay it off."

"Two years!" Annie looked livid. "That just be wrong! The whole thing be wrong." Her face sobered. "What's it like in them mines?"

Logan's eyes narrowed with fury and pain. "It be worse than any tobacco field, even with an overseer that likes the lash. I didn't see sunlight for more than a year. They sent us to a prison that makes a slavery shack look real good. They dug a tunnel between the prison and the mine. We went down that tunnel early in the morning and didn't come back out till late at night. We only got a few hours of sleep every night. They beat us real regular with the whips. They didn't have no trouble with torture. Any of the men who tried to get away got shot. A bunch more got killed when mine shafts collapsed, or equipment didn't work right. I don't figure they cared, 'cause the police were out there rounding up more of us all the time."

Matthew saw tears streaming down the face of every woman on the porch. Anthony, Thomas, and Moses had tears glittering in their eyes, their faces set in stoic lines. He understood.

"Did you finish your time and get set free?" Carrie asked as she brushed the tears from her cheeks.

"No. Not many men get set free. They find a way to extend your sentence if you manage to stay alive.

Once you get sent down in the mines, you most likely gonna die there." Logan took a shuddering breath. "Not many of us live that long. If we ain't shot or beat to death, we die from some kind of disease. Things be real bad in the mines, but new men keep coming."

"How did you get away?" Rose demanded shakily.

Logan took a deep breath. "There was a barge that had come down the Alabama River with a bunch of coal. When it came time to send it back up, most of the men who worked that ship were sick with dysentery. They pulled some of us outta the mine to work the boat. They kept us chained most of the time, but when we were shoveling coal into the steamers, they had to take 'em off. I wasn't gonna take no more of being in the mine, so I ran and jumped over the side of the boat into the river."

Carrie held a hand over her mouth. "Did they see you? Did they come after you?"

"They couldn't turn that boat around," Logan replied. "They tried to shoot me, but I kept diving under water and changing the way I be going. I was real lucky," he said. "Bullets got close, but they didn't get me. I got to shore and disappeared into the woods. I headed north."

Silence fell over the porch again.

Moses was the one to break it. "How did Matthew and Harold find you?"

The first glimpse of a smile flashed on Logan's face. "The war been over a long time now, but a few places down in Alabama still have stuff out that shows they been part of the Underground Railroad. Only us who were slaves know what it means, so it's been mostly safe from the KKK. One mornin', right before it was gettin' light, after a whole night of thrashing through the woods, I found one of them places." His lips tightened. "I didn't have no way of knowin' whether they was friendly or not, 'cause the place could have been bought up, but I decided to take my chances. I was in pretty bad shape by then."

Matthew could tell by the looks on everyone's face that they were envisioning precisely how bad of shape he was in.

"Anyway," Logan continued, "they be some real nice folks. White folks even. Carpenter is their name. They hate what be going on in Alabama. They took me in and got me some food. It took a while for me to get all healed up, but I did. Then the Carpenters tole me about Matthew and Harold. They said two men had come through asking about what was happening with black convicts. I told the Carpenters I wanted to tell my story, so they got word to them." He smiled at Matthew and Harold. "After they heard my story, they got me out of there. Got me a train ticket and asked me if I would come talk to y'all. So here I am. I'm gonna go on north soon."

Logan fell silent, staring out into the night. "I hope you folks know how good you got it here. After more than a year down in them mines, it be real nice to smell fresh air and hear the crickets." He looked hard at Moses and Rose. "Y'all got to be real careful. You and your kids. America ain't a place to be black right now. Least ways, not down here in the South."

"It's happening in Virginia?" Moses asked sharply.

Matthew shook his head. "So far, Virginia hasn't taken part. From what we have determined, Virginia is the only state in the South to not use leased convict labor."

"Leased?" Rose asked bitterly. "Is that how they're covering up what they're doing?"

Harold nodded. "They can call it what they want. It's slavery, pure and simple. While some white men are being used in the mines, our research reveals it's nearly one hundred percent blacks."

"It's the way to solve the *Black Problem*," Moses said angrily. His massive hands clenched into fists.

"I'm afraid that's true," Matthew agreed. "It's taken us weeks to gather the information we needed to prove it was happening, but I don't really think it will do much good," he said heavily. "The men who run these companies believe they've found the best way to bridge the era of slavery with new economic opportunities. They're determined to rebuild the economies that were destroyed during the war. They're convinced that, like it was in slavery, using blacks under the whip is the key to rebuild the industrial South."

"The whole thing is evil," Harold continued. "Whites have realized that the combination of trumped-up legal charges and forced labor as punishment has created a good business model." His voice roughened. "They also realize it's an effective tool for intimidating freed blacks and doing away with their most effective leaders."

Moses leaned forward in his chair even more, his eyes glittering with fury. "*Do away with their most effective leaders?* What do you mean?"

"They're making up charges against black leaders of the Republican Party," Harold said angrily. "Instead of killing them, the states recognize they can make money from them, and make sure they can't have any influence. Too many of them are being sold as convict labor."

Moses exchanged a long look with his wife and gritted his teeth. "Can it be stopped?"

"I don't know," Matthew admitted. "Supposedly, the South is in Reconstruction so that blacks are guaranteed equality. We've seen what the KKK is doing in South Carolina. It's gotten better since President Grant sent down troops, but the violence certainly hasn't stopped. It's going on throughout the South, with the KKK and other vigilante groups. There were plenty of whites who were uncomfortable with slavery before the war. Now that the war is over, they seem to be equally as uncomfortable with the idea of black equality, so they're turning their backs on what's happening. Since what the states are doing is technically legal on a federal basis, it will take each state to abolish the practice."

"Or a new amendment!" Abby said fiercely. "Certainly, our government won't turn a blind eye and continue to let this happen."

"Unfortunately, a new amendment will be hard to push through. Our country is in turmoil. The Republican Party is fighting many battles. The Thirteenth, Fourteenth and Fifteenth Amendments passed during the emotional fervor of the war, and in the immediate aftermath."

"You don't think an amendment closing the loophole on the Thirteenth would pass now?" Carrie demanded.

"I believe it would be an uphill battle. I can't honestly say I believe it would pass." Matthew shook his head slowly. "I hate to even hear those words come out of my mouth, but I know you want an honest answer."

A hush settled on the night.

Moses broke the silence. "You've seen it for yourself. What would you tell blacks to do?"

Matthew sighed. "Don't go south," he said bluntly. "Our best guess, from what we've learned, is that soon there will be tens of thousands of leased convicts. What we've learned reveals there is virtually no accountability. Too many people are making money, and the corporations have no reason to stop what they're doing. At least not a legal reason. We know what happens when greed is in control."

"The resurgence of slavery," Thomas said angrily. "What you are really telling us is that slavery continues to exist in this country. It's merely taken a different name."

"That's the bottom line," Harold replied regretfully. "I would tell every black man on this plantation, and every black man you know, to not go further south. If they want to leave the plantation, they need to go up north. It's not perfect there either, but their odds of staying free are infinitely better."

"So," Anthony said slowly, his voice seething with anger, "you're telling us that this country fought a war for four years—a war that ended with the death of hundreds of thousands of people—but nothing has really changed?"

"I wouldn't go that far," Matthew said thoughtfully. "What's happening is horrible, but there are positive things being done." He swept his arm outward. "Look at Cromwell Plantation. Things are happening here that no one could have envisioned even ten years ago. Black children are in school. Black colleges are cropping up across the South. Things *have* changed."

Rose nodded, her eyes glistening with tears. "Mama always told me that hope was the only thing that kept her going. She told me that I could never let go of hope."

"She was right," Harold said. "The last weeks were disheartening, but we have to hold onto hope. Hope doesn't mean you don't acknowledge how far you have to go to change things. It doesn't mean you ignore how hard things are going to be. It doesn't mean we don't fight with everything we have to make life better for everyone in this country."

Abby nodded. "I've learned that hope, no matter how bad things look at the moment, is the thing that gives us the ability to believe in something better. We have to choose the courage to reach for it. We have to work for it and *fight* for it. So many times, during the decades-long fight for abolition, there was reason to believe it would never happen. We had to decide over and over that we could make things change, providing we had the courage to continue."

Carrie reached over and took Rose's hand, her expression full of sympathy. "What are you feeling?"

"Terror," Rose replied honestly. "Not so much for me, but for my children. What kind of world are they going to grow up into? Felicia is going out to do something brave and courageous this summer. A lot of people are going to hate her for it. The North is better than the South, but there are plenty of racist people there. I have to try to accept that she'll be in danger every day." She twisted her hands in her lap. "John, Jed, and Hope are young, but everything I hear about what's going on in the country says their lives will still be hard when they're grown. Slavery may have been abolished, but people are finding ways to make sure blacks stay enslaved."

"Your children are going into the world educated and strong," Abby protested.

Rose met her eyes evenly. "Which might make them even more of a target," she replied flatly. "White people want blacks who *know their place*. My children are determined to be treated equally. How much danger will that put them in?"

Moses reached for her other hand, squeezing it firmly. "I won't pretend I'm not angry at what's happening, and I'm as frightened as you are, but we can't give up fighting for change. However much I want it to, change doesn't happen in a moment. It takes a lot of people, willing to do the hard things, to make change. Abby is right. Freeing our people took decades. It took a lot of people fighting for it to happen. It's only been seven years since the end of the war."

His eyes swept the porch while his strong voice rang out. "Things will only get better if we refuse to stop fighting for change." He grew thoughtful. "Fighting for change also means being wise. I'm not going down South. I'm going to tell every black man I know to not go down South. I'm going to make sure John and Jed don't ever head down South, not until this new form of slavery has been abolished. I'll protect every single person I can."

Moses turned to Matthew and Harold. "Thank you both. It's because you had the courage to go down there that we now know the truth of what's happening." His eyes shifted to Logan. "And because of what you did our new friend has the chance to start over." He looked quizzical. "Where are you going, Logan?"

Logan shrugged. "I hear there might be a factory in Philadelphia that will hire me. I reckon that could be as good a place as any." He glanced at Matthew and Harold.

Matthew smiled and turned toward Thomas and Abby. "If there is room for one more employee…"

"Of course," Thomas and Abby replied simultaneously.

"Business is doing well right now," Abby added.

Thomas turned to Logan. "When you head to Philadelphia, you'll have a letter to Jeremy from us. My brother manages our factory there. He'll have a job for you."

Logan sagged with obvious relief. "Thank you," he said fervently. "I have a hankering to get some more schooling, but I gotta have a job first."

"You'll have a job," Thomas said firmly.

Rose smiled. "You're going to love my brother," she said warmly. "We're twins."

Matthew swallowed his laugh at the confusion on Logan's face.

"Twins?" Logan asked slowly. His eyes moved back and forth from her to Thomas.

Rose laughed. "It's a rather long story. I can tell you later, but the short version is that Thomas' father raped my mother when she was a slave. I came out black, but Jeremy looks white." She exchanged an affectionate look with Thomas. "So, yes, Thomas is my half-brother."

Logan stared back at Thomas, clearly finding it difficult to believe what he was hearing. "And you be alright with that?"

Thomas chuckled. "It took me some time to come around, but I'm a fortunate man to have Jeremy and Rose in my life. They're family."

Logan shook his head but didn't say anything else.

Matthew knew he and Harold were going to be answering a lot of questions.

Rose snuggled into Moses when he slipped into bed. "How are you?" she asked softly.

Moses scowled. "I'm angry. I'm disgusted. I'm afraid," he responded honestly. "I also meant what I said about refusing to give up the fight. I look around the plantation and I see what can be if people are willing to change. I look at Russell and see what happens when a little boy is exposed to the truth about people. I saw those children from under the bridge go to new families who have learned to look beyond color, and instead create a community."

He shook his head and turned to stare out the window for a moment. "I know there aren't many places in the country that have what we have, but it gives me hope that perhaps more people can change." He sighed. "Your mama was right. We can't ever let go of hope."

Rose snuggled deeper into his rock-hard chest. "I was thinking tonight about when we escaped the plantation. When we almost died crossing the river in that icy rainstorm. That was a long journey, but it ended in joy for us. Back then, we never could have envisioned that we would return to the plantation and have the life we have. All we can do is keep moving forward."

Moses kissed the top of her head. "We don't really have a choice, do we? We live in this country. We're black. It's going to be hard for a long time...maybe forever. Too many white people aren't ever going to see us as anything but inferior, but that doesn't mean we have to see ourselves that way."

"And we can make sure our children *never* see themselves that way," Rose said firmly. "Day by day, moment by moment, and person by person, we'll do what we can."

## *Chapter Twelve*

Carrie glanced over at the wooden cradle in the corner of the clinic. A gurgling sound told her Bridget was awake, but she evidently wasn't hungry, and her diaper must be dry. She smiled but continued working. Abby would be there soon to play with her granddaughter while they waited for Patty to come nurse her.

"How long before I can play baseball again?" Paul asked, his eyes flashing with impatience.

Carrie considered the question as she finished applying the cast to her patient's right forearm. "Didn't you break this arm playing ball?"

Paul shrugged with his left shoulder. "I reckon," he answered reluctantly, as if not admitting it would mean it wasn't true.

Carrie swallowed her smile. "Are you right-handed?"

"Yes."

"How do you feel about being left-handed?"

Paul frowned. "Why would I do that?"

"Because you're not going to be able to throw a ball with your right arm for a couple months. If you want to play ball, you'll have to use your left arm."

Paul's eyes widened. "You mean you would let me keep playing ball?"

Carrie smiled. "*I* wouldn't stop you from playing, but your mama and daddy have to say it's alright." She'd seen Paul play baseball in the school playground. The twelve-year-old boy loved the game, and he was good at it. She could well imagine the misery of two months without being able to play.

"You cannot however, hit the ball," she said sternly.

Paul stared at her. "I'm supposed to play baseball but not hit the ball?" His tone of voice showed how ludicrous he found her statement to be.

"That's right," Carrie said calmly. "It takes both arms to hit. Your bone will be weak until it heals. If you hit a ball hard, you could break the bone again. If that happens, you won't be able to play for the entire summer." She gazed directly into his eyes. "More importantly, if you do extra damage, your arm may never be the same again. You might *never* be able to play baseball."

Paul blanched and gulped. "What can I do?"

"You're the pitcher, aren't you?"

"Yep."

"Then you can keep throwing the ball with your left arm." Carrie knew he needed some persuasion. "Do you remember meeting Mr. Jeremy when he was on the plantation a couple years ago?" Jeremy was the one who had introduced the children to the game.

"Of course!" Paul said eagerly. "He's a real good baseball player!"

"He is," Carrie agreed. "When I was in Philadelphia last summer, I saw him play with his team. The team pitcher is considered the best in the league." Watching Paul's face, she knew she had his complete attention. "Do you know why?"

Paul shook his head. "No."

"Their pitcher is naturally right-handed, but he can throw the ball equally as well with his left hand as he can with his right. The ball comes across the plate differently, so he can keep the batters confused." Carrie hoped she was saying the right thing. It was what she remembered from what Jeremy had told her after the game, but she made no pretense of being an expert about baseball. Regardless, she could tell she had the boy thinking.

Paul cocked his head thoughtfully. "And I can throw with my left arm all I want to?"

"That's right," Carrie replied. "I'll tell your parents you have my permission if you think it will help."

"Oh, it will help," Paul answered. "They listen to everything *you* say."

"You send them in after school," Carrie said, biting back a smile. "For now, you need to go back to class."

"School is almost out!" Paul protested. "Why do I gotta go back?"

Carrie raised a brow. "Gotta?"

Paul groaned. "Why do I *have* to go back?" he said clearly, and then grinned mischievously. "You can see how much I'm learning. Missing some of today won't hurt me any."

"And putting more information in your brain can only help you," Carrie retorted with a grin. "Get back to school, Paul. A broken arm doesn't hurt your brain."

Paul groaned but managed a smile as he jumped down from the treatment table. "I'll see you later, Dr. Carrie. Thanks for fixing up my arm."

"You're welcome."

As Paul ran out the door, Carrie heard the wagon approaching. At that exact moment, Bridget began to fuss. She walked over and scooped her daughter into her arms. "Hello, little one. Everything is alright," she crooned, cradling her gently.

Bridget gazed up at her. Her cry turned to a hiccup as she smiled.

Carrie could hardly believe Bridget was the same little girl she had rescued from under the bridge more than a month ago. She wasn't quite what Carrie expected should be normal size, but Bridget had gained weight and had a healthy glow to her skin and eyes. Her curly black hair was thicker, and her green eyes never missed a thing. When she was awake, she was seldom quiet, carrying on conversations with everyone who was in sight. It seemed to not bother her at all that no one understood any of the sounds she made. She was simply happy to make them.

Abby appeared in the doorway. "Where is that wonderful granddaughter of mine?"

Bridget's eyes flew toward her grandmother. Her smile turned to a delighted laugh when Abby peered down at her.

"There you are," Abby said, her laugh matching Bridget's.

Carrie kissed Bridget on what was rapidly becoming a pudgy cheek and handed her to Abby.

Abby reached down and tickled Bridget's tummy, grinning with joy when Bridget laughed even harder. "Did I see a boy with a cast going out of here?"

Carrie nodded. "That was Paul. He broke his arm playing baseball."

Abby looked sympathetic. "That's too bad."

"Perhaps," Carrie said with a chuckle. "I believe he's determined to now become the best switch- pitcher in the area. Probably the *only* one. He'll be alright. He's young, so his arm will heal quickly."

The sound of another wagon took her to the clinic door.

"Another patient?" Abby asked.

Carrie nodded. "Janie had to go into Richmond for supplies, and Polly is helping deliver a baby, so I'm on my own today. I just have to change Ava's bandage."

"I'm going to take Bridget for a walk," Abby responded as she pulled the little girl into her eager arms. "I'll have her back in time for Patty's feeding and then her nap." She kissed Carrie on the cheek and hurried down the steps.

As Carrie watched, she could hear her daughter laughing joyfully. They had a little wagon that Abby could have pulled her in, but she insisted she was going to hold the baby in her arms for as long as possible.

Ava smiled as she walked up the stairs. "That sounds like a happy baby."

Carrie grinned. "Almost as happy as her mama. I still can't believe she's mine."

"Douglas and me can't believe Clara is going to be ours, either," Ava said. "One of the happiest days of our lives was when you pulled up to the schoolhouse with that wagon of children."

Carrie examined Ava's eyes. "It's going well with Clara?" She hadn't wanted to ask last week when Ava had come to the clinic in terrible pain from a bad cut.

"That little girl is a jewel," Ava declared. "I can't believe her mama walked away from her."

"We don't know her mother's story," Carrie said softly.

Ava placed her hands on both hips and looked at her levelly. "Is there a reason that would make you walk away from any of *your* children?"

"No," Carrie admitted, thinking of the lovely little girl with blond braids and brown eyes. She remembered Russell's description of how often the girl cried from hunger and fear under the bridge the past year. "These are desperate times, though. We don't know if her mama left her, or if something bad happened to her."

"I suppose you're right," Ava admitted grudgingly, the scowl on her face saying she wasn't truly going to change her mind anytime soon. "All I know is that me and Douglas ain't never going to let her go."

Carrie smiled with delight. "I'm so glad! Clara seems to be a special little girl."

"Oh, she's special alright," Ava said enthusiastically. "When that girl got here, she couldn't sleep through a night without crying and calling out for us. Now she sleeps through the night without making a peep. She used to eat everything she could see, but now she knows there's going to be plenty, so she stops when she's full. I reckon she's put on at least ten pounds in the last three weeks. But that ain't all," she continued with barely a breath. "She hadn't ever been to school in her life. Now she's reading some of the beginner books and she's writing some. She stays up reading everything we can get our hands on. Miss Phoebe says she's real smart."

"She's very lucky to have you," Carrie said sincerely. "I hope all the other children are as happy." She stiffened when she saw an odd expression cross Ava's face. "What is it?"

Ava hesitated for a long moment before meeting her eyes. "I know my bandage needs changing so you can check my cut, but I really came in for another reason."

Carrie knew she needed to let Ava tell the story at her own pace. "Alright."

Ava stared out the window and then swung her gaze around. "It's Emma."

Carrie waited for Ava to continue, but her uneasiness was increasing.

"I don't think she's happy," Ava said.

"She went home with Charlotte and Abe," Carrie remembered. "They seemed excited that day. Why do you believe she's not happy?"

"Clara told me," Ava replied. "She says Emma cries every night. Emma told her at school."

Carrie frowned. "Did she say why?"

Ava hesitated again, her face red with emotion. "Emma said Abe hits her," she finally blurted. "Not every day, but more than a few times."

Carrie stiffened. "Why haven't you told me before now, Ava?"

"I didn't find out until last night," Ava replied. "When Clara found out I was coming here today, she asked me if I would talk to you. She said she was afraid to tell me because she didn't want Emma to get in more trouble."

Carrie felt sick. After all the little girl had been through, she couldn't believe Emma was somewhere she was being hit. She knew Abe was a rough man, but she'd seen him with his other children before. He appeared to be a good father. She didn't believe he hurt his children, but if he was hiding what he was doing to Emma, he might be hiding what he was doing to the others. She thought through her options, her mind spinning.

"Can you go over to the school and ask Clara and Emma to leave with you? I'll write a note to Phoebe. I'd like to talk to them alone, here at the clinic."

Ava nodded. "Yes, but can I tell you one more thing?"

Carrie nodded. "Of course."

"If Clara is right and Emma is real unhappy, me and Douglas would like to adopt her too. She's been at our house a few times and she's a fine little girl." She took a breath. "We always wanted two little girls. We ain't been able to have children of our own. We already love little Emma, and Clara and her are thick as thieves. As far as I'm concerned, they're sisters."

Carrie thought it was a perfect solution, but she didn't want to make promises until she talked to Emma. She knew children would sometimes tell stories to get sympathy, and she didn't want to make accusations without proof. "Let's talk to her," was all she said. "But first, let's change that bandage of yours."

It took only a few minutes to change the bandage and determine the cut was healing nicely. She put another salve of honey, garlic, and onion on the cut, and then wrapped it securely. "You're changing the bandage every day?" Carrie asked.

"Just like you told me," Ava assured her. "I made up a salve to use like you make. Douglas helps me. He cleans the cut, puts the salve on it, and puts the bandage back on."

"After he boils the bandage to clean the germs?"

"Yes, ma'am," Ava said promptly. "We know better than to not follow your orders, Dr. Carrie." Her eyes glimmered with amusement.

Carrie chuckled. "Well, I'm not going to apologize for giving you the best care possible." She secured the wrap, stood, and quickly wrote a note. "You can give this to Miss Phoebe. I've written that I need to do a quick check-up on the girls, so there'll be no reason for anyone to suspect anything else is wrong."

Ava nodded and disappeared.

Abby arrived as she was leaving. Her brow furrowed with concern when Carrie told her what Ava suspected. "Sweet little Emma is being hit?" she asked with outrage.

"We don't know yet," Carrie said, but she felt strongly that Emma wouldn't make up a story like that. She easily interpreted the look on Abby's face. "The trial month for the families and children to make their decisions is about over. I think it's wise if one of us meets with each child privately, in order to find out what they want to do. It won't be solely up to the adults."

Abby nodded. "I agree with you. If the children are afraid of their new families, they probably won't be able to tell us in front of them."

Carrie scooped Bridget into her arms. "How's my girl?"

"She's perfect," Abby said promptly. "I can say that because I'm her grandma, but it also happens to be true. I introduced her to many new birds today, and she also saw two deer."

Carrie leaned down to kiss Bridget's velvety cheek. "One day, you're going to know just how lucky you are to have this woman as your grandmother. I know that's true because I'm lucky to have her as my mother."

She looked into Abby's glowing eyes. "Thank you," Carrie said softly. "Patty should be here any minute for Bridget's feeding. Why don't you take this little girl into the back room and wait for her? She'll come in the back door, as always. I'd rather nothing interrupt my conversation with Emma."

She could hear Ava coming with the girls as Abby closed the door to the back room. Both girls looked apprehensive as they entered the clinic.

Clara walked right up to her, her blue eyes shining with concern. "Are we in trouble, Dr. Carrie? I didn't mean to do nothing bad."

Carrie gave her a warm hug. "You're not in trouble, Clara. It's good to see you." She reached over to take Emma's hand, shocked when the little girl trembled and drew back before allowing her to take it. "You're not in trouble either, Emma," she said gently. "I'm glad to see you, too."

Emma watched her closely, her brown eyes losing none of their fearfulness.

Carrie felt a surge of anger at Abe, but also at herself for not keeping better watch on the children they had entrusted to these families. "Girls, can we talk for a little bit?"

The two girls nodded but remained silent.

Carrie hoped she could get Emma to open up to her. "Emma, how do you like being with your family?"

Emma ducked her head and refused to meet her eyes. "It's alright," she said, her voice barely audible.

"Is it?" Carrie asked gently. "You don't seem like you're very happy."

Emma's head shot up, fear gleaming in her eyes again. "I'm sorry," she whispered. "I'll do better."

Carrie fought the tears swelling in her eyes, realizing that as unhappy as Emma might be, it was better than being under the bridge. She was terrified of returning to that life. "You have nothing to be sorry about, Emma. I want you to be happy. Is something making you unhappy?"

Emma stared at her for a moment before she looked back down. "No," she said softly.

"You know that ain't true, Emma," Clara protested. "Dr. Carrie is a good person. You can tell her the truth."

Emma gulped and began to tremble.

"Honey, whatever you have to say is alright," Carrie assured her. "You know, when Russell agreed for all of you to come out here to see if you could find a family, we promised him we wouldn't let anyone stay with a family that doesn't love them as much as we love Russell. Do you believe the Cummings love you like that?"

Emma started to nod her head but stopped when Clara squeezed her hand. She looked up slowly, tears seeping from her eyes. "No ma'am," she whispered. "I don't reckon they do."

"Can you tell me why you believe that?" Carrie asked. She hated to keep asking questions that were obviously causing distress, but she had to know the truth.

Emma peered into Carrie's face, trying to decide if it was safe to tell what was happening.

"Tell her," Clara said firmly. "Remember how we used to talk under the bridge last winter 'bout how it would feel to be safe and warm? What it would be like to have a family? Enough to eat?"

Emma locked eyes with her friend. "Yes," she said softly.

"Well, that's what I got Emma. You got to have the same thing."

Emma sighed deeply and turned to Carrie. Her seven-year-old face held far too much pain for her years. Carrie's heart tightened with agony. Minnie could have been Emma if they'd not been there to give her a family after the fire.

"I don't reckon they love me," she said haltingly. "Mr. Cummings...he hits me sometimes." She took a deep breath. "He says it's because I'm bad. I try real hard to be good, but I guess I keep messing up." Emma's face was twisted with emotion.

Clara sidled closer. "Show Dr. Carrie, Emma."

Emma reluctantly pulled up the sleeve on her dress. There was a dark bruise that looked fresh.

Carrie swallowed. "Are there more bruises, honey?"

Emma sighed and nodded. "Yes, ma'am."

Carrie clenched her fists but fought to keep her voice calm and comforting. "Will you show them to me? I want to make sure you're alright."

Emma nodded slowly. "He hit me on my back, Dr. Carrie," she managed to say in a choked voice.

Carrie locked the clinic door and then slid Emma's dress off her too thin body. Several large bruises, spread across her shoulders and back, were beginning to yellow. "Oh, Emma. I'm so sorry this happened to you." She fought to control her tears.

"I was bad," Emma whispered.

Carrie felt the fury rising in her throat. "Honey, you're not bad. Mr. Cummings is the bad one because he hits you." She pulled Emma into her arms. "I promise you it's never going to happen again."

"How?" Emma breathed. "I don't want to go back under the bridge. I ain't got nowhere else to be."

Carrie looked up at Ava and nodded. "Yes, you do, Emma."

Ava stepped forward. "Emma, you're going home with me and Clara," she said lovingly.

Emma, safe in the security of Carrie's embrace, looked up with wide eyes. "What?"

Ava knelt down so she could look into the little girl's face. "You're going home with me and Clara," she repeated. "Me and Mr. Blackstone already talked about it. We want you to be our daughter so much.

We've always dreamed of having two little girls. It would mean so much to us if you would agree to be our daughter."

Emma began to cry great gulping sobs of relief.

Carrie released Emma so Ava could pull her into her arms.

"It's gonna be alright," Clara told her friend. "You ain't never gonna be hit again."

"But..." Emma started, her eyes brimming with both relief and confusion.

Carrie knew what the little girl was thinking. "I'm going to talk to Mr. Cummings. You'll never see him again." Then she paused. "Emma, can I ask you one more question?"

Emma leaned into Ava's warm body, obviously drawing strength from the love she felt there. She nodded bravely.

Carrie waited until the tears had slowed. "Does Mr. Cummings hit his other children?"

Emma shook her head. "Not that I seen. I reckon I got hit 'cause I was bad." She stared up into Ava's kind eyes. "I'll try real hard to not be bad."

"You're not bad," Ava said fiercely. "Mr. Cummings is a stupid man who doesn't know a wonderful little girl when he has one."

Carrie couldn't have agreed more.

Emma looked startled but managed a smile.

Clara giggled. "Mama's right," she said stoutly. "Mr. Cummings is a stupid man who doesn't know a wonderful little girl when he has one."

Carrie knew she was right, but she also expected Clara probably shouldn't say that to anyone else.

Ava reached over to pull Clara close with her other arm. "We'll make that our little secret, alright? We can know the truth and be glad that Emma is going to be part of our family now."

Clara threw back her head with a laugh of delight. "Emma, we're gonna get what we talked about. But it's even better than we thought 'cause now we're going to be sisters for real!"

Emma's smile broadened as the fear ebbed from her eyes. She smiled into Ava's face. "Thank you," she whispered.

Anthony was livid when Carrie told him about Emma. "Have you talked to Abe?"

"No," Carrie admitted. "I was hoping you could go with me."

"Of course," Anthony said promptly. "Or I could go over and teach him a lesson about how it feels to be hit," he growled. "I would rather enjoy beating up on that puny little man."

Carrie smiled. She had savored envisioning the same thing during her ride home. "As much as I would like that, it's probably not the best solution. I want him and Charlotte to know Emma won't be coming back to their house. I want him to know exactly why, too." Fresh anger rolled through her as she remembered the fear shining in Emma's eyes.

"We've got to talk to every child," Anthony said. "I promised Russell no family would get a child that doesn't love them as much as we love him."

"Abby and I talked about that," Carrie replied. "We're going to have each child come into the clinic over the next few days. Today is Monday. The month is up on Friday. We'll have time enough to talk to each of them." She paused. "I'd like Russell to be there for the meetings. I've talked to Rose. She's fine with him missing school for the rest of this week."

"That's a brilliant idea," Anthony agreed. "They feel comfortable with Russell, so it will be easier to be honest."

"Clara being at the clinic helped Emma to tell the truth," Carrie told him. She felt another wave of fury sweep through her. "When I think of Abe hitting that little girl, I want to..." She could barely form words. "After all she has been through, I hate thinking there was even a single moment when she felt afraid and unsafe." She shook her head. "I should have seen it," she muttered.

"*We* should have seen it," Anthony said. "We wanted to believe each of the families who took the children would be good to them. We'll never make that mistake again." He reached for Carrie's hand and grasped it tightly.

Carrie sighed, relishing the feel of his warm strength. "No," she agreed. "We'll never make that mistake again."

Abe Cummings had a scowl on his face when he opened the door to Anthony and Carrie. "Where's Emma?" he snapped. Angry dark eyes peered out of a pinched, narrow face.

Carrie could feel Anthony's body tense. He was so angry; it wouldn't take much to make him lose his temper. He was normally an easy-going man, but he wouldn't tolerate abuse of either animals or people.

"Emma won't be coming back here," Anthony said tightly.

Charlotte appeared, gazing over her husband's shoulder. Her face was a mixture of sorrow and nervousness. "Why not?"

"I think you know why," Carrie said softly. She didn't know what was going on in this house, but it was obvious Charlotte was frightened.

Abe stepped out onto the porch. "We got Emma until Friday. We're planning on keeping that girl."

Anthony stepped forward until he was towering over the shorter man. "Are you also planning on continuing to hit her?"

Abe's eyes darted nervously. "What are you talking about? I ain't never hit that girl."

"I suppose those bruises on her back and her arm got there by themselves?" Anthony asked. "Abe, you're never going to lay another hand on that child." He moved closer. "If I hear of you touching one of your own children, or your wife, you'll have me to deal with."

"Who do you think you are?" Abe sputtered. "What I do in my own house ain't none of your business."

"Until I make it my business," Anthony snapped. "I understand you get paid pretty well for repairing the wagons and the carriages on the plantation."

Abe froze, his face a mask of concern. "I'm good at what I do," he managed.

"I suppose you are," Anthony said calmly. "I would hate to see your wife and children be hurt by you losing your job." His voice tightened. "It's a bad time to be without a job, isn't it?"

Abe gulped and nodded.

Anthony reached out and took Abe's shirt in his large hand. "You stay away from Emma. If I hear of you even being close to her, you will lose your job." He smiled slightly. "More than that, I will do what I really want to do right now." He gripped Abe's shirt more tightly. "I will beat you until you realize you should never touch another child." He shook Abe and then stepped back. "Am I making myself clear?"

Abe nodded again but remained silent.

"*Am* I making myself clear?" Anthony growled.

"Yeah," Abe muttered. "I ain't gonna go anywhere near that little troublemaker."

Carrie felt a surge of fury. "Why you..."

Anthony held up a hand to silence her. His fist shot out and connected with Abe's face. The man crumpled onto the porch.

"Abe!" Charlotte cried.

Anthony looked down at the slight figure of the man staring up at him fearfully. "You're pathetic," he growled. "Consider that a deposit on the beating you'll get if I hear anything about you touching anyone."

Carrie could feel nothing but satisfaction. The image of Emma's bruises would always be ingrained in her mind. She tried to lock eyes with Charlotte, but the woman refused to look at her. She'd have to wait until she could have a private conversation with the frightened woman.

"Let's go," Anthony snapped. "We're done here."

They were almost home before Carrie could get her emotions under control enough to speak. "I'm proud of you, Anthony."

Anthony shook his head. "I tried to not lose my temper," he said ruefully.

Carrie smiled. "If you hadn't hit him, I would have. Abe Cummings is a despicable man. Your punch was far more effective than mine would have been."

Anthony chuckled. "I don't know. You can be quite fierce when you're angry."

Carrie shook her head. "Sometimes brute strength is the only language a bully will understand."

"Brute strength and the threat of unemployment," Anthony replied. "If I knew it wouldn't hurt Charlotte and his other children, I would make sure Abe was out of a job now. For the moment, I'm satisfied with what I did, but if I find he touches even one more person, he'll be gone."

Carrie nodded. "You're right. I'm going to find a way to talk to Charlotte alone. It's obvious she's afraid, but we'll help her if she wants to leave him."

## Chapter Thirteen

Carrie kissed Granite on his muzzle and released him out into the pasture with the other colts and fillies that had been born in the last month. She grinned when he bounded away from her, bucking and leaping, to go meet his friends. No Regrets nuzzled her and then trotted over to join the other mares, who watched their babies with tolerant patience.

"That little man is somethin'," Miles said, striding out of the barn to stand beside her.

"He is," Carrie agreed, her heart swelling as she watched him. "I can't believe he'll be five months old soon."

Miles chuckled. "I'll never forget him being born on Christmas Eve. That boy always did know how to make an entrance. Ain't nothin' changed." His voice turned serious. "You done anything about finding out who his sire really is? We know it ain't Lexington like we first thought."

Carrie shook her head. Their belief that Granite's sire was the famous Lexington had been disproven when they realized Granite would be gray. A bay stud and a bay mare couldn't produce gray offspring. "I don't care who his sire is. He's beautiful and perfect. That's good enough for me."

"You can't register him," Miles warned, but ended with a chuckle. "Course, I know you don't care nothin' about that."

"I don't," Carrie agreed. "Granite will live out his entire life right here on the plantation. Papers will mean nothing to him or me." She smiled as she watched him spin on his hind legs and then leap off in a new direction.

Miles changed the subject. "I went and looked at some horses today."

Carrie turned to him in surprise. "Why? We're not buying any more brood mares this year."

"Didn't say nothin' about brood mares, now did I?" Miles replied calmly. "But the last I checked, we got a couple little boys that need their own horse."

Carrie gasped. "You found horses for Jed and Russell?"

"I reckon I did," Miles responded, his eyes glowing with satisfaction. "Two right nice geldings from a place not too far from here."

"Tell me about them," Carrie demanded, turning to give her friend and mentor her complete attention. "Jed has been waiting a long time for you to find him the right horse."

"He has," Miles agreed. "I weren't gonna put my grandson on any ole horse. He needs a horse he could grow with. One he can keep forever. The same for Russell." He smiled. "The one I figure for Jed is a buckskin named Tucker. He's five—young enough to be around for a good long time, but old enough to be done with most of his nonsense."

"Granite was thirteen when you brought him to me," Carrie remembered.

"Yeah, but that horse of yours never did get over his nonsense," Miles said with a grin. "He always figured on doing things his way, except when it came to you. He would do anything you wanted." He shook his head. "I still ain't never seen nothing quite like it."

"Perhaps Tucker will be like that."

Miles shrugged. "Tucker's a mighty fine horse, but he ain't got the fire that Granite had when he came. That's for the best though. Jed is a fine rider, but he ain't got the same somethin' you had when you were a girl. He needs a steady horse he can always count on."

Carrie nodded thoughtfully. As usual, Miles was right. "What about the horse for Russell?" She could envision the delighted joy on Russell's face when he discovered he would have his own horse.

Miles grinned. "It's another gelding. His name's Bridger."

Carrie stared at him. "You're making that up."

Miles shook his head. "I'm not," he insisted. "His name's Bridger. I figured it was meant to be some kind of sign seein' as how we got that boy from under a bridge."

Carrie laughed joyfully. "It certainly seems to be a sign. Tell me about Bridger."

"Bridger's seven. He's got a little more fire than Tucker has, but Russell can handle it. He's a natural, just like you was. I could see it in him the first week."

Carrie smiled. "He loves horses as much as I did."

"He does," Miles agreed. "Bridger is solid black, 'cept for a white blaze down his nose. He's a fine-looking animal. Mostly Quarter horse, but with enough Thoroughbred to give him the height Russell's gonna need. He's right at sixteen hands. Russell is gonna be tall, but he ain't gonna be too big. He'll need a mountin' block in the beginnin', but the rate he's growin', I don't figure he'll need it long."

"Gentle?" Carrie asked.

Miles gave her a mock scowl. "You figure I'd give them ten-year-old boys horses that aren't gentle?"

Carrie shook her head, instantly regretful. "I'm sorry. I know if you picked out horses for Jed and Russell, they're perfect."

"That's better," Miles grumbled, his eyes dancing with amusement. "You sound like a protective mama."

"Which is what I am," Carrie retorted. "But I know every child on the plantation is safe with whatever horse you choose."

"Yep."

"When are they going to get them?" Carrie asked eagerly.

"Well, I figure that be up to their parents," Miles replied. "I told the seller that we want them, but y'all need to let me know when to get them."

Carrie nodded thoughtfully. "Let me talk to Anthony, Moses, and Rose. We'll let you know." She wanted to get the horses as soon as possible, but she also wanted to finish the week of interviewing the children.

Friday evening was clear and beautiful. A late afternoon thunderstorm had cleared the air of the earlier heat and humidity. The lilacs and banks of honeysuckle were bursting with blooms, perfuming the air with their fragrance. The oak trees bracketing the porch were in full leaf, creating dense shade during the day. The deep hoots of the great barred owl lent a solemnity to the dusky sky. Fireflies flashed through the woods, starting low to the ground where they emerged from their daytime leafy beds, and rising into the branches of the surrounding trees.

"They're magical," Abby sighed, her head resting against the back of her rocker as she watched the fireflies' evening journey. The longer she lived on the plantation, the more she loved it. The beauty and peace seemed to embrace her every day, no matter what else was going on.

"You're right, Grandma," Frances replied softly. "The fireflies are my favorite part of spring." She leaned forward in her chair to get a better view as the fireflies drifted higher. "Do you know fireflies flash their light mostly to attract mates?"

"I didn't," Abby replied.

Frances nodded seriously. "There's more than one reason. Sometimes they're defending their territory or warning predators away." She shrugged. "Still, mostly they're looking for a mate."

Abby chuckled. "I knew you were becoming an expert on birds, but I didn't know you were studying fireflies." She was constantly amazed by her oldest grandchild.

Frances continued to gaze up into the trees as she replied. "I want to be as smart as Felicia, Grandma. She told me once that I can learn anything I want to from books."

"Which is why you spend so much time in the library," Abby said. "I'm proud of you."

Frances shrugged. "Everyone should want to know as much as they can. Knowledge is power, you know."

"Is it?" Abby asked. She completely agreed, but she was intrigued where Frances had gotten that belief. "Where did you hear that?"

Frances leaned back in her chair and gave Abby her full attention. "Grandpa has a copy of *Meditationes Sacrae* in the library. He showed it to me one day. It was written by Sir Francis Bacon in 1597. He said, '*knowledge itself is power.*'" She furrowed her brow. "I believe he was saying that having and sharing knowledge is crucial to having reputation and influence." She turned to stare at Abby. "I believe it's the only way women will have power."

Abby reached out to grasp her hand. "You're quite extraordinary, you know."

"Do you agree with me?" Frances demanded.

"Absolutely," Abby replied, grateful for this time alone with her granddaughter. With a household full of people, it didn't often happen. Annie, Minnie, and Hope were in the kitchen creating a new cake that they were keeping a secret. John, Jed, and Russell were in the barn with Miles, awaiting the birth of a new foal. "I was able to accomplish so much with the factories in Philadelphia because I was determined to learn everything I could."

Frances looked at her closely. "Isn't that what made you such a threat to the men who harassed you after your first husband died?" She paused. "Mama told me about it."

"You're right," Abby agreed. "Knowledgeable women are often a threat - not only to men, but also to many women who fear intelligence." She leaned forward to look at Frances intently. "Don't ever let that stop you from learning all you can. The world will change for women when we refuse to let anyone dictate to us what and who we can become."

Frances nodded vigorously. "I completely agree, Grandma. That's why I want to know everything I can. About medicine. About plants. About birds. About...*everything*!"

Abby chuckled. "There is endless knowledge to be had, Frances. There may be times when you believe what you're learning will be useless to you, but that isn't true. Many times, you'll find yourself in situations where you'll be surprised that your knowledge is useful. But..." She held up a finger. "Regardless of whether that ever happens, everything you learn will expand your brain cells."

Frances stared at her. "Is that really true, Grandma? My brain will really get bigger?"

Abby nodded. "The study of the brain is relatively new, but they do know that much. The more you learn, the better your brain will work. They say your brain actually expands from the knowledge. It will also keep your brain working well as you get older."

Frances cocked her head. "Is that why you and Grandpa spend so much time in the library?"

Abby chuckled. "Partly. We do a lot of reading, but we also spend time there because we write so many letters."

"To politicians? Mama told me you and Grandpa do that."

"Yes," Abby agreed. "We write to politicians, but also other people who have influence in our country. We both want to live here on the plantation, but that means we're not in the middle of things like we used to be. Our letters keep us involved with fighting to create change."

"Do you really believe they make a difference?"

Abby shrugged. "I hope so, but the most important thing is that we're making sure our voice is heard. There are far too many people who want to complain about what's happening in America, but they aren't willing to do anything to change it. Your grandpa and I don't want to be part of those people."

Frances mulled over her words. "I want to be like you and Grandpa," she said at last. "I know you're not simply writing letters. You do the Bregdan Women meetings for the same reason, don't you?"

"I do," Abby agreed. "No matter where you live, I believe you can do something to make a difference."

"Do you believe *I* can make a difference? Even though I'm only fifteen?"

Abby chuckled. "My dear, you *are* making a difference. The articles you wrote for the *Philadelphia Inquirer* were powerful. The work you do with Carrie in the medical clinic is amazing. You're a wonderful daughter and big sister. I will hate the day when it comes time for you to leave the plantation, but I know you're going to create so much change for our country, and for women."

Frances straightened her shoulders and grinned. "Thanks, Grandma!"

Abby reached over and took both of the girl's hands. "I'm not saying this because I'm your grandma. I'm saying it because it's true. *You are extraordinary.*"

"Thanks," Frances murmured, her eyes bright with pride.

The sound of wagon wheels in the distance ended their conversation.

Frances jumped up and moved to the edge of the porch. "They're back," she called over her shoulder. "The meeting must be over."

Abby had wanted to attend the adoption meeting but had wanted to spend time with Frances even more. She knew she would hear the details soon.

Carrie was weary, but happy, as she climbed the stairs to the porch with her father, Anthony, Moses, and Rose. The week had seemed endless, but the final results made it worth it.

"You look contented," Abby observed.

"Yes," Carrie answered as she eased her fatigued body into the rocker. She would tell her mother everything, but she was hoping Annie would soon arrive with hot tea.

As if conjured by her thoughts, Annie, Minnie, and Hope pushed open the front door and emerged onto the porch.

"Look!" Minnie cried. She proudly held a cake platter where everyone could see it. "We made this tonight!"

"I helped!" Hope said. "I got to break up all the nuts and put them in!"

Everyone clapped their congratulations but had puzzled looks on their faces.

"What kind of cake is that?" Rose asked, leaning forward to examine it more closely. "I don't believe I've ever seen anything like it."

"It's an election cake!" Minnie announced.

Abby smiled. "My grandmother used to make that cake, Minnie. I haven't had it in years."

Minnie's face grew serious. "That's because it doesn't get baked as much as it used to. I read something that says it fell out of favor."

Carrie stifled her laugh. *Fell out of favor?* Where did her youngest daughter learn some of the things she said? She received her answer quickly.

"I found a cookbook in the library," Minnie continued. "The front of it says it's the first cookbook ever authored by an American. Her name was Amelia Simmons, but the book doesn't say much about her. She calls herself an American orphan on the title page."

"American orphan?" Frances asked. "That's interesting. I bet there's a great story there."

Minnie shrugged. "Maybe. Anyway, it was published in 1796 but another edition came out in 1800." She turned to Thomas. "Grandpa, you have that cookbook too. Your library is wonderful!"

"Happy to be of service," Thomas replied with a smile. "Did this cake come from the second edition?"

"Yes. Election cake wasn't in the first edition."

"Election cake?" Carrie asked. She was intrigued, but most importantly, she was hungry. "Are you going to let us have some?"

Annie chuckled. "I thought I saw a hungry look in your eyes."

"In all our eyes," Anthony corrected. "Dinner wore off about halfway through the meeting."

Annie scowled. "I ain't feedin' y'all enough then."

"You're feeding us plenty," Rose corrected. "We've simply been thinking about cake all evening. Minnie told us the three of you were going to bake tonight." She eyed the cake longingly.

Annie shook her head. "Ain't no way to keep you people fed." She looked down at Minnie. "You tell them the rest of the story, Minnie. I'm gonna go get us some hot tea and plates."

"Alright, Annie," Minnie agreed happily. "When people first made election cake, it was meant to serve a whole bunch of people. The recipe I found in the cookbook called for fourteen pounds of sugar, three dozen eggs, ten pounds of butter, and thirty quarts of flour." She rattled it off quickly before stopping to take a deep breath.

"Oh my word!" Abby exclaimed. "That would make enough cake for an army."

Minnie laughed. "You're right, Grandma. That's what they started with, but then they added lots of spices, nuts, and dried fruits. Then they fed it to groups of soldiers who came through town for training days. At least, some people say that. I read some more about it in another book. The reason it's called election cake is because it used to be fed to the men who traveled into towns to vote." She frowned. "Of course, it should have been fed to women, too. They should have been there to vote!"

"I completely agree," Carrie said as she looked toward the house. "How many more cakes are inside? How long did it take you to bake all the cakes that would come out of that recipe?"

Minnie giggled. "We didn't use all that, Mama." She looked at Rose, her eyes shining with pride. "I used the arithmetic you been teaching, Miss Rose. I divided up the recipe until it was just enough to make two cakes."

Rose clapped her hands. "Well done!" she cried. "I'm very proud of you."

Minnie grinned again. "We ain't tasted it yet."

Rose slapped a hand to her forehead dramatically. "You used arithmetic to make it, but then dare to utter a sentence like that?"

Minnie giggled again. "I'm seeing if you're paying attention," she teased. "We haven't tasted it yet," she said primly.

Carrie laughed loudly. Her daughter was a bright ray of sunshine, always finding ways to make people laugh.

Annie pushed through the door with a large tray that held a silver teapot, teacups, plates, and silverware.

Anthony leapt up to take it from her. "I'm sorry, Annie. I should have come in to help you with that."

"Me too," Moses said remorsefully.

"Nonsense," Annie scoffed. "I reckon the day ain't come when I can't carry my own trays."

"Hey! Are y'all eating without us?" Russell dashed onto the porch. "Is that cake?" he asked eagerly.

John and Jed were right behind him. "Cake!" they cried.

A glance toward the barn told Carrie that Miles was making his way across the front yard.

"Did Jolly Molly give birth tonight?" Carrie asked.

Moses raised a brow. "Jolly Molly? Is that a real name?"

Carrie chuckled. "We thought the same thing, but the name is on her registration papers. Someone had a good sense of humor."

"Or just didn't know how to name a horse," Moses said ruefully. "I don't know a man alive who would ride a horse with that name."

Miles stepped onto the porch with a smile. "Jolly Molly is a new mother," he confirmed. "Dropped out a real fine bay filly."

"We're calling her Golly Molly," Russell informed them.

Carrie laughed but shook her head. "There will not be a foal born at Cromwell Stables named Golly Molly," she said. "I have my limits."

Russell grinned mischievously as he shook his head. "And here I thought I came up with the perfect name, Mama."

Carrie held back her gasp. This was the first time Russell had called her mama. She knew he was teasing about the name, but hearing it would make sure she forever remembered this moment. She pulled him into a warm embrace and ruffled his hair, smiling over his shoulder at Anthony. "Golly Molly it is," she said softly.

Laughter rang around the porch as Annie cut generous pieces of cake.

When everyone had cake and tea, Abby held up her hand for silence. "I've waited patiently to hear the results of tonight's meeting. Would someone care to fill in those of us who weren't there?"

Carrie swallowed a bite. "It was perfect," she said happily. She looked at Russell and John. "Thanks to these two boys being at our meetings this week, we know the children are happy and safe in their homes." She frowned briefly. "Abe and Charlotte weren't there, of course, but Douglas and Ava said Emma was happy to be with them."

Rose nodded. "She's a different child in school now. Phoebe told me she's laughing and smiling for the first time. I see it for myself when they're on the playground."

"And the other children?" Abby asked.

"They're happy!" Russell and John said in unison.

Carrie smiled at the boys. "The two of you were invaluable this week during the meetings with them. Thank you."

Russell shrugged. "It weren't hard."

Rose cleared her throat.

Russell's brow creased for a moment before it cleared. "It wasn't hard," he said carefully.

"Excellent!" Rose said enthusiastically. "You're learning fast."

"Hard not to, when everybody here is on you like a duck on a June bug if you don't talk right," Russell said wryly.

Carrie joined in the laughter.

"Anyway," Russell continued, "it wasn't hard because everyone *is* happy." He smiled brightly. "When we were all freezing under that bridge last winter, we didn't dream we would end up like this. We used to talk about life being better, but ain't a one of us really believed it would happen."

Rose didn't bother to correct him this time.

Carrie knew she was trying as hard as she was to not burst into tears.

"So, every child is staying with their family?" Abby asked, her eyes shining with delight.

"They are," Carrie confirmed.

Russell grinned. "I can't wait for Paxton to find out. If it weren't for him, I don't reckon any of us would even be alive." He looked at Anthony. "You really think Paxton is happy at the stables? I sure do wish he could go to school and live like the rest of us."

Anthony put a hand on his son's shoulder. "I promise you that if Paxton isn't happy, we'll bring him back out with us when we return from Boston."

"Promise?" Russell asked keenly.

Anthony nodded solemnly. "I promise, son."

"I believe you, Daddy," Russell said as he leaned into Anthony's side.

Carrie knew without looking that no one was controlling their tears any longer. After far too long of having to survive on his own, Russell was a little boy again.

Carrie was startled by a figure concealed in the woods when she rode up to the clinic the following week. She stiffened, wondering if an attack was imminent. Her hand reached for the pistol at her waist. Past experience had taught her it was unsafe to not be protected. She knew Rose would soon be arriving at the school with Jeb, but it might not be soon enough. It was best to be prepared.

"Who is there?" she called sharply. "Come out or I will shoot." She raised the pistol to show she was serious.

"Don't shoot!" A female voice called out.

It took a moment for Carrie to recognize the woman as she left the protection of the woods and walked closer. "Charlotte!"

Charlotte's eyes darted around fearfully. "Can we go inside?"

"Of course," Carrie responded. She swung down off the mare she was riding, released her into the small corral they had behind the clinic, and unlocked the door to the back entrance. "Please come inside," she urged.

Charlotte followed her, casting a desperate look over her shoulder when she edged inside.

Carrie realized she was afraid Abe had followed her. She latched the door securely, deciding to leave the front door locked, as well. She was there early, so no patients would be arriving right away. She turned to Charlotte. "Does Abe know you're here?"

"No," Charlotte whispered. "He left real early to go repair some wagons. I don't figure he'll be back until this afternoon."

Carrie relaxed. "What can I do for you?"

"I got to tell you how sorry I am for what happened with Emma," Charlotte said earnestly.

Carrie considered her response. Though Abe had done the hitting, Charlotte hadn't said anything. "Why did you let it happen, Charlotte? Emma is a little girl."

Charlotte flushed, her face turning bright red. "I didn't know how to stop him," she blurted. "I ain't never known how to stop him," she added hesitantly.

"Who else does he hit?" Carrie asked. "You? Your children?"

"All of us," Charlotte whispered. "I wanted to tell you the truth when you came over, but... I knew we would pay the price. Abe wants everyone to think he's a good father."

"Why do you stay?" Carrie asked gently.

Charlotte stared down at the floor for a long moment before she looked up. "I don't know what else to do. Me and the children barely made it through the war. They were babies when he left to fight, and we almost starved while he was gone. It ain't good since he got back, but at least my children eat." She shook her head. "I don't know what's worse. Starving, or being beat."

Carrie took a deep breath. "How would your children answer that question?"

Tears spilled down Charlotte's cheeks. "They hardly remember the days they didn't have anything to eat. They might answer different if they remembered." Her eyes were haunted.

Carrie prayed for wisdom. "Charlotte, you're part of the Bregdan Women's group. Are you making quilts?"

"Yes," Charlotte said, a glimmer of pride shining in her eyes. "I've sold ten of my quilts now. Henrietta, my daughter, helps me."

"What happens to your money?" Carrie asked.

Shame replaced the pride in Charlotte's eyes. "Abe takes every penny," she admitted. "Says we need it for the family, but..." Her voice faltered again.

"But what?"

"He makes good money repairing things at the plantation. I want to use the money I make from the quilts to buy some things for my children, but he won't let me."

Carrie sighed. "He's taking the money to keep you under his control, Charlotte."

"I reckon he is."

"What do you want to do about it?" Carrie asked quietly.

Charlotte's eyes widened. "*Do* about it? There isn't really anything *to* do about it."

"Why not?" Carrie pressed. "If you've sold ten quilts, you're making enough money to take care of yourself and your children. You know the Bregdan Women will help you if you leave Abe."

"He'll kill us," Charlotte said flatly, her eyes glazed with fear. "He said he would kill us if I tried to leave. I believe him."

Carrie's mind raced. She had seen women suffer at the hands of men before. She had seen a woman almost killed by her husband for daring to stand up to him. She understood the threat was real, however she couldn't stand by while Charlotte and her children were beaten. "Charlotte, where are you from?"

"Philadelphia," Charlotte replied.

Carrie stared at her with disbelief. "What?" She'd believed the woman was from the South.

Charlotte nodded. "It's true. I grew up in Philadelphia. A few years before the war started, Abe was up there doing some work. That's where I met him. Back then, he was real handsome and nice." She sighed. "He talked me into coming down here with him. We had our two children real close together. We were happy in the beginning, but the war changed him. I thought things would be better when he got home, but they've been real bad." She sighed again. "Or I've been real bad. That's what he tells me when he beats me," she admitted.

Carrie gripped Charlotte's hands. "That's what he told Emma too."

Tears filled Charlotte's eyes. "I know," she whispered. "I'm real sorry, Dr. Carrie."

Carrie made a quick decision. "Being sorry isn't enough, Charlotte," she said kindly, but firmly. "Being sorry isn't going to keep your children from being beaten. It's not going to keep you from being beaten. Being sorry isn't going to make life any different for you, or for your children."

Charlotte gasped and pulled back. "Dr. Carrie..."

Carrie raised a hand. "Is your family in Philadelphia?"

Charlotte nodded. "I believe they're still there, but Abe won't let me send them letters or nothing."

"How long has it been since they heard from you?"

Charlotte looked down. "Since before the war," she whispered. Tears began to stream down her face. "They ain't heard from me since the war started. During the war, I couldn't get letters to them. Since Abe got home, he won't let me send any." She shuddered. "I reckon my family thinks I'm dead."

Carrie gasped. "They must be worried sick."

"I know," Charlotte replied. "I've tried to send them something a few times since the war ended, but Abe always found out."

Carrie didn't have to ask her what had happened. The answer was in her eyes.

"I have a plan," Carrie said firmly.

## *Chapter Fourteen*

Carrie wanted to tell Anthony her plan as soon as she arrived home, but she knew there wouldn't be time until they went to bed. There was something very important to take care of.

Russell met her at the barn when she rode up at the end of the day. "Mama, Mr. Moses wouldn't let me ride with him into the fields today," he complained. "He wouldn't tell me why either. He said he had some important things that he needed to do by himself."

Carrie smiled. "It sounds to me like he told you why you couldn't come, Russell."

Russell shook his head. "He weren't telling the truth."

Carrie decided to not correct his speech. She could tell he was truly upset. She understood his distress, but also knew it wouldn't last long. "How do you know?"

Russell shrugged. "I could just tell."

Carrie believed him. He'd had to learn how to read people in order to survive. "Well, I'm sure he had a good reason."

Russell frowned and didn't look convinced but didn't say anything else.

"Where is Jed?" Carrie asked.

Russell nodded toward the barn. "His grandpa asked him to clean out a couple stalls," he said, shifting his eyes evasively.

"Miles only asked Jed?"

Russell squirmed but didn't lie. "He asked me to help, but I didn't feel like it."

"I see," Carrie said slowly. "So, Miles has done everything he could to help you with your riding, but you didn't feel like helping him?"

Russell stared down at the ground. "I was mad because Mr. Moses rode off and wouldn't take us."

Carrie raised a brow and looked at her son steadily.

Russell looked up as the silence stretched out, saw the expression on her face, and flushed. "I guess that wasn't right."

"I guess not," Carrie said calmly. "What do you think you should do about it?"

Russell sighed. "Go help with the stalls."

"I think that's a good idea," Carrie replied. It was the right thing to do, but equally important, he needed to not be out in the open when Miles and Moses returned. "Where's your daddy?"

Russell shrugged. "He went off to wherever Mr. Miles went."

Carrie had the information she needed. "I think you should go help Jed now," she said. "Since you haven't done your share, how about if you clean out No Regrets' and Granite's stall too?"

"Yes, Mama," Russell sighed, but gave her a quick smile before she turned away.

Carrie went up onto the porch, sank down into a rocker, and sighed gratefully. It had been a long day. The clinic had been full of patients after Charlotte had gone home. Thankfully, both Janie and Polly had been with her, but she was ready for a little rest before the men returned.

Annie appeared beside her with a glass of lemonade. "Jed and Russell got any idea what's about to happen?"

Carrie smiled. "No. Right now, Russell is pouting because Moses rode off without him. He can't stand not being out in the tobacco fields."

"That boy got a head for tobacco, sure 'nuff," Annie said. "John and Jed like to ride out with their daddy, but they don't care much about why they be out there."

Carrie chuckled. "I know." She glanced over her shoulder at the house. "I found Russell in the library last week, reading about tobacco farming. I know there were many words he can't understand, but he's picking up what he can and improving his vocabulary every day. He told me he wants to learn everything so that one day he'll know as much as my father and Moses."

Annie grinned. "I reckon he plans on taking over things sometime."

Carrie smiled. The same thought had crossed her mind. "It's a fine idea." A noise in the distance made her stand and move closer to the edge of the porch.

Annie stepped up next to her. "You reckon that's them?"

"We'll know in a minute," Carrie replied, her eyes glued on the last curve of the driveway. What she saw made her clap her hands. "They're here!" she said excitedly. She gulped down the rest of her lemonade and hurried down the steps. She wanted to make sure the boys stayed in the barn until the right moment.

She hurried into the barn, blinking her eyes to adjust to the sudden change from the late afternoon sunshine.

"Hey, Miss Carrie," Jed called. "Did you come to help?"

Carrie laughed at his quick grin. "Not a chance. Why would I want to help when I have two strong boys to do the work? Besides, I had to clean out stalls when I was your age too. I've already done my part."

Jed looked at her closely and shook his head. "I don't reckon that's true, Miss Carrie. Grandpa Miles told me that when you were my age, there were slaves that done all the work. You wouldn't have had to do stall cleaning."

Carrie laughed. "Well, you're partly right, Jed. It's true that back then we had slaves, but it's also true that your Grandpa Miles made me clean stalls. He told me if I really wanted to know horses, I had to know every aspect of their life." She chuckled. "My father never knew I cleaned stalls, and my mother certainly didn't know, but I did it anyway."

Jed's eyes widened. "Really?"

"Really," Carrie assured him. "You keep doing everything your grandpa tells you. No one knows horses and how to care for them better than he does."

Russell poked his head over the side of Granite's stall. "Mama, I know I haven't been here very long, not nearly as long as Jed, but do you think I'll get a horse of my own someday?"

Carrie hid her smile, pretending to consider the question seriously. "If you keep listening to Miles, I believe it could happen."

Russell's eyes brightened. "I'm real sorry about before. I won't let that happen again."

"Good plan," Carrie said, listening carefully to the noises outside the barn. When she was fairly certain they were close enough, she beckoned to the boys. "Will you come outside with me for a minute?"

Eager to leave their stall-cleaning chores, the boys were at her side quickly.

Russell spotted what she had brought them out to see immediately. "There's Daddy, Mr. Miles, and Moses," he said. "And they have some new horses with them." He squinted his eyes against the setting sun. "Daddy didn't tell me they were going after horses."

"No," Carrie agreed, biting back her smile. When Russell looked at her sharply, she knew he must have heard the stifled amusement she hadn't been able to hide. "Maybe he wanted it to be a surprise."

"A surprise?" Russell echoed. "Why?"

Carrie shrugged. "We're not supposed to know surprises until it's the right time."

Jed pointed toward the approaching group. "Look at that buckskin. That's a real fine horse."

"No," Russell said. "That big black one is the best!"

Carrie breathed a sigh of relief. None of them had known what they would do if the boys wanted the other boy's horse. "They both look like fine horses," was all she said.

"Hey!" Jed suddenly exclaimed. "Is that John? What's he doing with them?" Hurt crossed his face. "He told me Mama needed him to do something at the school. Why did he lie to me? Why did he get to go, and I have to clean stalls?"

"I'm sure there was a good reason," Carrie said gently, willing the group to get there so they could explain. She needn't have worried though. John heard his brother's questions and urged Cafi into a quick trot. "I got to go with them because I already got my surprise. I wanted to be a part of you getting your surprise!"

Jed stared at him with confusion. "Huh?"

John grinned. "Daddy and Miles brought my horse to me the exact same way." He turned to Russell. "Same for you!"

Jed's mouth dropped open.

He and Russell spoke simultaneously. "You mean...?"

"Yep," John said excitedly. "We're all going to have our own horses now!"

Russell and Jed seemed frozen in place as they watched the group approach.

Russell tore his gaze away long enough to look up at Carrie. "You mean...?" His voice was hoarse with disbelief.

Carrie grinned down at him. "Yes, that's exactly what we're saying."

The men reined their horses to a stop, bringing the horses they were leading to a stop, as well.

"Anybody here named Russell?" Anthony called seriously.

"M...me..." Russell stammered.

"Seems there is a mighty fine horse here named Bridger that says a boy named Russell is his new owner. He would like to meet you." Anthony dismounted and led the tall black gelding forward. Bridger's ebony coat gleamed in the sunlight as he held his head proudly and looked around, before lowering it to nuzzle Russell.

"Bridger," Russell breathed. "It's real nice to meet you, boy."

Bridger nickered and pawed the ground lightly.

Moses dismounted and led the shiny buckskin gelding to them. "I've got a horse here that says he came to meet a boy named Jed. His name is Tucker. Anyone here want to meet him?"

Jed broke out into delighted laughter. "Me! I want to meet Tucker!" He moved forward slowly, holding out his hand so Tucker could smell it.

Carrie was proud of the little boy for knowing how to approach a new horse, despite his eagerness.

Tucker lowered his head gently and blew on Jed's hand. Jed laughed more loudly as he began to stroke the horse's nose. "Hi, Tucker," he said softly. "Hi, boy." He looked up with wide eyes. "Tucker is really mine, Daddy?"

"All yours," Moses agreed. "As long as you take good care of him," he added.

"He'll get the best care in the whole world," Jed promised. Then he looked over at Russell. "We both got us a horse."

Russell stopped stroking Bridger long enough to look at both Anthony and Carrie. "Really? Bridger is mine? I really got me a horse?" His dazed look said he was clearly finding it impossible to believe.

"Yes," Anthony assured him. "But it's under the same condition. You have to take good care of him."

Carrie knew the words needed to be said, but she was confident Bridger was going to be well cared for. The adoration on Russell's face was clear.

"I'll take real good care of him," Russell promised. He pressed his face against Bridger's forehead. "You and me are gonna be real good friends, Bridger."

Carrie made no effort to control the tears in her eyes. She remembered with vivid clarity the day she had gotten Granite. It had been love at first sight.

She looked at Miles. "You did good," she mouthed silently.

Miles nodded, a pleased smile on his face as he watched the boys and their horses.

Russell looked up. "Can we go for a ride?" he asked eagerly. "Or are they tired?"

Carrie smiled and wrapped an arm around his shoulders. "That's an excellent question, Russell." She looked at Anthony.

Anthony smiled. "We haven't come that far. I would love to go for a ride with you, son."

Moses grinned. "Same here, Jed. Want to go for a ride?"

"Yes!" the boys cried in unison. "Yes!"

It was long past dark when Anthony, Russell, Moses, Jed, and John climbed the stairs. They looked tired but exhilarated.

Russell rushed over and threw his arms around Carrie. "Thank you, Mama! I can't believe I have my very own horse."

"Did you have fun?" Carrie knew the answer but wanted to hear him describe it.

"It was amazing!" Russell cried. "Even though it was gettin' dark, Daddy said we could ride down to the river because there's enough of a moon to give us light. We even saw a family of deer come out of the woods to get a drink."

Jed nodded his head vigorously. "There were two baby fawns," he added. "But the very best animal was Tucker!"

"No, it was Bridger!" Russell said. "Mama, he's so smooth. He didn't make me bounce around at all."

"I'm sure of that," Carrie responded. "Miles rides every horse before he buys it, to make sure their gaits are smooth."

Annie pushed through the front door. "Anyone hungry out here?"

"Starving!" Jed called.

"Starving!" John echoed.

"Starving to death!" Russell added.

Annie chuckled. "I'm here to save you with some fried chicken. Since you done missed dinner to go out on them new horses of yours, I figured you might wanna eat."

Moses reached out and snatched the plate from her hands. "Those boys don't get to demolish that food before Anthony and I have some. They won't leave us a single morsel if they have their way."

John jumped high in a futile effort to grab the plate that was out of his reach. "Daddy! You're the one who always eats the food."

"True," Moses conceded with a grin. "But since you were good tonight, Anthony and I decided to let you have some. Once we have what we want," he teased. He grabbed three crispy pieces of chicken and three biscuits, holding them easily in his huge hand, before he passed the plate to Anthony. "Take what you want, friend."

The boys groaned, watching the huge pile of chicken shrink considerably.

"Don't worry, boys," Annie said good-naturedly. "There be a bigger platter of chicken on the dining room table. Along with some cookies. Why don't y'all go on in and take what you want."

"Chicken!" the boys yelled as they dashed in the door.

"Hey!" Moses protested. "We didn't get any cookies."

"Oh, for Pete's sake," Annie scolded. "Since when did I ever not give you enough food to fill you up?" She reached into the big pocket of her apron and pulled out a handful of thick molasses cookies.

Anthony grabbed them before Moses could hold out his hand. "Sorry to be rude, Annie, but I know this is the only way I'm going to get to eat any of these."

Rose appeared at the door. "You're a smart man, Anthony Wallington," she said with a laugh. "And Annie is my personal angel. I shudder to think what my life would be like if I had to feed this man all the time."

"What do you mean?" Moses asked plaintively. "You used to feed me before Mama came to the plantation. And when we were in school at Oberlin."

"And it took practically every minute of my day," Rose retorted. "It's a miracle I had time to study. Now that I run a school, I'm afraid you'd go hungry if it were left to me."

Carrie laughed. "You're right, Rose. Both our husbands would go hungry if it were up to us. I'm afraid that neither of us would ever be considered good *Southern women*," she said with an exaggerated drawl. "I know my mother would be appalled."

Thomas strode out on the porch. "She would have no reason," he said. "Your mother never lifted a finger in the kitchen. She just gave orders," he said fondly.

Carrie knew that was true. In her mother's world, being a good Southern woman had meant being able to give orders to the slaves that performed the work. Her father had talked about it being a blessing that her mother had died before the war began; he was certain she could never have adapted to a new reality. Carrie sobered. "I'm glad the world has changed."

"So am I, my dear," her father said, sitting down next to her. "Are you ready to tell us why you look so worried?"

Anthony paused in his demolition of a chicken breast. He moved closer to gaze at her. "Your father's right." He took a final bite and sat down in a rocker. "What's going on?"

Carrie had planned on talking to Anthony alone, but there was no reason not to include everyone. After all, it would take everyone to make it happen.

"Charlotte Cummings came by the clinic this morning."

Thomas stood. "Wait a moment." He crossed the porch, opened the door, and stuck his head inside. "Abby," he called. "Will you come join us?"

The laughter of the children rolling from inside the house assured him they would have privacy for a while.

In less than a minute, Abby walked onto the porch.

"I want you to hear this," Thomas said, and then looked at Carrie. "Go on, my dear."

Carrie began again. "Charlotte Cummings came by the clinic this morning. She told me the truth about what's going on in their home."

"Abe beats her and the children," Rose said flatly, her eyes sparkling with anger.

"Yes."

"Will she leave him?" Abby asked, her face filled with concern. "Charlotte is a lovely woman, but I've seen fear in her eyes many times when she comes to the Bregdan Women meetings. At least now I understand why."

"She's terrified," Carrie told them. "Abe threatened to kill her and the children if they try to leave."

Anthony clenched his fists and started to stand.

Carrie put a hand on his leg. "I have a plan."

Anthony growled under his breath as he sat back. "I'm listening. I hate the idea of that man having even one more minute to abuse Charlotte or his children."

Carrie laid out her thoughts.

When she was done, Anthony had a smile and a look of admiration on his face.

"I believe that will work," Thomas said thoughtfully.

"It has to," Carrie stated.

The moon was cresting past its zenith in the sky, slightly more than a half moon, when Miles climbed the stairs to the porch.

Annie looked surprised. "I thought you was gonna go on up to bed?"

Miles glanced behind him. "Come on up here, Logan."

Anthony was surprised when their guest from Alabama climbed the stairs. "I thought you were staying with Matthew and Janie?"

"I am," Logan confirmed. "I needed to talk to Miles though."

Everyone waited to hear what Logan and Miles had to say.

Miles gazed at Anthony. "Y'all gonna leave for Boston pretty soon, ain't ya?"

"Three days," Anthony replied. "Why?"

"Got room for one more?" Miles cast a glance at Logan.

Anthony was surprised. "You know we do. We're already planning on taking Logan to Philadelphia." He turned to Logan. "Has something changed?"

"I reckon it has," Logan answered. "I suppose Philadelphia be better than down in Alabama. Maybe even better than here." He took a deep breath. "But I done decided to go on up to Canada."

"Which is why he came to see me," Miles said. "He heard I took off for Canada before the war."

Logan looked at Thomas and Abby. "I be real grateful for the letter you wrote to Jeremy about that job up in Philadelphia, but I reckon I want to get farther away than that." He sighed. "I've had time to do some more thinkin'. I figure things gonna get harder for black folk, not easier. I been a slave, I been a free man, I been a soldier, and I been a slave again. I don't wanna wait around to see what might happen next."

Anthony took a deep breath. He understood what Logan was saying. It was terrifying to think what it could mean for all his friends.

Moses leaned forward. "Can you get him a job up there, Miles?"

Miles nodded. "I sent a letter to Mr. Carson. He ain't running things up there no more, 'cause he be pretty old, but he still owns the stables. I ain't heard from him, but I know he'll give Logan a job." He stared hard at Logan. "You got any idea what it be like in Canada, Logan?"

Logan shrugged his narrow shoulders. He had put on some weight, but he needed more time before he fully recovered from the mines. "I know it ain't in America," he said bluntly. "I heard they don't treat black folks as bad as this country does. I reckon that's all I need to know."

"It's real cold," Miles warned.

"It was real cold down in the mines. At least up there I'll be able to wear shoes and more than a torn-up pair of pants."

Anthony winced as Logan described his experience.

"You gonna miss the fireflies and the honeysuckle," Miles stated.

"Probably," Logan agreed. "I don't figure they make up for whips and chains, though."

"Yeah," Miles agreed. "There's that." He turned to Anthony. "Can Logan go all the way to Boston with you? He'll catch another train on up to Canada after that."

"Of course," Anthony agreed. As he watched the play of emotions over Logan's face, he knew what he was thinking. "Don't worry about the train fare, Logan. We're more than happy to pay it."

"I'll pay you back," Logan said quickly.

"Alright," Anthony answered. "There's no hurry, though." It would hurt Logan's pride not to return the money, but he didn't want him to feel any pressure.

"I have a better idea," Carrie said quickly.

Anthony turned to her. "You seem to be full of them tonight," he said with a smile.

Carrie grinned at him. "Susan and I are planning on buying three or four more of the Cleveland Bays this summer to breed with Eclipse. It's a long trip from Carson Stables. We need them to be in perfect condition."

"I'm not coming back here," Logan protested immediately. "I reckon I would do just about anythin' for y'all, but I ain't comin' back once I get up to Canada. I'm real sorry."

"I don't want you to," Carrie said quickly. "It would mean a lot to Susan and me if you were to check out the condition of the horses and make sure they're ready to travel. Maybe you could go with the stable hands to make sure they get on the train safely. If you can do that for us, it would cover the cost of your ticket to Boston. It would save us the expense of having to send someone else."

Logan looked puzzled as he nodded. "I reckon I can do that, but I don't need no money for it. I don't reckon I'll really be doin' much. There ain't no need to pay me for it."

Miles stepped in. "Carrie's idea is a real good one. It's also a real important job. Puttin' horses on a train can be real hard on 'em. It's gotta be done right."

Anthony bit back his smile, working hard to keep a serious look on his face. "They're right, Logan. If we have to find someone up in Canada, or send someone from here, it would cost us more than your ticket." He prayed for Logan to accept what they were saying, so he wouldn't have to start his new life in Canada in debt. "Would you be willing to do that for us?" Anthony knew the time would come when Logan would realize what they were asking for was unnecessary, but hopefully it would be long after he arrived.

"Sure," Logan said promptly. "We leave in three days?"

"Three days," Anthony confirmed.

Their simple trip to Boston was becoming more complicated, but if all went right, everyone would be safe.

## Chapter Fifteen

Three days later, Anthony and Thomas had finished loading everything in the wagon.

Carrie stepped out onto the porch and shielded her eyes against the early morning sun cresting the perimeter of oak and maple trees that lined the far pasture. "Are they here yet?"

Anthony shook his head and pulled his pocket watch out. "They have another twenty minutes before they're supposed to arrive."

Carrie sighed. She didn't think Matthew and Janie would be late, but she was anxious to be on the road.

"Are the girls and Russell ready?" Anthony asked.

"The girls will be out any minute," Carrie replied. "Russell's in the barn saying good-bye to Bridger." She understood the sympathetic look in Anthony's eyes. Separating Russell from his horse so soon after the gelding arrived was difficult. Only Anthony's strong wish for Russell to join them during their trip to Boston had convinced him to leave Bridger.

"Have you said good-bye to Granite?"

Carrie nodded. "I was in the barn early this morning." She smiled, pushing down her own sadness. She knew she couldn't always be on the plantation, but other than her trip to get the children, she and Granite hadn't been apart since his birth. Saying good-bye for three weeks was hard.

Rose appeared on the porch, smiling brightly. John and Hope followed close behind. "Are we ready to leave?"

"Almost," Anthony replied. "Your bag is in the wagon."

"Jed didn't change his mind?" Carrie asked.

"No," Rose said ruefully. "I tried once more to tell him what a fun trip we're going on, but he insists he wants to stay here on the plantation with Moses."

"And Tucker," Carrie added with a smile.

"Boston and New York City don't stand a chance against Moses and Tucker," Rose agreed. "I suppose I should be grateful my other two children want to go."

Abby walked outside, Bridget nestled in her arms. "This baby girl wants one more kiss from her mama and daddy."

Carrie rushed over to give Bridget a noisy kiss, delighted when her daughter erupted into giggles. It was much harder to leave Bridget than it was to leave Granite. Once again, she wondered if she was doing the right thing.

"Stop thinking," Abby commanded.

"I can't," Carrie admitted. She didn't have to ask what her mother meant.

"You think I can't take care of my granddaughter?"

"It's not about Bridget," Carrie answered. "It's about me. I can't believe I'm leaving her for three weeks. When we made plans to attend Peter and Elizabeth's wedding, I didn't have a little girl. I don't want to miss anything!"

Abby gazed at her with understanding compassion. "I know, but they'll be so disappointed if all of you don't come. The reason they agreed to a wedding in Boston, instead of here on the plantation, is because everyone promised to be there."

"You promised too," Carrie reminded her.

"I know she'd like us to be there, too, but it's not the same as having you, Janie and Florence. I've written Elizabeth a letter, and one of those bags in the wagon has our present to them. I know she'll understand," Abby said confidently.

Carrie knew Bridget couldn't be away from Patty. While eating more solid food, she was thriving off Patty's breastmilk, and needed it to catch up on her growth, but it didn't make leaving her daughter any easier. "Are you sure Bridget won't be too much?"

Abby narrowed her eyes. "Your father and I might be getting older, but we are completely capable of taking care of our grandbaby."

Carrie sighed. "You know that I know that, right?"

Abby's expression softened. "I do. I also understand that you're nervous to leave."

"More sad than nervous," Carrie responded. Her eyes swept the plantation. More and more, she hated to leave the peace of her home. She knew the congestion and noise waiting for them in Boston and New York. "This is ridiculous," she said impatiently, pushing her thoughts away. "We're going. I need to stop whining about it."

"You'll have a wonderful trip," Abby replied. "Boston is beautiful this time of year."

Frances stepped outside. "So is New York City," she said excitedly. "Mrs. Stratford said she was going to show us all around the city. I can't wait!"

Carrie smiled. "It's going to be wonderful," she said cheerfully. She wouldn't allow her reluctance to taint the other's trip. "You're going to love Boston and New York City."

"Me too," Minnie said brightly as she appeared. "I've been reading about them. There are so many things I want to see." She frowned when she looked around. "Where's Russell?"

"In the barn," Frances informed her. "I said goodbye to Peaches already. I don't think Russell is happy about leaving Bridger."

Minnie looked sympathetic but also puzzled. "He'll be back. Bridger will be waiting."

"You just don't understand," Frances said impatiently.

Minnie looked hurt. "Mama, is there something wrong with me?"

"No," Carrie assured her. Even though she admitted to Anthony in private that she didn't understand Minnie's lack of interest in horses, she certainly accepted it. "Your passion lies elsewhere, honey."

"In the kitchen!" Minnie said promptly. "I'd rather be cooking with Annie than doing anything else." She frowned. "I like to ride, though."

Abby walked up and pulled her into a hug. "Not everyone is the same, Minnie. You happen to be surrounded by people who are crazy about horses. These same people would miss your cooking, though, if you were to stop."

"That's true," Frances piped in. "I give you a hard time about not loving horses like the rest of us do, but I love the fact that you want to cook all the time."

Minnie remained troubled. "I'm the only one without my own horse, though."

"Do you want a horse of your own?" Carrie asked gently. Up until now, Minnie hadn't been interested.

Minnie cocked her head and looked out at the pastures thronged with horses. "No," she admitted. "I like having horses that I can ride, but I don't want one I have to care for all the time."

"That's perfectly fine," Carrie assured her. "The one thing Daddy and I care about is that you're happy."

Minnie smiled and then looked at Abby with a question in her eyes.

"That's exactly how Grandpa and I feel," Abby told her. "If everybody here on the plantation was horse-crazy, we would never eat. I, for one, am so glad you love to cook. You may find other things you're interested in as you get older, but you'll always be a great cook."

Minnie smiled brightly, obviously convinced. "Alright!" She pointed down the driveway. "Is that Matthew and Janie?"

Matthew and Janie, with Robert and Annabelle looking over their shoulders, called good morning to everyone as they pulled to a stop at the porch.

There was a flurry of activity to get everyone into their own wagon, already loaded with luggage and baskets of food.

Logan, settled down on a nest of blankets in the back of the wagon, waved his hand and smiled.

"We're off to Boston!" Janie cried, exchanging a conspiratorial glance with Carrie.

Frances was the first to question their route. "Daddy, where are we going? We always turn left out of the driveway to go to Richmond."

Anthony glanced at Carrie. "You're right, Frances."

"We're making a stop before we go to Richmond," Carrie explained.

"We are?" Frances asked.

Carrie could tell by the expression on her daughter's face that she suspected trouble of some kind. They worked together too closely in the clinic for Frances to not recognize when her mother was hiding something.

Now that they were away from home, and no one could reveal anything that would create danger, it was time to tell the truth. Carrie turned in her wagon seat so she could see the children. She assumed the children had heard some things at school, but they'd been careful to not discuss Emma and the Cummings at home. "Do you know why Emma is living with Mr. Douglas and Miss Ava now?"

Frances nodded. "Because Mr. Cummings hit her," she said promptly. "Everyone knows, Mama. We're very glad Emma doesn't have to live there anymore."

Carrie didn't know whether to be relieved or sad that the children knew the truth, but she realized her feelings didn't really matter. "Mr. Cummings also hits his wife and other children," she said gently.

"What?" Minnie cried. "Mama, that's horrible. Henrietta and I play together in the playground. She looks sad sometimes, but I didn't know she's being hit." Her eyes blazed with anger. "We have to stop that bad man from hurting her. Henrietta is real nice."

"Josiah and I play baseball together," John added. He turned to Rose. "Mama, please tell me we can do something."

"We can do something," Rose assured him gently. "That's what Carrie is trying to tell you."

John, along with the other children, turned to look at her eagerly.

Carrie took a deep breath. "We're going to the Cummings' house right now, so we can take Charlotte and her children to Richmond with us." She saw the protest flare in Frances' eyes. It took very little effort to interpret her daughter's knowledge that taking them into Richmond wouldn't guarantee their safety. It would be too easy for Abe to find them. "And then we're taking them to Philadelphia with us. Charlotte's family lives there. We haven't heard from them, but we sent someone into Richmond to send a telegram so they would know Charlotte, Josiah, and Henrietta are coming home."

"They'll be safe there?" Frances asked sharply. "You don't think Mr. Cummings will go after them?"

"I don't," Carrie said. She didn't think it was necessary to tell the children that their grandfather was going to have a conversation with Abe once they were in Richmond. "Charlotte and the children will be safe once we get them away."

Frances remained tense. "It's quite early, Mama. How do you know Mr. Cummings won't be home?"

"Because Moses sent over one of his men to tell Mr. Cummings we needed him to work on some wagons this morning. I received word before we left that Mr. Cummings is there."

"That's real smart," Russell said admiringly.

"All your mama's idea," Anthony said.

"But it wouldn't have happened without everyone working together," Carrie added. "So," she continued, "we'll be there soon. Rose and I are going to sit in the back with Mrs. Cummings once we pick them up. I'm counting on the four of you to reassure Josiah and Henrietta. They're going to be very frightened."

Minnie nodded. "I'll hold Henrietta's hand all the way to Richmond, Mama. I'll let her know that she doesn't have anything to worry about with Daddy and Mr. Matthew to take care of things."

"Thank you," Carrie said softly.

"I'll stay with Josiah," John said firmly. "He'll be alright. He and I are good friends."

"Thank you," Rose replied, reaching over to give her son a hug. "You're just what he needs."

Frances hadn't lost her worried look. "What if Mr. Cummings tries to hurt Grandpa? Won't he be mad that we took his wife and children away?"

Carrie understood her fears. She had felt every one of her daughter's fears as she'd worked through the plan. "He won't be alone, Frances."

"Is my daddy going with him?" Hope asked eagerly. "He won't dare do anything if Daddy's there."

Carrie glanced at Rose as she shook her head. They had initially thought about sending Moses, but with the racial tension in Virginia, they thought it wise to not have a black man confront a white man. "No, Hope, but some of the parents from the school will be with my father. Mr. Cummings won't hurt him."

"Also, he won't be working on the plantation again," Anthony said. "We don't want someone like him around here. I don't imagine he'll stay in the area if he loses his job."

Frances finally looked at peace. "How far are we from their house?"

"Less than ten minutes," Carrie answered. She wasn't going to say anything about how nervous she was. Even though Abe was at the plantation, it was possible he would return home. He could have forgotten something or...

She brushed aside her fears impatiently. They had devised the best plan possible.

It simply had to work.

Charlotte rushed outside with her children the instant Anthony pulled the wagon to a stop.

Matthew and Janie pulled in close behind.

Charlotte's eyes were wide with fright. "Is Abe at the plantation?"

"He is," Carrie assured her. She stepped down from the wagon and hugged the terrified woman. "Are the children's things ready?"

Charlotte looked around helplessly. "I didn't have a chance to pack bags, Carrie. Abe was supposed to be gone yesterday, but he stayed home all day. He got angry last night..." Her voice trailed off. "Nothing is packed," she whispered in a defeated tone.

"That's not a problem," Carrie stated firmly. "We'll get everything you need in Richmond."

"But..." Charlotte looked toward the house. "I could go in and gather up some things real fast."

"I don't think that's a good idea," Anthony said. "I think we should start toward Richmond right away."

Josiah pulled away from his mother and went to stand in front of Anthony. "Where are we going?" he demanded.

Carrie shot a look at Charlotte. Hadn't she told the children what was happening?

Charlotte crumpled under her gaze. "I'm sorry. I didn't know how to tell them."

The swelling on Charlotte's face told Carrie everything she needed to know. Abe had beaten what little courage she was holding onto right out of her. "It's alright," she said gently, and then turned to Josiah and Henrietta.

"You're going on a shopping trip to Richmond with us," she said. "Your mama told me how much you needed new clothes, so we're going into town to get you some."

Josiah looked suspicious. "We don't have money for new clothes. My daddy said so."

"I sold a quilt," Charlotte said, obviously trying to pull her emotions together. "I have some money now to buy you some clothes. Won't that be nice?" Her attempt to sound cheerful fell flat.

Josiah looked uncertain. "I've heard Daddy talk about that. Won't you get in trouble, Mama?" He gazed at her swollen face. "I don't want you to get into trouble."

Carrie's heart ached at the troubled expression in the boy's eyes. She wondered how often he tried to protect his mama and little sister.

"It's going to be alright," John called. "Come on, Josiah. We're going to have fun in Richmond. Have you ever been there?"

Josiah stared up into the wagon, noticing the other children for the first time. "John! Are you going too?"

"I sure am!"

Carrie wanted to hug the little boy who was trying so hard to help his friend.

Minnie's smiling face appeared beside John's. "Come on, Henrietta. It's going to be so much fun. I know you like to shop!"

Henrietta shook her head doubtfully, her eyes gleaming with fear. "I ain't never been shopping before."

"That makes it even better!" Minnie replied, without missing a beat. "You're going to find out just how fun it is." She held out a hand. "Come join us."

Henrietta turned to stare into Charlotte's face. "Mama?"

Charlotte locked eyes with Carrie and then reached out her hand.

Carrie grasped it tightly, praying her strength and courage would flow into the terrified woman.

Charlotte nodded slowly. "Yes, Henrietta. We're going on a shopping trip to Richmond."

Carrie knew Charlotte was thinking about how she would explain to them that they would never be back—that they would never see their father again. "One step at a time," Carrie murmured.

"Don't we need to take anything?" Josiah demanded. "What about Daddy? He don't know about this trip does he?"

Charlotte took a deep breath and straightened her shoulders. "No, Josiah, but he's gonna be real happy that you two have some new clothes. I wanted it to be a surprise for him."

Josiah, obviously doubtful, opened his mouth to continue the argument.

John stopped him. "Come on, Josiah. We have to get going. Richmond's a long way. We need to go!"

Josiah's lips snapped shut before he could say anything else.

"Go on," Charlotte urged. "Get in the back with your friend."

Josiah glanced back at his house for only a moment before climbing into the back of the wagon.

Charlotte followed more slowly, her eyes taking in the house she would never see again. She turned beseeching eyes to Carrie.

"It's alright," Carrie whispered so the children couldn't hear. "Your family knows you're coming. Abe will never find you."

Charlotte took a long shuddering breath, and then climbed into the wagon.

Two hours into the wagon ride to Richmond, Josiah moved over to sit next to his mother.

Carrie and Rose had bracketed her tense body but recognized she wanted silence. Not a word had been spoken since the wagon pulled away from their simple house. Charlotte had faced the back, her eyes scouring the road the entire time. Carrie knew she was watching for Abe.

"Mama?"

"Yes, Josiah?" Charlotte replied. Her eyes were watchful, but her voice was calm.

"We're not going back, are we?" Josiah asked quietly.

Henrietta was laughing and talking with Minnie. There was no worry she would overhear the conversation.

Charlotte sucked her breath in sharply. "Josiah..." It was obvious she was searching for words. "I..."

Josiah reached out and gripped her hand. "Thank you," he said softly.

Charlotte gasped. "What?"

"I said, thank you," Josiah repeated. He looked at Carrie and Rose. "My daddy beats us."

"I know," Carrie replied. "I'm so sorry."

Josiah held her eyes. "I hate it, but I mostly hate it for Mama and Henrietta." He shook his head, his lips twisted bitterly. "It ain't right."

"No, it's not right," Carrie agreed, her heart swelling with sympathy.

"I'm sorry," Charlotte whispered. "I'm real sorry, Josiah."

"I know," Josiah assured her. "Daddy beat you the worst, Mama. I'm glad that ain't gonna happen anymore." He turned and looked down the road. "Where are we really going? Won't he find us in Richmond?"

"Philadelphia," Charlotte said softly, her voice almost caressing the word. "Your grandparents are expecting us. We'll be safe there."

Josiah turned wide eyes on her. "Grandparents? You mean...?"

"You and Henrietta don't know anything about your grandparents. I haven't seen them since the beginning of the war. When the war ended, your daddy didn't want me to talk to them or see them."

"Cause he didn't want anyone to stop him from beating us," Josiah said bitterly. His eyes turned hopeful. "Are my grandparents nice? Do they want us?"

Charlotte nodded. "They're wonderful, honey. Dr. Carrie sent them a telegram. They want us."

Carrie considered whether she should correct her but opted to remain silent. One of Moses' men had sent the telegram, but he'd returned before a reply had arrived in Richmond. Carrie could only hope Charlotte's parents had received it, and that they wanted her to come home. With no communication with her parents for eleven years, Charlotte didn't even know if they were still alive.

Josiah mulled over his mother's words. "Daddy won't find us?"

"No," Charlotte said firmly.

Josiah didn't look convinced. "Didn't you meet him up there? Doesn't he know where they live?"

"No, honey," Charlotte repeated, her own voice growing stronger as she talked with her son. "My family moved after I left for Virginia. It was the last communication I received just before mail service shut down during the war. Your father never knew."

Josiah cocked his head. "Was Daddy this mean before the war?"

"No," Charlotte said quickly. "Your father was a good man before all that fighting." She took a deep breath. "He came home changed. I kept hoping he would become the man he used to be but..." Her voice trailed off as tears clogged it. She shook her head sadly. "I'm sorry I waited so long to realize he would never change."

Josiah straightened his shoulders and held his head high. "I'm thirteen, Mama. I'll be the man of the house now."

Charlotte smiled gently. "I know I can count on you, son, but you've had to handle far too much. When we get to Philadelphia, things will be different. You won't have to worry about me anymore."

Josiah met her eyes but didn't look convinced.

Carrie doubted Josiah would ever feel he didn't have to look after his mother, but perhaps he would regain his childhood. She looked toward the front of the wagon where Henrietta was laughing happily. She was twelve, but Carrie hoped she would have years of joy before her. It would take time to heal from the abuse, but Frances was evidence it was possible.

The odds were in their favor that Abe wouldn't track them down in Richmond, but until they got on the train, Carrie knew she wouldn't relax.

## *Chapter Sixteen*

Russell leaned back against the massive maple tree shading the Church Hill house. He couldn't comprehend that he was now part of a family that owned a plantation, a beautiful home in Richmond, *and* factories.

He watched lazily as Minnie, John, Hope, Robert, Annabelle, Josiah, and Henrietta ran around the backyard in a game of tag. Frances was inside. They'd tried to convince Russell to play, but he didn't feel like it. There was a lot on his mind.

"What ya doing, Russell?"

Russell gasped and jumped up, a wide grin spreading across his face. "Paxton! What are you doing here?"

"Came to see you," Paxton said, his gray eyes examining his friend keenly. "Spencer came down to

River City Carriages to tell me you be here. You look pretty good."

"I'm great," Russell replied. He stared at his friend. Paxton's hair had been cut and it looked clean. "You look pretty good too. Especially for someone who works and lives in a stable," he teased.

Paxton shrugged. "I like being there. The drivers treat me real good. I work hard, but I got me enough to eat for the first time in a long time." His shoulders straightened beneath a new shirt. "I'm even learning how to read. Willard and Marcus been teaching me."

"That's great!" Russell said. "I'm in school now."

Paxton nodded. "That's what I hear."

"I also got adopted."

Paxton smiled. "I heard that too. I'm real glad."

"Did you hear about everyone else?" Russell asked, wondering if he knew what happened with the rest of the kids from under the bridge.

"Yep." Paxton's gray eyes glittered with happiness. "Everybody done got themselves a home now. That's real good."

Russell took a deep breath. "Why don't you come out to the plantation too, Paxton? You'd like it out there." He threw in the one thing he knew might convince his friend. "You'd even get your own horse. I have one now. His name is Bridger."

Surprise crossed Paxton's face before he grinned again. "That's real good, Russell. Having your own horse is really something."

"You could have one too," Russell said persuasively. "It's real nice out there. You ain't never seen anything like it." He wanted the boy who had saved his life to have what he had.

Paxton shook his head firmly. "Nope."

"Why?"

Paxton motioned for Russell to sit down against the tree again, and slumped down to join him. "I'm too old to join a family now, Russell. I'm gonna stay right here in Richmond and make a life for myself."

"You ain't too old," Russell protested. "You made sure all of us stayed alive so we could have this new life. I reckon now that I know just how hard that was. I want you to have what me and all the others have."

Paxton smiled but shook his head again. "I don't want to, Russell. Someday, I'm gonna have my own family—one that I'll take care of." His eyes grew serious. "I'm helping some more children here in the city."

"You are?" Russell's mouth gaped open. "How?"

Paxton smiled. "The drivers helped me find an orphanage that treats children real good. I walk around the city every night, looking for children who are in trouble. When I find them, I take them there."

Russell eyed him. "What about the black children? I ain't seen an orphanage that has both."

"I take them over to the Asylum for Colored Children. Marcus told me about it. He said your new grandma sends a lot of money there. They be good people over there."

Russell had to ask. "There ain't nobody living under the bridge again?

"Nope," Paxton said promptly. He leaned forward. "How's Bridget?"

Russell laughed. "She's doing great! I like having her for a little sister. She don't look anything like what she did when we were under the bridge. She laughs all the time and talks up a storm. None of us know what she's saying, but that doesn't stop her. My mama and daddy love her like crazy." He looked down. "Just like they do me," he added quietly.

Paxton slapped him on his arm lightly. "Hearing that makes me real happy, Russell. You're a good one. You deserve a good family." His eyes scanned the yard.

As he was getting ready to open his mouth again, the rest of the children ran up and collapsed into the grass, their breathing ragged from their running.

Minnie looked up into Paxton's face. "Who are you?"

Paxton smiled easily. "I'm Paxton. Who are you?"

"I'm Minnie," she said brightly. "I'm Russell's sister." She looked at him closely. "Are you the one who took care of him under the bridge?"

Paxton nodded, looking slightly uncomfortable.

"Thanks," Minnie said seriously. "I really like having a brother. If you hadn't taken care of Russell, I wouldn't have one." She grinned. "I'm ten, too. Russell and I are the same age. It's almost like having a twin!"

Paxton, obviously charmed by the outgoing little girl, smiled at her.

"My big sister is in the house," Minnie continued. "Her name is Frances. She's fifteen."

Russell didn't miss the flash of interest in Paxton's eyes.

"Frances is going to be a doctor," Minnie told him. "Just like my mama."

"That's good," Paxton murmured as he glanced toward the house.

"Emma was almost my sister," Henrietta said.

Paxton looked away from the house and gave Henrietta his full attention. "What do you mean? Why almost?" He shot Russell a concerned look.

Henrietta looked down, her blue eyes full of quick shame. "My daddy was real mean to Emma," she confessed. "I'm sorry."

Russell saw the flash of anger in Paxton's eyes. "Emma is with a good family now, Paxton. The same one that adopted Clara. The two of them be real sisters now."

Paxton took a deep breath and looked at Henrietta. "What about you? Was he mean to you?"

Henrietta nodded but kept her eyes on the ground. The sound of bobwhites and warblers filled the late afternoon air.

Josiah reached over to take his sister's hand. "We left," he said fiercely. "Daddy ain't gonna hurt us anymore."

Henrietta took a deep breath and began to cry quietly. "I miss Daddy," she whispered.

"No, you don't," Josiah said matter-of-factly. "You miss what you wanted him to be. He ain't never been that Henrietta. You can't forget all the times he beat on us and Mama."

"It was 'cause we were bad." Henrietta tried to gulp back her tears.

Russell shook his head. "I heard Mama and Daddy talking about it one night. They said there ain't never an excuse for beating on children. I heard Daddy say that your father just said that to make you feel even worse."

Minnie nodded. "Adults shouldn't ever beat children," she said firmly.

Henrietta looked at her friend. "How do you know? You're even younger than me."

Minnie looked her friend in the eyes. "Because families are supposed to love each other." Her voice was resolute. "My first mama told me that. She said my first daddy used to hit her. I can kinda remember him hitting me too." She hesitated. "I haven't ever told my new mama and daddy about that," she said softly. "I knew how sad it would make them. Anyway, Mama left him after he lost his job at the factory and made me work there. She said she wouldn't put up with him hitting his children anymore."

Henrietta stared at her. "Didn't you miss him?"

Minnie shrugged. "Sometimes," she admitted. "But I didn't miss him hitting me. I was real glad my mama left him. We didn't have much money. We were real hungry sometimes, and in the winter our room was really cold, but it was still better than being hit."

Henrietta leaned closer. "What happened to your family? I didn't know you wasn't always a Wallington."

"My daddy died in some kind of accident, not too long after my mama left. She didn't tell me anything else but that. My mama and my brother and sisters died in a fire," Minnie replied, tears glistening in her eyes. "One night there was a big fire in our boarding house. I wasn't there, or I would be dead too. Daddy took me home that night, and I've been their daughter ever since."

Russell looked at Henrietta. "I heard Daddy and Mama talking. You're going to live with your grandparents up in Philadelphia. They're gonna treat you real good."

"How do you know?" Henrietta whispered. She reached over and grabbed her brother's hand as if it were her only lifeline. "What if they hit us? What if I keep being bad?"

Josiah shook his head fiercely. "I asked Mama about that. She said her parents were always real good to her. They never hit her. They never yelled at her, either. I reckon things are gonna be a lot better there."

Paxton nodded his agreement. "Mr. Wallington is a fine man. He wouldn't let you go somewhere that wasn't going to be good."

"Like all the children who lived with you under the bridge?" Henrietta asked.

"Just like that," Paxton assured her. "It was real hard for a while, but now everyone has a family." He smiled at the girl. "I know it seems like things will always be hard, but we gotta believe life can be good."

Josiah stared at him. "Do you believe that?"

Paxton nodded. "I do. I didn't used to believe it, but then good things started happening. Miss Hannah, she's married to Marcus, told me she went through a whole bunch of hard years. More hard years than I been alive. She said she kept hanging onto the hope that things could be better. Then, one day, they were." He took a deep breath. "My life is already a whole lot better, but I'm counting on it getting even more so.

Miss Hannah talks about hope a whole lot. She says I just have to keep believing."

"That's right," Hope piped in, her little face set in serious lines. "My mama and daddy named me Hope because they said we always have to have hope. I reckon they had to hold onto hope real tight for a long time. They were slaves for all their lives before the war. Now they're not."

Hope took a breath and looked toward the house. "Mama always tells me that she's gonna make sure I get to do all the things she could only dream about when she was my age. She tells me I'm very lucky."

"She's right." Paxton looked toward the house again. "I know Mr. Wallington stays here when he's in Richmond, but who owns this house?"

"Our grandpa," Minnie replied. "He bought it right before the war started, after his first wife died. Now he has a new wife. She's our grandma."

"You like your grandma?" Paxton asked.

Minnie smiled brightly. "I *love* Grandma. And Grandpa!"

Paxton looked at Russell.

"Me too," Russell replied. He knew Paxton was trying to make sure he was alright. "I ain't never been so happy in my whole life. I reckon I never even thought about this kind of happiness."

Paxton stared at him hard, and then the lines on his face completely relaxed. "That's good."

Simon stepped out onto the back stairs. "May wants to know if there are any hungry children in this backyard. What should I tell her?"

"Yes!" the children called in unison as they leapt to their feet and raced toward the house.

Everyone's stomachs were full, and the children tucked in bed before Anthony brought up the topic he'd had on his mind. It would have been disturbing at any time, but after his lengthy conversations with Logan that afternoon, he was intensely troubled. From the way Carrie had been watching him all night, Anthony guessed she knew something was on his mind.

"Let's go into the parlor," Carrie suggested. She looked toward Micah, May, and Spencer. "Please join us." When May opened her mouth to protest, Carrie held up a hand. "We don't need another thing to eat or drink. I rarely get to town anymore. It would mean a lot to me if you would join us."

Anthony smiled when the three agreed. Micah and May had been purchased as slaves at the beginning of the war to run things in Thomas' new house on Church Hill. Now free, they worked for good wages, and were considered part of the family. Spencer, May's husband for the last six years, had been Carrie's driver through the years of the war. He, more than anyone, had protected her from danger during those turbulent years. Anthony had become good friends with all three of them during his many stays in

Richmond. He knew their presence in the parlor would make Logan feel more comfortable.

"I imagine you want to talk about what you read in the newspaper today," Matthew said astutely.

Anthony locked eyes with his friend, seeing the same unease he was feeling. "Yes." He looked around the room when they were settled in the parlor, the windows open to allow the sweet fragrance of magnolia blooms to waft inside. When he saw Carrie close her eyes, a smile of reminiscence on her lips, he knew she was thinking about the day she'd married Robert in this very parlor during the war, a single bloom off the magnolia tree her only flower.

As Anthony thought about the unimaginably high price that many had paid to win the war, his anger grew. "Three days ago," he began, "President Grant signed the Amnesty Act of 1872."

"What does that do?" Logan asked.

"It means that the constraints put in place by the Federal government after the war, which kept most of the Confederate leaders from holding office again, have been lifted," Anthony answered.

Logan's lips tightened.

"There have been other overtures of amnesty since the war started," Matthew added, "but this is definitely the most far-reaching."

Micah and Spencer exchanged troubled looks.

"So, what you're telling us," Spencer said slowly, "is that the vast majority of white former Confederates are free to own land, vote, hold office, and make laws in the Southern states."

"That's my understanding. Does that bother you?" Anthony asked. He didn't want to lead anyone to the conclusion he had reached after learning about the Amnesty Act.

Micah snorted. "Reconstruction is gonna end someday, probably not too far into the future. What you're telling us is that these white supremacists who be hurting so many all over the South are going to be in a right good position to seize control of their states again." His voice deepened. "What's gonna stop them from taking away any new rights we got down here?"

Anthony sighed. Micah had just verbalized what had been bothering him since he'd read the newspaper.

"They already be doing it," Logan said angrily. "They ain't waitin' until the end of Reconstruction."

"What are you talking about?" May asked. "We ain't heard nothing about you, Logan."

"Logan has quite a story," Matthew said quietly. "Harold and I met him when we were doing research down in Alabama."

Spencer shook his head. "Alabama isn't a good place to be black right now." He looked at Logan with sympathy. "What happened to you?"

Logan told his story.

There was a shocked silence in the parlor when he was finished. Micah, May, and Spencer stared at him, their hands clenched into fists on their laps.

"And now they gonna give them Confederates even more power?" Logan spit the words into the silence. "Things be bad enough for blacks, but they about to get worse." He sighed heavily. "I'm surer than ever that Canada is where I want to be."

Carrie looked appalled. "How is this happening? Why is the Republican Party acting like the war never happened? It's only been seven years since it ended."

Anthony agreed with her sentiments but knew Matthew would give a clearer explanation.

"The Republican Party is fighting to hold onto its identity," Matthew began. "I received a long letter from an old friend today. Just a couple weeks ago, the Liberal Republican Party was formed. There are a lot of people who are dissatisfied with the leadership of President Grant."

"Because of all the corruption?" Carrie asked.

"Partly," Matthew replied. "Political corruption is rampant in every party, though. It's hard for people to trust what's happening. It's more than that, though," he said thoughtfully. "There are prominent liberal politicians who were leaders in the fight against slavery, and they fought for the first stages of Reconstruction. The difference now is that they believe the job of Reconstruction is done. They believe continued radical policies are *oppressive.*" He made no effort to hide the sarcasm in his voice. "They're demanding an end to Reconstruction and a restoration of self-government to the South."

"Have they been down south recently?" Logan asked bitterly.

"I'm sure they have not," Matthew replied, his own eyes sparkling with anger.

"How much power do you think they'll have?" Spencer asked.

Matthew shrugged. "I doubt they can stop Grant from being reelected, but that doesn't mean they can't create havoc while they're trying," he said honestly. "I've seen other parties start up like this. They don't last very long, but the consequences of what they do last far longer than their actual existence."

Anthony watched his black friends carefully. "Spencer, what are you thinking?"

Spencer had moved to the window. His back was rigid, his fists clenched at his side. "Nothing good." He turned and looked around the room. "There are people who want to think that slavery ended with the Emancipation Proclamation, but it ain't so. Just because Lincoln wrote it, doesn't mean people believe it. I guess I thought those amendments would change things for good, but that ain't so either. People who don't want blacks to be free are figuring out ways to keep us as slaves." He glanced at Logan. "Like him. Now that those white men who started the war are going to be back in power in the South..." He sighed heavily. "If our government can't stop what's happening right now, how are they gonna stop what will happen next?"

"There are people who will fight this, Spencer!" Carrie protested.

Spencer met her gaze levelly. "You and I both know the government is getting tired of trying to fight for us blacks to have rights. The writing is on the wall, Carrie. They needed folks up north riled up about freeing the slaves in order to get them to keep fighting, but now that they won the war, there ain't enough of them politicians to keep fighting this battle. They have other things they believe are more important."

"Do you really believe that?" Matthew asked quietly.

Spencer turned around and stared at him. His eyes blazed with emotion. "I do, Matthew. More importantly, I think you believe that too."

Silence fell on the parlor. The sounds of crickets and frogs tuning up their orchestra flowed in through the window, but they did nothing to alleviate the tension.

Matthew shook his head. "I wish I could say I didn't, but my weeks down south have made it hard for me to believe things are going to get much better. I'm afraid you're correct that people don't have the same passion they had before and during the war. Now that the war is over, they want to get on with their lives. They're not realizing, or just don't want to see, that the battle is far from over, because they *want* it to be over."

Anthony scowled, unwilling to accept what he was hearing. "We can't give up."

Rose finally entered the conversation. "No one is talking about giving up, but at some point, we have to face reality."

Anthony turned to her. "What does that mean?"

"It means preparing ourselves for what could come," Rose replied. "I don't know how many years we have, or how many months before the fight will get worse, but we have to be ready." She shook her head. "Virginia has made it impossible for me to teach white students. They've made us build a new school, so our white students don't have to study with black students. What else will happen? We may be the only Southern state that doesn't use convict labor, but we know that could change, because the Thirteenth Amendment makes it legal. What if they decided Moses was a threat because of his influence? What if he ended up a slave again?"

Carrie reached over and took her hand. "I'm sorry, Rose." Her scowl matched Anthony's. "I hate this for you."

Rose turned and stared at her. "And, I hate it for you. You've already found yourself the target of the KKK. You lost Robert because you and your family look at blacks as equals. When things get worse for us, they're going to get worse for you, too."

Anthony stiffened. He couldn't deny the raw truth in her words. He watched as the truth of it hit Carrie as well, but it simply make her expression more determined.

"Then we'll fight it together," Carrie said firmly. "You are my best friend. I love you and Moses, and your children with all my heart. Nothing will make me stop fighting for your equality."

Rose smiled her thanks, but Anthony couldn't miss her bleak expression. He wanted to find a way to make her feel better—to make every person in the room feel better—but at the moment he couldn't think of any words that would accomplish that.

A knock on the door interrupted everyone's thoughts.

Micah stood immediately. "There shouldn't be no one here this late," he said. "I'll go see who it is."

Anthony joined him at the door. After the discussion they'd had, he wasn't going to take chances with his elderly friend.

A telegram boy was on the porch. "I'm sorry to come so late, but I found this telegram on the floor of the office when I was closing things up. I realized it could be important."

Anthony accepted the envelope. "Thank you, son. I know you didn't have to do this so late in the evening. I appreciate it very much." He reached into his pocket, pulled out a bill, and handed it to the boy.

"Wow! Thanks mister!" The courier shoved the money in his pocket, ran down the steps, and disappeared into the shadows.

Anthony opened the telegram and smiled. He walked over to Charlotte. "This is for you."

Charlotte reached for the telegram with trembling hands. "Thank you," she whispered. She took a deep breath before she opened it. Moments later, a glowing smile spread across her face.

"Is it from your family?" Carrie asked.

Charlotte nodded eagerly. "The telegram says they'll be waiting for us at the train station when we arrive. And...that they love me." Tears filled her eyes. "It's been eleven years since I've seen them or had any contact."

Carrie rushed over to hug her. "That's wonderful!"

Charlotte laughed shakily. "I was afraid they wouldn't want to have anything to do with me."

"Have they ever met their grandchildren?" Rose asked.

"No. Josiah and Henrietta were too young to travel, and then the war made it impossible." Charlotte's face darkened. "Abe made it impossible after that."

"Abe is no longer around to cause problems," Carrie said cheerfully. "You're about to start a brand-new life."

Charlotte smiled and nodded, but fear shadowed her face.

"What is it?" Janie asked gently.

Charlotte lifted her eyes. "I'm afraid."

Janie nodded. "I was too."

Charlotte looked confused. "Afraid? What do you mean?"

Janie took a deep breath. "My first husband was abusive, Charlotte. He separated me from my family and my friends who loved me. He kept me a prisoner in our home down in North Carolina. When I ultimately ran away and came to Carrie on the plantation, I was covered with bruises. I was a mess."

Charlotte gasped. "I had no idea!"

"It's my past," Janie replied. "It's not something I enjoy talking about."

"Why are you talking about it now?" Charlotte whispered.

Janie smiled gently. "Because you need to know that Abe can become a part of your past that you never need to talk about. I understand your fear, but you are being courageous. You've left. You're making sure your children can't be hurt anymore. I know you think Abe is a powerful man, but he's not. He's nothing but a bully," she said forcefully.

Charlotte gazed at her. "Did your husband come after you?"

"He did," Janie admitted.

Charlotte gasped again. "What happened?"

Janie's eyes glowed with satisfaction. "Robert was Carrie's first husband. He met Clifford outside the house when he arrived on the plantation, punched him a few times, told him if he ever returned it would be worse, and watched him ride off again. I never heard from him after that."

"It was quite wonderful," Carrie added brightly. "Clifford was nothing but a coward. We never heard anything about him again."

"Not true," Matthew corrected with a smile. "I saw him sitting in a prison cell down in North Carolina after one of the KKK incidences down there. His influence as an attorney didn't protect him from being jailed for Klan activity."

"I remember that now," Janie said. "You never spoke to him."

"Well..." Matthew drawled.

Janie lifted a brow. "You spoke to him?"

Matthew smiled at her tenderly. "He asked me for help in getting out of jail. I'm quite sure he didn't recognize me." His eyes sparkled. "I might have told him he could rot in there for the rest of his life. When he looked surprised, I told him who my wife was and repeated that I hoped he rotted in his prison cell. I might have also told him that Robert was my best friend, and that if he ever dared to show his face around my family, I would finish what Robert had started." He grinned. "From the look on his face, I don't think Clifford was used to being talked to that way. It was quite satisfying!"

Laughter rang through the room, Charlotte laughing as hard as the rest of them.

## *Chapter Seventeen*

Carrie breathed a sigh of relief when Logan's train pulled out of the Boston train terminal, bound for Canada. Charlotte was safely with her family in Philadelphia, and now Logan was on his way to a new life as well.

"Now do we get to have fun?" Minnie asked, her blue eyes sparkling with anticipation.

"Now," Carrie agreed.

The older children grinned happily, gathered up their luggage, and headed for the exit. Anthony and Matthew, little Robert perched on his father's shoulders, had gone ahead to secure two carriages for them.

"I can't believe we're finally here," Rose said, gazing around her as they followed the children. "Boston!"

"I've never been here either," Janie said excitedly, holding Annabelle firmly by her hand. The little girl toddled by her side, her head moving back and forth to take in the chaotic activity. "I've read so much about this city. I'm thrilled to see it for myself."

"I can't wait to see Elizabeth," Carrie said. "It feels like forever since she was in Richmond."

"And Florence," Janie added. "I can't believe the four of us are going to be together again."

"And then there is me," Rose said morosely. "The lowly schoolteacher among the mighty doctors."

Carrie snorted and waved her hand. "Oh, please. The lowly schoolteacher who is educating the next girls who will become doctors!"

Frances had drifted back to join them. "Like me!" she exclaimed.

Carrie slipped her arm around her daughter's waist. "Just like you," she agreed.

"Mama," Frances said excitedly, "did you know the first medical college in history was the Boston *Female* Medical College? It was founded in 1848 by a homeopathic physician named Samuel Gregory. Twenty years ago, it changed its name to the New England Female Medical College."

Carrie smiled. "Where did you learn that?"

Frances cut her eyes toward Rose.

"Oh, you mean the *lowly* schoolteacher is finding you books on homeopathic medicine?" Carrie teased.

Rose laughed. "Frances and I have learned that Boston is truly the seat of homeopathy in America."

Janie chuckled. "Aren't we the ones who should know this?"

"No," Rose said quickly. "My job is to educate. Your job is to use homeopathy to heal patients and change lives."

Carrie breathed a sigh of relief. "Thank goodness. I feel much better about my ignorance already!"

They emerged from the confines of the train station onto the cobblestone streets of Boston. The cacophony of noise assaulted them immediately. The rest of the children had stopped, set their luggage down, and were waiting for them.

"It's loud!" Minnie yelled.

Carrie smiled. "Not any louder than Philadelphia, where you grew up."

Minnie shook her head vigorously. "I've forgotten how loud it was. The plantation is never this loud."

"Thank goodness!" Frances exclaimed, her eyes wide with alarm as she looked around. "I know cities are wonderful places, but I think I miss the peace of the plantation."

Carrie had expected her oldest daughter's reaction. Frances had spent a lot of time with her in Philadelphia, but the noise and congestion always bothered her. As her daughter got older, she seemed to find it more distasteful. Carrie felt much the same way, but she was determined to make the most of their time there.

"Boston is a fascinating place, my dear," Carrie said cheerfully. "In fact, you're standing on top of water right now."

Frances looked down at the expanse of cobblestone street stretched out before them and raised a brow. "Has my mother disappeared into a fantasy land?" she teased.

Carrie shook her head. "I'm happy to report I have not."

Russell moved closer to her side. "What are you talking about, Mama?"

Carrie scanned the loading area in front of the terminal but didn't yet see Anthony and Matthew with carriages. They'd arrived at a busy time of day and had anticipated they may have to wait. The children had gathered around for the explanation of her mysterious statement.

"There's no water that I can see," Minnie piped in. She stared down at the landing as if she expected a torrent of water to suddenly appear.

"When Boston was first founded, it wasn't actually very big," Carrie began. "It was little more than a peninsula that jutted out into the bay. The Indians called it Shawmut. It was way less than half the size of Cromwell Plantation—only eight hundred acres. When the tide came in, Bostonians couldn't make it to the mainland because the water was too high."

Russell's eyes widened. "So, it was like an island?"

"Yes," Carrie agreed. "They didn't like being trapped by the rising tide, so they decided to make it bigger." She waved her hand in front of her. "Do you see those hills around us?" She waited for the children's nods before she continued. "They used to be higher. The Bostonians took dirt and rock off the hills, and from areas outside the city, so they could fill in the water." She pointed down. "Where you are standing used to be water, until they filled it in with dirt and rocks. It was called a tidal estuary."

"And they put buildings right on top of it?" John asked doubtfully. He looked down nervously, almost as if he expected everything around him to suddenly sink.

"Well, it was a little more complicated than that," Carrie admitted. "It's not safe to put buildings right on top of landfill, so they had to put them on pilings."

"Pilings?" Minnie asked, her fascination obvious as she gazed beneath her. "Are we standing on pilings right now? I only see a platform."

"We are," Carrie informed her. "Before they put any buildings in, they cut down lots of trees from the forest. They brought in a whole bunch of tree trunks and drove them through the landfill until they hit solid ground."

Russell frowned. "They drove big trees through the dirt. How?"

Carrie loved her son's curiosity and his willingness to ask questions. "They used a thing called a drop hammer. It's how they do it now, too. They put a giant hammer on a wooden rig, drop it down on top of the trees, forcing them into the dirt. Evidently, it's quite important that the trees stay below water level. It's the only way it will work. If they're exposed to air, they'll rot."

"Wow!" Russell looked suitably impressed.

"They put many big trees in as pilings. After they are in place, they put foundation stones on top of them. Once they've done that, they begin to build."

"My wife is an engineer?"

Carrie turned to look into Anthony's amused eyes. "Surprised?"

"Impressed," he corrected. "How did you learn this?" He answered the question in her eyes. "We've been listening since you began your explanation."

Carrie shrugged as she grinned at Frances. "You're not the only one who knows how to read, dear."

"Yes, but I'm reading medical history because I want to be a doctor. You're a doctor who is reading about construction in Boston!"

"You can never know too much," Carrie replied. "One of the books in the plantation library talks about it. I love learning about different things."

"That's what Grandma said," Frances replied with a thoughtful expression.

"She helped me learn that valuable lesson," Carrie answered. "I hope I never forget that learning is fun." She looked up at Anthony. "How long before we have carriages?"

"Right now."

Janie looked around. "I don't see them."

"That's because they're around the corner," Matthew replied. "Peter and Elizabeth ignored our instructions to not send carriages. They found us down at the loading area a few minutes ago."

Janie looked around with delight. "Elizabeth is here?"

Anthony grabbed both his and Carrie's bags. "She is indeed. Right this way!"

Elizabeth fell into Carrie's and Janie's arms as soon as she saw them. Then she hugged Rose tightly. "You're here! I'm so happy you've finally arrived!"

Carrie stepped back and gazed into her friend's face. Elizabeth's olive skin and dark eyes glowed with happiness below the tousle of dark curls escaping her hat. "You look marvelous."

Elizabeth grinned as Peter swept Carrie and Janie up into an embrace. "My soon-to-be husband is responsible for this happiness," she proclaimed. She shook her head dramatically. "I can't believe I'm going to be married!"

"I highly recommend it," Janie said with a laugh. "It's wonderful to see you again!"

Carrie pulled Russell forward. "I want you to meet our new son. His name is Russell."

"Hello, Russell!" Elizabeth and Peter said in unison. Their warm welcome almost covered the surprise on their faces.

"I'll explain everything," Carrie promised.

"As usual, Carrie is full of surprises," Elizabeth said with a chuckle. She hugged the children before she looked behind them. "Where are Abby and Thomas?"

Carrie couldn't stop her wide grin. "Taking care of my baby daughter."

Elizabeth stared at her with disbelief. "What?" She stepped closer to peer into Carrie's face. "Did you say *baby daughter*? What are you talking about? I know you can't..."

"You're right," Carrie agreed. "I can't have a baby, but that doesn't mean I can't find one under a bridge."

"Like she found me!" Russell said.

Elizabeth looked more confused than ever.

Carrie wrapped her arm around her friend's waist. "I'll tell you about it on the way to your house."

"Every detail," Elizabeth demanded.

Florence and her husband, Dr. Silas Amberton, arrived the next day.

Carrie, Janie, and Elizabeth rushed out to greet her.

Florence, radiant with happiness, stepped from the carriage. Tall, angular, and red-headed, her beauty had bloomed during her soul-wrenching time in Paris during the Revolution. She had met and married Silas during the worst of times. After the Revolution, they had returned to America. Both she and Silas were working with her father, also a physician, in Philadelphia.

The house rang with laughter as the four friends caught up on all that had happened.

Frances watched them closely and waited for a lull in the conversation. "The four of you really lived together during medical school in Philadelphia? In Grandma's house?"

"We did," Elizabeth assured her. "That is, until Florence, Alice, and I decided Carrie and Janie were completely wrong about homeopathy. We moved out of Abby's house, and our friendship almost ended over it." She shook her head sadly.

"Over homeopathy?" Frances asked with astonishment. "Why?"

Carrie remained silent, letting her friends explain. Their rejection of her and Janie had been one of the most painful moments of her life.

Florence frowned. "Homeopathy has been controversial almost from the beginning of its existence in Germany by Samuel Hahnemann. It was so different from traditional medicine that regular doctors reacted rather negatively. Hahnemann's real problems, though, came from the apothecaries. They disliked him especially because he recommended the use of one medicine at a time and prescribed limited doses. Because of that, they weren't making much money from his patients. There were also many times they weren't making the medicines correctly, or were giving out the wrong medication, so he decided to make his own." She shook her head. "Finally, they complained to the authorities. They had him arrested, he was found guilty, and forced to move."

Frances looked at her closely. "You sound sympathetic. I thought your friendship almost ended over homeopathy?"

"Oh, it did," Florence said with a chuckle. "I've changed though. I provide homeopathic care at my father's medical clinic." She waved a hand. "Back to our history... When we were together in medical school at the Women's Medical College in Philadelphia, the American Medical Association decided homeopathy should be banned. They forbade its students from practicing it or learning it."

Carrie watched her daughter, knowing she was learning valuable information about the battles she would fight in the future. Frances had never known anything but treating patients with herbal and homeopathic remedies, but the AMA was still fighting homeopathy.

Elizabeth joined in. "Homeopathy came to America in 1825."

"Almost fifty years ago," Frances observed.

"Correct. It expanded so rapidly that the homeopaths decided to create a national medical society in 1844. The American Institute of Homeopathy was our country's first national medical society," Elizabeth continued. "In response to the growth of homeopaths, a rival group formed that vowed to slow the development of homeopathy."

"The American Medical Association," Frances guessed.

Florence nodded. "Yes. AMA physicians don't like us," she said bluntly. "Shortly after the organization was formed, they decided to purge homeopaths from the local medical societies. That purge worked everywhere but here."

"Here?" Frances asked. "You mean in Boston?"

"All of Massachusetts, actually," Elizabeth answered. "Homeopathy is so strongly accepted by the Boston elite that they decided to make an exception. As long as the AMA didn't allow any new homeopathic physicians. Until last year," she said ruefully.

Carrie was surprised. "What do you mean?"

Elizabeth shrugged. "Last year, the eight remaining physicians were expelled from the AMA for the heinous crime of being homeopaths," she said sarcastically.

"That means your father...?" Carrie said.

"Yes," Elizabeth replied before Carrie could finish her question. "He's no longer in the AMA."

Alexander Gilbert walked into the room just as she was talking. "Which we know is no real loss, darling daughter."

"You don't regret it?" Frances asked.

Alexander gazed at her serious expression. His dark eyes crinkled with compassion as he settled down into the chair across from her. "I don't," he assured her. "My priority is helping my patients to the best of my ability. That means treating them homeopathically. I have no need to be part of an organization that would block me from doing that. I fought many battles to become a physician in the beginning, simply because I'm Italian. My real name is Allesandro." He shrugged. "I changed it when I got older, because I knew it would make it much harder to get into medical school. Looking Italian is one thing, but having an Italian name would only have made it harder."

Carrie had never heard this. She looked at Elizabeth with surprise. "I thought you said it was easier to be Italian in Boston."

Elizabeth nodded. "I did say it was easier. I did not, however, say it was *easy*. I watched what my father dealt with as I was growing up. It's easier to be Italian here now, but combine being Italian, a homeopathic physician, *and* a woman?" She laughed lightly, but there was a hint of bitterness in her voice. "I prefer it to what I experienced in the South, but we'll be fighting battles for a long time."

Carrie understood completely. She looked back at Elizabeth's father. "Has being banned from the AMA made practicing medicine harder?"

Alexander tilted his head. "In some ways, but we've had no reduction of patients. I've talked to many physicians who have been dealing with this for years. Seventeen years ago, in 1855, the AMA established a *code of ethics.*" The tone of his voice made it clear how he felt.

Carrie was familiar with the code of ethics that had driven her out of the Women's Medical College of Philadelphia, but she wanted Frances to hear it from an older physician who had seen far more.

"Orthodox physicians could lose their membership in the AMA if they even consulted with a homeopath," Alexander continued.

"Even if it helped their patients?" Frances demanded.

"Even if," Alexander informed her. "At the time, if you lost your membership in the local AMA, it meant that you couldn't practice medicine in some states. There have been instances where a medical society wouldn't admit a homeopathic physician. The result was that they would be arrested for practicing medicine without a license."

"That's wrong!" Frances exclaimed.

"It gets worse," Alexander said as he looked at Frances with approval. "Even though the code isn't regularly enforced, there have been some ridiculous examples of doing just that. An old friend of mine in Connecticut was expelled after consulting with a homeopath's wife. Another physician I knew from New York was expelled for purchasing milk sugar from a homeopathic pharmacy."

Carrie shook her head. "Unbelievable."

"I agree," Alexander replied. "The one that shocked me the most was when Joseph K. Barnes, the Surgeon General of the United States, was denounced for aiding in the treatment of Secretary of State Seward on the night he was stabbed and President Lincoln shot, simply because Seward's personal physician was a homeopath."

"But homeopathy heals far more people than orthodox medicine!" Frances protested.

Alexander leaned forward and looked at her squarely. "I love your passion, Frances. I believe you're going to be a magnificent homeopathic physician, but you can't ever forget that you'll never be allowed to merely practice medicine. You'll always have people to fight. First, because you're a woman. Second, because you're a homeopathic physician."

Frances stared at him, obviously processing what he'd said. "So, healing patients takes a lower priority than the money that can be made?"

Carrie knew how protected Frances was on the plantation. She also knew her daughter would have the freedom to become what Alexander had said—a magnificent homeopathic physician—before she had to fight the battles waiting for her. Carrie was grateful Frances had time before following her passion became a complicated challenge to forge through.

Alexander nodded regretfully. "I would be lying to say that isn't true sometimes." He paused and gave them a brilliant smile. "But, Frances, you have the advantage of working with women who have already done much to pave the way for you. It's always the people who go first who are forced to pay the highest price. Your mother, and the other women surrounding you, have done precisely that."

Frances nodded thoughtfully. "Do you think it's going to get easier?"

Alexander took a deep breath. "I didn't say that," he answered honestly. "There's no way to know what the future holds. It could get easier, but it could also get harder if the AMA decides to try to make it even more difficult for homeopathic physicians. What I do know," he said forcefully, "is that the women in this room have shown you it can be done. You may be forced to fight ignorance for your entire career, but if you believe in what you're doing, you keep fighting."

Frances took her own deep breath. She gazed around at Carrie, Janie, Elizabeth, and Florence. "Thank you," she said softly. "I promise I will keep fighting."

Carrie grinned and swept her into a hug. "I know you will, darling. And we will keep fighting with you."

At that moment, the front door opened. All the children raced into the parlor, followed by Anthony, Matthew, Silas, Rose, and Peter at a more sedate pace. They'd decided to take the children on an outing so the four old friends would have some time together.

"Mama!" Minnie cried. "Boston is wonderful! Daddy took us to the Public Garden. It's beautiful!"

Russell nodded vigorously. "Remember telling us about how they filled in water so they could build on it? Well, Back Bay is part of that. It's not totally filled in yet, but they've done lots of it."

"That's where the Public Garden is?" Carrie asked.

John rushed forward. "Yes! We got to run around. They have a lake in the middle of it. We got to walk across a suspension bridge, and we saw a big statue of George Washington."

Hope wrinkled her nose. "Part of the Public Garden stinks. Mama didn't make us stay there."

Alexander nodded his understanding. "That was a good idea." He turned to the rest to explain. "The entire area of Back Bay hasn't been filled in. Originally, the Charles Street side was used as an unofficial dumping ground because it's the lowest lying portion of the garden." He wrinkled his nose and smiled at Hope. "Combine that with the fact that the garden used to be a salt marsh, and you end up with what closely resembles a moist stew. It is a mess to walk over, and it stinks."

"Are you going to fix it?" Hope demanded. "Your Public Garden would be much nicer if parts of it didn't stink."

"We're going to fix it," Alexander confirmed with twinkling eyes. "The city doesn't know when they'll be able to move enough dirt to fill it in, though. It costs a lot of money to move that much dirt."

Hope shook her head. "That shouldn't be a reason," she stated seriously. "My daddy and the men who work for him cleared a whole big bunch of forest last winter so they could plant more crops. It was real hard work, but I heard Daddy say that if something is important, you do what it takes." She put her hands on her hips and stared at Alexander. "Isn't it real important?"

Carrie watched as the adults stifled their laughs. Hope was a tiny replica of Rose, but at that moment, she looked exactly like her daddy.

"It's important," Alexander assured her gravely. "I'll bring it up at the next City Council meeting."

Hope stared at him a moment longer before relaxing her stance and smiling. "That's good." She looked around the room. "Are y'all done talking? I'm hungry!" she announced.

Gertrude, the family cook who had been with the Gilberts for over thirty years, appeared behind her. "Did I hear a little girl say she's hungry? Is anyone else interested in eating?"

"Yes!" the children cried.

"So are we, Gertrude," Elizabeth said. "There are a lot of us though."

Gertrude waved her hand. "You know your mama made plans for every little thing about this wedding. She hired some more kitchen help for this week. I'm not doing much more than giving out orders." Her Irish blue eyes gleamed beneath her graying hair.

"That's perfect," Elizabeth replied. "What are we having?"

"Sandwiches."

Carrie smiled. "I've heard sandwiches are good." She didn't add this would be her first time being served sandwiches at a meal.

Gertrude, turning to leave, swung back around, and stared at her. "You've never eaten a sandwich?" she asked with disbelief.

"Guilty," Carrie replied with a laugh.

"Neither have I," Janie confessed. "It sounds like I've been missing out on something special, but I don't actually know what they are."

"You mean you've never taken a slice of meat and stuck it between two slices of bread?" Gertrude demanded.

Carrie and Janie shook their heads at the same time.

"No, of course I've done that," Janie replied.

"Then you've had a sandwich," Gertrude announced. "They're getting a lot fancier in the last ten years, but you still have to start out with some slices of bread. Listening to this is yet more proof you Southerners don't know how to cook." She winked. "I've had women slicing bread all morning. They've also been slicing meat and cutting up cheese and vegetables."

Carrie could feel her stomach grumbling.

Rose heard it and leaned closer. "Someone hungry?"

"Starving!" Carrie admitted.

Looking around the table later, she acknowledged the sandwiches had been a big hit. The children had loved putting their choices between the bread, creating exactly what they wanted. Not a crumb of food remained.

Elizabeth's wedding day dawned bright and clear.

Matilda Gilbert clapped her hands brightly at the breakfast table. "My daughter got the perfect day she hoped for."

Elizabeth grinned. "I don't believe the weather gods would have dared mess up your carefully planned day."

Matilda scowled at her daughter playfully. "I expect nothing but perfection for you, my dear."

Carrie watched the exchange, grateful that Elizabeth seemed genuinely happy to be in Boston. It had been a hard decision for her to return home for the wedding, rather than having it at the plantation.

Anthony, Matthew, and Silas had left early that morning in order to be with Peter until the ceremony.

"I've never been to a church wedding," Carrie said. "I'm looking forward to it."

Matilda turned startled eyes to her. "You've never been to a church wedding? How is that possible?"

Carrie smiled. "My first husband and I were married in the parlor of our house in Richmond during the war. There was no time or money for something fancy. When Anthony and I married, we chose to have the ceremony on the plantation so we could be with everyone we loved. It was also where we met. Every wedding I've been to has been on the plantation."

Matilda nodded. "Elizabeth has told me a great deal about Cromwell Plantation. I can't imagine there's a more beautiful place to be married."

"Except Old North Church here in Boston," Elizabeth said loyally.

Matilda gazed at her lovingly. "Oh, my darling daughter, don't think I don't realize that you're marrying here in Boston in order to make your mother happy."

Elizabeth's mouth dropped open. "I..."

"You are the most wonderful daughter in the world, is what you are," Matilda finished for her. "I've dreamed of your wedding since you were a girl. Now that you're a grown woman, and a doctor, I'm even more eager to show you off to everyone before you dash off on your honeymoon."

Carrie gasped. "We've been so busy talking about the wedding that we have no idea where you're going on your honeymoon."

"Speak for yourself," Janie said smugly.

"You know where they're going, but I don't?" Carrie demanded.

"Evidently," Janie replied with a satisfied smile.

Carrie turned to Rose and Florence. "Do both of you know?" She was partly mollified when they both shook their heads, looking as mystified as she did. She turned on Elizabeth. "Why don't we know?"

"You haven't asked," Elizabeth replied, her eyes glimmering with amusement.

Carrie shook her head and rolled her eyes. "Elizabeth, where are you and Peter going on your honeymoon?" she asked slowly and succinctly.

Elizabeth grinned. "Our favorite place in the country," she said happily.

Carrie started to ask where that was, but snapped her lips closed. "Really?" she breathed. "You're coming to Cromwell?"

"We are!" Elizabeth replied. "Matthew and Janie have agreed to let us stay in their home for two weeks."

Carrie clapped her hands and turned her attention to Janie. "Where...?"

"We're staying in the guest house for those two weeks. The children are thrilled because they'll be so close to everyone."

"And we'll have privacy within close distance to our favorite people," Elizabeth finished.

Rose laughed with delight. "It will be like the old times when we were all together."

"Exactly," Elizabeth replied.

Carrie looked toward Florence. "Are you and Silas coming?"

Florence shook her head regretfully. "I'm afraid not. As much as we would like to, we have to return to Philadelphia. Some friends we met at the hospital in Paris during the Revolution are coming to spend a month with us at the clinic. They're determined to learn more homeopathic options to use in their practices back in France. Evidently, France has decided to follow the American practice of decrying homeopathy. They want to learn everything they can, because they saw how many people Silas and I helped." She gazed around the table. "If we were able to change the timing, we would join you in an instant. Unfortunately, their boat was halfway across the Atlantic before we knew of the plans."

"Which is my fault," Elizabeth said remorsefully. "I should have let you know earlier."

"We'll have more opportunities," Florence assured her. "The important thing is that you have a wonderful honeymoon."

"It wouldn't take much for it to be better than the original honeymoons," Janie commented wryly.

Curious eyes turned her way.

"It's true," Janie informed them as she smiled at Matilda. "I discovered a book in your library that talks about honeymoons. Evidently, the idea of a honeymoon dates back to the fifth century in Europe, when time was measured in moon cycles."

"Moon cycles?" Carrie asked with amusement.

Janie nodded. "Yes. At their wedding, couples were presented with a month's worth of mead. A month's worth was called a *moon*. The mead was an alcoholic honey wine believed to be an aphrodisiac," she said mischievously. "The couples were expected to binge on mead for thirty days so they would get drunk enough to establish sexual intimacy. The hope was that the couple would conceive their first child during this time."

"Oh my," Matilda said, laughing as she covered her face.

Elizabeth chuckled. "My mother isn't used to being around a group of female doctors and educated women. I'm afraid this conversation isn't acceptable fodder for most Victorian-era women."

Matilda raised her head quickly. "On the contrary, Elizabeth. I find it quite refreshing to be around women who discuss the things the rest of us only dare think about."

Laughter rolled around the table.

## Chapter Eighteen

The sun was sinking low behind the trees when the caravan of carriages rolled their way through the tree-shaded streets of Boston, on their way to Old North Church. The azure sky was dotted with banks of fluffy clouds that caught the sun's rays and shot them outward in a glorious spiral of light. The heat of the day was dissipating as a soft breeze cooled the air.

Carrie smiled at Elizabeth. She looked radiantly happy, but also apprehensive. "It's alright to be nervous, my friend. This is a momentous occasion."

"I'm not nervous about marrying Peter," Elizabeth replied. "I'm afraid I'm going to do something wrong at the ceremony that will embarrass my mother. She has worked hard to make this day perfect." She shook her head. "At least I wouldn't have embarrassed anyone at the plantation."

Rose smiled. "Don't be so sure. You could have fallen down the steps during your grand entry."

"You could have said 'I do' at the wrong time," Janie added.

"Or perhaps your dress would have torn during transit," Carrie added in a dire voice. "Could you imagine what your mother would have done?"

Florence grinned. "Or..."

Elizabeth held up her hand, laughing helplessly. "Alright. Enough. You've made your point."

"The important thing," Florence said seriously, "is that at the end of this day, you will be Dr. Elizabeth Wilcher."

Elizabeth cocked her head. "Not Dr. Peter Wilcher?"

Florence shrugged. "I took Silas' last name, but that doesn't mean I'm giving up my whole identity. I don't care what proper *Victorian protocol* mandates. Besides, Peter wasn't the one to graduate from medical school."

Elizabeth eyed her. "That's true. I suppose there are many ways to claim our independence as women in this country."

"Do you know Dr. Mary Edwards Walker?" Carrie asked, knowing a discussion about one of her medical heroes would keep Elizabeth distracted during the carriage ride.

"The only woman to receive the Medal of Honor for Meritorious Service for her work during the war? Of course," Elizabeth replied.

"Did you also know that when she married her husband, a fellow medical student named Albert Miller, she refused to agree to obey Albert in her wedding vows, she kept her last name, and she wore a short skirt and trousers instead of a traditional wedding dress?" Carrie loved telling this story.

Elizabeth gaped at her. "I did not." She chuckled as she shook her head. "Whatever I might do today, I won't come quite as close to shocking my mother as she would have."

"Then you have nothing to worry about," Carrie assured her.

"What happened to Dr. Walker?" Florence asked. "I've heard her name but know very little about her."

Carrie smiled. "Dr. Walker takes great pride in being a nonconformist. She's strongly opposed to traditional woman's dresses. She believes they're uncomfortable, they inhibit mobility, and spread dust and dirt."

Elizabeth sighed. "Who can disagree with her?" She gazed at Carrie and Janie. "At least the two of you can wear breeches on the plantation."

"I can't imagine riding a horse in a dress," Janie said passionately. "I can't imagine riding sidesaddle in a dress like most proper Southern women still do. I wear dresses more than Carrie does, but I feel the freest when I'm in breeches and astride a horse. I'm not sure I would have been courageous enough to do it, until I saw Abby wearing breeches. I decided if a woman of her generation could spurn societal expectations, so could I!"

Elizabeth turned to Carrie. "Do you wish you could dress like Dr. Walker all the time?"

Carrie considered the question. "Dr. Walker's typical clothes used to be trousers with suspenders worn under a knee-length dress. She refused to wear women's clothing during her years volunteering with the Union Army because she said it made her job easier. My understanding now is that she only wears trousers and a jacket, along with a top hat," she said with a smile. "She's quite insistent that she doesn't wear men's clothing—she wears her *own clothing*."

"Again, who could argue with her?" Elizabeth asked wistfully. "The only times I've worn anything but a dress is when I've been with you on the plantation. Breeches really are rather wonderful."

"Carrie, you haven't answered Elizabeth's question," Florence observed.

"I've thought about it a great deal," Carrie said, realizing they wouldn't let her escape without an answer. She knew she wore breeches far more than any of them, but she also spent more time in the barn and with the horses. "Dr. Walker has been arrested many times for being dressed in men's clothes. I believe her arrests are completely wrong and that she should be free to dress how she wants, but I'm not eager to take on another battle. It's quite enough for me to be a female homeopathic physician. I would be more than willing to fight that battle, if I believed it would make me a better doctor, or give me access to more patients, but I don't think that would be the result." She paused thoughtfully. "At this point in my life, I'm content to live in breeches on the plantation, but wear dresses when I'm out in society." She grinned. "I reserve the right to change my mind, however."

"That I'm sure of," Florence said.

Carrie wanted them to know more about the woman who had made it easier for them to become doctors. "Dr. Walker was a surgeon during the war. In 1864, she was arrested when she crossed the lines to treat some civilians, and was thrown into Castle Thunder in Richmond with about one hundred other women prisoners."

Janie shuddered. "Such a horrible place!"

Carrie completely agreed. "She was only there four months, but before she was released in a prisoner exchange, she became quite ill. It resulted in muscle atrophy that made it impossible for her to continue to practice. She no longer works as a doctor, but she's become a passionate advocate for women's rights."

"What happened with her husband?" Elizabeth asked.

Carrie frowned. "Albert wasn't faithful. When Dr. Walker found out about his many affairs, she asked him for a divorce. He suggested that they should instead both have affairs, yet stay married."

"No!" Elizabeth gasped. "I know that kind of thing happens, but I can't imagine a woman like that would agree."

Carrie nodded. "You're correct. Dr. Walker wasn't interested. It's difficult to get a divorce in New York state, but in 1859 it was even more challenging. After obtaining divorce papers, you have to wait five years before it's official. Their divorce wasn't final until three years ago."

"And people wonder why women are fighting for rights," Janie muttered. "I'm glad Dr. Walker is on our side."

Elizabeth looked up. "We're almost there!" She reached over and took Carrie's hand. "Well done, my friend. I haven't thought about wedding nervousness since you started the discussion about Dr. Walker."

Carrie smiled. "Good. I accomplished my mission." She looked up admiringly. "Old North Church is beautiful!"

Elizabeth followed her gaze. "It's the oldest church in Boston. Next year it will be one hundred and fifty years old. Its name is actually Christ Church, but everyone in Boston knows it as Old North Church."

Carrie gazed up at the imposing brick building with the towering white steeple that threatened to puncture the clouds hovering above it.

"The steeple is quite impressive," Janie said.

"It is," Elizabeth agreed. "It was destroyed in 1804 by heavy winds from an October hurricane. Evidently it was quite a storm. It took out the church steeple, damaged many buildings, and took a heavy agricultural toll. There was a lot of rain here in Boston, but by the time the storm reached Vermont, it was cold enough to produce almost four feet of snow."

"Oh my!" Florence exclaimed. "I can't imagine that much snow. It snowed a lot during our time in Paris, and was brutally cold, but it never got that deep."

"Peter wrote an article about it once," Elizabeth replied. "Not only was it a lot of snow, it was also very early in the fall. It froze most of the potato crops, destroyed a large amount of the fruit trees, and took out a lot of timber. Old North Church wasn't the only church to sustain damage, but most houses seemed to be spared. He learned that the winds were at close to one hundred ten miles per hour when it hit here."

Carrie shook her head. "I'm glad the plantation is far from the coast. Storms have hit the Virginia coast, but by the time they reach us, the winds aren't strong enough to do that kind of damage."

The carriage pulled up to the church.

Laughing and talking, the friends ducked in through the service entrance to finish Elizabeth's preparations.

Despite Matilda Gilbert's pleas that Elizabeth and Peter choose bridesmaids and groomsmen for their wedding, they had insisted they wanted it to be just them for the ceremony. They'd agreed to a church wedding, but they were determined to do it their way.

The pews were full of family and friends, many of them from the Boston elite.

Carrie was glad there was nothing to detract from the stunning beauty of Elizabeth gliding slowly down the long aisle of Old North Church on her father's arm, her billowing wedding dress providing the perfect foil for her dark, Italian beauty.

Peter, tall and handsome, had eyes for nothing but his bride. His face glowed with happiness as Elizabeth approached, the organ music accompanying her with a crashing crescendo as she reached his side.

Tears filled Carrie's eyes as she watched her friends exchange their wedding vows, their voices strong and sure as they rang through the church. The two had already been through so much together. Their union would be strong and solid.

Carrie clasped Anthony's hand, grateful for the strength of their own marriage. She wondered what the future held but wasted little time with her thoughts. Whatever she could imagine, she would never truly know what was coming. The only thing any of them could do was attempt to live each day the best they could, adjusting to each new situation that came their way.

Abe Cummings cursed as he slammed his fist against the solid dining table in his echoingly empty house. He couldn't believe his life had spiraled so out of control. Charlotte was a meek little wife until the

Cromwells had decided to involve themselves with his family. His children had been easy to control with a strategic slap or punch when needed. They weren't bad children; they just needed a tough hand of discipline when they misbehaved.

Charlotte had taken good care of his house and his children, but there were times she had to be reminded who the man of the house was. Since joining those Bregdan Women, she'd gotten ideas that didn't sit well with him. He had thought he was enforcing submission in his household, until she'd taken his children and disappeared. He never imagined she would do such a thing.

Abe scowled as he thought of Emma. If that worthless little girl hadn't opened her mouth, none of this would be happening. He'd offered his home to the orphan child, and she'd repaid him with tales that had made him lose everything important to him. He cursed again as he kicked aside a chair that dared to be in his way as he stalked around the house.

He stopped and took a gulp from the bottle of moonshine perched on his fireplace mantle. It had been his only solace in the days since he'd lost his family and his job.

He kicked another chair as he thought about Thomas Cromwell showing up at his door the evening they had disappeared. He'd had four men with him. He supposed he should be gratified that Cromwell knew he would need a lot of backup, but thinking about it enraged him even more. None of those men had any business getting involved with his family. He could do what he wanted with his own wife and children.

Thomas Cromwell had assured him those days were over. Charlotte, Josiah, and Henrietta were gone. He would never find them. Cromwell had told him he didn't deserve such a fine wife and children, and that it was nobody's fault but his own that he would never see them again.

Abe's teeth ground in anger and frustration as he remembered Cromwell telling him that his services would no longer be wanted at Cromwell Plantation. It didn't matter that Abe was a master ironsmith and expert wagon and carriage repairman; they didn't want anyone around the plantation who beat their wife and children.

He slammed his fist against the table again, ignoring the pain that shot through his hand and wrist, and grabbed the bottle of moonshine. Each day since Cromwell's visit had passed in a blur of fury and alcohol. Today, though, he was determined to not drink too much. He had planning to do.

The group of men who had dared to come to his house believed they'd frightened him. Oh, he knew he would never see his family again, but that wasn't much of a loss as far as he was concerned. His job was a much bigger worry.

There were other plantation owners who would hire him when they needed work done, but most of them were struggling to make money again after the war. They needed him, but they had little to pay him. They hated Cromwell because he hadn't fallen in line with how white Virginians believed the freed slaves should be treated. It infuriated them that Cromwell paid fair wages to his workers, when all they wanted was to keep blacks in poverty and beholden to them. Many of their field hands, despite the threats heaped on them, had simply walked off and gotten a job with Cromwell.

In his more lucid moments, Abe recognized that Cromwell and Moses Samuels had paid him better than anyone else in the area would have, but that didn't abate his rage at the man for taking his wife and children. They might not be a big loss, but they were his to control. It didn't matter that he knew Charlotte wouldn't have taken his children and left if she hadn't wanted to. Without help, she never would have had the courage to leave. The blame rested squarely on Thomas Cromwell's shoulders. His, and the Wallington's. He didn't know exactly how it had been accomplished, but he was certain Anthony and Carrie Wallington had been involved.

A knock at the door disrupted his furious stalking. He moved to the door and ripped it open. "What?" he shouted.

A stranger stared at him calmly. "Having a bad day, Abe?"

Abe scowled at him. "Who are you? What are you doing at my house?"

Instead of answering his questions, the stranger asked another of his own. "I hear you have good reason to hate Thomas Cromwell. That true?"

Abe stared at him. "So what if I do? What's it to you?" His mind raced as he tried to place the face of the burly man at his door. He was certain he'd never seen him before.

"I got good reason to hate him too," the man replied, his eyes burning with a deep fury.

"What'd he do to you?" Abe asked. He had planning to do, but he was curious enough to ask.

The man seemed to be in no mood to answer questions. "What are you gonna do about it?"

Abe was quickly losing whatever little patience he had. "What's it to you? Why do you think I'm gonna tell you anything? I don't even know who you are."

The stranger shrugged. "My name is Rawlings. Me and some boys decided to pay Cromwell a visit a few years back to teach him a lesson about how blacks oughta be treated around here." His eyes darkened with an expression that almost frightened Abe. "They shot my brother. Killed him."

Abe was glad he hadn't drunk as much alcohol that day. His mind was at least partially functioning. "That ain't got nothing to do with me," he said bluntly.

Rawlings' features darkened even more. "Me and some of the boys figure it's about time for someone else to pay Cromwell a visit."

Abe looked at him hard. "And you figure that someone oughta be me?"

Rawlings shrugged. "From what I hear, you got good reason to. I don't figure they'll be expecting you. I reckon they figure they've scared you off."

Abe couldn't deny that observation, but he hadn't decided what he was going to do about it. The reminder fueled his own fury. "So?"

"It will be easier for just one man to slip into the plantation," Rawlings drawled. "They won't be expecting you."

"One man can't do much," Abe snapped.

"Not true," Rawlings replied. "One man can do plenty."

Intrigued, Abe hesitated. Some part of his brain told him he should shut the door in Rawlings' face, but the part of him that craved revenge couldn't bring himself to do it. "What are you talking about?" he finally asked.

Thomas and Abby had sat down to dinner moments earlier when there was a loud knock at the front door. Bridget was cooing from the wooden cradle they had placed in the corner of the dining room.

Moses, who had arrived with Jed from a day in the fields, looked at the door. "Are you expecting anyone?"

Thomas shook his head. He rose immediately and moved to answer it. Moses was right beside him. "Jeremiah. Welcome. What are you doing here?" Thomas was surprised to see the man in front of him but held the door open. "Come on in. Is everything alright?"

Jeremiah shook his head. "Thank you, Mr. Cromwell. I'll stay out here." Tall and lanky, his blond hair shaded light brown eyes. "I came to warn you."

Thomas stiffened. "Warn me about what?" He felt Moses move closer.

"One of the men rode by Abe Cummings' house today."

Moses scowled. "That man is still in his house?"

Jeremiah nodded. "Ain't nobody seen him since Charlotte and the children took off, but we done seen lights on at night."

Thomas eyed him. "You've been keeping a watch on him?"

"Yes, sir," Jeremiah replied. "I saw the look on his face the day we went with you to tell him his family was gone. Abe is a man who lives for revenge."

Thomas recognized the truth in what he said. "What did you see today?"

"Weren't me," Jeremiah said. "It was Smitty. He saw another man going into Abe's house as he was passing by."

Thomas waited, knowing there was more.

"Man's name is Rawlings," Jeremiah stated coldly. "Lots of us have had dealings with him. He's been after us for a while to cause you trouble, Mr. Cromwell."

"Why?" Moses growled.

"You remember that winter night a bunch of those KKK fellas tried to attack the house, but they didn't get no further than the gate?"

"Yes. It was Christmas Eve," Moses said. "We convinced them it wasn't a good idea to do that."

Jeremiah nodded. "Some of those men died that night." He took a deep breath. "One of them was Rawlings' brother. Rawlings got away that night, but his brother died."

Thomas took a deep breath, wishing Jed wasn't close enough to hear what was being said. The little boy had been terrorized by the KKK. Jed would never forget the night his mother had been killed and his father beaten so badly he had died from the wounds. They'd assured Jed he was safe here.

"What does that have to do with us?" Thomas asked, impressed that his voice remained calm.

"Maybe nothing," Jeremiah admitted. "But I got me a real bad feeling about it. I reckon Rawlings was there to get Abe to do his dirty work. He's tried to get a bunch of us to join up with the KKK. He's too scared to come over here himself, but he's been after some of us to create trouble," he repeated. "Ain't none of us gonna do it, 'cause we don't have any reason to. We all got good work. Our children are in school, and Dr. Carrie takes good care of us. Rawlings ain't figured out that the country is changing. That includes down here in the South."

"You believe Abe is going to cause trouble," Thomas said slowly, grateful that not every white man in the South was eager to join the KKK. He had hoped that when a force of men arrived at Abe's door, he wouldn't have the courage to attempt retaliation. It was possible he had miscalculated.

"I think it's likely," Jeremiah responded. "Me and the others thought it was best to warn you."

Moses stepped out onto the porch. "I'm going to increase the guard, Thomas. I'll be back soon."

Thomas nodded, making no attempt to stop him.

Jed appeared at his side. "Is the KKK coming here, Mr. Thomas?"

Thomas looked down into the little boy's frightened eyes and put a comforting hand on his shoulder. "If they do, they'll be sorry." He managed a smile, wondering if the threat from the Ku Klux Klan would ever end. He turned to their visitor. "Thank you for coming, Jeremiah. We appreciate it very much."

"You're welcome, Mr. Cromwell." Jeremiah turned to leave but swung back around. "You need some extra help to watch over things?"

Thomas hesitated. Just how much trouble might they be facing?

Abby stepped up next to him. "There is strength in numbers, dear," she said quietly.

Thomas knew she was right. "We would appreciate that, Jeremiah. Moses will put some extra men at the gate and around the house, but if you and some other men would put a guard around the school and clinic, it would be helpful. If Abe gets it in his head to cause trouble, we have no way of knowing where he'll strike."

"Yes, sir, Mr. Cromwell," Jeremiah agreed. "I'll go round up some men now. We'll take turns watching the school and clinic until Abe moves on."

Thomas frowned. "That may not be for a while."

"That's true, but our children need that school, and every one of us needs the clinic. We ain't gonna let nothing happen to it," Jeremiah promised. The look in his eyes said he would do whatever was necessary to make sure he delivered on his promise.

Thomas felt a surge of relief. "Thank you."

He stepped onto the porch as Moses strode out of the barn holding Champ, his towering gelding. He called Moses over and explained what Jeremiah was going to do.

"Thank you," Moses said quietly. He turned and urged Champ into a gallop. If there was going to be trouble that night, he didn't have much time to strengthen the guard. They were never without men watching the plantation, but the number had been greatly diminished as time had passed with no trouble.

It appeared their luck may have run out.

## Chapter Nineteen

Moses galloped through the woods, intent on returning home before the sun completely set. The long shadows cast by the trees seemed to hide danger around every curve. He peered into the encroaching darkness, even though he realized he probably wouldn't see trouble until it was too late to stop it.

He had alerted several of his men, who were riding to other homes to activate the guard for the plantation. Once again, he was grateful that most of the Cromwell field hands were also Civil War veterans. There wasn't a single man who wasn't exhausted after a long day in the fields, but he knew they would respond immediately.

Thomas was waiting for him on the porch when he arrived back at the house.

"Everyone will be in place soon," Moses assured him.

"Good," Thomas said fervently, his eyes scanning the clearing around the house.

"How's Jed?" Moses asked. He knew how frightened the little boy must be. He was furious that the KKK was once again terrorizing a defenseless child. All during his long ride, his brain had worked tirelessly. It wasn't that anyone believed the KKK would leave them alone forever, but the long period of respite had been wonderful. Having had a season of peace somehow made the threat of new violence that much more difficult to deal with.

"I had Abby take Annie, Jed, and Bridget into the tunnel."

Moses breathed a sigh of relief. Whatever happened, Abby, his mama, and the children would be safe. He knew Jed would be frantic with worry for them, but at least he would be spared any sounds of violence if whomever was coming managed to reach the house. He glanced toward the barn.

"Miles has brought Eclipse, No Regrets, and our other personal mounts into the barn," Thomas told him. "Clint hadn't left the barn before we received the warning, so he's going to bunk down in the tack room to provide extra protection."

"Amber?" Moses asked tersely. He would never forget the night Robert had been killed while shielding Amber from gunfire during a KKK attack five years earlier.

"She's home with Gabe and Polly."

Moses spoke his mind. "If something happens to All My Heart, she'll never forgive us for not letting her know there could be an attack. I don't want her in danger, but she's not a little girl anymore. Cromwell Stables is her life. She should know."

Thomas frowned and hesitated, before nodding. "You're right, of course." He shook his head. "I'm sick of this," he said bitterly.

Moses echoed his sentiment. "Me too. I suppose we can be grateful that most of the house is empty, and the rest of the children are safe."

"Yes, I'm glad that Carrie and Rose aren't here, but I know they would be stationed at the windows with rifles if they were."

Moses managed a smile. "They're fierce," he agreed.

Thomas looked east. "What about Susan?"

"One of my men is alerting her," Moses replied. "I'm confident she and Harold will be here soon."

A few minutes later, a cloud of dust on the horizon told them Harold and Susan were arriving.

"Any sign of Abe?" Harold asked tersely as his horse slid to a halt in front of the porch.

"No," Thomas replied. "This might all be for nothing, but we can't take the chance."

"I'm going into the barn," Susan said. She eyed Harold sharply when he opened his mouth to protest. "We had this discussion. I'm not going to hide in the tunnel while the barn and horses might be in danger." She turned Silver Wings, her tall black mare, and trotted off.

Harold rolled his eyes at the men and followed her. "We'll be in the barn," he called over his shoulder.

Moses glanced at the woods. Glimpses of movement told him his men were taking position around the house. He knew there were others stationed at the gate, but his gut told him that whoever was coming wouldn't make another attempt to breech the entrance to the plantation.

Which meant they had no idea what direction the danger would come from.

Abe, dressed in dark clothes, edged his way through the woods. He'd ridden his horse as far as he thought was safe, and then tied him to the low-lying branch of a tree. The last thing he needed was his horse getting free and giving him away. He readjusted the burlap sack on his back and continued to move as quietly as he could. He longed to be on horseback, but the noise would assure he was a target.

At first, he'd thought Rawlings' plan was crazy, but the man eventually convinced him it could work. The KKK member had stressed that it *would* work, but Abe was only willing to admit it *could* work. The plan could also go very wrong, but his fury and desire for revenge was driving him onward.

He had not left his house until midnight, easing out through the back door very quietly. If his house was being watched from the road, they wouldn't know he was gone. Earlier that afternoon, he'd tied his horse about a half mile from the house. Fifteen minutes after leaving, he had mounted his gelding and ridden as quietly as possible down a trail concealed from the road.

Now he was on foot, staying as deep in the woods as possible. Rawlings had warned him that the plantation was always under guard, but it wasn't possible to guard every inch of such a huge place. He had but one destination in mind. It may take him hours to reach it on foot, but as long as he had the cover of darkness, he believed he held the advantage. He always took the trails through the woods when he rode to the plantation for work. He knew them like the back of his hand. Even in the darkness, he was making good time.

The night wore on as he worked his way from trail to trail. Every few minutes he would stop to listen carefully. So far, he'd heard nothing but the expected night animals and the song of the breeze through the trees. He knew the breeze could hide the sound of men, but it would also be his friend tonight if he reached his destination.

Susan stiffened when she heard the sound of hoofbeats, but relaxed when Amber led her horse into the barn. "Hey," she called softly.

Amber slid off the mare she was riding, removed the saddle and bridle, and opened the barn door to set the horse free in the pasture with the other mares and foals. "Anything?" she whispered.

"Nothing," Susan assured her. The barn was so dark she could only see Amber's dim outline, but it was enough to tell how tense she was. "Are you alright?"

"I'm alright," Amber whispered tersely.

Susan's heart surged with sympathy. It had been five years since the now sixteen-year-old had almost died in another KKK attack. Despite Amber's answer, she could hear the tension in her voice. "You're not alone this time."

Amber took a deep breath. "I know. What's the plan?"

Susan admired Amber's courage. She knew the girl would do anything to protect the horses she loved so much. "Annie, Abby, Jed, and Bridget are in the tunnel. Miles is upstairs watching out the window from his and Annie's room. Clint is in the tack room. You and I are going out into the pasture so we can watch for any movement coming toward the barn and house. If we see something, we'll call out a warning."

"Is everyone armed?"

Susan hesitated, unsure how to answer.

"I know Miles and Clint have their rifles," Amber stated flatly. "Clint taught me how to shoot, and I already know you can. If we're going out to act as guards, it seems rather foolish that we not be prepared."

Susan hesitated a moment longer. She hated to put a rifle into a sixteen-year-old's hands, no matter how mature they were.

Susan felt, rather than saw, Amber edge closer. Her whisper grew more intense. "I know everyone is worried because of what happened the last time the barn was attacked. Robert died that night, his body covering mine when the bullet ripped through him." Emotion shook her voice as the memories assailed her. "He didn't save me so I could cower in fear when there's danger. He risked everything that night. Now, I'm going to do whatever it takes to protect what I love." She paused. "Where is my rifle?"

Susan, hearing the conviction in the girl's voice, knew she was right. Amber was surrounded by strong women. They had to let her be strong now. It was hard to acknowledge that some of the plantation children were growing into adults, but it was true.

Moments later, the two slipped from the barn, staying close to the shadows as they worked their way toward the large oak tree in the middle of the pasture. They sat down, their rifles propped on their knees, and began to scan the countryside.

Abe cursed under his breath as he stumbled over a root and fell to his knees. Freezing in position, he turned his head slowly, straining to hear anything unusual. He remained motionless until he was confident no one had heard him. He stood, adjusted the bag on his back, and continued to press forward. As far as he could tell in the darkness, he was less than ten minutes from his destination. That meant he had to be quieter than ever. Where he was going would be more heavily guarded the closer he got.

The fact that he was so close had greatly increased his confidence. He was sure there were guards, but Rawlings had insisted no one had ever attacked the plantation from deep within the woods. Cocky and arrogant, the KKK had assumed their strength was in numbers. Their attacks from main roads, and through the gate, had each been too easily thwarted.

Abe stopped again on the dark edge of the woods. He wasn't a member of the KKK; his plan had nothing to do with race. Instead, it was fueled by the rage burning in his heart and mind.

He was alert to every noise and every movement.

He froze when he heard rustling in the growth close to him, holding the breath that might give away his position. Moments later, a doe stepped out of the woods with a fawn by her side. Abe sagged with relief but stayed where he was. Anyone watching the woods would spot the animal's appearance. He wouldn't give them anything else that would catch their attention.

The doe and fawn faded back into the woods, but Abe patiently waited for ten minutes to pass by. While he waited, he scanned the area.

His destination loomed in front of him.

He was relieved to see the big pasture outside the barn was full of horses. The noise they made would help cover his approach. He looked up as a huge bank of clouds scuttled across the sky. In a few minutes, it would cover the half-moon illuminating the field.

He used those minutes to continue to scan the area around the barn. His gaze sharpened when he saw a dark shadow crouched at the bottom of the big oak. He couldn't tell if the shape was human, but he had to assume it was. He carefully pulled his pistol from his waistband, laid it on the ground within reach, and knelt to untie the burlap bag he had placed at his feet.

He counted methodically, satisfied when he confirmed there were twelve kerosene-soaked fire sticks. The ends of the stick were thickly wrapped with cloth that would burn quickly. He fingered the matches in his front pocket, knowing it would only take a moment to light the sticks when he was within throwing range.

Getting within throwing range was his next challenge.

Abe moved out of the woods as soon as the clouds swallowed the moonlight. It was now or never. He kept his eyes on the shadow by the tree as he began to move through the field, doing his best to remain soundless. Horses whinnied or nickered as he passed, but that was no different from their normal sounds.

Every moment, he expected there to be a shout, or the crack of pistol fire, but the night remained eerily silent.

Amber kept her eyes trained east, forcing herself to breath evenly and steadily. The night had passed slowly. She had no way of knowing exactly what time it was, but the position of the moon indicated it was several hours past midnight. The sun would start to illuminate the horizon in a few hours. Her body was exhausted, but her mind was screaming at her to stay alert. She couldn't see anything but darkness, but her nerve endings had started vibrating minutes earlier.

She'd learned to not question the warning system that would go off in her mind and heart at unexpected moments. It was always wise to pay attention.

She stiffened when she spotted a movement that seemed different from the horses roaming in the field in search of grass and hay. Most of the foals were sleeping soundly, but the mares were taking advantage of their freedom.

Amber leaned forward, her eyes trained on the spot that had captured her attention. She longed for the clouds to part, but the moon remained securely tucked behind a dark bank. That knowledge made her more suspicious. If she were planning an attack on the barn, she would have waited until just this moment.

*There!*

Amber caught the movement again. She couldn't be certain what it was, but her job was to raise the alarm if she suspected danger.

"Attack!" Amber yelled at the top of her lungs. "Attack!"

Abe froze, cursed beneath his breath, and then darted closer to the barn. Someone had spotted him, but he was close enough. He dropped to his knee, quickly lit a match, ignited a fire stick, and heaved it as high as he could. He wanted to cheer when he saw it land on top of the barn, igniting the surrounding wood immediately.

Not waiting to see any more, he darted to the right, ignited another fire stick, and threw it.

The crack of a rifle made him run again, but he wasn't done. As long as he kept moving, it was too dark for them to get a bead on him.

He ran farther, threw another fire stick, and quickly followed it with another before he ran again. He stopped barely long enough to see the barn ignite in each location.

Shouts of alarm sounded through the night.

Abe fingered the pistol on his belt, but he didn't feel the need to shoot anyone. His goal was to destroy the barn. Hopefully, the horses stabled within would also be killed. Rawlings had been right. Aiming a strike against the prestigious Cromwell Stables would make a powerful statement and grant him the revenge he desired.

He continued running, hurling firesticks as he went. When he tossed the last one, he turned to race across the pasture. He heard more gunshots, but none of them whistled by his head. He laughed as he reached the protection of the woods. He had done what groups of KKK members had failed to do.

Alone, he had launched a successful attack against Cromwell Plantation.

Amber watched in horror as the barn ignited and burst into flames. "All My Heart!" she screamed. "Eclipse!"

Susan grabbed her arm and pulled her toward the barn. "We'll never get the fire out!" she yelled. "We have to save the horses!"

Amber raced after her, ducking through the open barn door as the fire spread. She sped to All My Heart's stall, released the gate latch, and pulled her reluctant mare forward. She wanted to cry when All My Heart reared backward, terrified by the flames casting an orange glare through the barn. "Come on, girl!"

Miles appeared at the door with a pile of horse blankets in his arms. He threw her one. "Put this over her head," he hollered. "She ain't gonna be afraid if she can't see it!" Then he was gone.

Amber forced herself to breathe as she edged toward her terrified horse. "It's alright," she said soothingly. Praying All My Heart wouldn't fight it, she threw the blanket over the mare's head, completely covering her eyes. All My Heart froze, but her ears flicked toward her. "That's right," Amber crooned. "Come with me, girl."

Talking nonstop, she led All My Heart to the door leading out to the pasture. As soon as they were free of the barn, she removed the blanket, released the lead line, and slapped her mare on the rump. The terrified horse leapt forward into the dark embrace of the night.

Amber turned and ran back into the barn.

Thomas was watching from a bedroom window when he heard Amber's yell. He and Moses reached the front door at the same time.

"Watch the house!" Thomas yelled to the men pouring from the woods.

Moses was in front as they raced across the yard toward the burning barn.

Thomas groaned as he heard the whinnies and screams of terrified horses. He knew how quickly the old barn would burn. He envisioned falling rafters and burning hay as he and Moses ran through the door.

Amber was leading All My Heart out to the pasture. Clint was pulling No Regrets out, but the mare was fighting him. Miles had a blanket over Eclipse's head, but the powerful stallion refused to move forward.

"I'll help Miles!" Moses yelled. "You get Granite!"

Not until that moment did Thomas realize Granite wasn't following his mama out into the safe, cool night. He turned and dashed into No Regrets' stall. Granite was huddled in the far corner, his dark eyes wide with terror as he screamed for his mother. The colt, confused by the flames and noise, had not left with her.

Thomas moved forward. "It's okay, boy," he said calmly, trying to keep the fear from his voice. He glanced up and saw the rafters burning overhead. They didn't have long before they would fall. He'd not thought to get a horse blanket before he entered the stall. Knowing they didn't have much time, he peeled off his shirt and wrapped it around Granite's head. He grabbed the lead line from the stall door and secured it around the colt's neck. "Come on, boy," he commanded, praying his voice had the right amounts of command and comfort to release Granite from his frozen terror.

Granite screamed again as he pulled backward.

Thomas winced as hot embers fell across his exposed skin, but his entire focus was on the colt. He refused to allow anything to happen to Granite while Carrie was gone.

"Come on, Granite," Thomas commanded again. He pulled harder on the lead line as he prayed. "Come on!"

Granite began to edge forward haltingly, tossing his head with fear.

Thomas gasped with relief. "That's right, boy. It's time for you to get out of here."

Granite followed him slowly, his entire body trembling with fear.

Thomas brushed away the flaming embers as they landed on both of them, but never stopped talking to the frightened colt. "We're almost there, boy. We're almost there."

The night air embraced them as they moved past the barn wall. The crackling and roar of the fire was no less intense, but at least there were no embers assaulting them. He continued to move forward, aware that every horse had dashed to the far edge of the pasture.

A shrill whinny rang through the night.

Granite bolted forward as No Regrets called for her son.

Thomas barely managed to hold onto him long enough to untie the shirt and release the lead line. He sagged with relief when the colt ran off into the darkness.

He pulled on his shirt, ignored the pain radiating through his upper body, and dashed back into the barn.

There were other horses to save.

Thomas sagged against the back of a rocking chair as he stared at the smoldering remains of the barn.

Moses gulped the lemonade Annie handed to him, his face a mask of stern lines and exhaustion. Jed sat on his lap, his head burrowed in his father's shoulder.

Amber and Susan clutched hands as they sat on the steps and gazed at the destruction of their lives.

Harold sat close to Susan, his arm thrown over her shoulder in an attempt to comfort her.

Clint remained close to the barn, determined that no embers would fly free and ignite the woods.

Moses' men hauled bucket after bucket of water to douse the remaining embers. There was nothing left to burn, but they wouldn't relax until every spark had been extinguished.

Abby walked out with a huge tray of ham biscuits and hot coffee. "Food will help," she declared.

Everyone lifted exhausted eyes to her, their faces streaked with black soot.

Thomas shook his head as she offered him a biscuit. "No, thank you," he managed. "I'm not hungry."

"You have to eat," Abby said softly as she laid a hand on his shoulder.

Thomas winced and flinched away.

"Thomas!" Abby cried. "What's wrong?"

Thomas shrugged. "I suppose I have a few burns."

"More than that," Miles said as he stepped onto the porch, his elderly face almost collapsing with fatigue. "You took Granite out of the barn without a shirt on." He looked at Abby. "I suspect he's got some real bad burns."

Thomas was too tired to register much of the pain he was feeling, but he allowed Abby to lead him into the house, and up the stairs to their bedroom. Moments later, Annie arrived with a basin of cool water and some flannel rags.

"Take off your shirt," Abby commanded. She undid the buttons and helped him as he slid it off his skin.

Thomas swallowed his whimper, but it still came out as a moan.

Abby whitened and looked at Annie. "Please go into the basement and get some of the aloe salve. And please ask Harold to go to the clinic and get some Hypericum. It's in the medicine cabinet on the third shelf."

Annie nodded and disappeared.

Thomas managed a brief smile. "Are you a doctor now, my darling wife?"

"I'm smart enough to pay attention when Carrie is treating patients while I'm at the clinic with Bridget," Abby retorted. "The good news is that these aren't third-degree burns. The bad news is that they're second-degree burns. You're going to be in a lot of pain, and you'll most likely scar."

"Not as much pain as I would be in if I'd had to tell Carrie that Granite died in that fire," Thomas replied, wincing as jolts of pain shot through his body. "The burns will heal."

Abby's face was set in tight lines. "We've got to get these cleaned up before we put the salve on them. It's going to hurt."

Thomas set his lips. "Best to get it over with."

Susan and Moses stood as close to the smoldering remains as they could.

"It's gone," Susan murmured as tears filled her eyes. "It's all gone."

Moses shook his head. "Abe didn't destroy the most important thing, Susan. We saved the horses. Not one of them was even injured. Barns can be rebuilt and tack can be purchased."

Susan glanced up. "Are they sure it was Abe?"

"They're sure," Moses said tightly. "One of my men saw him in the light of the flames when he threw his last fire sticks. He tried to shoot him, but he missed."

Susan sighed. "We'll never see him again."

Moses knew she was right. "Probably not," he admitted. "But, it could have been much worse."

Susan stared at him. "Worse?" she asked disbelievingly. "The barn is gone. All the tack has been destroyed. The grain is gone."

Moses knew this wasn't the moment to vent his own anger and frustration. "All that is true," he said quietly. "But not a single horse was lost." He repeated what he'd said moments before; words she hadn't been able to hear. "Abe didn't destroy the most important thing, Susan. We saved the horses. Barns can be rebuilt. Tack can be purchased."

Clint appeared out of the darkness. "You won't have to purchase tack. It's safe."

Susan turned disbelieving eyes to him. "How?"

Clint managed a brief smile. "When Amber came in to get her rifle, she told me to start moving tack down the ladder into the tunnel. Until she said something, I hadn't even thought of it. Some of it got tossed down the hole, but I believe every bit of it will be fine."

Susan shook her head and gazed around. "Where's your sister?"

"Daddy and Mama took her home for some sleep."

"I'll thank her tomorrow for being the smartest one of us," Susan said. "She saved the stables a small fortune!"

"Now all you have to do is rebuild the barn," Moses said, amazed at Amber's clear thinking.

Susan met his eyes and slowly nodded her head. "You're right," she said at last. "Carrie and I had planned to buy more horses and increase our reserve with the extra profits we've made, but that won't happen now. At least we have the money to rebuild."

"That's right," Moses said encouragingly. "When we lost the crop two years ago, I was afraid we'd never recover from the flood. We have. In fact, the fields that flooded are bearing the best crops. The silt from the river enriched the soil."

Susan stared back at where the barn had been. "I hardly think the soot and remains from the fire are going to help us in the future."

"No," Moses agreed. "But I've heard you and Carrie talk about wishing you had a bigger barn."

Susan remained silent for several minutes as she stared at the destruction. "I'm too exhausted right now to see the good that can come out of this, Moses."

Moses gripped her hand. "I understand." He knew he'd planted the seed, just like Thomas had done for him when the flood destroyed the crop and almost killed John. After some rest, Susan would be able to see it differently.

Moses led her toward the guest house. "You and Harold are staying here tonight. He'll be over as soon as he returns with the Hypericum from the clinic. Miles and Annie are asleep. Clint is going home to Hazel."

Susan allowed herself to be led as docilely as a child. "Good night," she said as they reached the door.

Moses was ready for the day to be over, but he knew it was only beginning. The sun was about to crest the horizon, daring to shine brightly on the remnants of a long, terrible night.

Abe had moved quickly as he made his way back through the woods, his heart pounding with exhilaration. He'd longed to stay and watch the results of his efforts, but escape was primary in his mind.

Surely, everyone would be too busy fighting the fire to take the time to come after him, but he knew it wasn't safe to return to his house. When he'd pulled the back door closed that night, he knew he'd been saying good-bye to the life he'd known. There was nothing there for him anymore. No Charlotte. No children. No work. As he drew closer to where he'd tied his horse, he thought about where he would go next.

He didn't have a destination in mind, but he knew he had to get as far from Cromwell Plantation as he could. The sun would be up soon, but he knew of more trails through the woods that would keep him off the main road. If he was careful, he would escape detection.

His life here might be over in this area, but he was leaving with the knowledge he'd successfully executed revenge on the Cromwell family. It wouldn't make up for what he'd lost, but it would help.

He breathed a sigh of relief as he reached his horse. He'd been afraid it might have worked its way free during the night, taking his chance of escape with him. He reached eagerly for the canteen tied to his saddle. The long night had left him parched.

"Going somewhere?"

Abe stiffened as a voice sounded through the night. He reached quickly for his pistol.

"Touch that gun and I'll shoot you."

Abe's hand froze as his mind raced. It took him a moment to recognize the voice. "That you, Rawlings?"

Rawlings stepped closer. "That's right."

Abe was confused but certain an explanation would resolve any misunderstanding. "I did it," he said triumphantly. "Cromwell Stables has been destroyed."

"Yep," Rawlings said abruptly.

Abe reached again for his horse's reins. "I got to be going."

"I don't think so," Rawlings said coldly.

Abe was more confused than ever. "Why? I need to be gone before it gets light."

"You ain't going nowhere."

"Why not? I did what you asked." Abe itched to grab the pistol at his waist, but he was almost certain any movement would result in Rawlings firing his gun.

"The boys don't want you to point anyone back to us," Rawlings said flatly.

"I won't say anything," Abe replied, fighting to keep the desperation from his voice. Men like Rawlings fed off others' fear. "I just want to get out of here and start a new life."

"That ain't happening," Rawlings said.

Abe swore he could hear something like regret in the other man's voice. He felt a flash of hope.

Until he saw the flash of the pistol.

The breeze was the only sound in the woods when Rawlings rode off, leading Abe Cummings' horse.

## Chapter Twenty

June 1872
New York, New York

"Mama!" Minnie cried. "Look at that church! It's so beautiful!" She leaned far out of the carriage to get a better look.

Anthony chuckled as he pulled her back onto the seat. "It won't look as nice after you fall onto the road, honey."

Carrie gazed around as the carriage continued to roll down Fifth Avenue. The wide, smooth road was shaded by trees. The sidewalks were thronged with well-dressed pedestrians clad in elegant dresses and suits. Top hats bobbed on almost every man's head. Far from the industrial section, there was none of the cacophonous noise she'd come to expect from New York City. "This is a part of the city I haven't been in before, Nancy."

Nancy Stratford, her blond hair gleaming beneath her stylish hat, waved a hand toward their surroundings. Her blue eyes shone with pleasure. "I wanted to show you the best of what our city has to offer. I do wish Abby and Thomas could have come on the trip. It's been years since Abby has seen this part of town. The last time she was here, most of this area was nothing but farmland and cow pastures."

"She wanted to come," Carrie assured her, knowing how eager Abby had been to see her close friend.

Nancy laughed. "I know Fifth Avenue doesn't stand a chance in comparison to taking care of Bridget. In the letter she sent me, she told me she had never dreamed of having an infant granddaughter. She's in heaven."

"I think *I* might be in heaven. It's quite magnificent," Rose said breathlessly as she craned her neck back to examine the towering buildings. "Philadelphia is a wonderful city, but it doesn't have anything like this."

"Mama! Look at that big building. It's completely white!" John called as he pointed up the street.

"That's the Fifth Avenue Hotel," Nancy told him. "It was the very first building out here. People thought the owners were quite crazy to build out in rural farmland, but their gamble paid off when the city grew to encompass it. The outside of the hotel is white marble."

"It's shiny!" Hope said, her eyes wide and round as she tried to take in everything. "Do you think that's what Heaven will look like, Mama?"

Rose chuckled. "I believe it will be as beautiful as that hotel, Hope. Probably even more so!"

"The hotel came close to burning down," Anthony said.

"Another fire?" Carrie asked with dismay. "Obviously, they were able to save it. I'm glad."

"It never actually burned," Anthony said. "There was a plot near the end of the war to set Manhattan and Fifth Avenue on fire. A handful of Confederate conspirators met in Canada to hatch a scheme to firebomb the city's main hotels. Their goal was to liberate Confederate prisoners, disrupt elections, and scare the nation into believing the North's biggest city continued to be vulnerable to the South. Their ultimate goal was that their actions would spark an uprising by Southern sympathizers in the city that would prolong the war the South was so obviously losing."

Carrie grimaced. "You said they wanted to disrupt the elections. When was it?"

"November 1864," Anthony replied. "They'd planned to do it on November second, but the city was tipped off by a telegram from Secretary of State Seward. Thousands of Union soldiers were positioned around the city on the lookout for Rebel terrorism. There were enough of them that the conspirator's plan was pushed to the end of the month. They hoped the city would let its guard down if the attack didn't materialize."

"It was the day after the first official Thanksgiving," Nancy told them. "November twenty-fifth. The conspirators set fire in thirteen of the city's finest hotels here in Manhattan. One of them was the Fifth Avenue Hotel."

"I'm glad it didn't burn!" Russell said. He hadn't taken his awestruck eyes off the gleaming structure.

"The conspirators weren't very good at what they were attempting to do," Anthony said wryly. "They chose one of the rooms in the hotel to burn. Bedroom furniture was stacked together and doused with turpentine and resin. They also added liquid phosphorous."

"And it didn't burn?" Carrie asked. She knew how quickly white phosphorous could spontaneously combust into flame. "Why not?"

Anthony smirked. "Because whomever was given the job of setting fire to the hotel forgot to take the corks out of the bottles of liquid phosphorous. When someone opened the door the next morning, the phosphorous had barely begun to smoke. They were able to quickly extinguish it."

"What about the other hotels?" John asked.

"They successfully ignited the other fires," Anthony replied, "but none of them caused serious damage or injuries. Thankfully, the city had maintained vigilance in case the saboteurs really did try to pull off their diabolical plot."

Carrie thought about what Peter had endured eight months earlier. "It could have been another Chicago," she said with a shudder.

"It indeed could have been," Nancy said grimly. "If everything had been set on fire at the same moment, and if each fire had been well kindled, the fire department wouldn't have been strong enough to extinguish them all. Michael told us the confusion would have been so great that the best portion of the city would have been destroyed."

"That's terrible!" Frances exclaimed. "So many innocent people would have died."

"That's true," Anthony said solemnly.

"Like my family did," Minnie said shakily. The wonder was gone from her voice, replaced by a stark horror.

Anthony pulled her into his strong arms. "Honey, I'm sorry. I shouldn't have been talking about this."

Minnie burrowed into him.

Carrie stroked her daughter's hair gently, knowing she would carry the memories of that terrible night for the rest of her life.

"Minnie, look!" John came to the rescue as he excitedly pointed to something coming down the road.

Minnie lifted her head and followed John's pointing finger. Her eyes widened with confusion. "What is that thing?"

Nancy started laughing. "That, my dear, is a bicycle. They call it a penny-farthing, or an ordinary bike."

Carrie stared at it in wonder. "I'm afraid it doesn't look very safe."

"Yet jumping a horse over a fence is?" Nancy asked with a raised brow.

Carrie laughed. "I'm fairly certain I have far more control over a horse than a person has over that contraption."

Nancy sobered. "I suspect you're right. Michael has one, but my wonderful daughter-in-law, Julie, does her best to talk him out of riding it. She is successful only part of the time. There are only a few of these bicycles in New York City right now, but they're quite the craze in England."

Carrie gazed at the thing Nancy called a bicycle. It had a towering front wheel, with a much smaller wheel close behind it. The tiny seat was perched high in the air on a long metal bar that connected the two wheels. "How in the world does someone get on top of that thing?"

Nancy shrugged. "Michael has explained it to me, but I honestly have no idea how it's possible. Supposedly, you stand behind it, straddling the rear wheel while holding onto the handlebars with both hands." She pointed toward the bicycle. "See those two steps? You're supposed to put one of your feet on the lower step. Then you use your other foot to scoot you forward. Once you're moving, you move that foot to the higher step. Then you slide forward onto the saddle and put your feet on the pedals."

"I see," Carrie said faintly. She watched as the young man pedaled down the road. "How do you get off once you get up there?"

Nancy shook her head. "I'm told you do everything I just told you, except in reverse. Needless to say, I haven't felt the need to try it."

Carrie loved adventure and new things, but she didn't feel the urge to try a bicycle. She continued to examine it. "What happens if you fall off?"

"It hurts," Nancy said bluntly. "Michael loves them because they're fast. Julie hates them because they're unsafe. Being high up in the air is treacherous if you hit a bad spot in the road. Many riders are thrown over the front wheel and seriously injured. Or killed," she added grimly.

Russell was staring intently at the bicycle. "The rider's legs are underneath the handlebars. What happens if they fall, but ain't able to get off?"

"They get hurt," Carrie said grimly.

Russell continued to study the contraption. "It'd be a lot safer if the wheels were the same size," he said slowly. "And a whole bunch easier to pedal."

Carrie exchanged a surprised look with Anthony.

Rose watched Russell with a broad smile on her face. "We might have an inventor in our midst."

Russell looked up with an embarrassed shrug. "Ain't so hard to see when something can be better."

"*Isn't* so hard," Rose said gently.

"That's what I said," Russell replied with a grin. "I'm glad you can see it too, Miss Rose."

Everyone laughed as they continued down the road. Russell's speaking was getting much better, but there were times, like now, when it wasn't as important as what he was saying. Carrie saw evidence of his strong intelligence almost every day. He saw things with a clarity she'd never seen in such a young boy. She and Anthony were determined he would have every opportunity to explore his abilities.

"Where are we going now?" Minnie asked eagerly.

"Central Park," Nancy answered.

"Oh, good!" Frances exclaimed. She had been avidly observing everything, but this was the first time she'd spoken. "I've read about Central Park. Is it as beautiful as it sounds?"

"It is indeed," Nancy replied. "It's getting more beautiful every year. I wish Matthew was with us. He's written several articles about the park. He knows far more than I do."

"Matthew was eager to meet with his friend, Thomas Nast, to hear the latest on Boss Tweed," Anthony said.

Carrie was sad Janie was missing their excursion through the city, but her friend had decided little Robert and Annabelle needed a break after their whirlwind visit to Boston.

"William Tweed is a blight on our city," Nancy said angrily. "It seems like every day reveals some new way he's tried to destroy it."

Anthony eyed her. "I know he's no longer in prison."

"Not yet," Nancy said flatly. "Tweed was arrested but released on a million-dollar bail. Then, would you believe that detestable man was reelected to the state senate last November? Despite what he's done, he remains very popular in his district. It boggles my mind how many people refuse to see the truth about him."

"I've heard that many within his inner circle are fleeing the area. Surely that will change things?" Anthony asked.

Nancy smiled. "Many of them have gone overseas to separate themselves from what is being discovered. He was arrested again and forced to resign his city positions late last fall but was once again released on an eight-million-dollar bail."

Anthony whistled. "That's a huge amount. How could he pay it?"

Nancy shrugged. "He's stolen far more than that from the city of New York." She scowled. "His first trial will be early next year. I hope they throw him away for good."

Carrie was surprised at her vehemence.

Nancy saw the expression on her face. "Wally has kept me informed about what Tweed has done to the city. Let me tell you one small example. The cost of building the New York County Courthouse, begun in 1861, grew to thirteen million dollars." She snorted in a very unladylike manner. "*Thirteen million dollars*! That's nearly twice the cost of the Alaska Purchase five years ago!"

Carrie stared at her in astonishment. "One building? How is that possible?"

"Oh, it's very possible when a carpenter is paid almost three hundred and ten thousand dollars for one month's labor," Nancy said sarcastically.

Anthony's mouth dropped open. "That's unbelievable."

"Even more unbelievable when you realize there's very little woodwork in the courthouse," Nancy answered. "A plasterer was paid over one hundred thirty-three thousand dollars for two days' work. Part of Tweed's ring approved the charges. It was paid through a go-between who cashed the check, paid the contractors the going rate, and divided the remainder of the money between Tweed and his inner circle." Her face tightened. "Tweed even bought a marble quarry in Massachusetts to provide much of the marble for the courthouse."

"At a great profit to himself, I'm sure," Anthony said ruefully. "It's astounding the city could absorb that much corruption."

"That's but a tiny example of what he's done. Wally tells me he's been responsible for the embezzlement of close to one hundred million dollars."

Rose gasped. "One hundred million dollars? I can't even wrap my mind around that amount of money."

"How could the city afford to lose that much?" Carrie asked faintly.

Nancy shook her head. "It can't. As the newspapers have exposed what he's done, it's created an international crisis of confidence in New York City's finances. There's huge concern about the city's ability to repay its debts. European investors are heavily positioned in the city's bonds, which has resulted in a massive concern that there will be a run on the securities." Her lips tightened. "If the city's credit collapses, it could potentially bring down every bank in the city."

Anthony stared at her. "New York City would be like Richmond after the war."

"Exactly," Nancy agreed. "There's much happening to create political reform right now. Wally is part of a group of the city's elite who have formed the Executive Committee of Citizens and Taxpayers for Financial Reform. They call themselves the Committee of Seventy. Their first step against Tweed's political machine was to cut off the city's funding. Property owners have refused to pay their municipal taxes."

"Because if no money is coming in, there won't be new money for Tweed to steal," Rose observed.

"Correct. One of the men, George Barnard, is a judge. He's put a stop to issuing bonds and spending money until things are right again." Nancy sighed. "Of course, however necessary, it's hurting people because workers aren't being paid. The positive thing is that they've turned on the man they used to be such avid supporters of. The workers marched to City Hall, demanding to be paid. Tweed doled out fifty thousand from his own funds, but it hasn't been nearly enough. Needless to say, his political base is weakening," she added with satisfaction.

"The people he used are turning against him," Anthony said.

"Far past time," Nancy replied. "He used the Irish of the city to build his power. Tweed was appalled when Nast started posting his cartoons. He didn't care so much what the paper *said*, because most of his constituents can't read, but he knew the pictures would be easily understood."

Anthony nodded. "Matthew told me Tweed tried to buy Nast off. He offered him a large sum of money to leave the city and quit putting out his cartoons. Nast refused."

"As far as I'm concerned, Nast's cartoons have saved the city," Nancy said bluntly.

"Tweed was counting on the ignorance of his followers to keep him in power," Rose stated. She looked at the children who were listening avidly to the conversation. "This is why I stress the importance of learning, children. Ignorance makes it easy for people to take advantage of you, and also gain power over you. Education and learning give you the ability to control your own life."

Frances nodded her head. "Do you think Boss Tweed will have to pay for what he's done? Will he get away with it?"

Nancy gazed at her. "I believe he'll be held accountable, but it may take time. Men like him have spent their life outwitting the system, but it usually ends badly. He'll do everything he can to put the blame on others, but the evidence against him is piling up."

"You always pay the price for greed," Carrie said quietly. "Greed is a bottomless pit. Greedy people exhaust themselves with the endless effort to satisfy their need, but they're never actually satisfied."

Frances grimaced. "What a terrible way to live." Then she cocked her head in thought. "Didn't he need a lot of help to do so many bad things? He didn't do it by himself, did he?"

"No," Nancy agreed. "When you've got someone who will lead the way into illegal behavior, there will always be people who choose to follow him." She smiled slightly. "Of course, those are also the same people who will turn against him to protect themselves. The closer he got to being exposed, the more of those people came forward. People who choose to use each other have no loyalty. In the end, they'll always do what they believe is best for them."

Frances shook her head. "I'm glad we don't live that way on the plantation." She gazed around the bustling streets. "It seems to me that the more people have, the more they want." She reached out to take Carrie's and Anthony's hands. "Thank you for showing me the right way to live. I like knowing that we give back more than we take."

Carrie swallowed hard as she squeezed her daughter's hand. "You're welcome, honey."

"Central Park!" their carriage driver called.

"We're here!" Hope squealed. "Mama, this is the park you told me about!"

"It is!" Rose agreed, her expression as excited as her daughter's.

Carrie took a deep breath as they passed through the gates into the park. The longer she lived on the plantation, the less tolerance she had for big cities. She was ready for something other than towering buildings.

"How big is Central Park?" Anthony asked.

"Eight hundred and forty-three acres," Nancy said proudly. "I know it's not as big as the plantation, but it's amazing to have it right here in the heart of the city."

Carrie felt relief sweep through her when they entered the park. She recognized the same look on Frances' face. The rest of the children had been delighted with every minute of their adventures in Boston, and now in New York City. Carrie had enjoyed the trip, but her soul longed for the peace and quiet of the plantation. The noise in the cities made it almost impossible to think.

She leaned back against the carriage seat and took another deep breath, absorbing the almost instant peace as they moved into the park. You could hear distant city noises, but it was far enough away to offer a reprieve.

"Central Park is the country's first large urban park," Nancy told them, taking her role as tour guide very seriously. "You'll find every kind of landscape here, but it's not entirely natural. It's been carefully designed to incorporate a variety of types of landscapes and experiences."

"What do you mean?" Russell asked quizzically.

"Central Park has meadows, woodlands, lakes, hills, and streams," Nancy told him. "Some of it was here, but much of it had to be built. They moved tremendous amounts of dirt, they blasted rock, and they installed miles of underground drainage pipes. The work continues."

"It's fake?" Russell looked disappointed.

"We prefer to see it as deliberate," Nancy replied.

Russell stared at her. "Why?"

"Being in a big city can be hard. Central Park was designed by Frederick Olmsted and Calvert Vaux. They believe parks like this are necessary to keep people healthy. People come here to breathe fresh air and exercise, but also to be together to socialize. The designers believe the park can provide tranquility and rest to the mind."

Russell nodded slowly. "I reckon we get that on the plantation every day."

"I completely agree with you," Nancy said.

Russell looked up at Anthony. "I reckon I get lots of rest to my mind when I'm out in the tobacco fields."

Anthony chuckled. "That you do, son."

Russell continued to gaze around. "I like Boston and New York City just fine, but I like the plantation most of all."

Carrie couldn't have agreed more. Russell's life under the bridge and within Richmond had torn at his soul on a daily basis. She had seen him relax a little more with each day on the plantation.

The next few hours passed in a haze of laughter and delight. The carriage stopped often to let the children out to run and play. They dashed across meadows and rolled down steep hillsides, their peals of laughter ringing through the air. They removed their shoes and splashed into streams, spraying water as they flung it with their hands.

Carrie, longing to roll down the hillsides with them, hated the confines of her dress.

Rose leaned close. "Wishing you had on your breeches?"

Carrie smiled. "You too?"

"Of course! I want to roll down that hill with John and Hope."

Carrie laughed with delight. "I was thinking the same thing. I wish there was a hill steep enough on the plantation to do that."

"Is anyone hungry?" Nancy called.

"Yes!" The children scrambled back to the carriage.

Nancy had large picnic baskets in the back of the carriage. They stopped by the Central Park Lake, spread blankets on the ground, and feasted on bread, sliced beef, cheeses, vegetables, and fruit. They finished off the meal with thick slices of chocolate cake.

The sun beat down on them, but the temperature was comfortable.

"If it was winter, you could go ice skating on the lake," Nancy said.

"Ice skating?" Minnie asked wistfully. "That sounds fun."

"It is," Nancy replied enthusiastically. "We've been coming for many years. I'm not a very good skater, but I don't fall down anymore."

Russell looked at the water dancing in the sunlight, casting glimmering droplets of water as the breeze caught it. "It must get awful cold here for that lake to freeze."

"It gets cold," Nancy agreed.

"Does it have to be cold for a long time?"

Carrie was constantly amazed by Russell's curiosity and desire for knowledge. She hoped he would never lose it.

"Yes," Nancy admitted.

"How long?" Russell pressed.

Anthony answered when it was obvious Nancy didn't know. "It takes about two weeks of overnight temperatures near zero for a lake or pond to freeze enough for safe skating."

Russell's eyes widened as he shook his head vigorously. "No, thank you," he said emphatically. "I was plenty cold enough under the bridge this last winter. I don't ever want to be that cold again!" He looked at Carrie. "Have the lakes ever frozen on the plantation?"

"There's a shallow pond in the woods on the east edge that will sometimes freeze hard enough to slide around on, but I never want any of you to go there by yourselves," Carrie added sternly when she saw the children's faces light with anticipation. "If it gets cold enough this winter, we'll take you there. Miles taught me that just because it looks thick enough to go out on, that isn't always true. It's very easy to fall through and drown."

Russell nodded. "I saw someone drown in the James River one time."

Carrie's gut clenched. She hated how much pain her son had experienced. "What happened?" she asked gently.

Russell frowned, opened his mouth, but closed it again as he looked down.

Carrie waited. If he didn't want to tell them, she wouldn't force him. Some things were simply too hard to talk about.

Minnie didn't know that. "Who died, Russell?"

Russell looked at her, his eyes dark with haunted memories. "It was a girl who lived under the bridge," he finally said. "Her name was Sylvia. She was real nice. She got tired of being under the bridge, so she decided to go sit down on the rocks near the water. Paxton told her it wasn't a good idea, but she didn't listen. It was real cold, so I reckon there was some ice on the rocks." His voice faltered. "Anyway, I was watching her when she slipped off where she was sitting. The water was running real fast. I saw her head bobbing, but not for very long..."

Carrie reached out and pulled him into a hug. "I'm sorry you lost your friend, Russell."

Russell sniffed and looked up at her. "We never saw her again. I guess the river carried her down a long way."

"It probably did," Carrie agreed. She knew there were no words to assuage that kind of pain, so she pulled him into a tighter embrace.

Minnie looked shattered. "I'm real sorry, Russell." Her own eyes were haunted. "I guess that was like the night my family died. One minute they were there. The next, they were all gone."

Russell pulled away from Carrie to put an arm around Minnie. "I guess we both lost a lot," he said.

Minnie laid her head against his shoulder. "Yes, I guess we did."

Carrie locked eyes with Anthony, before turning to gaze at Rose. The two children had suffered unimaginable losses, but they would help each other heal.

---

The carriage driver turned to Nancy once the picnic gear had been repacked and stowed. "Is it time for roller skating?"

The children turned round eyes toward their hostess.

"Roller skating?" Hope asked. "What's that?"

"New York City's newest craze," Nancy replied with a chuckle. She nodded to the driver. "Yes, Milo. Please take us to the skating rink."

Carrie was as mystified as the rest. Her mystification grew when, thirty minutes later, the carriage pulled up in front of a furniture store.

Frances was as confused as her mother. "Why are we at a furniture store, Mrs. Stratford?"

Nancy smiled. "It's only partly a furniture store. It's also a roller-skating rink. Mr. Plimpton owns the furniture store, but nine years ago he designed the four-wheeled, turning roller skate. He opened the first rink right here in his store. Another opened in Newport, Rhode Island with his support. That rink started out as the dining room in a large hotel." She turned to the carriage driver. "Milo, you're much more familiar with roller skating than I am. Will you explain it to them?"

Milo smiled brightly and turned to the children. "I'll be happy to. I bring my son and daughter here every week. They love skating." He turned to Russell. "I know you're interested in how things are designed, young man."

"I am," Russell said eagerly.

"I love to know where things come from too. The very first roller skate was invented in London, back in 1760, or thereabout," Milo began. "Back then, roller skates had the wheels in a straight line, much like ice skating. John Merlin was the inventor, and he was also an accomplished musician, but he wasn't actually a very good skater. He decided to debut his invention at a fancy masquerade ball." He rolled his eyes.

"I take it the debut wasn't entirely a success," Anthony observed.

Milo chuckled. "Not entirely. As his costume, he donned his roller skates and a violin, skating around the party while he played music. At first, people were impressed...until he lost control of his skates and crash-landed into a huge and expensive mirror. He smashed it to bits, severely wounded himself, broke his violin, and sent roller skating design back to the drawing board."

Carrie laughed as she envisioned the chaotic scene. "I take it the design has come a long way?"

Milo nodded. "Thankfully, yes. Mr. Plimpton created the first two-by-two roller skates. Instead of being attached directly to the sole of the skate, the wheel assembly was fastened to a pivot and had a rubber cushion. It allowed the skater to—"

"Curve by shifting his weight," Russell said excitedly.

Milo's eyes widened. "Yes, that's exactly right. How do you know that?"

Russell shrugged. "It just makes sense."

"To you perhaps," Anthony said admiringly. "Where did you learn all that you know?"

Russell shrugged again. "My uncle liked to tinker around in his workshop and make things before he died. He let me hang out with him. I reckon I learned some things."

"I reckon you did," Milo replied. "I think, though, that you also inherited your uncle's skill at inventing."

Russell smiled. "I hope so. That would be great."

"I think you can be sure of it," Anthony said. "I'm going to set you up a shop when we return home. You can tinker to your heart's content."

Russell smiled brilliantly. "Really? Thanks, Daddy!" He turned back to Milo. "Did Mr. Plimpton do anything else?"

"Six years ago, Plimpton added leather straps and metal side braces. My children claim they can now move around the floor as easily as they can skate on ice," Milo answered.

"I wish they could teach us," Minnie said wistfully. "It would be fun to learn how to roller skate."

"That's why we're here!" Nancy told her. "Milo's children are waiting to teach all of you how to skate."

"What?" Minnie's eyes opened even wider.

"We can skate?" John cried. "I don't know what it is, but it sure sounds fun."

"Let's skate!" Hope squealed. "Skate!"

Nancy turned to Carrie, Anthony, and Rose. "What do you think?"

Carrie looked down at her dress and grimaced. "Will I survive if I try to skate in a dress?"

"Definitely," Nancy assured her. "You'll find as many young ladies and women in there, as you'll find boys and men."

Carrie grinned. "Let's skate!"

Within thirty minutes they were making their way across the wooden floor on their skates.

Within an hour, everyone was moving fairly smoothly. There were falls, but no one was hurt. Laughter abounded as the children became more secure on their skates.

"Look at me, Mama!" Hope called.

"I see you!" Rose called back, concentrating on keeping her balance.

Carrie rolled up to her. "You're doing great!"

Rose looked less than pleased. "I've never been on anything but my own two feet. I'm not certain I'm supposed to be rolling around on wheels."

Carrie laughed. "You're a teacher. You're all about learning new things."

"Things that go in your head," Rose retorted, reaching out a hand to grip the rink wall when she started to teeter. "I'm happy to explain about the invention of roller skating. That doesn't mean I have to attempt to kill myself by trying it."

Carrie was laughing so hard she had to lean over and grasp her knees.

"Mama!" John skated up to Rose and held out his hand. "Come skate with me."

Rose gave Carrie a helpless look. "If you find my body in a bloody pile on the floor, don't say I didn't tell you it might happen."

John cocked his head. "Mama, you might hurt a little if you fall down, but I don't think there will be blood," he said seriously.

Rose shook her head as she took his hand and skated off beside him, her lips set in a grim line.

"Your best friend is very brave."

Anthony's amused voice sounded over Carrie's shoulder. "I'm not sure that's courage," she said with a laugh. "Rose just doesn't see a way to escape with any dignity." She watched as Rose skated stiffly beside her young son, who was already comfortable on his skates.

"She'll be fine," Anthony replied as he held out his hand. "Would you care to skate with me, Dr. Wallington?"

Carrie took his hand gladly. "The pleasure will be all mine, Mr. Wallington."

Everyone piled out of the carriage, laughing and talking as they arrived back at the Stratfords' home. Their day of fun and adventure had been a huge success. The sun was sinking lower in the sky, but dark clouds over the harbor warned of an incoming storm.

"What are we doing tomorrow?" Minnie asked as she stifled a yawn.

"We're going on one of the ferry boats," Nancy told her.

Minnie gaped at her. "I've never been on a big boat on the water."

"You're going to love it," Nancy assured her. "It's so much fun for me to have you here. I'm glad we've got another week."

Wally was waiting for them. He lifted an envelope when Carrie and Anthony reached the porch. "This telegram came a few minutes ago."

Carrie felt a sense of foreboding as Anthony quickly opened it. Her dread deepened as his somber green eyes found hers.

"We have to go home tomorrow," Anthony said grimly.

## Chapter Twenty-One

Carrie's hand went to her mouth as the wagon rounded the last curve. The children, laughing and talking, fell silent as the destruction unfolded before them. They'd been assured all their horses were safe, but the realization of what had happened silenced them.

"It's completely gone," Carrie whispered.

Anthony took her hand. "The barn can be rebuilt."

Carrie's eyes searched the pasture. She relaxed slightly as she saw Granite grazing in the field. As if called by her thoughts, his finely shaped head shot up. His eyes searched the distance until they settled on the wagon. Moments later, his shrill whinny cut through the air as he took off at a run for the fence. Just like the many years before, her horse was welcoming her home.

Carrie's heart caught in her throat as tears filled her eyes. Even though the telegram had said Granite was fine, she hadn't truly believed it. The terse lines had revealed so little. They'd gotten on the train to Richmond the day after they received the message, and on the road to the plantation just four hours ago. It was sad to have had to cut their trip short, but they'd all been in agreement that home was where they wanted to be.

Anthony pulled the wagon to a stop as they came even with the pasture. Carrie climbed down from the seat and ran over to the wooden fence, laughing through her tears as Granite shoved his head through the rails. He wasn't tall enough yet for his head to clear the wooden slats, but he was determined to reach her. She stroked his soft muzzle until her emotions were under control. She slowly walked along the fence line to where the barn had once stood. All that remained was a blackened area.

Carrie stared at the blank spot, her mind swarming with memories from her entire life.

"Welcome home, honey."

Carrie turned to gaze at her father and then melted into his arms. "What happened? How did the barn burn?"

Thomas' lips tightened. "Abe Cummings. We were warned, and had guards all around, but we couldn't stop him from coming through the woods and setting fire to the barn."

Carrie's mind continued to spin. "All the horses?" The telegram said the horses had been saved, but she needed to hear it from him.

"All safe," her father assured her.

Carrie leaned into him, needing the feel of his solid comfort. She was alarmed when he winced and drew back. "Father! What's wrong?"

Miles arrived as they were talking. "Your daddy saved Granite, Carrie Girl. But he got himself burned pretty good while he be doin' it."

"Father!"

"I'm fine," Thomas insisted. "Abby treated me. Evidently, she's learned quite a lot from the clinic. Peter and Elizabeth arrived four days ago. She took up where your mother left off. There's some lingering pain, but everything will heal."

Carrie narrowed her eyes. "I believe I'll be the one to decide that."

"Didn't I tell you that's what she would say?" Abby's amused voice sounded from behind her.

Carrie turned to hug her, but hesitated. "Are you alright?"

Abby pulled her into a warm embrace. "I'm fine, my dear. I was in the tunnel with Annie, Jed, and Bridget during the attack."

Carrie sagged into her arms. "The attack..." The truth of what had happened was slowly sinking in.

Abby put an arm around her waist and turned to lead her to the porch. "There's nothing to see here. Annie is bringing out drinks and food. We'll tell you the story when we're together."

Carrie allowed herself to be led, but looked at Miles. "You and Annie?"

"We're fine, Carrie Girl. Ain't nothin' but stuff burned. Stuff can always be re-got. We be living over in the guest quarters till the barn gets built again. Your daddy offered to build us a cabin of our own, but I be happiest when I be right there with the horses."

Carrie knew that was true. Other than the years after his escape to Canada, he'd spent his entire life above the barn. The reality that it was gone took her breath away once again.

Abby led her up the steps and settled her into a rocking chair.

The children had been taken inside to feast on cookies and milk. Moses, Susan, and Harold had assembled on the porch by the time she arrived.

Carrie, Anthony, Rose, Matthew, and Janie listened quietly while the group shared the story.

"Did they catch Abe?" Anthony asked angrily when they were finished.

"Somebody did," Moses said in his deep voice. "One of the men found him dead in the woods a couple days ago. Had a bullet in his head."

Carrie winced but couldn't find it in her heart to feel sympathy. "He tried to burn the barn with the horses inside." She couldn't stop envisioning what might have happened.

"Stop that!" Miles commanded. "I know what you be doing. Ain't no use trying to imagine what could have happened, 'cause it didn't. Ain't a single horse lost."

Carrie knew he was right, but it was going to take time for her vivid imagination not to conjure what she hadn't experienced. She turned to Susan. "All the tack?"

Her partner smiled. "Amber is smarter than all of us. She and I kept watch in the pasture, but before we went outside, she told Clint, who was guarding the tack room, to toss the tack and grooming supplies into the tunnel. Somehow, that girl knew what would happen. The tack was a tangled mess when we got down there, but not a single thing was lost. We've got it sorted out and stored away down in the tunnel. No one who has come by guessed where it went. They assume it was burned up."

Carrie was relieved that the plantation secret hadn't been revealed to everyone, but she suspected workers had wondered what happened to the metal bits and saddle pieces

Susan read her mind. "Clint and Amber cleaned that area first so no one wondered how metal could have burned. The tunnel secret is safe."

Carrie looked out over the yard to where the barn had once stood. A soft breeze carried the aroma of soot and charred wood, but the horror was lessened by the soft whinnies and nickers of horses. "Where is Eclipse?"

Miles laughed. "We built the king his own paddock farther away from the rest of the horses. He's not overly pleased, but he's fine. Moses' men have built close to two dozen lean-tos to protect the horses from the heat. They're good. The lean-tos will be a welcome addition even after the barn is rebuilt."

Carrie took a deep breath. "So, we rebuild."

"We rebuild," Susan agreed. "At least we have the reserves."

Carrie nodded and looked at Abby. "Thank you for teaching us the value of having emergency funds available."

Abby reached out for her hand. "You're welcome, but all I can do is teach. You and Susan listened and took action."

Susan smiled and stood. "Hold on a minute. I have something to show you." She disappeared into the house.

Anthony gripped Carrie's hand tightly. "It's going to be alright."

Now that the initial shock was over, Carrie's mind was spinning with possibilities. "We've talked about wanting a new barn."

"That we have!" Susan said cheerfully, stepping back onto the porch with a large roll of paper. "Turns out my husband is more than a reporter. He evidently is also an architect."

Harold shrugged. "It's rudimentary, but I think it will give you the idea."

Matthew laughed. "Whenever my twin says something is *rudimentary*, it means he's put his best effort into it. He's been drawing and designing things since we were boys, but he insisted reporting was his first love."

Carrie eagerly unrolled the thick paper. Her eyes pored over the detailed drawing with increasing delight. She sucked in her breath and turned to Susan. "Is it bad to tell my business partner that I I'm glad the barn burned down?"

Susan smiled brightly. "I told Harold the same thing when he showed me. I don't know how long it would have been before we thought we could afford to build what we've dreamed of, but now that we've been forced into it..."

Carrie beckoned to Anthony. "Look at this! Susan and I have talked about building a barn like this for the last few years."

Anthony moved his chair closer to her and examined the drawing. When he was done, he gave a long, low whistle. "Impressive." He turned to Harold. "Where did you learn to do this?"

Harold shrugged modestly. "It just comes to me. I'm glad Susan and Carrie like it."

"Like it?" Carrie asked. "I *love* it!" She took a deep breath. "How long before we can start building?"

Susan chuckled. "I suspected that would be your response, but nothing could be started until you got home. Now that you've given approval, Moses will send his men with wagons to get the materials from Richmond."

Carrie turned to Moses. "It will take a lot of wagons to get all this lumber and tin." She sighed. "If we'd had a tin roof, the barn wouldn't have burned so quickly."

"Yes, but tin wasn't readily available when my great-grandfather built the barn," Thomas replied. "That old thing stood for a long time, but it's life was over."

"It will have a tin roof now," Susan said. "And twelve more stalls. And a larger tack room and grain room."

"And a higher pitched roof that will allow better air circulation and protection from heavy snows," Carrie added excitedly.

"And every stall will have outside doors that lead to the pasture so that air will flow through better. Susan's eyes shone with anticipation. "Eclipse even has his own private paddock!"

Carrie suddenly thought of something. "Who's going to build this? I know you'll offer your men, Moses, but we're in the middle of tobacco season. They need to be in the fields. It will take weeks to build something this massive."

"I would normally agree with that," Moses answered "But I imagine one hundred men can build it in far less than two weeks."

Carrie sucked in her breath. "Excuse me? *One hundred men*? Where are they coming from?"

Thomas grinned. "All the plantation workers and every man from the surrounding area has volunteered to help. They started showing up here as soon as they heard about the fire."

Carrie stared at him. "One hundred men." She couldn't wrap her mind around that number. "That's difficult to believe."

"No, it isn't," Abby said quietly. "We were warned about the fire by the father of one of Rose's students."

"Who?" Rose asked.

"Jeremiah Hutchinson."

Rose smiled. "He's a good man."

"He is," Abby agreed. "Without his warning, we wouldn't have lost only the barn. It's very likely that Miles, Annie, and the horses would have been lost, too."

Tears filled Carrie's eyes as she once again considered what could have happened.

"Jeremiah said he was warning us because of how much the school and the clinic mean to the community. They weren't going to let anything bad happen to Cromwell Plantation. Once they learned of the fire, every man who benefits from the school, the clinic, and the plantation signed on for the barn raising." Thomas said.

"The Bregdan Women are going to provide the food," Abby continued. "As big as the barn is, it will probably take at least two days to complete it. At the end, we're going to have music and dancing."

Carrie laughed. "You're turning it into a party?"

Abby grinned. "Why not? Abe planned to do us great harm, believing he could destroy Cromwell Plantation by destroying the stables. Instead, you're going to build the barn you always dreamed of, and the community is coming together to work and celebrate."

Rose chuckled. "My mama would be proud. She always said that you could make honey out of even the most bitter things."

"If you look hard enough for the goodness," Carrie added. "When I was younger, I thought she'd lost her mind, but she was right."

"My mama was always right," Rose said softly.

Carrie, hearing the catch in her voice, reached over to take her friend's hand.

"I'll miss her for as long as I'm breathing," Rose said. "I believe she knows what has happened here though."

"Just like Robert knows," Carrie added. She looked out at the barren area. "Long before Susan and I started talking about it, Robert dreamed of having a bigger barn. He believed that one day Cromwell Stables would be the largest and most successful stables in the South."

"We're well on our way," Susan said. "He'd be proud."

Carrie clapped her hands, determined to push away the memories bearing down on her. "When does the barn raising happen?"

Moses shook his head. "Not a patient bone in your body, woman."

Carrie stuck out her tongue. "As I've told you many times, I don't particularly believe patience is a virtue. It's merely an excuse for mediocrity." She glared at him playfully. "When does the barn raising begin?" she repeated.

"I'm sending in men with the wagons tomorrow," Moses replied. "I don't know that they can bring it all back at one time. It may take two trips, but I believe that in eight days we'll be ready to start building."

Carrie jumped up, pulled Susan from her rocking chair, and began to dance her around the porch. "In less than two weeks we'll have a new barn, partner!" she exclaimed.

"And a party!" Janie added happily. Suddenly, she paused. "We haven't even asked about Peter and Elizabeth. How are they?"

"Deliriously happy," Abby replied. "They're enjoying their solitude in your and Matthew's home. They'll be here later for dinner."

Carrie turned to her father. "Which means I have time to examine your burns." She held up a hand when he opened his mouth to protest. "Don't even try," she warned. "I'm confident Abby and Elizabeth did a wonderful job in treating you, but I'm your daughter, and it was my horse you saved. It's barely been four days since you were burned. I have to see for myself."

Thomas snapped his mouth closed and nodded. "Have it your way, my dear."

"How are your father's burns?" Anthony asked when they were snuggled in bed together that night. "I didn't want to ask until we were alone."

"They're severe second-degree burns," Carrie said grimly, as she fought back tears. "I can only imagine how much pain he was in when he was getting Granite out of the barn. He took off his shirt to wrap it around Granite's head. There was nothing to shield him when the embers were falling." She gritted her teeth. "I can hardly believe Abe set fire to a barn full of horses. Valuable or not, they were living beings that didn't deserve to burn to death!" Carrie had been fighting fury ever since she had pulled back the bandages to examine her father's burns.

"Will they heal?"

"Yes," Carrie replied. "But there will be scarring."

"Do you regret helping Charlotte and the children get away?" Anthony asked gently.

Carrie took a deep breath and shook her head. She'd thought about nothing else while she'd been treating her father. "No."

"You don't sound certain," Anthony observed.

"I'm certain they needed to get away from that monster," Carrie said quickly. "I suppose I'm glad I didn't know the price that would be paid for getting her and the children to safety. I hate to think I might have reconsidered my actions. We did the right thing. All of us."

"Doing the right thing doesn't mean we're protected from negative consequences."

"I know," Carrie agreed readily. "But it's alright to wish we were, isn't it?"

Anthony laughed and pulled her closer. "Absolutely." He hesitated and then said, "It wasn't solely Abe, Carrie."

Carrie pulled back to gaze at him. "What do you mean? No one said anything about seeing more than one man. Abe set fire to the barn."

"He did," Anthony replied, "but evidence suggests he was prodded into it by a KKK member."

Carrie stiffened. "What are you talking about? What evidence?"

Anthony told her what he had learned from further discussion with Thomas. "He didn't want to say anything on the porch, or at dinner, because he didn't want Jed to overhear. Jed was traumatized enough by the attack. When Jeremiah came to give the warning, Jed heard him talking about the KKK."

"And it invoked all the memories of the attack that killed his mother and father," Carrie said softly. "Poor Jed."

Anthony nodded. "Moses said he's had nightmares every night since the fire, and he won't let Moses out of his sight. He's convinced they're going to come back."

"None of us can really assure him they won't," Carrie said wearily. She was exhausted to her core. "Do you think it will ever end?"

Anthony hauled her back to lie against his warm body. "I don't know," he said gently. "I do know, however, that we've beaten them back every time."

Carrie felt tears welling that she couldn't control. "Not every time," she choked. "Not when Robert was killed." She wasn't sure if she wanted to scream with fury or weep with abject despair. "Please tell me it will end, Anthony," she whispered as she burrowed as close to his solid chest as she could manage.

"What I can tell you is that we'll face everything together," Anthony whispered. "Always together."

Carrie knew that was all he could honestly promise. For tonight, it would have to be enough.

## *Chapter Twenty-Two*

The morning of the barn raising was hot and steamy, but at least it was dry. Miles assured Carrie and Susan that it wouldn't rain that day, despite the clouds on the horizon that seemed to be scuttling their way. Carrie believed him. Her elderly friend was never wrong about the weather.

Men had begun to arrive as soon as the sun lightened the horizon at six o'clock.

The women had arrived by nine o'clock. They were plying the workers with cold well water and ham biscuits, all while they were loading food onto the tables for lunch. Children played under the shade of the backyard trees, flopping down to cool off when it got too hot.

The sound of sawing and hammering filled the air. Men called to each other, laughing and talking as they worked. The horses had moved to the back of the pastures but were watching the activity with great curiosity.

As promised, at least one hundred men swarmed over the barn site. Carrie was amazed that it wasn't a chaotic scene. Somehow each man seemed to know what his job was. Moses was managing the building, with Harold directing the placement according to his design. Her father, Anthony, and Peter worked with the men.

"This is unbelievable," Susan said.

Carrie stared at the progress. "I really didn't think it was possible to build a barn in two days. Now that I see how fast they're working, I actually believe it can happen. Look how fast the frame is going up. They'll have the roof on by the end of the day!"

"Dr. Wallington!"

A shout interrupted their talking. Carrie moved toward the man beckoning her. "What's going on?" She didn't know the man's name, but she recognized him as the parent of one of Rose's students.

He pointed to another man close to him that was holding his hand tightly, a blood-soaked shirt wrapped around it. "Elijah cut himself with the saw."

Carrie walked to the injured man. "Hello, Elijah. Do you mind if I take a look at that?"

Elijah looked up, his face a mixture of embarrassment and pain. "Can't believe I cut myself this bad. I only looked away for a moment."

Carrie smiled calmly. "Don't worry. I'll fix it up for you."

Elijah returned her smile, his narrow face showing his appreciation. "Ain't never had a doctor standing by when I was out working."

"It's a good thing I'm here." Carrie could see almost to the bone once she'd pulled the shirt away from his wounded hand. "Your wound is going to need stitches."

Elijah scowled. "That ain't no good. How am I gonna work with one hand?"

"You're not," Carrie responded evenly. "If you try and work with this hand, you could do permanent damage." She took his arm and guided him toward the house, motioning to Anthony what she was doing. "I'll get you fixed up inside. Is your wife here?"

"Yes, ma'am."

"Perhaps she'll let you help with getting lunch ready," Carrie said gently. "I know you want to help build, but I'm sure the women will appreciate your help. I know you will appreciate using your hand for the rest of your life."

"I reckon," Elijah grumbled, but he allowed her to lead him inside and treat the cut.

When Carrie was finished suturing, coating the wound with a honey-garlic mixture, and giving him some herbal tea for the pain, she went back outside, anticipating she would be needed again. She smiled when she saw both Janie and Elizabeth tending to different workers. Indeed, she wasn't sure there had ever been a barn raising with this many doctors present.

By the time the sun set, the frame had been completed and the roof was finished. The workers finished pounding in the last sheet of tin on the roof before they packed up their tools and left, promising to return the next day.

Carrie and Susan roamed beneath the rafters, relishing what had been done.

"It's exactly like I dreamed," Susan said reverently as she peered up at the towering roofline.

Carrie breathed in the fresh scent of cut wood that had obliterated the burned smells. "It's a new beginning," she said softly. "I can't believe so many people came to help. The men, the women, even the children who were carrying scraps of wood to the kindling pile for this winter's fires."

"It's because of the clinic and the school," Susan reminded her. "Everyone here is grateful for their community."

"Partly," Carrie agreed. "It's also because of the plantation providing jobs and work to at a fair wage. It's astonishing to see how fast the barn is going up, but it's also such a confirmation of the benefits of simply treating people right."

"That's true," Susan said thoughtfully. "If every plantation owner and farmer in the area paid people fairly, and gave them a share of the profits, they would always have the help they need and they would make more money. It boggles my mind that they refuse to comprehend such a simple truth."

"They've always done it one way," Carrie said with a sigh.

"So did your father," Susan observed. "He changed."

"And he'll tell you how hard it was for him," Carrie replied. "Father told me today that even though he's changed, it is unbelievable to him that one hundred men came to help today. Barn raisings are commonplace around the country in rural communities, but to see such an open-hearted willingness for whites and blacks to work together, without slavery being in the picture, is still amazing to him."

Susan fell silent for a long moment and then said, "I'm glad my parents taught me that it's not our differences that divide us. They told me often that it's our inability to recognize, accept, and celebrate those differences. There was much to celebrate here today."

"Your parents were very wise." Carrie stepped into where the tack room was going to be and looked down. "You would never dream there's an entrance to a tunnel here. Father, Anthony, and Moses will create the opening when the barn is complete."

Susan smiled. "The tunnel has saved so many. I wonder if your great-grandparents had any idea how often it would be used."

Carrie chuckled. "I'm quite sure they didn't. They thought it would only be used for Indian attacks. They could never have envisioned a Civil War in their new country, nor imagined protecting themselves from white men who wanted to destroy what they'd worked for." She sobered as thoughts of the newest attack filled her mind again.

"Don't," Susan said firmly.

Carrie raised a brow. "Don't?"

Susan gripped her hand. "Don't focus on the attack. It could have easily been far worse. If it wasn't the KKK, it would be someone else who wants to attack what's been created here. My father used to tell me that there will always be people who hate other people's success. Especially now, after so many people in the South have lost everything, they're going to fight back against people who are succeeding. It's easier to fight against success than to take responsibility for the fact that you aren't successful."

Carrie thought about her words. "I agree with that mostly, but I also understand the helplessness people feel. We're surrounded by people, both white and black, who had nothing to do with starting the war they were forced to fight. Now, because the South isn't helping them the way they should be, they're forced to fight to rebuild a life they weren't responsible for losing. I understand their frustration and anger."

Susan was the one to raise her brow.

"I don't agree with what many of them are doing," Carrie added. "I just understand why. Until people can find a different way to vent their frustration, or until they have a way to rebuild their life, the South will continue to be in turmoil."

"Which puts the entire country in turmoil," Susan said sadly.

"I'm not sure of that," Carrie said slowly. She thought of all she'd seen the last two weeks. "Boston and New York City don't seem to be impacted by what's happening down here. The war decimated the South, but it seems to have brought great wealth to the North. Their cities and countryside weren't destroyed. They aren't having to rebuild. They don't have to carry the weight of defeat. They're moving on."

It was Susan's turn to fall silent. "The North fought to keep the country united, but they're moving on without making sure the South is recovering? Where is the fairness in that?"

"There is none," Carrie said swiftly. "The North is tired of Reconstruction already, but the job is far from finished. I see it in many ways, but Logan's being enslaved in the Alabama coal mines is another horrible example. I shudder to think what will happen if the North completely turns its back."

Susan nodded. "Has anyone heard from Logan?"

Carrie smiled. "Yes. He sent a telegram to the Stratfords while we were in New York. He made it to Canada and loves it. He's working at Mr. Carson's stables and planning on going back to school."

Susan smiled. "I'm glad there are glimmers of good news in the midst of darkness."

Carrie looked around her and felt a genuine surge of joy. "There is more than a glimmer here, Susan." She raised her arms. "This is a whole barn full of good news. In two days, Cromwell Stables will be what we've dreamed it could be." She shook aside her dark thoughts and chose to focus on the miracle that was coming to life.

The next afternoon, the barn stood completed, its new wooden sides glowing red with a fresh coat of paint. The setting sun made it look as if it were on fire.

"That's the kind of fire I can live with," Rose said as she stood arm in arm with Carrie on the porch.

Carrie took a deep breath of the fresh air. A wind had blown in during the night, pushing aside the hot, steamy air. It was warm, but the air no longer felt suffocating. The huge oak tree in the pasture seemed to shine as the breeze tossed its leaves. The horses stood in formation as they stared at the new barn, their heads lifted proudly.

Suddenly, Granite broke free and did a series of bucks across the pasture.

Carrie laughed as she watched him. "He always has to be the one to do things his own way."

"Just like you," Rose said with a chuckle. "You two are made for each other."

"Yes," Carrie whispered as she watched him cavorting around the field. "I can hardly believe I have Granite. I can hardly believe there's a brand-new barn standing on the plantation. When Granite died... When the barn burned..."

"You thought things had ended," Rose said.

"I did." Carrie gazed out at the beauty surrounding them. "I remember your mama telling me once that life is a journey, and where that journey ends is up to us." Carrie remembered the moment Sarah had said those words to her. They'd been deep in the plantation woods, looking for the healing plants Sarah assured her were there. Every time they went into the woods, Carrie had learned something new — knowledge she was now using every day.

"Mama told me the journey could lead to joy if we'd let it," Rose added, her eyes shining with her own memories. "Mama lived through so much pain. So many hard times. But in the end..."

"In the end she had joy," Carrie said softly. She looked around the plantation with a sense of wonder. "So much has happened since your mama died. So many things I could never have dreamed." She paused. "Do you think the journey ever ends, Rose?"

Rose shook her head immediately. "No. Mama told me that as long as I be breathin', I gonna be travelin' through dis here life. She told me the journey don't neber end till I take my last breath."

"I'm not sure if I find that comforting or discouraging," Carrie replied.

"Don't matter none," Rose quipped. "It just be what it be. You got to embrace it and find joy anyways you can."

Carrie chuckled and shook her head. "You sound exactly like your mama."

"Her voice is always in my head," Rose said. "I hope it always will be. I don't think I could stand it if I lost her voice. It would be like losing part of who I am."

"You'll never lose it," Carrie assured her. "Your mama planted herself in you as surely as that big oak tree is anchored in the ground."

Rose smiled and changed the subject. "I received a letter from Felicia today. She arrives in Washington, DC next week to join Sojourner Truth."

Carrie smiled. "And now her new adventure begins. How are you doing with it?"

"Just like before," Rose replied. "Both excited and terrified. I want this to be a wonderful experience for her, but I'm under no illusion that it will always be fun and easy."

Carrie heard something in her friend's voice that she couldn't quite identify. "What aren't you telling me?"

Rose sighed. "I got a letter from Sojourner, as well."

Carrie waited.

Rose stared out at the plantation, her expression deeply troubled. "The suffrage movement is getting more complicated. Women used to be united in fighting for the right to vote, but it's not that simple now."

Carrie had talked with Nancy Stratford about this exact issue, but she continued to wait to hear what Sojourner had written.

"It's bad enough that there are many women who don't believe women should have the right to vote, but now those who do want it can't agree on how it should happen," Rose continued.

"I understand Susan B. Anthony and Elizabeth Stanton refused to support ratification of the Fifteenth Amendment because it refused the right for women to vote, even though it gave black men the right to vote," Carrie replied.

"That's right," Rose agreed. "Of course, the amendment passed anyway, but it created a wide split in the women's rights movement. Stanton and Anthony started their own organization, the National Woman Suffrage Association. Lucy Stone and Henry Blackwell started the American Woman Suffrage Association. The National organization opposed the Fifteenth Amendment. The American Association championed it."

"Which one has Sojourner aligned herself with?" Carrie asked.

"The National Woman Suffrage Association, with Susan B. Anthony and Elizabeth Stanton," Rose said heavily.

"You disagree with her?" Carrie asked carefully. Her instincts told her there was something more going on.

Rose shrugged. "I have very mixed feelings quite honestly. I'm glad black men have the right to vote, but I also believe women should have the right to vote. However, the Fifteenth Amendment has passed, so my opinion doesn't really matter. We simply have to move forward from where we are, which is fighting for the right to vote for all women."

"Then what's bothering you?"

"It's more what Sojourner is concerned might bother Felicia. She's gotten to know Felicia quite well at Oberlin, but so has Lucy Stone. She's afraid Felicia will feel torn between the two organizations."

Carrie fell silent as she mulled over Rose's statement. "I don't think you have anything to worry about."

"Why not?" Rose demanded.

"Because Felicia isn't on that stage to debate the Fifteenth Amendment. She's telling her story to give people hope. She went through a horrendous experience when she was young, but she's grown into a powerful young woman. She chose to not let her parents' murder define her. Yes, she will support women's right to vote, but that's not her entire message. Her most important message is that you can choose to create the life you want for yourself, no matter what happens to you," Carrie said firmly. "Felicia knows the conflict within the suffrage movement. There's no way she could be at Oberlin and not be aware of it. Still, she chose to travel with Sojourner. Why do you think that is?"

Rose hesitated before she answered. "Because Sojourner asked her?"

"Exactly. If Lucy Stone had asked her, she would probably be on the stage with her. Felicia is a bright, strong young woman. She knows what she's getting into."

Rose managed a wry laugh. "You nearly had me convinced, until that last statement."

Carrie frowned. "What did I say?"

"That she knows what she's getting into. Felicia has no idea what she's getting into. *I* don't know what she's getting into. I doubt Sojourner knows what my daughter is getting into, because she's never been a sixteen-year-old on stage," Rose said. "I agree that Felicia has a message of hope, but I pray her experience this summer doesn't destroy that message."

"It won't," Carrie replied, convinced what she was saying was true.

Rose eyed her. "How can you be certain?"

"Because I know her parents," Carrie answered. "It's because of you and Moses that Felicia has her message of hope. It's because of the two of you that she has the opportunity to stand on that stage and talk to people. Felicia has already seen the worst life has to offer. No matter what she experiences this summer, she'll come out of it stronger and more certain of her message."

Rose sighed and gave Carrie a hug. "Alright, *now* you have convinced me." Her laugh was shaky. "Thank you."

The sound of music erupted from the back of the house.

"I do believe that's our cue," Carrie said. "It's time for a party to celebrate all those who worked to build that beautiful barn."

The evening passed in a whirl of dancing, music, and food. Laughter filled the air as everyone celebrated what they had accomplished.

A full moon slowly rose over the plantation, casting a brilliant glow over the scene. A bonfire crackled merrily as a breeze kept the mosquitoes at bay. Fireflies decorated the tree and the sky as they blinked into the darkness.

Anthony appeared next to Carrie, slipping an arm around her waist. "Happy?"

Carrie gazed up into her husband's eyes. "Gloriously happy," she admitted. The music ended and then changed into the Virginia waltz. "Care to dance, Mr. Wallington?"

Anthony laughed, pulled her into his arms, and joined the others in the waltz.

## *Chapter Twenty-Three*

Late July 1872

Felicia, accompanied by one of her Oberlin professors, stepped off the train in Washington, DC. The late July air, even in the station, was hot and humid—much warmer than Oberlin, Ohio. She took a deep breath, uncertain if she was feeling excited or simply nervous. Now that the day had finally arrived, her emotions felt like water rushing over a towering waterfall. Her heart pounded as fast as a runaway train.

"It's going to be alright," Connie Gallery soothed.

"Do I look as overwhelmed as I feel?" Felicia managed a shaky laugh as she pushed back stray strands of hair from her braided bun.

Connie smiled. "I'd be surprised if you weren't feeling overwhelmed, Felicia. What's most daunting? Being in Washington, DC for the first time? Meeting Sojourner here? Speaking on stage tomorrow?"

"Do I have to choose merely one?" Felicia asked shakily.

Connie laughed. "You don't. If I were you, I believe all of them would be daunting, especially if I were only sixteen. Of course," she added lightly, "every professor at Oberlin has decided you're sixteen, going on thirty." She smiled, but then sobered. "We also realize it's because of what you've been through. Everyone who lived through the war had to grow up quickly, but not many experienced what you did."

Felicia knew that was true. Her experiences were what drove her to accomplish everything she had to date.

"You know you're special, don't you?" Connie asked. Her light gray bun was pulled back to frame a kind face with sparkling blue eyes. She was both shorter and rounder than Felicia.

"I'm not special," Felicia protested. "I do what I do because I have to."

"Have to?"

Felicia nodded. "The day my parents were murdered, I knew I had to make it have purpose. I was only ten, so I didn't really know what that meant. I figured out, though, that having a purpose gave me a reason to live." Her eyes darkened. "When they were killed, I wanted to die too. Moses saved me, but I often worried that my life hadn't been worth saving. I do everything I do to make sure my life was worth the risk he took."

Connie took her hand. "That's a heavy burden to bear, Felicia. I believe your life was worth saving simply because you *are*. It's not about what you do. The things you've accomplished are remarkable, but they're less remarkable than who you are as a person."

Felicia shook her head firmly. "I don't believe that." There was a part of her that perhaps thought she should believe it, though the reality was far different. She'd agreed to share the stage with Sojourner because she hoped it would help her clarify her life. She knew she was intelligent, but simply being able to absorb huge amounts of knowledge wasn't enough. As she increasingly saw and experienced how difficult it was to be black in America, she felt compelled to give people hope that it could be better.

First, though she had to find and hold on to her own hope. She prayed her time with Sojourner would enable her to do that.

Their conversation halted as the flow of passengers from the train moved out onto the open platform. Felicia gazed around, excited when she saw the towering rotunda of the Capitol building in the distance. She knew it was white, but at the moment it was glowing gold from the late afternoon sun sinking toward the horizon. "It's beautiful," she said softly.

"That it is," Connie agreed.

"Have you been here before?" Felicia asked.

"Once. I was here right after the war ended."

Felicia caught the sadness in her professor's voice. "When President Lincoln was assassinated?" she guessed.

"Yes. I'd thought I was coming to join in the celebration of the end of the war. When Booth shot President Lincoln, the entire city went immediately into mourning. Businesses were closed, there were black buntings hanging from almost every window, and everyone was in a state of disbelief." Connie lapsed into silence as she stared at the Capitol. "He laid in state for three days before they took his body to Illinois for the funeral. There were tens of thousands of us who passed through the Rotunda to pay our respects before he was gone. The whole experience remains utterly surreal. President Lincoln was a great man."

Felicia remained silent, trying to imagine what a sad time it must have been. She'd been too young to understand what had happened. She'd heard her parents talk about it and had understood that President Lincoln had set the slaves free, but the long-term consequences of his assassination had certainly not been on her mind. Now she was faced with them every day.

"The city has changed," Connie said in a determinedly cheerful voice. She looked out over the streets radiating from the Capitol. "An extensive amount of construction has been done since the war ended."

Felicia listened but was suddenly aware of her acute fatigue after so many hours on the train. Her whirlwind departure from Oberlin, along with her nervousness had made sleep impossible during their travels. While her teacher had slept, she'd stared out the window at the passing countryside, lush with summer growth. She pulled out a handkerchief to wipe the sweat from her face and wished her light blue dress wasn't so wrinkled from the cramped conditions on the train.

A man appeared in front of them. "Mrs. Gallery? Miss Samuels?"

"Yes," Connie replied brightly. "Are you taking us to Sojourner Truth's lodging?"

"I am," the portly black man agreed. "My carriage is right over here." He reached down and picked up their luggage. "Please follow me."

Felicia tried to relax on the narrow twin bed in her allotted bedroom. The air was hot, but a slight breeze blowing in off the Potomac River made it bearable. Sojourner Truth had not been there when she arrived, so she'd escaped to her room with the hope of getting some rest.

Felicia forced her eyes closed, but her mind would not acquiesce quite so easily. She tried to envision what the next day would be like. Her prepared speech might not be well received. She'd spoken many times in front of classmates or younger students, but she'd never addressed an audience she didn't know well. What if she froze and couldn't find words? The idea of humiliating herself was more palatable than the possibility she would humiliate Sojourner. She bit back a moan as she thought of disappointing the renowned abolitionist and women's rights activist.

Felicia rose from the bed and walked to the window overlooking the river. She took long, steady breaths, hoping they would settle her heart and mind. She could tell very little difference when she stopped breathing. She leaned far out the window, looking out over the streets in the direction of the Capitol

Rotunda. She relished the stronger breeze, wondering if she could hang out the window for the rest of the evening, or at least until it cooled off.

A tap on the door made her pull her head back in. She hurried across the room and pulled the door open. "Hello, Mrs. Gallery."

"Did I wake you, Felicia?"

Felicia shook her head. "I'm afraid I can't sleep."

"Understandable," Connie responded. "I'm going out for a stroll. Would you like to join me? I'm told it will be at least two hours before Sojourner returns."

Felicia cast a practiced eye at the sky. Though the sun was hovering close to the horizon, there would be daylight for at least an hour. "I'd love to join you." At least if they were out walking, she might be given a reprieve from her thoughts.

Moments later, they were outside on the sidewalk. Trees provided welcome shade as they walked past Georgian and Colonial style homes bedecked with brilliant flowerboxes. The street was busy, but the sidewalks weren't overly crowded.

"We're walking down Pennsylvania Avenue," Connie told her. "It will take us by the President's house, the Smithsonian Institution, and the Washington Monument."

Felicia welcomed anything that would take her mind off her speech the next day. "The Smithsonian Institution?"

Connie nodded enthusiastically. "Yes. It's really rather wonderful!"

Though Felicia had questions, she decided to wait until they were actually at the Institution before she asked them. A few minutes later, her mouth dropped open. "What is that?" A towering, reddish building loomed in front of them.

Connie laughed. "That, Felicia, is the Smithsonian Institution."

Felicia eyed it with wonder. "It looks like a castle. Not that I've seen a castle. I've seen pictures, though," she said hastily.

"You're right," Connie replied. "The Smithsonian Institution building is popularly known as 'The Castle.' It's constructed of red sandstone from a quarry in Maryland. I'm no expert on architecture, but I'm told it's a twelfth-century combination of late Romanesque and early Gothic motifs. All that really means to me is that it's beautiful and quite impressive! When it was first built, it was isolated from the rest of Washington, DC by a canal, but the city has grown up around it in the years since."

Felicia continued to examine the structure. "What happened to it? It looks like it was damaged."

"Indeed. In January 1865, a few months before the war ended, a fire broke out that destroyed the upper story of the main segment. It also destroyed the north and south towers. Work has been done to restore it, but it's not complete."

"What's the building used for?" Felicia asked.

"The story behind it is rather fascinating," Connie replied. She stopped under a tree in front of the building while she talked. "The Smithsonian Institution was established with funds from James Smithson. He was a British scientist who left his estate to America to begin an establishment for the increase and diffusion of knowledge."

Felicia's interest grew. "He was British? Why did he leave his estate to America?"

"No one really knows for sure," Connie told her. "He never actually even visited our country. Smithson was the illegitimate son of a wealthy Englishman who never acknowledged him and who refused to leave his legacy to him. When Smithson became wealthy on his own, some believe he gave his money to the United States to spite his father. However, there are others who believe he was inspired by America's experiment with democracy. They think he wanted, even in his death, to be part of an American identity rooted in exploration and innovation."

"How wonderful!" Felicia said excitedly. "That's what the building is for?"

Connie nodded. "Smithson was a well-regarded chemist and mineralogist. He made many field trips in Europe to collect specimens, and published many reports. The Institution is home and office for Joseph Henry, the first Secretary of the Smithsonian. The administrative offices are there. There are also lecture halls, exhibit halls, a library and reading room, chemical laboratories, and storage areas for specimens." She sighed. "Unfortunately, when the top floor burned seven years ago, the losses included Smithson's diaries and papers, and his mineral collection. I had hoped to see them when I visited last time, but they were all gone when I arrived. The loss was quite a tragedy."

"How sad," Felicia said, her gaze locked on the building as she considered the wonders it held. "I wish I could go inside."

"You can," Connie told her brightly. "The Institution is open to the public. I'm sure there will a day when I can bring you back. As marvelous as it is now, the Smithsonian will continue to grow and expand. Let's keep walking."

Felicia reluctantly allowed herself to be led further down Pennsylvania Avenue. The evening air had become quite pleasant. The temperature had dropped along with the sun. She relished the refreshing breeze off the water as they continued to stroll along. The Potomac sparkled blue in the distance. She stopped, though, when she saw something that seemed out of place. "What is that thing?"

Connie chuckled. "That *thing* is the beginning of the Washington Monument."

Felicia eyed it doubtfully. "A monument? It's not very impressive," she said bluntly.

"Not yet," Connie agreed. "But if it's ever finished according to design, it will be."

"Why isn't it completed? Was it because of the war?"

Connie shook her head. "No, work began on it in 1848. It was stopped six years later because they ran out of funding. It's hard to tell right now, but the design has it completed in the shape of an Egyptian obelisk. It's meant to evoke the timelessness of ancient civilizations."

"It's not exactly invoking that right now."

Connie laughed again. "It's supposed to be five hundred and fifty feet tall. Right now, you can see little more than the foundation and the beginning of the structure. It's actually one hundred and fifty-six feet tall, but because they had to stop where they did, it's hard to tell what they envisioned it would become. Right now," she admitted, "it's more of a national embarrassment than a beautiful monument to our Founding Father."

Felicia continued to gaze at the tall, squarish column of rock, unable to envision what Connie had described. "Do you think it will ever be finished?"

"I think so," Connie said. "There have been congressional attempts to get the construction moving again, but the tension with the South halted progress. The war completely brought it to a stop."

"It's been seven years since the war ended," Felicia observed.

"Yes, but there have been many things that have seemed more important as we rebuild the nation," Connie replied. "As important as I believe the Washington Monument will be someday, I agree there are higher priorities."

Felicia turned away from the incomplete monument and looked at Connie. "You're a wonderful professor, Mrs. Gallery. How do you know so much about this?"

"You and I share something in common, Felicia. Benjamin Franklin once said that an investment in knowledge always pays the best interest. I believe that completely. I suspect you do too."

"Oh, I do!" Felicia said enthusiastically. "The more I learn, the more I want to know. I don't think I'll ever be able to learn everything I want to."

"I assure you that you cannot," Connie replied promptly. "The amount of knowledge in the world is too vast for one person to ever absorb. If you ever got close, there would be so much more knowledge obtained by then, that you would once again be far behind."

Felicia knew that was true. "Still, it's fun to try," she replied.

"That it is!" Connie agreed. "I think we should get back before it's dark. Washington, DC is mostly safe in this part of the city, but it's probably not wise for two women to be out on their own."

Felicia felt, more than heard, what Connie wasn't saying. "Especially when one of them is black?"

Connie sighed. "We can discuss that question when we're back at the house."

The two women walked quickly through the darkening shadows. Felicia didn't relax until they were safe inside, with the locks secured.

"Hardly good for a black woman to be out at night by herself, Felicia."

Felicia smiled when Sojourner walked into the parlor. The tall woman, nearly six feet, took her hands warmly. "Hello, Sojourner." Felicia felt uncomfortable calling this formidable icon by her first name, but she had insisted that if they were going to share a stage, they should be on a first-name basis.

"I'm sorry," Connie said contritely. "We were discussing the Washington Monument and I lost track of time."

"You're back," Sojourner said calmly. "That's what counts." She looked at Felicia keenly. "You're tired."

Felicia shrugged, not bothering to deny what must surely be obvious. "A good night's sleep will take care of it."

Sojourner continued to eye her. "You as nervous as I was before I took to the stage for the first time?"

"Did you feel like you might throw up?" Felicia had begun to relax as soon as she heard Sojourner's voice. The simple English, spoken with a Dutch accent, never failed to charm her. The power of Sojourner's voice never failed to comfort her.

Sojourner chuckled. "I sure did. Course, I was a whole lot older than you are. You ain't nothing but a girl, but you be one of the strongest girls I ever met. We got a lot of work to do to make this country right for women, Felicia."

Felicia met her penetrating gaze. "I know we do." She took a deep breath. "I hope I don't let you down."

"Let me down?" Sojourner scoffed. "Ain't no chance of that. All I want you to do is get up there and tell your story. I heard that story, Felicia. I know the power in it."

Felicia sighed and decided to opt for honesty. "What if I get up there and freeze? What if I can't tell it?"

"You'll tell it," Sojourner said with solemn confidence. "The good Lord didn't give you the stage without him knowing you could do it."

Felicia struggled to believe her.

"I remember the first time I took to the stage," Sojourner continued. "I weren't nothing but a freed slave woman who had a story to tell. I wanted other slaves to be free, so I swallowed my fears and got up on that stage. I prayed mighty hard before I opened my mouth. I reckon I had nothing but faith that I would make words come out of my mouth. When I opened it and started talking, it came to me." She chuckled. "It's been coming ever since."

Felicia listened closely. "Did you ever write down your speeches?"

Sojourner shrugged. "Couldn't. I can't read and I don't write. I open my mouth and talk. The good Lord takes over. From what I hear, what he has to say is real good. Least ways, people listen, and it seems to do some good in the world."

"It does!" Felicia assured her. Could it really be that simple? Just open her mouth and talk?

"Felicia, if it makes you feel better to write it down, you go ahead and write it down, girl." Sojourner encouraged. "But know this, what the good Lord planted in your heart to say will always find a way to come out if you let it."

Felicia thought of the things she'd heard about Sojourner and thought of the times she'd heard her speak at Oberlin. She couldn't deny the power the woman had on a stage. She sucked in her breath and nodded.

Sojourner settled down into a parlor chair, arranging her simple, gray Quaker-style dress around her. As always, she had on a white collar and wore a white peaked hat. Her strong face radiated caring and strength. Her eyes, framed by simple wire spectacles, shone with compassion and purpose.

Felicia felt herself relaxing. If such a formidable woman believed she could tell her story on the stage, she had to be confident of that as well.

Felicia swallowed hard and stepped behind the simple podium that had been placed on the platform at the front of the church where she was about to begin her speaking career. Sojourner smiled at her warmly, squeezed her hand, and moved to take a chair at the front of the church.

Felicia gazed out at the audience of close to two hundred people. Every pew and chair were full. Their faces were turned to her expectantly, their eyes offering encouragement. She'd watched as Sojourner had spoken, finding nothing but support from every person there. If they hadn't heckled Sojourner, certainly they wouldn't harass her. At least, she hoped they wouldn't.

She closed her eyes, prayed, and began. She had notes in front of her in case she needed them, but doubted she would because she had lived her story.

"Hello. My name is Felicia Samuels. That wasn't always my name, though. I was simply called Felicia. My parents, the ones who gave birth to me, were slaves in Tennessee for most of their lives. I'm sixteen now, but until the war ended, I grew up on the plantation as well. When the war was over, and my parents realized we were free, we moved to Memphis to begin a new life."

Images swarmed into Felicia's mind as she spoke. "I was only eight when we moved to Memphis. My parents wanted me to have a better life than they'd had, so they made sure I went to school at one of the Freedmen's Bureau schools in the city. I loved to learn, and I loved to go to school. My daddy and mama both got jobs, but they didn't make much money. Still, we were happy. We lived in a very simple shack, but we had enough to eat, and there was love and laughter in our home."

Felicia paused as the memories took a dark turn. "That is, until May of 1866. I didn't understand it at the time because I was so little. I know now that racial tensions had been increasing in Memphis ever since the end of the war. It was like a keg of gunpowder ready to explode. It exploded on May 1st." Her insides tightened as the images exploded in her mind as violently as the keg of gunpowder had exploded that day.

Felicia took a deep breath, fighting for control. When she looked down, she saw Sojourner staring at her steadily, her dark eyes offering strength and courage. Felicia gazed into her eyes until she felt her insides settle again. "The Memphis riots started on May 1st. There were three days of killing and violence," she said steadily. "The Irish policemen of Memphis decided to teach the blacks what they believed their place should be. I went to school that morning because no one knew what was about to happen. My teacher, when he became aware of the violence, sent us back home."

She backtracked, knowing she'd left out an important part of the story. "A couple days earlier, while I was at school, I met a man named Moses. He came by the school with some out-of-town reporters who were writing about the situation in Memphis. I didn't know then who he would become in my life, but I knew he was very kind." She paused, collecting her thoughts.

"When our teacher told us to go home, I ran back to our house as fast as I could. We thought we would be safe if we stayed inside, but that wasn't true. Sometime in the afternoon, we heard someone pounding on our door. A minute later, they kicked it open." Felicia let the pain in her voice flow freely. "It was some Irish policemen. They demanded my daddy come outside. My mama begged him to not do it, but he knew that if he stayed inside, they would only come in after Mama and me."

Felicia closed her eyes briefly, engulfed with pain as she remembered. Taking a deep breath, she forced herself to continue. "Daddy heard one of the policemen say he was going to rape my mama. When he heard that, he did what any husband would do, and he tried to protect his wife. He had a knife with him. He attacked the policeman who said he was going to rape my mama. He stabbed the policeman, but the others shot my daddy and killed him. My mama and I were inside, watching what happened."

Felicia blinked away the tears filling her eyes and forged on. "My mama raced outside to help my daddy.

She threw herself down on the ground beside him. I guess she believed the policemen wouldn't shoot a grieving wife. She was wrong. They shot her in the head."

Felicia stopped again to collect herself. She had relived that experience countless times since it happened, but standing here in front of these people and telling her story brought it back with a vividness she could hardly bear. She risked a look at her audience. Every person she saw was staring at her with looks of horror and grief, tears streaming down every woman's face. Their compassion gave her strength to continue.

"All I wanted was to be with my mama and daddy when they were shot. I started screaming and ran outside, demanding to know why the policemen shot them. I remember now that they raised their pistols to shoot me too, but they stopped before they killed me. Two other men appeared out of nowhere. I recognized one of them as one of the reporters who had come to the school. His name was Matthew Justin. I didn't know who the other one was. I know now that his name was Robert Borden. At about the same time, I saw Moses hiding in the shadows beside the building across from my house. Moses is black, so he knew better than to come out in the open. He was the very kind man I had met at school. I didn't know what he was doing there, but he motioned for me to stay quiet. I was so terrified I did what he told me to do."

Complete silence followed her shocking statements.

"Matthew and Robert pretended they were out to kill black people too," Felicia said quietly. "When they got close to the police, they knocked them out with heavy pieces of wood they were carrying. As soon as the policemen fell, Moses dashed across the road and scooped me up into his arms. I imagine I was in shock. He told me to climb onto his back, so I did what he said. It took us a long time to get back to Fort Pickering, where he was staying. We had to duck into dark alleys and dodge between groups of rioters. I remember very little of that because I was focused on holding onto Moses' back. He told me I had to be quiet, but I cried silently for my parents the whole time."

Felicia wiped at her tears and straightened her shoulders. "While I grieved my parents, the entire city of Memphis was in chaos. Blacks were being gunned down in the streets. They were being raped, beaten, and robbed. When it was over, roughly fifty blacks had been killed. Almost three hundred were wounded. More than one hundred homes, schools, and churches were burned. I know all those numbers now. At the time, all I knew was that my mama and daddy were dead. I couldn't close my eyes without seeing them lying in pools of their own blood."

She looked up at her audience, fighting to keep her thoughts in order. "When the riot was over, Moses came to me and asked if he could take me home with him to Virginia. I didn't know where Virginia was, but I knew I didn't have any other family that would take me in. I didn't have any family at all. Moses Samuels was a kind man and he'd saved me, so I agreed to go. I had no idea what I was getting myself into."

When she smiled, it was genuine. "That was the day my entire life changed. Cromwell Plantation, outside Richmond, is beautiful. The Samuels, Moses and Rose, adopted me fairly soon after I arrived. I have a little brother named John, a little sister named Hope, and another little brother named Jed, who is also adopted. His mother and father were killed by the KKK down in North Carolina last year."

Felicia's smile faded as she thought of Jed's pain. "My daddy, Moses Samuels, used to be a slave on Cromwell Plantation. The plantation owner, Thomas Cromwell, changed his views on slavery during the war, and realized how wrong it was. He's a wonderful man whom I love very much. He's a mentor and teacher for me, and he lets me spend every hour I'm home in his library. He buys me new books that he knows I'll be interested in."

She paused to make sure she was telling the story correctly. "After the war, some things came to light. My mama found out that she was actually Mr. Cromwell's half-sister. Her mama had been raped by Mr. Cromwell's father. My grandmother, whom I never got to meet, had twins, but one of them came out looking white. He was sent away from the plantation and was adopted by a white man, but my mama eventually found him. I love my Uncle Jeremy."

She smiled. "I know you have many questions that I don't have time to answer. It's an unbelievable story, but every word of it is true. When Mr. Cromwell discovered the truth about everything, he decided to make my daddy half-owner of Cromwell Plantation."

Felicia understood the shocked looks on people's faces. "It's true," she assured them. "My daddy, Moses Samuels, is half-owner of Cromwell Plantation. They run it differently than other plantations. The workers are paid well, and they also receive a percentage of the profits at the end of the harvest. Everyone works hard, and the plantation is quite successful."

Felicia loved the excitement vibrating through the audience. "My mama, Rose Samuels, is a schoolteacher. She started and runs the school on the edge of the plantation, for both white and black students." She frowned. "The Virginia Board of Education mandated last year that black and white students can't go to school together anymore, so they built another building right next to the first one and made sure everyone shares the same playground."

Most members of the audience shook their heads with disgust, continuing to listen avidly.

"My mama grew up on Cromwell Plantation as the slave of Carrie Cromwell Wallington, but they've been best friends for all their lives.

Carrie is now a doctor. She and another friend, Dr. Janie Justin, run a clinic on the plantation that takes care of everyone in the area, regardless of their color. We realize we live a different existence than most areas of the South, but we hope that one day the entire South will be the same."

Felicia took a deep breath, knowing the next part of her speech was the most important.

## Chapter Twenty-Four

"My first mama used to tell me that education was the key to me having a better life. She made sure I went to school, and that I learned how to read and write, even though she never did. When I went to live on Cromwell Plantation, I decided I had to learn everything I could in order to make this country better for black people. I had to help change things so people like my parents wouldn't continue to die. I went to school, but I also spent most of my time in the plantation library. It is full of amazing books!" she said enthusiastically.

"I discovered that the more I learned, the more I wanted to know. I know I'm intelligent, because I'm a student at Oberlin College in Ohio. I was the youngest person to ever be admitted to study there. I'm not saying that to boast," Felicia said hastily. "It's to let you know how important I think it is for black people to learn everything they can. We live in a country that wants to keep us down. There are a lot of people who don't believe we should be slaves, but that doesn't mean they think we're equal."

Felicia smiled at her audience. "I know this room is full of people who view me as an equal, however I believe you would agree you're not the majority in the United States." She watched as most of the people nodded solemnly. "Like Sojourner, I have two strikes against me. I'm black, and I'm a woman. I suppose my third strike is that I'm so young, but I'll grow out of that."

The room rippled with laughter.

"I've had to fight for everything I've gotten. I've been extremely fortunate to be a student at Oberlin. I'm also quite aware that Oberlin doesn't represent the majority of America either. When I leave the grounds of the college, I realize I'm at risk."

Felicia stood straight and let her gaze sweep the room, feeling strength flow through her. "That has to change for *every* women. I know I'm young, but I also believe that what I've experienced has made me see things differently. I'm aware of the privileges I've been given by being adopted by the Samuels. I don't take that lightly. I believe I have a very serious responsibility to help make things better in the United States."

Her eyes swept the room. She took the time to let her gaze rest on every young person in the audience, gratified they were listening so intently. "I don't care how old you are. You can make a difference. No matter your color, if you're going to help change things in this country, you have to take it seriously. If you have a chance to go to a university, *go*. There are many people who don't have high expectations for women because they believe we're lesser than men."

Felicia's voice sharpened. "That's utter nonsense. It doesn't matter what expectations others have for you. What matters is the expectations you have for yourself. Set them high. What do you want for your life? Forget what anybody else says about your ability to achieve them. You have to believe in your own abilities."

She smiled as each person in the room nodded their confirmation, with some looking quite uncomfortable. "I knew I wanted to go to college, and I knew I wanted to learn all I could, but until recently I didn't really know what I wanted to do. I do now," Felicia declared. "I'm going to become a businesswoman." Saying the words out loud made her feel stronger.

Felicia had stepped onto the stage wondering what she would say. Hearing the words pour from her mouth had given her a confidence and belief she hadn't had before she started speaking. "Abby Cromwell is married to Mr. Thomas Cromwell, the owner of the plantation. She's a very powerful woman. She was living in Philadelphia, married to the owner of several textile factories, when her first husband died. Everyone expected her to hand over the ownership of the factories to men. She refused to do that. Instead, she decided to run them herself. That was fifteen years ago. She was threatened and harassed for not doing what others expected her to do, but she's been very successful. She and Mr. Cromwell run the factories together now, yet she has maintained sole ownership of the ones she had with her first husband."

Felicia took a deep breath. "I expect to be threatened and harassed for pursuing what I dream of doing. I don't yet know what kind of business I want to be in, but I believe it will become clear in time. What I do know is that money is power in this country. The more power I have, the more I will be able to help young black women fight back against the prejudice that exists in this country."

She gazed around at her audience. "Some of you listening to me right now are just beginning your lives. Others, probably most of you, are already successful. I believe you can give great opportunities to those who desire to move beyond societal restrictions. It doesn't matter if you help white or black women, though I hope you'll do both," Felicia said earnestly.

When she looked down at Sojourner, she was encouraged by the broad smile of approval spread across her face. Felicia lifted her eyes to the audience again. "I want to thank everyone who is here. I realize most of you in this room fought hard for the abolition of slavery. Thank you. I also realize you're fighting for equality and for women's right to vote. I won't add to what Sojourner Truth has already said today about that, because no one can say it quite as eloquently as she did, but I l thank you for joining in the fight for us."

Felicia paused, deciding how she wanted to finish. "My mother, Carrie Cromwell, Abby Cromwell, and other women in my life tell me that while they may never gain their ability to vote, they believe it will happen. They believe it will be my generation who makes it happen.

I hope with my whole heart that these powerful women I know, and those of you here in this room, will gain the vote in this lifetime. I promise I won't stop fighting until every woman can cast their ballot and have a say in this country. I promise I won't stop encouraging other young women to take a stand and carry on the battle you have started!"

Felicia smiled brightly. "Thank you for the opportunity to speak to you today." She moved away from the podium to take a seat by Sojourner, but the elderly activist held up a hand to stop her.

Moments later, everyone in the room was on their feet, applauding her.

Sojourner embraced her after the building had cleared. "You did good, Felicia." Her caring eyes shone with approval. "I'm real proud of you."

Felicia smiled. "I was so afraid, but you were right. Once I started talking the words just came."

Sojourner smiled. "You have a gift, Felicia. I knew it when I met you at Oberlin. You had those people right in the palm of your hand today. People tell me I do the same thing, but you're only sixteen." She shook her head. "I hope I live a long time. I want to see what you do with your life, and with your gift." She cocked her head. "You mean what you said about going into business?"

"Yes," Felicia answered firmly. "I've seen what Abby has been able to do with the money she's made. She's put people through school. She bought the first horses for Cromwell Stables, now one of the most successful stables in the South. She and Mr. Cromwell started a factory in Moyamensing, Philadelphia to give people jobs. There's so much good that can be done when you have money."

"I reckon that be true," Sojourner said thoughtfully. "I reckon that be true."

The portly man who had driven them to Sojourner's house the day before appeared at the door to the church. "You ready, Sojourner?"

"I'm ready, Aaron." Sojourner turned to Felicia. "How tired are you?"

Felicia was exhausted, but she could tell by the shine in Sojourner's eyes that if she admitted to it, she was going to miss out on something wonderful. "I'm not tired in the least. What do you have in mind?"

"Ever heard of the Fisk Jubilee Singers?"

"Never."

"Well, girl, you're in for a treat. They happen to be in Washington, DC for a few days of their tour. Mrs. Gallery is gonna join us."

Sojourner explained about the Fisk Jubilee Singers as they traveled across the city. "These young people attend Fisk University in Nashville, Tennessee."

Felicia was immediately intrigued. "Isn't Fisk a relatively new school?"

"It sure is. It was founded by the American Missionary Association, right at the end of the war. They aim to educate freed slaves and other black students. The problem was that they were real close to running out of money." She smiled. "If you were already a businesswoman, you coulda helped them."

"I wish I could," Felicia said instantly. "Is the school going to close?"

"Not now that them young people are singing," Sojourner replied. "There's a white man named George White. He loves music and proving blacks be the intellectual equal of whites. Anyway, he chose nine black men and women, and created an *a cappella* group to sing around the country. They been following the path of the Underground Railroad."

Felicia was delighted. "That sounds wonderful!"

"I ain't heard them yet, but I'm told they're right fine singers. They only been singing together for 'bout a year now, but they're sending money back to the college real regular. I imagine it will only get better." Sojourner chuckled. "Course, most white people don't know what to do with black people singing."

"What do you mean?" Felicia asked.

"Well, I ain't never seen black people singing on a stage," Sojourner answered. "I do some singing when I speak, but it ain't the same. White folks ain't used to seeing nothing but pretend black people singing."

Felicia was confused. "*Pretend* black people?"

"Yep." Sojourner cackled with amusement. "I heard the people get confused because there are actually genuine Negroes up on the stage. Up till now, the only black people on stage be white people who use burnt cork to make themselves *look* black while they sing our songs."

"Pretend black people singing our songs?" Felicia asked indignantly. "That's just wrong!"

Sojourner agreed. "Bout time they got some real Black folks up on the stage. I been looking forward to this ever since I heard about it."

"Where did the name Jubilee Singers come from?" Felicia asked. She was aware the music director had created an innovative business solution to a very real problem. She wanted to know all she could.

"Well, things didn't start out real easy for them. They weren't making much money, and they was getting real discouraged. Mr. White went off on his own to pray over it for a while." Sojourner's eyes shone with approval. "He done got the message that they needed a new name that would grab people's attention." She paused. "You know, Felicia, ain't no matter what you got to say if you don't first get people's attention."

Felicia knew that was true.

"Mr. White came back and told them young'uns that they were gonna be called the Jubilee Singers because of the Jewish year of Jubilee," Sojourner announced. "Jubilee be talked about in the book of Leviticus in the Good Book. When fifty Pentecosts go by, it is followed by a year of Jubilee. That be the time when slaves get set free. Since most of the young people going to school at Fisk University started out as slaves, the name seemed to be fitting."

As Sojourner finished her explanation, the carriage pulled up in front of the church hosting the performance.

Connie Gallery waited on the church steps for them. "Hello, Sojourner. Hello, Felicia," she called. She took Felicia's hand as she stepped down from the carriage. "How did your speech go? I'm sorry I couldn't be there for it, but I had another responsibility."

Felicia knew Mrs. Gallery had been meeting with Susan B. Anthony in regard to suffrage issues. "I think it went well."

"*Well?*" Sojourner scoffed. "This girl be a natural. Whole place stood up and clapped for her. She got a whole lot of people thinking, that's for sure!"

Connie clapped her hands. "Felicia, that's wonderful!"

"Thank you," Felicia said shyly. "Sojourner was the one who was spectacular, however. Everyone loved her."

"Been loving me a long time," Sojourner said casually. "That's good, but they needed to hear a new voice. A young voice. That's what they got to hear today." She turned to Connie. "You shoulda seen the young people in that room. They looked like they been struck by lightning when Felicia got near the end of her speech."

"Did you read it?" Connie asked.

"Not a word of it," Felicia replied. "Sojourner was right. When I started talking, my story just flowed out."

Felicia was certain she'd never enjoyed anything as much as she enjoyed the Fisk Jubilee Singers. To see people close to her age singing the spirituals she'd grown up with on the plantation was wonderful. Their voices blended together perfectly, and their faces glowed with purpose and joy while they sang.

One of the singers approached them at the end of the concert, her eyes wide with awe. "Are you Sojourner Truth?"

"That's right, miss. I have to tell you that tonight was a pure joy. All you young'uns got the voices of angels. I reckon God was singing right through you."

"Thank you, Mrs. Truth. That means so much to me. You've been one of my heroes for a long time. It's such an honor to meet you. I'm told we're going to get to hear you speak while we're here. I can hardly wait."

"What's your name, young lady?"

"I'm Ella Sheppard."

"Well, Ella Sheppard. I got someone right here you should meet." Sojourner pulled Felicia forward. "This here is Felicia Samuels. She goes to Oberlin up in Ohio. More important, though, she is speaking with me for the next month. You gonna get to hear both of us."

Ella smiled at Felicia brightly. "That's wonderful! I can't wait to hear what you have to say." She hesitated. "Were you a slave, too?"

"Yes, until the war ended," Felicia replied. "Your concert tonight was so wonderful! I closed my eyes and felt like I was back on the plantation, listening to the slaves sing late at night after a long day in the fields."

Ella nodded. "At first, I was uncomfortable with singing the songs. I could remember the same thing you do. These are songs that were sacred to our parents. It felt wrong to sing them for entertainment. When our people were slaves, they used them in their worship and the songs gave them the strength to keep going."

Felicia knew that was true. "Surely they must be glad the songs are making it possible for Fisk University to stay open."

"That's what we decided. When we realized how many hearts are being opened by our songs, we began to appreciate the wonderful beauty and power of them." Ella smiled. "It really is like being in church when we sing, no matter where we are."

"Course it is, Ella," Sojourner said. "God hears the cry of our hearts every single time we open our mouth in song."

Ella gazed at her eagerly. "Will you sing when we come to hear you speak? I hear you are an amazing singer."

Sojourner chuckled. "I reckon I'm real fond of singing, Ella. Since all you young'uns are gonna be there, I reckon I'll lift my voice in song for you."

"Will you sing *Valiant Soldiers*?"

Felicia cocked a brow. "You didn't sing that song today."

"I only sing it when I feel like I oughta." Sojourner turned to Ella. "How do you know about *Valiant Soldiers*?"

"My mama and daddy heard you sing it one time when they went to hear you speak. They talked about it for days. They told me you wrote it for the first Michigan regiment of colored soldiers."

"That's right," Sojourner replied. "The Lord gave me a real fine song."

Ella hesitated. "Can I ask you one more question?" When Sojourner nodded, she continued. "How did you get your name?"

Sojourner smiled serenely. "My name started out to be Isabella. I carried that name a good long time, but when I left the house of bondage, I left everything behind. I wasn't going to keep nothing of slavery in me, so I went to the Lord and asked him to give me a new name. The Lord done gave me the name

Sojourner because I was to travel up and down the land, showing people their sins and being a sign to them." She paused. "Sojourner is a real good name, but I told the Lord I wanted two names 'cause everybody else had two names. The Lord gave me Truth, because I was to declare truth to the people. The truth is powerful, and it will always prevail."

"Thank you," Ella said sincerely. "I agree it's a perfect name. I look forward to hearing you at the meeting we attend."

"That will be nice, Ella," Sojourner said. "Now, it's late, so we got to go on and head for home.

Sojourner had retired for the night, but Felicia was too excited to attempt sleep. She curled up on her windowsill and stared out at the lanterns glowing through the city. The entire day had been extraordinary.

Too exhausted to move, she called out to the person who tapped on her door. "Come in."

Connie poked her head in. "Too tired for a little talk?"

Felicia shook her head. "I'm too excited to even close my eyes." She decided to not mention the angst boiling in her. "Please come in, Mrs. Gallery." She was happy to see her professor. Perhaps talking about the day would allow her to relax enough to sleep.

Connie settled down on the windowsill beside her. "I'm very proud of you. Sojourner told me a little more about how extraordinary you were on the stage."

Felicia warmed with pleasure. "Thank you. I believe it helped me as much as it helped everyone else."

Connie raised a brow. "What do you mean?"

Felicia hesitated as she tried to order her thoughts. "I knew my job was to go up and give people a reason to hope. My problem was that I was struggling with my own hope." She paused, appreciative when Connie remained silent. She knew her professor was giving her time to decide how to say what she needed to say. "My years at Oberlin have been amazing. I've felt safe, and I've had a chance to do things and learn things that most black people haven't had. I appreciate all of it, but I will graduate in a few months." She took a deep breath. "When I do, I'll be just another black woman in America."

Felicia turned to gaze out the window, letting the wind caress her face. "Things are going to be hard for blacks for a long time, Mrs. Gallery." She picked up the letter that had been waiting for her when she arrived back at her lodging. "The Cromwell Stables barn was torched last week. It burned to the ground. If there hadn't been a warning, every horse in it would have died." Her voice choked as she thought about it.

"I'm so sorry," Mrs. Gallery responded, her eyes gleaming with compassion. "How did it happen?"

"A white man, egged on by a member of the KKK who tried to attack the plantation several years ago, snuck through the woods and set it on fire. He was angry because Anthony and Carrie rescued his wife and children from being beaten. They took them to Philadelphia and reunited them with the wife's family so they would be safe."

Mrs. Gallery nodded thoughtfully. "So even though it was done by a white man, it wasn't really a racial attack, was it? The KKK member may have used the opportunity to strike back against the plantation, but he wasn't really after black people. It sounds like he was striking back against the Cromwells."

"That's true," Felicia replied. "The KKK doesn't only go after blacks. There's a lot of hatred toward the plantation because they're employing freed slaves and paying them well. The KKK has tried to wreak havoc at the plantation many times." She scowled when she thought about Jed. "My little brother was traumatized again. It's bad enough that his parents were murdered. He thought he was safe on the plantation, but now he knows he's vulnerable."

"Jed is safe?" Connie asked keenly.

Felicia would never reveal the secret of the tunnel that had sheltered him during the attack. "Yes, he's safe."

Connie continued to gaze at her. "Something else is on your mind."

Felicia sighed. She should have known her professor would see more deeply into her thoughts. They'd had many in-depth conversations over the years. "My mother sent me an article that Matthew and Harold Justin wrote." Wordlessly, she handed it to her and watched as Mrs. Gallery's features tightened with anger and disgust.

"Unbelievable!" Connie snapped as she finished the article. "After all we've done to set the slaves free, people in the South have found a way to enslave them again?" Her eyes blazed with fury. "This has to stop."

Felicia sighed. "Unfortunately, until they change the Thirteenth Amendment, or write a new amendment that makes convict labor illegal, it won't change. America has found another way to wreak havoc on my people."

Connie eyed her more closely. "I'm sorry this is the country you're growing up in. You mentioned earlier that you'd found a way to have hope, even though you'd read this article. How did you do that?"

Felicia straightened. "As long as I'm breathing, I have a chance to change things. That gives me hope. When I was up on the stage today, I saw how people responded to what I was saying. They were really listening. After the meeting, I had the opportunity to talk to a group of girls close to my age. They thanked me and told me they were going to enroll in college. They told me they were going to join me in my fight for equality."

Connie grasped her hands and squeezed tightly. "That's wonderful, Felicia!"

"It's a small beginning," Felicia admitted. "I'm looking forward to talking to as many people as I can while I'm here with Sojourner."

"And after?"

Felicia managed a tired smile. "I'll give speeches every time I have the opportunity," she said.

"Sojourner also tells me you've decided to become a businesswoman."

"I have," Felicia said firmly. "I've seen how money can give you the opportunity to change things. It's going to be hard to be black in America for a very long time. I want to encourage and help other black people." She sighed. "I'm reminded every day how I have opportunities that most of my people don't have right now. It's not enough for me to be grateful. I have to make a commitment to change things."

Connie gazed at her. "I knew your mama and daddy well when they were in school at Oberlin. They attended many of my classes before they returned to the plantation. They would be very proud of you."

"I want them to be," Felicia replied. "If it weren't for them, I can't imagine where I would be now. Probably cleaning houses for some rich white person in Memphis." Her insides clenched as she thought of what her life would have become after her parents were murdered, if it hadn't been for Moses.

"How can I help you?" Connie asked quietly.

Felicia took a deep breath. She'd thought of this question ever since she'd made her announcement from the stage to become a businesswoman. "I want to meet successful black women business owners. Can you help me do that?"

"I can," Connie replied. "I would encourage you, though, to not limit yourself to just black women. All women are going against the tide to own businesses in America. You'll learn something from all of them."

"Like I have from Abby Cromwell," Felicia mused. "You're absolutely right. I know knowledge is power. I want to gain as much knowledge about business as I possibly can."

"Business knowledge is invaluable." Connie paused thoughtfully. "The most important thing you'll learn from women, however, is about how to stand against all the challenges that will be thrown at you to make you fail." She smiled. "Would you like to start day after tomorrow?"

Felicia gasped. "What do you mean?"

"I have a good friend here in Washington, DC. For right now, I'm going to keep her identity private. I believe she'll be more than willing to talk to you, but I want to ask her permission first."

"Of course," Felicia agreed. "Just the idea of it is quite exciting."

"While you're waiting to talk to a live person, I can tell you about a woman I find incredibly motivating. She's passed away now, but her legacy lives on."

"I can't wait to hear about her," Felicia said quickly, forgetting about her fatigue.

"Her name was Margaret Hardenbroeck. She was only twenty-two when she arrived in New Amsterdam in 1659."

"New Amsterdam became New York, didn't it?"

Connie nodded approvingly. "Very good. Yes, it did. When Margaret arrived, she was ambitious and ready to work. She already had a job lined up collecting debts for a cousin's business. Eventually, she married a wealthy merchant named Peter de Vries, but she was determined to continue to work. She became a business agent for several Dutch merchants. She sold cooking oil to the colonists and bought furs to send to Holland."

"Smart," Felicia said admiringly.

"Her husband died a little more than a year after their marriage. She inherited his estate and took over his business. She expanded her fur shipping operations in Holland, trading the furs for merchandise to sell back in the colonies. Of course, for the Dutch, it was not all that unusual for women to run businesses on equal footing with men." Connie smiled. "Dutch women called themselves 'she-merchants.'"

"*She-merchants*," Felicia murmured. "I love it!"

"Margaret went on to become the most successful and wealthiest she-merchant in the colonies. She purchased her own ship in order to increase her profits, and accumulated real estate holdings throughout the colonies."

"Brilliant," Felicia replied, her mind spinning with possibilities.

"Even more brilliant than you know," Connie said. "When she married again, she ensured that her wealth, properties, and independence were protected by choosing an *usus* marriage under Dutch law."

"*Usus*?" Felicia had never heard the term.

"Yes. Margaret rejected marital guardianship of her husband. She also rejected communal property and retained all that was hers prior to marriage. The only women who had that freedom were the Dutch inhabitants of New Amsterdam, because the colony operated under Amsterdam laws. The English women in every other colony would have lost their wealth to their new husband. It worked well for Margaret. When she died in 1691, she was the wealthiest woman in New York."

Felicia's eyes were wide. "What a woman! I wish she was around now to fight for equal rights."

"She would be cheering us on," Connie assured her. "She would also most likely be appalled at how little control women have over their lives now in the United States – including New York. She would have been at the forefront of our fight." Connie grinned. "Do you think you can sleep now?"

Felicia laughed. "I'm afraid I may never sleep again. You've given me so much to think about."

Connie stood. "I don't have the benefit of youth on my side, so I'm off to bed. I suggest you do the same."

Felicia's mind spun furiously as she thought about the events of the incredible day. To think that it was only her first full day in Washington, DC was truly unfathomable. She could only imagine what would happen in the month before she returned to Oberlin to finish her education.

Finally, somewhere around dawn, she slipped into an exhausted slumber.

## Chapter Twenty-Five

Felicia was thrilled to see another packed auditorium for the next day's meeting. She leaned over to talk to Sojourner. "Should I make my speech different today?"

Sojourner shrugged. "Speak what comes out of your heart, Felicia." She nodded over her shoulder. "I see some folks that were here yesterday. Only they got more people with them. Young people. I reckon they be here because of what you said. They want their friends to hear it because it struck them like that lightning I was talking about. Still, you got to say what God gives you to say. Nothing else matters more than that."

Once introduced, Sojourner stood and made her way to the front, warm applause welcoming her.

Felicia, not as nervous as she'd been the day before, was able to listen more closely. She leaned forward and fastened her eyes on Sojourner. She would never tire of the compassion and strength radiating from her wrinkled face.

"Good day," Sojourner began. "We got some real special young'uns with us today. For those of you who ain't heard of the Fisk Jubilee Singers, you need to find out where they gonna be in the city for the next few days and go hear them. I had me the pleasure of doing that last night. It was something I'll never forget." She waved a hand toward the singers seated in the middle of the auditorium. "Now, one of them be Miss Ella Sheppard. She asked me last night if I would sing *The Valiant Soldiers*."

Sojourner paused when enthusiastic clapping broke out. "I told her I would, so I reckon I'll start with that."

Her voice, strong and beautiful, filled the sanctuary.

> We are the valiant soldiers who've 'listed for the war;
> We are fighting for the Union, we are fighting for the law;
> We can shoot a rebel farther than a white man ever saw,
> As we go marching on.
>
> Glory, glory, hallelujah! Glory, glory, hallelujah!
> Glory, glory, hallelujah, as we go marching on.
>
> Look there above the center, where the flag is waving bright;
> We are going out of slavery, we are bound for freedom's light;
> We mean to show Jeff Davis how the Africans can fight,
> As we go marching on.
>
> Glory, glory, hallelujah! Glory, glory, hallelujah!

# Journey To Joy

Glory, glory, hallelujah, as we go marching on.

We are done with hoeing cotton, we are done with hoeing corn;
We are colored Yankee soldiers as sure as you are born.
When massa hears us shouting, he will think 'tis Gabriel's horn,
As we go marching on.

Glory, glory, hallelujah! Glory, glory, hallelujah!
Glory, glory, hallelujah, as we go marching on.

They will have to pay us wages, the wages of their sin;
They will have to bow their foreheads to their colored kith and kin;
They will have to give us house-room, or the roof will tumble in,
As we go marching on.

Glory, glory, hallelujah! Glory, glory, hallelujah!
Glory, glory, hallelujah, as we go marching on.

We hear the proclamation, massa, hush it as you will;
The birds will sing it to us, hopping on the cotton hill;
The possum up the gum tree couldn't keep it still,
As he went climbing on.

Glory, glory, hallelujah! Glory, glory, hallelujah!
Glory, glory, hallelujah, as we go marching on.

Father Abraham has spoken, and the message has been sent;
The prison doors have opened, and out the prisoners went

To join the sable army of African descent,
As we go marching on.

Glory, glory, hallelujah! Glory, glory, hallelujah!
Glory, glory, hallelujah, as we go marching on.

A hushed silence filled the room when the song ended.

Felicia took a deep breath, understanding anew why Sojourner had such a power over her listeners. Never had she heard a song sung with such passion and feeling. The glow on Sojourner's face was as forceful as her voice.

Sojourner smiled when applause broke out, but held up her hand to stop it soon after it began. "I wrote that song when I was enlisting black soldiers during the war. A war that was fought to grant freedom." Her bright eyes swept the room like a beacon. "Problem is, there ain't enough freedom in this country. Women are trying for liberty that requires no blood—that women shall have their rights. Rights that already belong to them. I reckon this country needs to give them what belongs to them."

Sojourner spoke eloquently for a long time. Her wit and wisdom, combined with solid common sense, held the audience spellbound. There was barely a stir while her voice rang out. "People figure I'm getting real old. I ain't ready to go yet, though. If you want me out of the world, you had better get the women voting soon. I shan't go until I can do that!" With those last powerful words, Sojourner nodded serenely and left the podium.

Felicia waited until the applause died down and took her place at the front. Her heart was beating fast, but this time it was from anticipation rather than nervousness. As her eyes swept the crowd in front of her, she wondered who was present that needed to hear what she had to say. Opening her mouth, she began to speak.

Halfway through her speech, Felicia noticed a white man seated near the back of the auditorium staring at her with hostility. His face was set in stern lines and his eyes were full of a fury that shocked her. She forced her eyes away from him, finding Ella Sheppard in the audience. Ella's brilliant smile helped to calm her nerves and enabled her to continue.

When the meeting was over and the auditorium was quiet, Felicia told Sojourner about the man who had frightened her.

"It happens, Felicia," Sojourner said calmly. "I lost track of the number of times men been sent in to scare me away from speaking. As long as we open our mouths and speak things they don't like, they're gonna try to stop us with fear."

"Have you ever been afraid?" Felicia asked, controlling her shudder as she thought of the man's eyes.

Sojourner gazed at her for a long moment. "Ain't a soul alive who hasn't been scared a time or two. You and I are probably gonna be scared more than that, 'cause we fighting a battle that men don't want us to fight. They for sure don't want us to win the battle. Being afraid ain't a weakness, Felicia. It's when you give into the fear that you let them win."

Felicia listened intently.

Connie Gallery was standing close by, listening to their conversation. "I hear you, Sojourner, but I believe Felicia has to be careful. You've never been sixteen when you were speaking. You're also tall and strong, even now. Felicia is none of those things, and she's quite young."

"That's true enough," Sojourner replied. "Connie makes a good point, Felicia. Besides that, things are changing in this country as fast as a storm approaching from the east. Now that all of us be free, white folks see us as more of a threat. They could make fun of an *old* black woman speaking on the stage, but you is a young, pretty girl. You're not so easy to make fun of. I reckon you best be careful."

Felicia listened but had no idea how to protect herself in Washington, DC. How would she *be careful*?

Connie endeavored to enlighten her. "It's not wise to go out by yourself, Felicia. It's probably not even safe to go out with just me, quite honestly. There are people who know what you look like now. As much as I would try, I don't know if I could protect you. If I were you, I would only go out when the driver is with you."

Felicia hoped her face didn't reflect her thoughts as she envisioned the slight, portly man.

Connie's chuckle told her she'd failed. "Aaron fought in the war and commanded his regiment. He's good with a gun, and he'll do whatever it takes to protect you. That's why Sojourner rides with him."

Felicia felt marginally better as she nodded her understanding. "Yes, ma'am."

Later that night, after an evening of laughter and talk with Sojourner and Connie, Felicia was ready for some much-needed sleep. First, she longed for some cool air to relax and refresh her. She slipped into a nightgown and a light robe before she moved to the windowsill. Leaning as far out as she could, she breathed in the night air.

She could smell the moisture that said a storm would soon descend upon the capital city. Her eyes scanned the horizon, but it was too dark to discern if there were storm clouds looming. She longed to watch the storm erupt over the city, certain lightning would illuminate the Capitol Rotunda in a spectacular way, but her body demanded sleep.

Felicia sighed and pulled her head back inside the window.

A loud crack of gunfire rang out. The window glass shattered, the fragments spraying toward her. Felicia dropped to the floor and covered her head with her hands just as another bullet tore through the room, lodging in the wall above her bed.

Felicia screamed and crawled frantically toward the door. She flung it open as Connie came racing down the hallway, her face white with alarm.

"Felicia!" Connie dropped to the floor, her wide eyes on the open door. "What happened?"

Felicia was shaking so hard she could barely speak. "Someone...shot through...my...window..." She shuddered and huddled close to her teacher.

"Are you hurt?" Connie cried. She leaned back and examined Felicia. "There's blood!"

"Blood?" Felicia whispered. She stilled long enough to determine if she felt like she'd been shot. The only thing she felt was a burning sensation. "The glass...it must have...cut me."

At that moment, Sojourner hurried down the hallway. "Felicia! Child, what happened?"

"Someone shot at her through the window," Connie said grimly.

Felicia shuddered again. "I was on the...windowsill. My head was outside." She began to tremble all over. "I had just pulled back inside. Another...second..." She covered her eyes and began to cry.

Connie pulled her close. "It's alright, Felicia. You're alright," she said soothingly.

Felicia tried to pull away. "I'll get blood on you," she gasped.

"Blood will wash out," Connie said, holding her tightly. "You're safe now. You're safe."

Felicia shook her head. "What if he tries to get in the house?" Her heart pounded with fear.

Sojourner knelt down and took Felicia's face in her hands. "Aaron went outside as soon as he heard the shots. Whoever it was won't still be there. Look at me, Felicia."

Felicia took a deep breath as she gazed up into the wise woman's face, tears continuing to stream from her eyes.

"You didn't get shot, Felicia. Another second and you would have been. Don't you know the Good Lord done protected you? I reckon it was God that pulled your head back in that window. It was God that kept those bullets from going into you. God ain't done with you." Sojourner's voice rang with confidence and strength.

Felicia tried to hear the calm words over the terror washing through her.

Sojourner continued to gaze into her eyes. "I should have been dead a whole lot of times, Felicia. I been beat hard enough to die more than once, but I be right here. God ain't done with me yet, just like he ain't done with you." She tilted Felicia's face so she could see into her eyes more clearly.

Felicia felt strength pouring into her through the old woman's eyes. She took steadying breaths as she peered into the dark pools of compassion. Finally, she nodded. "Alright," she whispered. "I'm alright."

Sojourner nodded. "That be the truth."

Aaron appeared behind them. "You alright, Miss Felicia?"

Felicia took a deep breath and wiped away the remainder of her tears. "I'm alright, Aaron. Thank you."

"That coward run off into the night?" Sojourner asked sternly.

"He did," Aaron assured her. "I walked all around. There ain't nobody out there." He patted his waistband. "Still, now that I know Miss Felicia is alright, I'm gonna sit out on the porch for the rest of the night and keep watch." He reached down and touched Felicia's shoulder. "You go ahead and sleep, girl. I ain't gonna let nobody hurt you."

Felicia nodded, aware that one more second with her head out the window, and she would most likely be dead. Still, it gave her comfort to think of the war veteran stationed on the porch under her window. "Thank you, Aaron."

Aaron turned to Sojourner. "I can't do nothing about that window until tomorrow, Sojourner."

"I don't reckon you can. I'm gonna put Felicia in the room next to mine." Sojourner eyed Felicia. "You ain't gonna stay in this room tonight."

Felicia managed a wan smile. "You'll get no argument from me." She couldn't imagine being able to close her eyes in that room ever again. Protected by God or not, whoever tried to shoot her knew where she was. "Do you think it was the man from the meeting?" she whispered, swallowing hard to block the memory of his furious eyes.

"Ain't no way of knowing," Sojourner replied. "It coulda been him, but it could have also been someone else. Might never know."

Sojourner was probably right, but there was no comfort in her words.

"I'm going down to get you some warm milk," Connie said. "You come on down with me so I can clean up those cuts."

For the first time, Felicia remembered the cuts from the breaking glass. She looked down with dismay. "I'm covered with blood." At that moment, she also became aware of the stinging pain.

"I have an extra nightgown and robe," Connie assured her. "I'll help you clean up and then we'll have that milk."

Felicia allowed herself to be led down the hall. She would never forget the night her parents had been killed, but this felt different. The men in Memphis had come in broad daylight and killed her parents out of hatred, simply because they were black and helpless. The man who had tried to shoot her had appeared in the dark of the night, attempting to kill her because she was trying to make things better for her race.

Bandaged and attired in a fresh gown and robe, Felicia sipped the milk Connie had prepared for her. The soothing warmth allowed her to finally relax.

Sojourner, after showing Felicia her room, had retired for the evening.

"Better?" Connie asked.

Felicia nodded, choosing to not mention the continued sting from her cuts. Connie had done her best to treat them. Felicia pushed away her longing for

Carrie. She was grateful none of the flying glass had gone into her eyes.

"You don't need to speak tomorrow," Connie said.

Felicia smiled. "I'm speaking," she said firmly. "Now, perhaps more than ever, I realize how important it is. I'm not going to let fear stop me."

Connie eyed her. "You're quite extraordinary."

Felicia shrugged. "No more than all the men and women who have fought this battle before me. I've been surrounded by brave people who refuse to let fear keep them from doing what they believe they're meant to do." Saying the words helped ease the fear lurking in the corners of her mind.

"You should let your parents know what happened."

Felicia considered Connie's declaration for a moment but shook her head. "All they'll do is worry."

"They're worried anyway," Connie told her with a smile. "Your mama wrote me several weeks ago. I promised I would take good care of you and let her know if something happened."

"That sounds like Mama. Still…" Felicia thought of the ramifications of telling her parents she'd almost been shot.

"If you don't tell them, I'm sending a telegram tomorrow," Connie said. "If you were my daughter, I'd want to know."

Felicia sighed. "What can they do? They'll only feel helpless and be afraid for me."

"They already feel afraid and helpless," Connie said gently. "They're letting you do this because they know how important your voice is to the world, and because they know how badly you want to do it."

Felicia knew that was true. "Telling them will only make them more afraid."

Connie eyed her. "Would you want to know if it were *your* daughter?"

"I suppose so," Felicia admitted. "I don't know how to tell them, though. Will you do it for me?"

"I will," Connie promised. "A telegram will go out tomorrow."

Felicia felt a combination of relief and worry, but she knew it was out of her hands. She swallowed the last of her warm milk and stood. "I'm going to bed. Thank you for taking care of me."

"Do you think you can sleep?" Connie asked. "If you need me, you know where my room is."

Felicia hugged her warmly. She doubted she would sleep anytime soon, but her professor needed rest after the long day and night. "I'll be fine," she replied.

Only she knew how untrue that was.

## Chapter Twenty-Six

Felicia took a deep breath and walked to the podium the next day. She faced the audience with a warm smile, understanding the alarmed looks on their faces. "Last night," she began, "someone tried to kill me."

She waited until the gasps died down. She and Sojourner had agreed she would be the one to explain the bandages on her face.

"Most of you haven't heard my story yet. Before I share it, I want to tell you what I realized at some point last night. I refused to sleep because I wanted to *think* my way through the fear that gripped me after a bullet exploded through my window. I'm used to utilizing my brain to accomplish what I want. I think the sun was close to coming up when I finally realized all my *thinking* wouldn't make my fear go away." Felicia straightened her shoulders. "The only thing that conquers fear is action. That's why I'm here today."

Felicia allowed her eyes to sweep the audience, taking strength from the encouragement and compassion she saw shining from people's eyes. "There isn't a person alive who doesn't feel fear, but I suppose black people in America feel it even more. We have a lot of reasons to be afraid," she said bluntly. "I realized something last night, though. Fear is the one thing that can truly defeat me." Her voice rang out with the conviction that had come to her during the night. "Only fear can defeat life."

Felicia took a deep breath before she continued. "I was so happy and relaxed when I went to my room last night. I leaned out my window to enjoy the fresh breeze and the incoming storm. I thought about waiting for the storm to erupt, but I was too tired, so I pulled my head back in so I could sleep. That was when a bullet shattered the glass above my head. Another one was stopped by my bedroom wall."

Horrified gasps sounded.

Felicia touched her face. "Whoever tried to kill me, they failed." Her eyes searched the room, wondering if she would see the same man who had stared at her with such fury the day before. She was actually disappointed when she didn't see him. She wanted him to know she wasn't going to let fear stop her. Perhaps he was the one who was too afraid to show his face again. Thinking that only increased her courage.

"Fear goes for your weakest spot," she continued. "It always begins in your mind." She thought about how happy she'd been as she breathed in the night air. "One minute you're feeling calm. Then fear comes into your mind like a spy and tries to steal your peace." Felicia took a deep breath and touched the bandages on her face. "I almost let the fear rob my peace," she admitted. "I wasn't sure I could get back on this stage and continue to make myself a target. Except, I knew whoever tried to shoot me was counting on that. When he didn't kill me, I know he believed I would be too afraid to do what I'm doing."

Felicia smiled. "I'm afraid he's going to be sorely disappointed. He failed to kill me, and he has failed to silence me." She met Sojourner's eyes. "God isn't done with me. Until he is, no one will be able to stop me."

Hearty *amens* broke out around the room.

"There's not a black person in this room who doesn't have reason to be afraid," Felicia said. "The truth is that there isn't a black person in this country who doesn't have reason to be afraid. Let me tell you my story."

Felicia spoke eloquently, fueled by the passion in her heart. Passion that burned more brightly after her near brush with death the night before. When she finished, she pulled out a sheet of paper. "I wrote something this afternoon. I want to share it with you now."

Felicia stood straight and tall. Her voice rang through the auditorium as she began to read.

Black In America

I stand before you now
In a country that hates me
In a country that wants to wipe me from existence
Because I am Black.

I stand before you now
In a country that wrapped us in chains
That lashed our bloody bodies
Because we are Black.

I stand before you now
In a country that says I am free
But knows not the meaning of free
Because I am Black.

I stand before you now
In a country determined to hold us yet as slaves
To control our destiny
Because we are Black.

I stand before you now
In a country that must hear our voices
That must see our courage
Because we are Black.

I stand before you now
As a woman
A Black Woman in America
Determined to be heard.

I stand before you now
And tell you I will not be silenced
I will lift my voice
And I will be heard.

I stand before you now
To tell *you* to raise your voice
To not give in to fear
To be proud of being Black.

I am a woman
A Black Woman in America
Lifting my voice with pride
Because I will be heard.

I am proud to be Black in America.

Felicia stopped reading and lifted her eyes. A hushed silence met her, but barely for a moment.

The entire auditorium rose to their feet and applauded. While Felicia appreciated the applause, there was only one opinion that mattered to her in that instance. When her eyes settled on Sojourner, she was warmed by the bright smile and the pride beaming on the elderly woman's face.

Sojourner was the first to come to her as she stepped down from the podium. "You are a wonder, child," she whispered as she wrapped her in strong arms. "I'm so proud of you."

Felicia hugged her fiercely. "You're the one who reminded me that I can never let fear steal my voice. Thank you."

Carrie walked into the barn, greeted by Granite's glad whinny. She inhaled deeply. The smell of the new wood, merged with the odor of horses, grain, and hay, never failed to delight her. She gazed around and smiled up at the new, high ceiling.

"You ever gonna quit doing that, Carrie Girl?"

Carrie grinned at Miles. "I don't think so. I can hardly believe Susan and I own this magnificent barn."

"It weren't so bad before," Miles protested mildly.

Carrie narrowed her eyes. "You know you love it every bit as much as I do. Especially that brand new apartment you and Annie live in. It's twice the size of your old one."

"The old one was just fine," Miles responded laconically.

Carrie waved her hand. "Oh, play your games with someone else. You know as well as I do that you and Annie are wildly happy up there."

Miles chuckled. "I reckon I never dreamed of living in a place like that in my whole life," he admitted. "My Annie is about to get a swelled head. She's thinkin' she's some kind of queen."

"I *am* a queen," Annie said loftily as she sailed down the stairs. "Course, this queen gotta go do a mess of cookin' for ever'body in my kingdom." She lifted her head high and disappeared out the barn door.

Miles stared after her. "She's something, ain't she?"

Carrie was warmed by the love shining in his eyes. "That she is, my friend. That she is. There isn't a single person on the plantation that would have a clue what to do without Annie to cook for us, look over us, and scold us when we need it."

"She's a keeper, that's for sure," Miles agreed.

Carrie looked at him more closely and saw the intensity shining in his eyes. "What are you thinking?"

Miles shrugged. "That night I run away from here, back before the war, I could never have dreamed that I would be back here with a beautiful wife, a job I couldn't never have dreamed up when I was a slave, and now a brand-new place to live in." He shook his head. "I be one lucky man."

Carrie hugged him tightly. "I still remember the night I discovered you had escaped. I was happy for you, but I didn't know what I was going to do without you. Cromwell Plantation was never the same without you here. I'm so glad you came back."

"Me too, Carrie Girl. Me too." Miles laughed when Granite pawed his stall and snorted impatiently. "My Annie might be the queen around here, but that little man be convinced he's the prince."

Carrie laughed. "I think he might have bypassed the princely part and gone straight to being king."

Granite snorted again and bobbed his head.

Miles laughed loudly. "Ain't nobody gonna convince him he ain't the center of the universe."

"That's because he is," Carrie said happily. She hurried over to open his stall door and threw her arms around his neck. Granite nickered and shoved his head into her, calming immediately as she stroked his face.

Miles shook his head. "You two are somethin'. Ain't never seen nothin' like it." He headed toward the tack room. "I got me some tack to oil in here. I'll be seein' you later."

Carrie strolled along the riverbank, Granite pulling chunks of grass from the clearing above the shoreline as he kept pace with her. Weaned from No Regrets until a month earlier, he had adjusted remarkably well.

She was glad it was high tide. She loved the sound of the waves lapping at her feet, pebbles rolling in and out with the little waves created by a brisk wind that made the high temperatures more bearable.

When she reached the sandy little cove that stretched further inland, she took off her boots and ran into the cool water. She longed to strip off her breeches and shirt, but wasn't quite able to bring herself to go that far. She plunged beneath the water, swimming until lack of air forced her to the surface. A shrill whinny made her look toward shore.

Granite stood on the beach, his ears pricked forward as he stared at her.

Carrie laughed. "I'm alright, boy! Would you like to come in?"

Granite snorted and pawed the dirt, sending it flying behind him.

Carrie laughed louder. "Come on, Granite! You'll love it!"

Granite snorted again and began to walk forward slowly. He shook his head when he was up to his knees in the water and began to paw again. He looked behind him with surprise when water sprayed all around and over him.

"It feels good, doesn't it?" Carrie treaded water, wondering if he would continue. At nearly eight months old, Granite was getting bolder, but he was also learning how to navigate life without his mother by his side. He had quit calling out for her, but Carrie could tell he missed her.

Granite took another few steps, plowing to a stop when the water lapped at his belly. He looked down, stared into the waves, and plunged his muzzle in to take a long drink.

Carrie continued to tread water out in the deeper part. The river felt splendid. She ducked under and allowed herself to lean back into a float. Instead of pulling her under, her breeches seemed to have transformed into a soggy flotation device.

Carrie gazed up at the puffy clouds piling up on the horizon. She knew it meant they were in for a late afternoon thunderstorm, but right now the sun shone brightly. It would take a few hours for the breeze to deliver the clouds to their location.

"Mama!"

Carrie righted herself in the water and grinned in the direction of the shoreline. "Minnie! Frances!" She frowned suddenly. "What are you two doing out here by yourselves?" She didn't mean to sound sharp, but even though they'd tightened security measures ever since the attack on the barn, she worried about safety. She tried hard to control her concern, but sometimes it got away from her. Abe Cummings was dead, but the KKK member who had prodded him into burning the barn, and most likely killed him, could still be in the area. None of them went anywhere without being armed now, and they had all agreed the children should always be with an adult.

"We're not alone," Frances called back. She glanced over her shoulder. "Abby and Hope are with us."

Carrie relaxed as Abby emerged from the woods.

"I'm sorry," Abby called. "I'm afraid my grandchildren are much faster than I am." She answered Carrie's unspoken question. "Russell, Jed, and John are all with Moses out in the fields. Annie is teaching Bridget how to make strawberry shortcake."

Carrie laughed at the image of Bridget demanding attention from within the enclosed area in the kitchen. Her daughter was just beginning to crawl but was quite determined to conquer the world immediately. Her favorite thing to do was wave her arms, while babbling endlessly. "I imagine she's quite a help."

Abby grinned. "Annie was happy to let Bridget direct her. That little girl is never quiet unless she's asleep, and if I don't miss my guess, she'll be conducting an orchestra one day. She never quits waving her arms."

Carrie returned her grin. The stronger Bridget became, the more her personality shone through. Perhaps because she had been forced to fight so hard for survival, she seemed to be determined to be in control of things. "It's cute now," she said wryly. "When she gets older…"

"She's going to be a force to be reckoned with," Abby agreed. "Of course, your father tells me he thinks it's quite fair. He claims every one of his gray hairs is directly attributable to you."

Carrie laughed. "I suppose there could be a dash of truth to that."

Moments later, the girls came splashing into the water with her. Granite snorted and dashed back toward the shore. He snorted again and returned to his grazing in the field.

"I'm sorry I scared him," Minnie said contritely.

"He's not scared," Carrie assured her. "He wasn't at all sure he wanted to come all the way in. You gave him a good excuse to go back to eating." She eyed Abby. "Speaking of which…"

Abby rolled her eyes. "Did you really think Annie would let us come all the way out here without food? I left it back in the shadows of the oak tree. The shade won't help much in this heat, but at least it will keep it out of the direct sunlight."

"Strawberry shortcake?" Carrie asked hopefully.

"Not unless Bridget turned herself into a leprechaun and spirited it away in the basket," Abby retorted. She relented when she saw Carrie's forlorn expression. "Strawberry shortcake is for dinner tonight. Annie did, however, send two loaves of zucchini bread, along with a bowl of fresh butter she and the girls churned.

Carrie's stomach growled loudly.

Abby chuckled. "Let me guess, you didn't eat lunch today."

Carrie shrugged. "The clinic was full, from the moment we opened the doors. I don't think either Janie, Polly, or I ever had a chance to sit down, much less eat. When we at last said good-bye to the final patient, all I could think about was coming for a swim." When Abby turned toward the woods, Carrie waved her back. "I'll get it. You get in the water. It's spectacular."

Abby leaned down to remove her shoes and plunged into the water happily.

The children were squealing and splashing, the sun catching the droplets of water and turning them into glistening jewels.

Carrie wolfed down two slices of bread before joining Abby and the children in the river. She didn't want to miss any of the fun.

Rose was waiting on the porch when they returned. Their clothes had long dried, and they were sweating again, but the fun of the river lingered in their hearts.

Carrie took one look at her best friend, ushered the children into the house with orders to change their clothes, and turned to her. "What's wrong?"

"Has something happened?" Abby asked.

"Someone tried to kill Felicia," Rose said hoarsely. Her eyes glittered with pain.

Carrie gasped and grabbed Rose's hands. "What? Where? How?"

Rose managed a weak smile. "Which question would you like me to answer first?"

Abby took each of them by a hand and led them to the rocking chairs. "Sit," she commanded. When they were all seated, she turned to Rose. "Tell us what happened, honey."

At that moment, Moses appeared from the barn, followed by the boys.

"Does Moses know?" Abby asked.

"Not yet," Rose answered. "The telegram came just a few minutes ago, right before you returned. Willard sent one of the drivers to deliver it. I thought Moses was still in the fields."

As Moses and the boys clomped up the stairs, Abby stood. "Boys, Annie has some warm zucchini bread waiting for you."

Russell eyed her. "Annie don't let us eat right before dinner."

"*Doesn't* let us eat," Rose sighed as she shook her head. "Force of habit."

Russell seemed to know this wasn't a time to joke around. "Annie *doesn't* let us eat right before dinner," he said carefully, watching Rose with a concerned look.

"It will be alright this time," Abby assured him. "You tell her I said so."

Russell nodded doubtfully but disappeared into the house behind John and Jed.

"What's going on?" Moses asked keenly. He turned to look at Rose, his expression darkening as he saw her distress. "What's wrong?" He moved to her and took her hands.

"Someone tried to kill Felicia," she whispered, obviously fighting to control her tears. She lost the battle as they leaked out and rolled down her cheeks.

At that moment, Thomas strode onto the porch. "I heard the children telling Annie that my wife gave them permission to have zucchini bread. I had to come find out for myself if that's true." His amused expression turned troubled when he saw Rose's face. "What's happened?" he asked sharply.

Carrie wasn't sure Rose could repeat herself a third time. "Someone tried to kill Felicia in Washington, DC. That's all we know so far."

Thomas took a deep breath and dropped into a chair. "Tell us."

Rose took several deep breaths as she fought for control. "I received a telegram from Connie Gallery a little bit ago."

"The professor from Oberlin?" Carrie asked.

"Yes. She's traveling with Felicia during her trip to Washington, DC. We agreed for Felicia to go, but insisted she needed an adult with her during her travels," Rose explained.

"Is she hurt?" Moses asked hoarsely.

"She has some cuts, but she's alright," Rose answered. "I don't really know that much because it was just a telegram. Someone tried to shoot her when she was looking out the window where she's staying with Sojourner. She pulled her head in a second before the bullet shattered the glass."

Carrie gasped and held a hand to her mouth. "Oh, Rose..." She knew how terrified her friend must be right now.

Thomas sat quietly for a moment before he walked to the edge of the porch and stared out over the fields.

Carrie could tell by the set of his shoulders that her father was furious.

"Go to Washington, DC," Thomas said firmly. He spun around before either Moses or Rose could respond. "Don't bother telling me it's not possible. I ran this plantation for a long time. The tobacco crop is coming along wonderfully. I'll make sure it stays that way. School is out for the summer." He raised his hand. "I don't want to hear anything either of you can come up with as an argument. I love Felicia like she's my own. She needs her parents with her right now."

Moses chuckled, though his eyes blazed with concern and anger. "I wasn't going to argue, Thomas."

Thomas stared at him. "You weren't?"

Moses shook his head. "I was going to say thank you." He reached over and pulled Rose into his arms. "We'll leave tomorrow. We'll be in Washington, DC within two days."

"One, if we catch an afternoon train," Rose replied. She dashed away her tears. "Our daughter needs us."

"Will you make her leave and come back to the plantation?" Carrie asked, surprised when Rose shook her head.

"No. Connie also told me how magnificent Felicia is. How people are responding. We won't take that away from her," Rose said.

"We'll just make sure she's safe," Moses stated quietly. "Anyone who wants to harm her will have to attempt to go through me."

"That should be effective," Thomas said dryly. "I can't imagine anyone daring to do that."

Everyone chuckled, but Carrie knew a bullet wouldn't be deterred by Moses' size. She also needed to know more. "The breaking glass must have cut her. Are the wounds bad?"

"I don't know," Rose admitted.

Carrie read the question in her friend's eyes that she knew would never be voiced. "I'm going with you." She held up a hand. "I'm not taking no for an answer. I want to see for myself that she's alright, and I want to treat the cuts so they won't scar."

Rose managed a smile. "I wasn't going to say no. I was going to say thank you. I'm not ashamed to admit my daughter and I need you."

"Oh." Carrie's voice was meek.

Thomas laughed. "We evidently don't listen well, daughter."

Carrie nodded, her mind spinning. "I'll need to let Janie and Polly know."

"I'll send one of my men," Moses replied. He looked between Rose and Carrie. "We leave at dawn tomorrow. With any luck, we'll get a seat on the afternoon train."

Suddenly, Carrie gasped.

Abby stood and came to her side. "Of course I'll take care of Bridget."

Carrie held her hands to her burning face. "How could I forget I have an infant daughter?"

"Because you've only had her for a few months, and because you love Felicia like a daughter," Abby said calmly. "I happen to adore taking care of my grandchildren. With you out of the way, I'll have her all to myself!"

Carrie managed a laugh. "Where's Anthony? I seem to have also forgotten I have a husband who might be interested in my plans."

Russell appeared on the porch behind her. "Daddy is in the backyard putting up a new rope swing. He said he thought the old one was looking frayed, so he decided to put up a new one." He looked excited. "We get to play on it tonight."

"No, you'll get to play on *two* of them."

Russell whirled around as Anthony strode up on the porch. "What do you mean?"

"I mean there are too many children living here now to have just one swing. I replaced the old one and added a new one."

Minnie ran onto the porch and threw herself into her father's arms. "Thank you, Daddy! That means I'll get to swing more. You're the best daddy in the world!"

Carrie couldn't have agreed more. It was going to be hard to leave the plantation again after such a brief time home, but she had to be sure Felicia was alright, and she wanted to give Rose the support she needed. That's what best friends were for.

## Chapter Twenty-Seven

Felicia was exhausted when she arrived back at Sojourner's house the next evening. The speaking had gone well, but the lack of sleep was weighing on her. Every time she tried to close her eyes and slip into slumber, the sound of shattering glass would jolt her awake. She yawned, hoping it portended some rest.

"You're exhausted, Felicia," Sojourner said sympathetically.

Felicia saw no need to deny the obvious. "Today went well, didn't it?"

"That it did," Sojourner answered. "That poem of yours is hitting a lot of people close to home."

"I'm glad," Felicia said softly.

"Are they hard to write?"

"The poems?" Felicia shook her head. "No, they just come to me. I write down what I hear swirling through my head."

Sojourner chuckled. "A poem-writing businesswoman. That might be a first."

Connie met them in the foyer when they entered the house. "We're having a visitor for dinner tonight," she said.

Felicia eyed her. "You look very pleased with yourself."

"With good reason," Connie replied tartly.

Felicia waited, but her professor offered no more explanation. "Are you going to tell us?"

"No," Connie replied with a smile. "Go to your room and get freshened up. You'll find out soon enough."

Sojourner shrugged. "I've learned how to wait in this long life I've lived." She headed for her room. "I'll see you at dinner."

Felicia, clad in a fresh dress after cleaning her wounds and replacing her bandages, hurried to the dining room.

Connie was waiting there with a stout woman whose ebony skin shone in the lantern light.

"Felicia, I'd like you to meet Clara Masterson."

Felicia smiled warmly. "Hello, Mrs. Masterson."

Clara shook her head firmly, her lined face radiating strength and confidence. "There's no *Mrs.* attached to my name, Felicia. I've heard good things about you. It's a pleasure to meet you. I would prefer you call me Clara."

"Alright, Clara. It's a pleasure to meet you, as well." Felicia sensed from the charged atmosphere in the room that the elderly woman had been brought to the house for a special purpose. She was used to that after a week in Washington, DC. Sojourner Truth was an icon in the women's rights movement. Since she'd arrived, not a single night had passed without them sharing their dinner table with someone important in the fight. Each one of the guests had taught Felicia something.

Sojourner entered the dining room and rounded the table to embrace Clara. "Hello, old friend. What a wonderful surprise! How are you?"

"Better than I have a right to be," Clara responded. "I heard your speeches in the city are being well received."

"I believe Felicia and I are having our say. It's far past time for women to have the vote, but that's not why we're here tonight."

Felicia was surprised. "Why *are* we here?"

"'Cause Connie brought Clara here for you," Sojourner replied.

Felicia turned to Connie, suddenly remembering their conversation days before. "Is this...?"

Connie nodded. "Clara is a very successful businesswoman. Actually, she's one of the wealthiest women in this city. When she heard about your decision to become a businesswoman yourself, she wanted to come."

Felicia smiled brightly and turned to Clara. "Thank you so much."

"You may not thank me when I'm done," Clara warned. "What you want to do isn't easy."

Felicia straightened her shoulders. "Not much of what I've done has been easy."

Clara gazed at her for a long moment before she asked, "Why do you want to become a businesswoman, Felicia?"

"To help other women, especially black women, have opportunities only money can bring them," Felicia answered. Every speech she'd given had solidified her determination. Every day she looked out at young black women determined to have a better life. She was determined to help them.

"You're sixteen."

"I'll grow out of that," Felicia said calmly.

The three women laughed.

"That you will," Clara agreed. "What do you want from me?"

"I want to know how you did it," Felicia said. "How did you become successful?"

"By realizing that any success I have probably won't last forever," Clara said promptly. "More importantly, failures won't kill me." She held Felicia's eyes. "All I could do was choose to have the courage to keep moving forward."

Felicia pondered her words, knowing deep in her heart that Clara was giving her a wisdom she probably had no ability to fully process at that moment.

"Let me tell you how I made my money," Clara offered. She exchanged an amused look with Sojourner and Connie. "I'm the finest laundress in Washington, DC," she said proudly.

Felicia stared at her, certain she'd heard incorrectly. "What?"

Clara cackled and slapped her leg. In that moment, Felicia could see the young woman she had once been.

"It's true," Clara assured her. "I was born a slave in Virginia, back in 1812. My owner had some kind of religious experience and decided to set my family free when I was fifteen years old. I'd been working in the fields for eight years at that point, but I also had to help wash the clothes. When my parents were freed, they decided they weren't going to stay around for whatever else was going to happen in the South. They chose to move up here to Washington, DC."

"What was the city like then?" Felicia asked.

"It wasn't hardly worth being called a city," Clara told her. "It was meant to be a grand city on the Potomac, chosen by President Washington, but designed to be similar to Paris. It was officially founded in 1790. Just twenty-two years later, in 1812, much of the city was burned to the ground during the war with England. The President's House was gone, the Capitol was destroyed, and the Library of Congress was burned, along with all the books."

Felicia thought about the city she had explored. "It's so different now."

"Sixty years can make a lot of difference," Clara agreed. "When I got here with my family, you could still see evidence of the war, although people were rebuilding. Course, Washington, DC didn't have all that many people for a long time. It started growing during the Civil War."

"Is that when you started making your money?" Felicia asked.

"No," Clara replied. "Felicia, one of the first things you need to know is that if you want to succeed, you have to want it badly enough to do it anywhere. You can't just go looking for an opportunity, you have to *make* that opportunity."

Felicia listened carefully. She was trying to envision a city without the vibrant growth and life she was seeing now. "How did you make your opportunity?"

"I found a need," Clara said. "Even though there weren't a lot of people here, there were lots of politicians and their wives. Those people don't like to do their laundry," she added with a smile. "Remember me telling you I learned how to do laundry on the plantation when I was a slave? I was twenty when I decided to start doing other people's laundry. But I wasn't just going to be a laundress, I was determined to be the best one in the city."

Felicia nodded, but she knew there had to be more. Clara hadn't become one of the wealthiest women in the city by washing clothes, no matter how good she was.

Clara read her thoughts. "I can see that brilliant mind of yours working. When I started making money, I kept living like I wasn't making any at all. Instead, I invested it."

Felicia stared at her. "Invested it?"

Clara nodded. "I started buying up land and houses. First time, it took me two years to save up enough to buy a tiny house. At that point, I was making my mark as a laundress, so I was able to ask for more money. I bought another house." She paused. "You see, if you want to be a success, you can't just look at what's around you today. You have to look beyond, and imagine what will be. Washington, DC is our nation's capital. I figured the country was going to keep growing, which meant this city was going to grow. I decided I was going to buy as many houses as

I could while they were cheap. I lived like a very poor woman for a long time, because I believed in what the future would bring."

Felicia leaned forward, letting every word from Clara's lips enter her mind and heart.

"I bought houses and I rented them out. I used that money to buy more houses. By the time the war came around, I owned one hundred and three homes."

"One hundred and three?" Felicia gasped and held a hand to her mouth.

"One hundred and three," Clara assured her. "I own more than that now, but when war broke out, Washington, DC became a beehive of activity. People needed a place to live. I was making a lot of money."

Felicia thought about what she knew of that time. "Weren't there a lot of newly freed slaves coming to the city?"

Clara smiled. "Now we're getting to why I agreed to come tonight. I know you want to be a businesswoman so that you can help our people."

"Yes," Felicia said eagerly.

"That's what I did," Clara informed her. "When our people started coming, they didn't have anything. I allocated some of my houses to *our* people. I got those people together and I taught them what it meant to be free—how to pursue opportunities."

Felicia grinned. "How wonderful!"

"That's just the beginning of what was needed. What *continues* to be needed... Howard University was founded here two years after the war ended. Education is the key to helping our people, so I set up a scholarship program." Clara smiled proudly. "So far, close to one hundred young people have graduated from college because of all those houses I own."

Felicia clapped her hands together. "That's exactly what I want to do!" Then she paused. "You started out by telling me you're a laundress. Why didn't you tell me that you own real estate?"

Clara leaned forward and grabbed her hand. "Because white Washington, DC doesn't want a wealthy black woman," she said bluntly. "This may be the town that created the Emancipation Proclamation, but the Democrats are taking power again. They know they can't take away our freedom, but they certainly don't believe we're equal. If you try to show them you are, you make yourself a target."

Felicia stared at her. "But…"

Clara held up her hand. "I told you that you wouldn't like some of what I had to say." She paused. "Connie told me someone tried to kill you a few nights ago."

Felicia squeezed her eyes together tightly as the memories flashed through her mind. "Yes."

"Somebody is trying to remind you of the proper place of black people," Clara declared. "You're stirring people up with your speeches. You're making them believe they can be something, and you're challenging them to do something about it."

"Because it's true," Felicia cried.

"Yes, of course it is," Clara agreed. "But you have to know that every time you do that, you're turning yourself into a target. I tell people I'm a laundress because they think that's what a black woman is good for. Only a few people know how wealthy I am." She shrugged. "It's not the money that's important to me, it's what I can do with it. I don't care where people think it's coming from. It's only important that I do it."

"You do it anonymously?" Felicia asked.

"I do," Clara replied. "I hope the day comes when I don't feel it's necessary, but I certainly don't feel that time is now. The only thing I would accomplish by telling people about my wealth, is to make it more certain I will die." She held Felicia's gaze. "Or that they'll find a way to take it away from me."

"But it's yours," Felicia protested. She was trying to wrap her mind around what she was hearing.

"That doesn't matter," Clara said grimly. "People have been doing illegal things against blacks since they brought us here as slaves. It's going to take longer than ten years of freedom for that to change."

Felicia thought about Clara's words, battling a sense of hopelessness.

Once again, Clara read her mind. "I want what I'm saying to make you careful, but I don't want to diminish what you're determined to do. I was determined to be rich. I am. I was determined to help our people. I'm doing that too." She put a hand under Felicia's chin and stared into her eyes. "You go out into the world, figure out how to make your money, and you make as much of it as you can. Just be careful." She talked slowly and deliberately. "You have to be wise."

"I understand," Felicia said finally. "Thank you."

Clara gazed into her eyes, until evidently she was convinced Felicia had received her message. She turned to Connie. "Didn't I hear something about tea and cake?"

Connie leapt to her feet. "You did indeed. It's coming right up." A firm knock on the front door made her halt in her tracks.

The women exchanged puzzled looks.

"Are you expecting anyone?" Connie asked Sojourner.

Felicia hated the fear vibrating through her as she awaited her answer. Surely, if someone was coming to cause harm, they wouldn't announce it by knocking on the door.

Aaron suddenly strode through the room. "I'll answer it."

While they waited for him, it was as if one collective breath had been taken in the room.

"Who are you?" Aaron's voice rang through the house.

"I'm sorry for the late hour," a man's voice began. "We are Felicia's..."

"Daddy! Mama!" Felicia jumped up and rushed for the door, falling into her father's arms when she reached them. "What are you doing here?" Next, she fell into Rose's embrace, laughing through the tears that insisted on coming.

"No one tries to shoot my daughter," Moses said, his deep voice booming. "I'm here to make sure it doesn't happen again."

Felicia saw another movement on the porch. She gasped again when she recognized who it was. "Carrie! You're here too?" She rushed forward to hug her.

Carrie held her back and gazed into her face, her eyes probing the bandages as if she believed she could see through them. "Did you think I would trust anyone else to make sure you're alright?"

Sojourner and Connie hurried into the foyer.

Sojourner embraced her parents. "Moses. Rose. It's so wonderful to have you here."

Connie laughed as she hugged them next. "You must have left the instant you received my telegram."

"It was brought to the planation last night by one of the men who works for Anthony," Moses told her. "We left at dawn and caught an early afternoon train."

"You must be exhausted," Connie exclaimed. She grabbed their hands and pulled them forward.

"Wait!" Felicia said, as she pulled Carrie forward. "I would like you to meet Dr. Carrie Wallington. She's my mother's best friend, and the finest doctor I know."

Sojourner stared at Carrie keenly. "I've met you," she said slowly. Her eyes cleared. "You were at Oberlin for Rose's graduation."

"I was." Carrie took Sojourner's hand and squeezed it warmly. "It's wonderful to see you again."

The rest of the introductions were made quickly.

Within minutes, they were in the dining room with hot tea and cake.

Felicia stared at her parents. "I can't believe you're here. When Mrs. Gallery sent that telegram..."

"What?" Rose demanded. "You thought we would ignore that someone tried to shoot our daughter?"

Felicia saw the raw fear on her mother's face. "I'm sorry you were frightened," she whispered.

"Frightened?" Rose retorted, her eyes blazing with anger as the fear retreated. "I was infuriated. I still am."

"I'm quite sure you know how I felt," Moses added wryly. His voice was calm but laced with steel.

Felicia did know. "I tell people at every speech how you saved me during the riot in Memphis." She took a deep breath. "Thank you for coming." Having them there, seated across from her, had done more to bolster her courage than anything else could have.

"Felicia is a power on the stage," Sojourner said.

Rose smiled. "I have no doubt of that. We're here to make sure she speaks every word she's meant to."

Felicia stared at her, certain she hadn't heard her correctly. "You're not here to take me home?"

Moses shook his head. "Why would we do that? You have something you started. You need to finish it. We're merely here for support."

Felicia sagged with relief. Leaving would have been hard, but if she was honest, there was a part of her that would have welcomed it. Fighting through fear every day was exhausting. With her father and mother by her side, she was confident she could do it.

"There's an extra room for you," Sojourner said. "You too, Dr. Wallington. We're thrilled to have you."

Felicia turned to Carrie. "How long will you be able to stay?"

"Until I'm quite convinced that beautiful face of yours is going to heal perfectly."

Felicia frowned. "It's already been four days since the cuts. Is there really anything that can be done if they're not healing well?"

Carrie held up the bag she'd brought. "I have everything I need right here. You doubt my miracle-working powers?"

Felicia smiled, despite the worry in Carrie's eyes. "Never."

"Can we go take a look?" Rose asked.

Felicia stood. "I'll show you where my room is." She knew there was no use in suggesting they wait until the next day. They were exhausted from their travels, but Felicia knew they wouldn't rest until they were convinced she was alright.

"She's going to be fine," Sojourner said calmly as she smiled at Carrie. "You think you're the only one who knows plant magic?"

Carrie smiled brightly. "I'm not at all surprised you know it. What did you use?"

"Connie took care of her. I just told her what to do. I keep a supply of marigold ointment. None of the cuts needed sutures, but we been putting the ointment on every day."

Carrie stared at Sojourner. "You have marigold ointment?" She held up her bag. "That's one of the things I brought. Marigolds are fabulous at healing surface wounds."

"Yep. I mixed me up some marigold with lard, just for that use. I carry it with me all the time."

Carrie reached into her bag and pulled out a small tin. "Are you familiar with petroleum jelly?"

Sojourner cocked her head and stared at the colorful tin. "Ain't never heard of it."

"It has wonderful healing qualities. I've learned about it just recently, though it's been around for hundreds of years. The Seneca and Iroquois Indians dug pits in the ground in Pennsylvania after they discovered the oil deposits there. They used it to set ceremonial fires, and they also used the jellylike substance to slather onto their skin as protective lotion," Carrie explained.

"How did you learn about it?" Felicia asked eagerly.

"About twelve years ago, workers at some of the first oil rigs in Pennsylvania started using the paraffin-like material they found forming on the rigs to treat cuts and burns. They were convinced it hastened healing. It was really Robert Chesebrough who made it available for use, however. He's a chemist who used to distill fuel from the oil of sperm whales. As petroleum has made that industry obsolete, he went to the petroleum fields to see what new materials had commercial potential."

Felicia stared at the tin Carrie was holding. "Brilliant! That's what he discovered?" She knew she had learned another aspect of being a successful businesswoman. The chemist had lost one source of income, so he went searching to find another.

Carrie nodded. "The miners showed him what they called rod wax, and told him how they used it. It was black and not very appealing, so he took it back to his lab. He discovered that by distilling the lighter, thinner oil products from the rod wax, he could create a light-colored gel."

"How did you find out about it?" Felicia asked, fascinated by what she was hearing.

"When I was in New York a few weeks ago. Chesebrough is traveling around the city, demonstrating the product." She grimaced. "His demonstrations have to be incredibly painful, however. He burns his skin with acid or an open flame, before he spreads the ointment on his injuries and shows the past wounds that have healed. I was impressed enough that I bought several tins. I've had a chance to use it many times since I've been back on the plantation. I'm a believer!"

"What's it called?" Sojourner asked curiously.

"He calls it Vaseline." Carrie held up the tin again. "It's a recent discovery. He opened his first factory in Brooklyn two years ago."

Felicia stared at Carrie with admiration.

Rose chuckled. "You're not the only one who can discover obscure things that no one else is aware of."

Felicia laughed. "You're right." She was eager to see the Vaseline. "Let's go to my room so we can try it out."

Moses grabbed her in a hug. "I'm going to give Aaron a break for the night. He's exhausted. I'm staying out on the porch to keep an eye on things."

"You're exhausted yourself," Rose protested.

Moses shrugged. "I came here to take care of our daughter. That's what I'm going to do. I'll sleep tomorrow, after Aaron has had some rest."

Felicia hugged her father again. "Thank you," she whispered.

Moses held her back and gazed into her eyes knowingly. "You haven't slept a bit since this happened, have you?"

Felicia's silence was all the answer he needed.

"You go get some sleep."

"I'm staying in your room with you tonight," Rose added. "You're not alone."

Felicia's heart swelled with love and gratitude. "Thank you," she whispered. "I love you both."

Carrie nodded with satisfaction after she examined Felicia's face. "You're doing well," she announced.

"You don't think there will be scarring?" Felicia asked.

"I don't believe so. The marigold ointment has done a wonderful job, but I'm going to exchange the new ointment I made using the Vaseline. I believe it will heal your face even faster and better." Carrie was incredibly relieved after her examination. She and Rose had both envisioned deep, jagged cuts that had become infected. Nothing could have been further from the truth.

"I've cleaned the cuts every day," Felicia informed her. "Then put the ointment on."

"You've done a wonderful job," Carrie assured her. She tilted the girl's face up so their eyes met. "The best thing for you, though, is to get some rest. You look exhausted. The body can't heal when it's tired."

Felicia's smile was genuine. "I'll sleep tonight," she said confidently. "With Mama beside me, and Daddy on the porch, I know nothing can harm me."

Carrie prayed she was right.

## Chapter Twenty-Eight

Rose stepped from the carriage in front of the church. She was excited to hear Felicia's last speech, but also grateful they were returning home the next day. Carrie had returned two days after they'd arrived, confident Felicia would completely heal. Rose missed her best friend and the rest of her children, and she knew Moses was eager to return to the tobacco crop. He'd received one telegram from Thomas, assuring him all was well, yet she knew her husband wouldn't be satisfied until he saw the crop for himself, and she knew he missed riding the fields with the boys.

Still, they'd had a wonderful time exploring the nation's capital during the last few weeks.

Connie slipped her hand through Rose's arm. "What's been the best part of your time here?"

Rose thought carefully. In the end, she shook her head. "I can't come up with just one."

"Alright, tell me some of your favorite things."

"Going through the Smithsonian Institution was wonderful," Rose said promptly. "While it was fascinating, seeing Felicia's excitement was the highpoint. Touring the Capitol Rotunda is something I will never forget, either." She thought of all the things they'd experienced as they traveled the tree-lined streets. "It's not actually any of the things I've seen that have meant so much to me, though. We've been able to meet a great many amazing people since we've been here. People I've only heard of. I never thought I would actually meet them. It's been such an honor and a privilege."

"Do you have a favorite?" Connie asked lightly.

Rose considered the question seriously before she shook her head. "Each one was special in their own way." She looked into Connie's eyes and realized the other woman was wanting to know more than she was actually asking. "Why don't you tell me what you really want to know?"

Connie stopped under the shade of a tree and stared at the auditorium for several moments. "I hate what has happened to the suffrage movement," she stated.

"The division over the ratification of the Fifteenth Amendment," Rose replied as she realized what was bothering her friend. "The decision to give black men the vote, without women also having the vote."

"Yes. Sojourner has aligned herself with Susan Anthony and Elizabeth Stanton. I love both those women. I admire and appreciate what they've done, but I question some of what they've said in the last several years."

Rose didn't have to ask what she meant. "They believe that if anyone is deserving of the vote, it should be educated white women. They've argued that blacks are ignorant of the laws and customs of the United States." She paused. "Wasn't it Elizabeth Stanton who said, *'it was a serious question whether we had better stand aside and see Sambo walk into the kingdom of civil rights first'?*"

Connie sighed. "It was."

Rose read the turmoil in her eyes. "Lucy Stone and Frederick Douglass supported the Fifteenth Amendment. They believe it's the Negro's hour, and that black male voting rights should come first."

"They got what they wanted," Connie replied. "They believe that now all men have the right to vote, we should fight for a separate amendment for women to have the vote."

"It doesn't seem to be happening." Rose said flatly.

"No, it doesn't," Connie said sadly. "How do you feel about that?"

Rose knew what she was really asking. "How do I feel about it as a black woman? And how can Sojourner support Susan Anthony after the things she's said about blacks?"

"I suppose that's what I'm asking," Connie admitted.

Rose thought about her answer, striving for fairness. "I see both sides," she said eventually. "Of course, I want blacks to have the vote, but I agree there's a very low level of education among the freed slaves right now. That will change in time, but it will definitely take time. On the other hand, you don't need education to know what has to happen for blacks to have a fair chance at equality in America. The whole system has to change. The country has a very long way to go."

Her thoughts took her in a different direction. "It's also fair to say that most whites aren't any more educated than blacks. The literacy rate among poor whites is extremely low. Without education, it doesn't matter what race you are. Knowledge is key to a true democracy. Without knowledge, it is too easy for people to be controlled."

Rose paused thoughtfully. "The sad thing is that everyone is being forced to take a side. The right answer to the whole issue is for *all* Americans to have the vote. And education. Black men. *All* women. We'll never live in a true democracy until everyone has a say."

"I suppose the split was inevitable," Connie replied. "This whole issue is volatile, and there are many viewpoints. The problem is that the division and strife among the movement's leadership will most likely delay suffrage even more."

"Then we keep fighting," Rose said firmly. She knew Connie was right. She thought of Felicia's speeches while they'd been in town. "There's a younger generation determined to make it happen. I don't know how long it will take, but I believe the time will come when women have the vote."

"I hope I live long enough to see it," Connie said ruefully.

"I do too," Rose agreed. She slipped her hand through Connie's arm. "Let's go hear this last speech.

Felicia gazed out at the audience as she stepped to the podium. It was the largest crowd she'd spoken before. Since it was Sojourner's last appearance before she left to return home to Battle Creek, Michigan, the auditorium was packed.

She took a deep breath and prayed for the right words.

"The last month has changed me," Felicia began. Her eyes swept over new faces and familiar faces that had become dear to her. "I've learned a great deal from all of you. I've learned what courage is, and I've learned what it means to take a stand for what you believe in, no matter what the price is."

Felicia smiled warmly at Sojourner. "I will forever be grateful that I had the opportunity to spend time with Sojourner Truth. She's taught me more than I will ever be able to express. I know she will continue to teach me and be a role model I will be proud to emulate. When she returns home to fight for President Grant's re-election, I know she'll be powerful. I have no doubt she will do exactly what she told you today, which is to try to vote on Election Day. Whether she succeeds or fails, she'll be doing what she's done for so long—

taking a stand for women everywhere." She took a deep breath. "Thank you," she said sincerely.

Sojourner nodded serenely, giving her the same encouraging smile she'd given her every time they shared the stage together.

Felicia looked back at her audience and began the story she'd shared every time she'd spoken, except this time she ended it differently. "I wouldn't be standing here right now if it weren't for my parents. I've told you how Moses Samuels saved my life in Memphis during the riot. I've told you about Rose Samuels, the most amazing teacher I've ever known. They gave me the courage to agree to this tour, and granted me the freedom to do it, even though they were frightened for me."

Moses and Rose gazed at her proudly.

"If you've heard me speak in the last few weeks, you've heard this part of my story. If you're here tonight for the first time, you don't know that someone tried to kill me during my first week here."

Felicia waited for the anticipated gasps to die down. "I wasn't sure I would have the courage to continue after the attempt to murder me. I kept speaking, but I was exhausted. Each time was harder than the one before. I couldn't sleep because I was afraid someone would try and kill me again. Until my parents came. As soon as my parents found out what happened, they got on a train and came to be with me. They haven't left my side in the last few weeks."

Sojourner stood and waved a hand toward Moses and Rose, sitting one row back. "You two stand up and let everybody see you."

Moses and Rose stood, turned slightly, and lifted a hand as applause broke out.

Sojourner laughed lightly. "I seen the look on most of your faces. Most of you ain't never seen a man as big as Moses Samuels. Now you know why there ain't been anybody bother to try and hurt Miss Felicia again. Moses Samuels was a hero during the war. As far as I'm concerned, he's a hero now."

Applause broke out again.

Sojourner wasn't done. "Ain't just one hero in their family, though. Rose Samuels be just as much a hero. She helped Felicia with her hunger for knowledge, because she's a mighty fine teacher. I met her at Oberlin not too long back, but she been a teacher long before that. When she was sixteen, the same age as Felicia now, she was teaching a secret school, hidden back in the woods of the plantation where she was a slave. After she ran away, she taught at the contraband camp at Fort Monroe. She ain't quit teaching since then."

More applause filled the auditorium.

"Now I reckon you know why Felicia is so special. Her first parents raised her to be strong and resilient. They got taken too soon. Her new folks gave her everything they couldn't." Sojourner nodded and took her seat.

Felicia blinked back her tears and reached into her pocket. "I wrote a poem for my last speech. Though I'm referring to me, I'm speaking to all of you. It will take *all* of us to change America. It will take *all* of us to fight for equality for every person in this country." She cleared her throat. "I'd like to read it to you now.

## I WILL SPEAK

When the world vows to silence me
When fear clogs my throat
I will speak.

When I want to shrink within
When I'm too afraid to expand
I will speak.

When courage is beyond my reach
When I tremble to utter the next word
I will speak.

When I'm scared
When I want to turn tail and run
I will speak.

When people try to stop me
When others ridicule and scorn
I will speak.

When the winds blow hard
When I'm far from safe harbor
I will speak.

I will take the risks
I will choose truth and compassion
I will speak.

I will speak.
I will speak.
I will never cease speaking.

Felicia raised her head, waited a long moment, and then added, "I ask each of you to join me."

## *Chapter Twenty-Nine*

Carrie was excited to celebrate Peter and Elizabeth's last night on the plantation before they returned to Boston from their honeymoon. She hugged the newlyweds tightly. "Being on the plantation was much different than you anticipated," she teased.

"It was perfect," they declared in unison. Though they'd only intended to stay two weeks, they'd been on the plantation for two months. Elizabeth's father had insisted the medical practice would run smoothly despite her absence and had encouraged them to make the most of their opportunity.

"I've never taken part in a barn raising," Peter said enthusiastically. "I actually have an assignment from the paper to write about my experience. At first, they were upset about my prolonged stay – until they realized how many articles I would write because of it."

"City folks," Carrie scoffed. "They have no idea how we live in the country."

"Which is exactly what I'm going to tell them," Peter assured her. "Mostly, I want to reveal what it's like to see nearly one hundred men, both black and white, working together in harmony to create something fabulous." He glanced in the direction of the barn. "I'm always going to be glad I played a small part in helping build that."

"And that I played a small part in keeping people working," Elizabeth added.

"A *small* part?" Carrie chided. "You treated close to a dozen men who were injured that day."

"Probably the only reason we have a barn standing there," Susan added. "Without you, Carrie, and Janie, we would have lost some of our men. You patched them up enough so they could keep building."

"All in a day's work." Elizabeth smiled brightly, her eyes shining with joy. "We weren't able to get married on the plantation but spending our honeymoon here was far better." She turned to look west. "I believe swimming in the James River was the best part for me."

Carrie grinned. "It's wonderful, isn't it?"

"More than wonderful," Elizabeth agreed. "I love Boston Harbor and the beaches, but I've only been in the water once. It's nothing like swimming in the James."

Frances looked appalled. "You've only been in the water once? Why?"

Elizabeth smiled. "You have no idea how fortunate you are to live here on the plantation, with parents who are open-minded. Swimming is not usually the object of visiting the Boston coast. Most women go so they can enjoy the promenade. They dress up in lighter clothes, wear large-brimmed hats they call *uglies*, and carry parasols to keep their skin safe from the direct sun."

"Do you wear that outfit?" Frances asked. She kept her voice neutral, but the distaste was obvious on her face.

Elizabeth sighed. "I do. Or, at least I *did*. I'm not sure I'll ever be able to bring myself to do it again, now that I've experienced the freedom here. Rather than hiding from the sun, it's been wonderful to feel it on my face and body. Proper Victorian women never expose themselves to the sun's rays."

"That doesn't sound like fun," Frances said dismissively.

"Oh, it gets better," Elizabeth assured her. "Women around Boston use bathing machines to swim."

Minnie screwed up her face. "Why do they need a machine to swim? We just jump in the water."

"Which is why I said you're so lucky," Elizabeth replied. "Bathing machines are the rule for *proper* ladies. The machine is actually a small cabana on wheels. The lady goes into the cabana to change into her bathing costume."

Frances interrupted. "Bathing costume?" She glanced down at her breeches. "These work just fine."

Elizabeth chuckled. "*Proper* bathing costumes are generally made of wool. The top is a jacket with short sleeves and buttons down the front. It hangs down far enough to turn the jacket into a knee-length skirt. Under the skirt, there are loose trousers that usually come to mid-calf. The whole outfit is finished off with a bathing cap that has ruffles."

Minnie looked more horrified. "That sounds terrible!"

"It's certainly not like the freedom you have here," Elizabeth agreed. "Though, if you were to appear on the Boston beach in breeches and a shirt, you would be escorted off by the police."

"Why?" Frances demanded.

"Because society people are very serious about their rules," Elizabeth told her. "Let me finish telling you about the bathing machines. The time I went swimming, I was escorted into the cabana to change into my swimming costume. While I was inside, the entire thing was wheeled into the surf. They made sure the cabana door faced away from the beach so that I was guaranteed privacy. I got out and splashed around in the water for a little while, but I felt very self-conscious. The water felt wonderful, even if I can't say it was fun." She rolled her eyes. "When I was done, I climbed back in my cabana, and they rolled me back to shore. I changed inside and went back to the promenade."

Frances frowned. "I wouldn't like that at all. No wonder you had so much more fun here."

Elizabeth nodded enthusiastically. "Exactly. I rode a horse down to the river in my breeches and jumped into the water in my clothes. The water was refreshing and warm." She smiled as she remembered. "It felt soft on my skin, and the sun was wonderful on my face." She looked down at her arms. "I'm afraid my mother will be quite horrified with how tan I've become, but I don't care in the least. I've had such a marvelous time."

Minnie gazed at her for several long moments. "Do you really want to go back to Boston? It's better here."

Elizabeth took her question seriously. "I wish I could stay here, Minnie, but I can't."

"Why?"

"Because I have a job to do in Boston. It's hard to be a doctor *and* be a woman in America. Those of us who are, need to be doctors everywhere we can. We need to show people we're good doctors, and we also need to show other women they can be anything they want to be."

"You didn't like being a doctor in Richmond," Frances observed. "Do you wish you had stayed here, though?"

Elizabeth took a deep breath. "Life in Boston might be restrictive, but it's far easier than living in Richmond. I loved working with your mama and Janie, but life is even more restrictive in the South if you're a woman."

"And Italian," Frances said astutely.

"Southerners are not fond of ethnic differences," Elizabeth agreed. "It's going to take all of us fighting for change in order for America to be better for women. I'm counting on both of you to do your part."

"You can count on it," Frances said firmly.

"Me too!" Minnie said.

Carrie hugged both her girls and looked around. "Where's your father?"

"Out in the fields with Moses," Frances told her.

Annie appeared on the porch. "I'm inside fixing a feast of ham hocks, grits, fried squash, fresh tomatoes, and strawberry shortcake."

"That sounds wonderful!" Elizabeth groaned and patted her stomach. "I'm going to miss your cooking when I get back to Boston. Peter will, too."

Annie sniffed. "Ain't a Northern cook alive that knows how to cook food the right way."

Carrie thought of the wonderful meals they'd eaten in Boston, but she knew better than to mention it. In truth, she would take Annie's cooking over anything she'd eaten there. She may not appreciate many Southern customs, but she freely admitted to loving the food.

"You're right about that!" Elizabeth said enthusiastically. "I appreciate that you've taught me how to cook like a Southerner. Well," she added quickly, "at least a little bit."

Carrie looked at Annie with surprise. Annie loved having Minnie in her kitchen, but she barely tolerated anyone else. This was the first she'd heard about Annie teaching Elizabeth to cook. "Cooking lessons? Did all this happen while I was at the clinic?"

Annie shrugged. "You can't be knowin' every little thing that goes on around here, Miss Carrie. I reckon it's a good thing for you to be surprised every now and then." She reached over and squeezed Elizabeth's hand. "I can't send you back up to that frozen land without knowin' how to cook some real food."

Elizabeth leaned forward and kissed Annie on the cheek. "Peter will be a happy man this winter when we're eating grits."

"Grits? In Boston?" Carrie laughed. "I'm afraid you'll be quite disappointed."

Annie shook her head. "Ain't nobody gonna be disappointed. Mr. Peter and Miss Elizabeth gonna go home with a big sack of grits."

Elizabeth gave her a smirk of satisfaction. "Boston will be a better place this winter," she announced.

Peter stepped out onto the porch in time to hear her statement. "Ahh...a wife who knows how to keep her husband happy."

Elizabeth laughed. "Don't think you won't be learning how to make them, too. Even a reporter can figure out the mystery of good grits."

Peter shook his head. "Don't be so sure, wife. Reporters have very limited skills."

"I don't think you want to open that bucket of worms," Carrie admonished him. "You'll end up making *all* the grits, if you want them."

Peter immediately looked remorseful, though his eyes shone with amusement. "Please forgive me, Elizabeth. I'll be quite honored to obtain the skill of making good southern grits," he said dramatically.

"I never doubted it for a second, husband," Elizabeth retorted.

Peter eyed her. "You do know your mother would be quite appalled at how you're treating your new husband, don't you?"

Elizabeth shrugged and grinned. "You're assuming I care? My mother is from a different generation. She'll have to adjust to change."

A distant yell made Carrie turn away from the amusing exchange.

"It's Daddy!" Minnie cried.

A few minutes later, Anthony and Russell rode up to the porch. Moses, John, and Jed waved before they disappeared into the barn.

"Mama!" Russell slid off Bridger and ran up the steps to fling his arms around her. "I missed you!"

Carrie hugged him fiercely, looking quizzically at Anthony. She'd only been gone for the day at the clinic. "I missed you too! Did you have fun riding?"

"I had the best time!" Russell pronounced. "Bridger and I went swimming in the river."

Carrie was delighted. "You rode him bareback into the river? That used to be my favorite thing."

"I know. Miles told me he took you riding into the river for the first time when you got Granite. He showed me how to do it. I loved it!"

Carrie hugged him back to her. She could hardly believe this was the little boy who had spent a year and a half under a bridge. "Tomorrow, we'll go together," she promised. "I'll leave the clinic in time to join you."

She looked at Anthony. "We received a telegram from Rose. They'll be home in two days. Felicia will be here for an entire month before she returns to finish school."

"Hurrah!" Frances cheered. "I can't wait to have her back home."

Abby opened the door and stepped out onto the porch. "Look who just woke up."

Carrie's grin widened as she scooped her daughter into her arms. "Hello, Bridget," she cooed. Nothing was better than coming home to her family after a long day at the clinic.

Bridget stared up into her face, waved her arms, and grinned.

"I'm never going to get tired of her chubby arms," Carrie said softly. "It's like a miracle every time I see them."

Abby nodded serenely. "This little girl eats all the time now. Pretty soon, she'll have made up for all the times she didn't have enough to eat."

"Ain't gonna have no skinny children in my house," Annie declared, her eyes soft as she peered down at the baby.

Carrie's heart was full as she gazed at her family and the people she loved so much.

Laughter rang through the house during the dinner to celebrate Peter and Elizabeth. Stories were exchanged as they talked about all that happened during their stay.

"You'll be back, won't you?" Minnie asked Elizabeth. "I don't want you to leave. I've had a lot of fun in the kitchen with you and Annie."

Elizabeth reached over to take her hand. "I'll be back, honey. Cromwell Plantation will always be my favorite place in the world. Nothing could keep me away."

"Me either," Peter said firmly. "I never imagined we would be here so long. Every moment has been special."

Minnie looked at Janie. "Does this mean you're moving back to your house? I really like having Robert and Annabelle right next door in the guest house."

Janie nodded. "We'll be moving home again, but you'll still see us a lot. I promise."

"We'd better," Thomas grumbled. "I don't like you taking those children away."

Robert jumped up, ran to Thomas, and crawled into his lap. "We'll see you real soon, Grandpa Thomas," he said seriously.

Carrie smiled at the exchange. Since Robert had no grandparents of his own, he had claimed Thomas and Abby. To say they were delighted would be putting it mildly. She knew she and Anthony could adopt as many children as they wanted. Thomas and Abby would embrace and delight in them all.

Minnie rose to stand next to Elizabeth. "Are you ready?"

Carrie watched them curiously. "Ready for what?"

Minnie looked at her but remained silent.

Elizabeth stood immediately, motioning for Annie to stay in her seat. "We've got this, Annie."

Much to everyone's amazement, Annie nodded serenely and settled back. "I know you do."

Carrie stared at her. She'd never seen Annie willingly relinquish her kitchen to anyone. She was seeing a miracle unfold before her eyes.

Minutes later, Minnie appeared at the kitchen door, Elizabeth right behind her. Both of them were holding tall chocolate cakes, the chocolate frosting gleaming in the lantern light.

"Elizabeth made her first chocolate cake!" Minnie cried. "I helped her!"

"I couldn't have done it without her help," Elizabeth assured them. "This little girl is quite the cook."

"Course she is," Annie said smugly. "I'm teaching her everythin' I know."

"Me too!" Hope cried.

"You too, grandbaby," Annie assured her as she scooped Hope into her lap. "Pretty soon, you'll be as good a cook as Minnie."

The rest of the evening flew by as they devoured the dessert everyone proclaimed a complete success.

Russell was sitting on the window seat in the room he shared with John and Jed when Carrie went in to tell him goodnight. The other boys were downstairs with Miles and Annie. Miles was regaling them with stories of earlier times on the plantation.

"Hello, Mama." Russell's voice was sleepy.

Carrie sat down next to him and ruffled his hair. "You had a very full day, son."

"Yep. It was a real good day."

They sat quietly, letting the night air sweep over them. The curtains billowed, carrying in the scents of honeysuckle and fresh cut hay from the fields.

"I love it here," Russell said quietly as he melted into her side.

Carrie wrapped her arm around his shoulders and pulled him close. "And we love having you here. There aren't words to express how glad we are that you're our son."

"Me too, Mama."

Another long silence passed. The breeze carried in sounds of frogs, crickets, and hooting owls. Flashes of light announced the nightly dance of the fireflies. Jagged streaks of lightning on the horizon promised rain before midnight.

"Mama?"

"Yes?" Carrie asked softly, wrapped in the peacefulness of the moment.

"What is joy?"

Carrie pulled back and gazed down at her son. What an interesting question. "Why are you asking?"

Russell gazed at her solemnly. "My first mama used to tell me that someday I would find joy." He cocked his head. "Have I found it?"

Carrie's heart squeezed. "Well, when I feel joy, it's like being swallowed by a feeling of great pleasure and happiness."

Russell cocked his head as he considered her answer. "Then, I reckon I found joy," he said decisively as he smiled up at her. "Will I always feel this way from now on?"

Carrie thought about her answer. She wanted to give Russell hope, but she also wanted to be honest. "I've learned that joy is more of a journey," she said slowly.

"A journey? What do you mean?"

Carrie chose her words carefully. "There are moments, like this one right now, when my heart is full of so much joy that I can hardly stand it. The thing is, I also know life has hard times. There will be days I feel sad. Days that I might suffer and cry." She gazed down into her son's earnest face. "I've also learned, though, that life has very many joyful moments. Getting through the hard times sometimes feels like an impossible journey. As long as you keep moving forward, though, you'll break free from the clouds and come back out into the sunshine of joy."

Russell turned his face to gaze back out into the darkness. The breeze rustled the leaves of the trees, creating a musical background for the chorus of frogs. "I reckon that sounds right," he said slowly. "I used to have moments when I was real happy, before my mama died. We didn't have much, but she loved me a whole lot. Once she died, I guess I started on that journey you're talking about. I didn't feel joy at all when I was under that bridge." He took a deep breath and turned a blinding smile on her. "Now, I got more joy than I think I can hold sometimes."

Carrie pulled him closer into her arms. "I know how you feel, Russell."

"Do I bring you joy, Mama?"

"More than you will probably ever know," Carrie answered. "I'll do my best every day to show you how much joy you bring me and the rest of our family."

"Does Bridget bring you joy, too?"

"You. Bridget. Frances. Minnie." Carrie stroked his hair. "Each of you brings me such great joy. That's something that will never change."

"And Daddy? He brings you joy?"

Carrie laughed. "Your daddy definitely brings me joy. I love him with all my heart."

Russell snuggled in closer. "I reckon this journey has been worth it," he said softly. "I suppose I'm glad I lived under the bridge. I'm glad Daddy caught me stealing. I guess all the hard times were just part of my journey."

"I reckon they were," Carrie said softly. The low rumble of thunder in the distance accentuated her words. "I'm grateful your journey led you to us."

"Me too," Russell agreed. He yawned as he fought to keep his eyes open.

"Let's get you in bed." Carrie waited until he crawled under the covers, and kissed him on his forehead. "Sweet dreams, honey."

Russell nodded. "And tomorrow we'll ride in the river together?"

"I promise," Carrie answered as she kissed him again.

Within moments, Russell was sound asleep.

# Book # 18 of The Bregdan Chronicles

As Carrie gazed down at his peaceful face, she recognized that her own journey had led her to a joy she had never imagined. Whatever came next, she knew the journey would continually lead her to moments of joy exactly like this one.

## To Be Continued...

**Coming Early 2022!**

***Would you be so kind as to leave a Review on Amazon?***

Go to www.Amazon.com

Put Journey To Joy, Ginny Dye into the Search Box.

Leave a Review.

*I love hearing from my readers!*

*Thank you!*

## The Bregdan Principle

*Every life that has been lived until today
is a part of the woven
braid of life.*

*It takes every person's story to create
history.*

*Your life will help determine the course of
history.*

*You may think you don't have much of an
impact.*

*You do.*

*Every action you take will reflect in
someone else's life.*

*Someone else's decisions.*

*Someone else's future.*

*Both good and bad.*

## The Bregdan Chronicles

# 1 - Storm Clouds Rolling In
1860 – 1861

# 2 - On To Richmond
1861 – 1862

# 3 - Spring Will Come
1862 – 1863

Book # 18 of The Bregdan Chronicles 519

# 4 - Dark Chaos
1863 – 1864

# 5 - The Long Last Night
1864 – 1865

# 6 - Carried Forward By Hope
April – December 1865

# 7 - Glimmers of Change
December – August 1866

# 8 - Shifted By The Winds
August – December 1866

# 9 - Always Forward
January – October 1867

*Book # 18 of The Bregdan Chronicles*

# 10 - Walking Into The Unknown
October 1867 – October 1868

# 11 - Looking To The Future
October 1868 – June 1869

# 12 - Horizons Unfolding
November 1869 – March 1870

\# 13 - The Twisted Road of One Writer
The Birth of The Bregdan Chronicles

\# 14 - Misty Shadows of Hope
1870

\# 15 - Shining Through Dark Clouds
1870 – 1871

*Book # 18 of The Bregdan Chronicles*

# 16 - Courage Rising
April – August 1871

# 17 – Renewed By Dawn
September 1871 – January 1872

March 1872 – September 1872

*Many more coming... Go to DiscoverTheBregdanChronicles.com to see how many are available now!*

## Other Books by Ginny Dye

### Pepper Crest High Series - Teen Fiction
Time For A Second Change
It's Really A Matter of Trust
A Lost & Found Friend
Time For A Change of Heart

### Fly To Your Dreams Series – Allegorical Fantasy
Dream Dragon
Born To Fly
Little Heart
The Miracle of Chinese Bamboo

All titles by Ginny Dye
www.BregdanPublishing.com

*Book # 18 of The Bregdan Chronicles*

## *Author Biography*

Who am I? Just a normal person who happens to love to write. If I could do it all anonymously, I would. In fact, I did the first go 'round. I wrote under a pen name. On the off chance I would ever become famous - I didn't want to be! I don't like the limelight. I don't like living in a fishbowl. I especially don't like thinking I have to look good everywhere I go, just in case someone recognizes me! I finally decided none of that matters. If you don't like me in overalls and a baseball cap, too bad. If you don't like my haircut or think I should do something different than what I'm doing, too bad. I'll write books that you will hopefully like, and we'll both let that be enough! :) Fair?

But let's see what you might want to know. I spent many years as a Wanderer. My dream when I graduated from college was to experience the United States. I grew up in the South. There are many things I love about it, but I wanted to live in other places. So I did. I moved 57 times, traveled extensively in 49 of the 50 states, and had more experiences than I will ever be able to recount. The only state I haven't been in is Alaska, simply because I refuse to visit such a vast, fabulous place until I have at least a month.

## Journey To Joy    526

Along the way I had glorious adventures. I've canoed through the Everglade Swamps, snorkeled in the Florida Keys and windsurfed in the Gulf of Mexico. I've white-water rafted down the New River and Bungee jumped in the Wisconsin Dells. I've visited every National Park (in the off-season when there is more freedom!) and many of the State Parks. I've hiked thousands of miles of mountain trails and biked through Arizona deserts. I've canoed and biked through Upstate New York and Vermont, and polished off as much lobster as possible on the Maine Coast.

I've lived on a island in the British Columbia province of Canada, and now live on a magical cliffside in Mexico.

Have you figured out I'm kind of an outdoors gal? If it can be done outdoors, I love it! Hiking, biking, windsurfing, rock-climbing, roller-blading, snow-shoeing, skiing, rowing, canoeing, softball, tennis... the list could go on and on. I love to have fun and I love to stretch my body. This should give you a pretty good idea of what I do in my free time.

When I'm not writing or playing, I'm building Millions For Positive Change - a fabulous organization I founded in 2001 - along with 60 amazing people who poured their lives into creating resources to empower people to make a difference with their lives.

What else? I love to read, cook, sit for hours in solitude on my mountain, and also hang out with friends. I love barbeques and block parties. Basically - I just love LIFE!

I'm so glad you're part of my world!  ~**Ginny**

---

Join my Email List so you can:

- Receive notice of all new books
- Be a part of my Launch Celebrations. I give away lots of Free gifts!
- Read my weekly BLOG while you're waiting for a new book.
- Be part of The Bregdan Chronicles Family!
- Learn about all the other books I write.

Just go to www.BregdanChronicles.net and fill out the form.

Made in the USA
Columbia, SC
10 August 2022